Cosmic Castaway

Cosmic Romance 3

Mars Quinn

Editor: Adie Hart

Cover Artist: Etheric Designs

ASIN: B0DR3869TJ

ISBN: 978-1-961972-06-3 (Paperback)

Content Warnings

Several hard and potentially upsetting topics are discussed in this book, and people with triggers might want to read the following. But be aware that these content warnings contain spoilers, so if you have no triggers, feel free to skip these. Remember your mental health is more important than reading any book, so be gentle with yourself and skip this book if one of the following is upsetting to you.

Please note: I am human. I have tried to list everything I could think of, but I might have missed some. Feel free to DM or email me if you have a specific trigger you want to know if it is in this book or not.

- Explicit sexual content (all consensual)

- Fellatio

- Frotting

- Felching

- Edging

- Biting

- Licking (including injuries/ no blood play)

- Spanking

- Tail Play

- Primal Play (light)

- Slavery

- PTSD

- Survivor's guilt

- Flashbacks

- Gore

- Abuse

- Freeze Trauma Response

- Mentions of emaciation and malnutrition

- Mentions of needing to gain weight

- Mentions of death

- Immolation (not explicit)

- Animal injury (no pet death)

- Hunting

- Mentions of field dressing and preparation of an animal for consumption.

- Swearing

- Alcohol consumption

- Arachnids

Chapter 1

ABDUCTION IS NEVER GREAT.

Bartholomew

Well, this wasn't ideal. I stood in a minuscule room made of rough metal with at least a hundred other humans. We were packed into the cramped space like cattle on the way to slaughter. I had no idea how I'd gotten here. One moment, I was getting ready for bed, and the next, an alien with a watermelon-shaped head on a toothpick body was screeching at me and shocking me with some kind of baton that sparked with green electricity.

Now, I was in this tiny room.

The room was so full that it was impossible to sit unless I flopped on top of the other people. I'd had to do that, though, when my legs grew too weak to support me, and the other people stuck with me had done it as well.

We'd had no choice.

Someone vomited and drew me back to the present hell we were all living in. The stagnant air from everyone's breathing was mixed with the stench of sewage, sweat, and general B.O. It was enough to burn my eyes and send my stomach lurching with every inhale. I might have puked if I'd had anything in my stomach, so that was one benefit, if I wanted to find the silver lining of this horror.

The toothpick aliens, which seemed anatomically impossible, hadn't provided food, water, or somewhere to go to the bathroom. As a result, we were all coated in things I refused to think about.

While I didn't know how long I'd been gone, as the hours blurred together, I had a sneaking suspicion we weren't on Earth anymore. Aliens. Weird ship. Humans in a hold. It wasn't hard to figure out what had happened. We'd been abducted, and probably not for a good reason, since the aliens were treating us like shit.

But oddly enough, I didn't care.

There was a disconnect between my emotions and my mind, like someone had snipped a thread connecting the two. I was frozen in place, unable to move. My heart was pounding and my breathing was shallow; all the while, a helpless feeling consumed me, but my body refused to move and my thoughts circled on the end of the journey.

Some of the people trapped with me cried, others chatted quietly, and some stared into the distance, rocking back and forth. Everyone was coping however possible. My method was not moving, I guessed. There was nowhere to go anyway, and perhaps being numb was better. There was no fear. No worries about what my family would think when they couldn't get a hold of me. No cares about the people trapped with me. No panic about the end of this trip.

None of it mattered.

The ship shuddered, knocking me out of my frozen stance and allowing me to take a deep inhale and move. I thumped into the wall, which was growing hotter by the second, as the ship jerked hard once again right before a loud grinding sounded. People screamed, trying to scramble to their feet. I pressed against the warm wall, struggling to remain upright.

A guy toppled to the floor with a yelp, and someone stepped on him, making him cry out. Shaking, I yanked him up, and he clung to me. Together, we fought to remain upright while people tumbled around us, trying to stand, trying to get away, trying not to get trampled.

The floor jolted, sending more people to the ground, and then all vibration ceased, which was more terrifying than the constant rumble I'd grown used to.

"I think we landed," the guy said.

I nodded.

"Vince," he said.

"Bartholomew Reginald," I replied.

His eyebrows lifted.

"My moms are weird. You can call me Teddy."

Vince glanced at the door through the sea of filthy people. He didn't act in a rush for me to let him go, and honestly, I wasn't ready to release him. When the doors opened, I was fairly certain we were going to die. It was nice not to die alone, even if I didn't really know the man beside me.

Panic, my first real emotion since this ordeal started, bolted through my veins and jump-started my pulse. I was going to die.

This was it. My last moments, filled with terror and the smell of piss, awaited me as soon as those rough metal doors opened.

My companion squeezed me in a bruising grip and his heart thudded powerfully against my chest.

We were going to die.

I studied him, hoping his human face was the last thing I'd see in this world. It was a sight better than the watermelon-head aliens, or the metal room filled with screaming people. Vince was attractive, almost giving me romance villain vibes, with sharp features that were somehow delicate. While we were both white and had black hair, his hung to his shoulders, perfectly straight, and his skin was deathly pale. His dark brown eyes were almost black to my light brown, and they were wide with fear. The one thing holding him back from being a true villain in the romance novels I enjoyed was his height. Vince was short.

"What do you think is going to happen?" Vince asked, his voice soft, though deeper than his thin frame suggested.

"Death."

"At least you don't sugarcoat it," he said, his words dripping in sarcasm.

I shrugged.

The doors opened and worse than death happened.

Serlotminden

I crossed the finish line marked by the lighted buoys, and a number flashed on the screens. Fifth. Not bad. Up from last cycle where

I took seventh in the annual Coalition Charity Race. I slowed to drifting speed, then directed my racing shuttle to the docking ring of the station to begin my post-flight checks. Many racers had their teams handle shuttle maintenance, but I preferred to do everything myself. While I wasn't an engineer, it was my ship and therefore my responsibility.

When I stepped onto the promenade, people cheered, and I waved, giving everyone a wide smile, but my eyes went to the terrace above. All four of my brothers and my sole cousin leaned against the railing. Kalvoxrencol, the youngest, cheered loudly, while his human mate, Seth, was bright red at his side, clapping in that human manner. Not to be outdone, Caleb shouted, jumping up and down, only to pause with a deep grimace. Zoltilvoxfyn, my next youngest brother, instantly checked on his mate.

Dontilvynsan, my directly older brother, politely lifted his hands in approval, as did my cousin, Monqilcolnen. Hallonnixmin, the eldest, yelled my name, and his mate, Gilvaxtin, matched him in volume, though she was significantly more animated, jumping and bouncing. They'd left their kids at home with Father and Mother; that was the requirement Father had given when all my siblings insisted on coming to watch me.

Father and Mother didn't often allow us all off the planet at the same time. We were royalty, and with that came risks. Hallonnixmin, the heir to the throne, left as little as possible, as did Zoltilvoxfyn because of his mental health and rare inner fire. However, Caleb, his mate of three cycles, assisted with both, allowing him to leave more frequently.

I lifted my fist, and the crowd grew louder. I flicked my long white hair over my broad shoulder and smiled, giving a few people winks. They screamed in response. I was a fan favorite for many species, as I was exceedingly attractive or, as Caleb liked to say in English, "Hot as fuck."

Monqilcolnen rolled his eyes while Kalvoxrencol pretended to fluff his hair. I laughed at their reactions. I didn't mind them teasing me for my vanity. They did it in good humor and with love; besides, I poked at their flaws as often as they did mine.

I spoke to a few reporters about the race and how I felt about my ranking, then finally snuck to the quarters my family had claimed. We were all in one suite with separate rooms for each of us. It made security easier on the station master and Dontilvynsan, who oversaw our safety, but we hadn't all been in the same crowded space like this many times in our lives, and it had gotten overwhelming fairly fast.

My family all beamed when I came inside; even Father, Mother, and my two nephews were on the large screen spanning the shared space. Everyone congratulated me, and I thanked them before slipping into my bedroom to change. I pulled off my racing jumpsuit and donned black trousers and a simple orange sleeveless shirt that showed off my muscular arms and contrasted excellently next to my purple scales.

Knees trembling, I sank to my bed and breathed deeply to calm the rapid beat of my soul. I loved racing. It was in my blood, but it sent my soul pounding like I'd been fighting for my life and made me exhausted afterward. I always had the urge to curl up and sleep, which my brothers understood, but today I wanted to party, so I took a single moment for myself, then rushed out.

Caleb was the first to greet me. He used to be a human spirit that wandered the stars, but the Crystal had placed him in a drakcol body, shocking everyone. His reddish-brown hair was cut short, no longer than his finger, and one side of his scalp had a massive scar showing his mottled gold and emerald skin devoid of light gray scales or hair—lingering evidence of what had happened to his body before he'd occupied it.

He squeezed me, making me grimace. Caleb didn't know his own strength, and he was taller and broader than most drakcol. I carefully patted his back so as to not injure him. "Air."

"Sorry, Mindy. I always forget. I used to be tiny, and now I'm huge. Fyn keeps trying to help me, but I swear I wake up and expect to be smaller. Three cycles later and it's still weird being in a different body. I never meant to hurt you, but—"

"I'm fine." I interrupted, smoothing my shirt. When Caleb started talking, he didn't stop. Zoltilvoxfyn had assured me that was simply how Caleb was, whereas I thought it had resulted from him being a spirit for over twenty cycles and being unable to speak to anyone.

"You did awesome," he said, switching to English. The ship's NAID—Network of Artificial Intelligence for Drakcol—didn't understand Caleb when he spoke in English, because of his rough accent, but he spoke Drakconese fluently, so it wasn't much of a problem for him.

Currently, I am attempting to perfect my English. Seth and Caleb were teaching me, as well as our friend Edith. I loved learning languages, rather than relying on a translator. This was my seventh language, and, according to them, I was basically fluent. Not surprising. I was that amazing.

"Thank you."

Seth moved to Caleb's side, and I greeted him with a smile.

Humans were odd creatures. Seth had round pupils, round ears like they had been docked—Kalvoxrencol had assured me they were natural—pinkish white skin, no tail, no wings, no sharp canines, and no claws. He was also short. Seth had told me he was the average height and frame for human males. His shoulders were far narrower than a drakcol's, and his stomach was pudgy. He was soft all over. I didn't think he was unattractive, just different in an overly squishable way.

Kalvoxrencol loved his little mate, and that was all that mattered.

I hugged Seth, and he squeaked. I released him instantly. I must have startled him. When I'd first met Seth, it had taken months to discuss permissions with him, because each time I'd brought it up, he became distinctly uncomfortable. But I'd wrangled him into a conversation eventually. He allowed me to hug and touch him occasionally, as long as I didn't suddenly grab him. All in all, Seth didn't like being touched by anyone except Kalvoxrencol, and sparingly by his close friends Urgg and Wyn.

He went bright red and buried his hands into his thick jacket pockets. "Good race, Mindy."

I fought a frown at the endearment, or nickname as my mate-brothers called it. I wasn't particularly fond of it, but Seth struggled with our long names. Also, humans shortened names with alarming frequency. I'd accepted it as inevitable and as a sign of affection. Not to mention, I would much rather have received one than be left out as the only person in my family without a human endearment.

"Thank you," I told him.

Kalvoxrencol wrapped his blue arms around Seth, tail winding up his calf. "Fifth." His silvery-blue hair fell over his mate's shoulder.

"Two better than last cycle, though this outlying location leaves much to be desired," I commented.

"The Coalition was trying to entice the Maykian Papacy by having the race near their territory," Hallonnixmin said as he moved to stand beside Kalvoxrencol. "It was discussed in the last Cohort meeting, which you missed. Father was hoping to send you to Voyk to discuss the proposal with them. He had to send Fynlincoxmin instead."

I was a diplomat, which I loved, but I hadn't wanted to go to Voyk so I'd skipped the Cohort meeting.

"I'm impressed with your ranking," Monqilcolnen interrupted, giving me an indulgent smile.

"Indeed," Dontilvynsan said. "It was well done, Speedy."

I beamed, tail writhing and wings shuffling.

Caleb, face scrunched, brought me a glass of graugg with his inner fire—telekinesis. The glass wobbled and spilled some of the maroon liquid onto the moss floor. He bit out a swear, and Zoltilvoxfyn dragged his tail over the back of Caleb's leg. Gripping his cane, Caleb grunted as the glass began to move again. He was still struggling to master his gift, but Wyn, a close friend of Seth's, had been teaching him.

I accepted the maroon liquid, tousling Caleb's hair, and took a deep drink, relishing the bitter tang. All of my brothers and my cousin, who was basically a brother, followed suit, and I grinned. I loved them more than anything.

The similarities between us were beyond obvious. All of us brothers, besides Kalvoxrencol, had deep green eyes like our mother. My white hair matched Zoltilvoxfyn's, though he had black scales as did Dontilvynsan. Kalvoxrencol and Hallonixmin both had blue scales, though Hallonnixmin was a shade darker. His purple hair matched Dontilvynsan's. I was the lone man out with purple scales, as was Monqilcolnen with dark green scales and silver hair. But we all shared the same wide foreheads, long noses, and strong chins.

With a grin, I basked in the glow of my family's attention. What more could I need?

Chapter 2

RACING BY.

Bartholomew

I fell onto one of the two cots in our cell and pulled my glasses off to rub my face. The black plastic frames had held up, but one of the lenses sported a crack from where I'd gotten smacked in the face. At least I was able to see well enough, not that there was much to look at. The cell was made of metal, rectangular in shape, and had two bare cots, a toilet, and nothing else.

Vince stumbled in a few minutes after me, covered in soot, blood, and general grime, much like I was. Both of our heads were shaved and our simple brown jumpsuits were ratty and thin, to the point of non-existent.

Almost two years had passed since our abduction and subsequent sale. Some of the humans who'd been kidnapped had been sold to a restaurant that catered to rare tastes, which turned my stomach, but I tried not to focus on it too much, as there was literally nothing I could do about it. Some had been sold to brothels—I actually spotted those humans every once in a while—and some to private households as servants or pets. Everyone else had been offloaded to different planets.

The only human I saw regularly was Vince. The others were distant figures ghosting through the city, trying to survive. When I did see another human, we gave each other the same helpless look. None of us was in a position to save the other.

Vince and I had been sold to a fighting ring. Not as fighters, thank god, because we were scrawny as fuck, especially since Agk, our xoi owner, saw feeding us as an unnecessary luxury, but as cleaners. We cleaned the refuse, vomit, or piss left behind by the audience and dead bodies after the fight concluded. Not glamorous, but we were alive.

Vince collapsed beside me, and I grabbed his hand, interlacing our fingers. I was perfectly content to never touch anyone or talk—I was fairly self-sufficient—but Vince needed physical reassurance to cope with our surroundings. He was a tactile person. Me? Not really, but touching didn't bother me either, so I gave him what he needed.

"The furnace is threatening to give out again," Vince said, dragging his free hand over his soft features. He was lovely. There wasn't any other way to say it. Vince was lithe and attractive, even with the grime. I was shocked someone hadn't made Agk an offer for him.

I nodded with a grunt. The massive machine had been sending out more plumes of smoke than usual and giving us error codes that we couldn't read.

"If it dies, Agk's going to sell one of us to pay for it."

I tightened my hold on him.

Our owner had been threatening to sell us since he'd acquired us. The restaurants would always buy us. Given how rough a shape I was in, I doubted a brothel, except the cheapest, would purchase me. Vince probably—that was the problem with being pretty. But then again, who knew what a xoi found attractive? They were purple watermelons with horns, stuck on to toothpicks in bad spandex.

In the end, if Agk sold us, it was to become food or a whore or fodder for some kind of monster.

"Come on," I said, tugging on him. "Let's go watch that race everyone was talking about. We can probably see it on one of the screens around town."

Vince groaned, but I dragged him up. He needed this. He needed to do things, to see people, to pretend that there was a life after this.

We were free to leave after our work was done. We both had an implant in our arms to translate for us, track us, and prevent us from going far. If we did try to escape, the implant would shock us until we fell unconscious, leaving us vulnerable to anyone who passed by. Besides, where was there to go? There was no escape from the planet's surface. And if I was honest with myself, I wasn't sure if I deserved to escape, let alone survive.

I shrugged off the memories and kept walking. The dirt streets were crowded with filth and smog. The buildings were all unfinished rusty metal. Aliens of all types pressed against us while hovercrafts flew overhead. Xome was where the watermelon-head xoi called home, and it was the ass of the universe according to the residents, though it was right next to Maykian space. Mayks were wealthy aliens with supposedly wondrous technology that everyone wanted, but they did not share.

We crowded around a screen behind a force field of a shop along with other aliens. The shuttles darted between the indicated lights as the drones followed them. I didn't know much about the universe we inhabited, except that it was larger, meaner, and a whole lot more horrible than I'd ever thought, but the technology was amazing.

I chewed on my lip, watching the race—well, a sped-up version. Vince and the rest of the crowd groaned and cheered, calling out who they wanted to win. A large busk—an alien covered in thick brown fur with two huge tusks pushing out of their mouth—shoved me to the side to see better.

"Watch it, asshole," Vince snapped, dragging me closer.

"You watch it, puny," the busk snarled, the pink spines on their back lifting.

Vince wasn't intimidated—he never was. It was a wonder he didn't have his ass handed to him on a daily basis. "Back the fuck up."

"Make me."

I snagged Vince before he attacked the busk and probably got beaten to a pulp. I held him against my chest and moved out of the busk's way. "It's not worth it."

Huffing, Vince turned to the screen to watch the end of the race.

The crowd roared when a sleek Maykian shuttle pulled in first. However, as the racers docked at a station, the feed focused on the person who took fifth. His long white hair was shaved on one side, and his royal purple scales had a sheen like a snake. Drakcol. I didn't know much about the species and I'd never seen one in person, but they had changed my life.

My gaze slid over the drakcol. He was handsome, with his strong chin, long nose, and full lips. His plump bottom lip had a single gold ring in the middle. That was not his only piercing. His tapered ears were pierced from tip to lobe; the lobe having long golden earrings that ending in emeralds the same color as his eyes.

Apparently, one of the drakcol princes had taken a human as their mate. I wasn't sure how it had happened, but that human was the reason we'd all been abducted. Humans had become hot ticket items to be bought and sold as the newest fad.

I really wanted to hate that human, but they'd been abducted like I had. For all I knew, they hated their mate and hadn't had a choice in the matter. In the end, it didn't matter. I was here now, and the last two years had happened; there was no changing that.

Vince slid his arm through mine and drew my focus away from the screen. He was clinging to me as he watched the crowd with narrowed eyes. He was always nervous when we left the ring, even though if someone so much as gave me the stink eye, he would snap and growl. He was practically feral about protecting me. But he worried about someone taking us whenever we left.

It wasn't that I didn't worry, because I did, but at the same time, we needed to leave our cell and see sunlight, even if it was filtered through smog. But Vince wasn't as calm as I was.

He constantly yelled and railed about Agk or the unfairness of our situation. Honestly, I was pretty sure if given the chance, he would straight-up murder Agk. Me? I wasn't sure. Agk might deserve it, but killing him didn't guarantee freedom and the thought of ending someone's life, even his... My stomach churned. No. I had enough ghosts without adding another one to the horde.

Vince often talked about his past, the people he missed, his home, and whatever else he was pissed about. I would nod along, occasionally sharing, but most of the time, I listened to him without giving anything back. Talking it out helped him calm down, which he often needed. Vince sometimes was an asshole in his aggression, but it didn't bother me—we were friends. The closest one I'd ever had. Of course, in this situation, we didn't have much choice but to band together.

We stayed for a few minutes after the conclusion of the race, listening to the interviews, before shuffling back to the ring. Our rations, if Agk had made enough money tonight, were going to be given soon and more fights were scheduled tomorrow, so we needed rest. I slung a bony arm over Vince's shoulders to keep him tucked against my side.

Serlotminden

The shared space was empty when I stepped out of my bedroom in the morning. I peeked into Dontilvynsan's room, but it was empty; he was probably occupied with navy business. He oversaw several science stations and was charged with monitoring the Immortal Planet—one of our most important studies. Monqilcolnen, Hallonnixmin, and Gilvaxtin were gone, probably exploring the station together.

Zoltilvoxfyn growled and Caleb released a sound that made me distinctly uncomfortable when I rang their door. They were fucking, again, and I had no desire to interrupt them, *again*. Last, I went to Kalvoxrencol and Seth's room. The door was ajar, so I peeked inside. *They* wouldn't fuck with the door open—I was safe.

Seth stood in front of a large screen depicting a tube full of green liquid. Lucy, his black cat, was in his arms. He rubbed her flabby belly, and she purred in what I assumed was cat contentment, but his focus never deviated from the screen.

I grinned and leaned against the doorframe. His and Kalvoxrencol's kit. Seth watched the fetus almost constantly—it was an obsession. He hated being away from their growing child, though it would be some months yet before the fetus was viable.

"Watching again." Kalvoxrencol snagged Seth around the waist, biting his neck.

"I can't help it. What if something goes wrong?"

"Nothing is going to go wrong," he answered. "This is common, Husband. Many couples use this service."

"I'm allowed to be worried. That's our kid."

I almost stepped forward at Seth's rough tone to protect my younger brother, who wasn't as confident as he acted, but I controlled the instinct. Seth wouldn't hurt Kalvoxrencol—not ever.

Kalvoxrencol kissed his cheek. "My apologies. Of course, you're worried. This is the first time for you. For us. But..." He pointed at the corner of the screen. "The baby's vitals are strong. Edith is monitoring them. You know she'll never let anything happen."

Edith was one of Seth's closest friends, and a NAID who had gained sentience when Kalvaxrencol first took Seth from Earth over three cycles ago. She had slowly forced her way into each of our lives. I quite liked how hilarious she was, even if she did impart unwanted advice frequently.

"Wyn is checking on the baby daily," Kalvoxrencol added.

Lucy seemed to sense the seriousness of the conversation, or Seth's stress, because she squeaked and wiggled until her head was pressed under his chin. The cat was an odd creature that Seth had brought from his planet, and I'd only seen her a handful of times, including right now, because she wasn't friendly. When she did make an appearance, she usually hissed at everyone and then hid.

Wyn, like he'd been summoned, appeared on the screen. His bright pink hair was shaved on both sides and braided down the middle of his scalp. His lavender scales were glorious, as were his delicate features. I had never seen a prettier person in my life, no matter the species, though he was too short for my preference. I liked taller people, regardless of their gender. Wyn sat and began to read to the fetus, who probably didn't have ears.

Kalvoxrencol held Seth tightly in his arms as they stared at their kit. A little family in the making.

My soul hurt at the thought. Both of my younger brothers had taken mates, as had my eldest. I wanted that but hadn't found anyone I enjoyed spending more than a few days with. As I watched my youngest brother and his mate, I felt as if I was being left behind. He, Zoltilvoxfyn, and Hallonnixmin were out pacing me. They were busy with their families, and Dontilvynsan was always busy with his duties.

This feeling was ridiculous. I wasn't being abandoned, and I had as meaningful responsibilities as any of them. Despite it all, the feeling persisted.

I stepped back to give Kalvoxrencol and Seth privacy and headed to my shuttle, personal not racing, and slipped into the void of space.

Chapter 3

A HUMAN? HERE?

Serlotminden

A few of my less reputable racer acquaintances had invited me last night to join them in watching some fights on a planet closeby. Xome was out of Coalition space, so I probably shouldn't go, but then again, I did many things I shouldn't do.

Recreational fighting was a hobby of mine. I was a warrior soul, after all. Me and all my brothers were experts in hand-to-hand combat as well as blasters, but none of us participated in paid or recreational fights, unless you counted Kalvoxrencol's challenges, though it had been cycles since he'd issued one. We were royalty, examples to our people, and while we originated from a warring species, we had worked hard to change our image. So having the empire's princes fight for fun was seen as unwise by the Cohort.

I docked at a planet I would describe as seedy. I wasn't shocked, because this was the xoi homeworld. The xoi procured as well as supplied nearly all of the products to the black market, not to mention operated it. They had very few laws and were generally seen as disreputable throughout civilized space.

A heavy cloud of yellow pollution hung in the air as I stepped out of my shuttle. People leaned out of open windows in dilapidated buildings, calling out their services to me and the others who landed at the minuscule port. The overwhelming stench of fumes, urine, and smoke made my nose twitch and my eyes burn. More than one person glanced at me and my sleek silver shuttle with narrowed eyes.

This was a bad idea. I'd been to similar planets more than any of my brothers would like or that I would tell them, but the calculating looks I received made me question staying here. I heard all of my brothers in my thoughts insisting I get back into the shuttle and return to their sides where it was safe.

I was about to follow their non-existent demands, but something made me hesitate. What? I didn't know. Some instinct insisted that this was where I was meant to be. I'd learned long ago to trust my instincts, though they'd led me astray more than once. Unlike Monqilcolnen, I couldn't predict the future. My inner fire was rather boring, and not worth mentioning in comparison to all of my brothers and cousin.

My fellow racers called my name, making me start, and I shook off my random thoughts and followed them, remaining prepared for any threat that might present itself. I was far from helpless.

Flashing signs with betting odds covered the front of the building, which had forcefields for windows and trash littering the illuminated entrance. I stepped over a pile of puke to go inside, ignoring the massive security guard at the door, and my acquaintances vanished from my side to the betting window. I leaned against a wall not far from the entrance to watch the crowd shuffle into the simple benches around a dirt circle that barely qualified as an arena.

When the first competitors came out, it became a slugfest between two aliens wearing compliance collars. They were owned by the arena. The Coalition of Planets had made slavery and indentured servitude illegal, but the xoi weren't a part of it. To try and get rid of either would be an act of war. The xoi didn't have to follow our laws, and nor did they wish to.

Disgust filled me as I watched the two aliens attack each other. I shouldn't be here. I would've never come if I'd known this was what qualified as a "fight" on Xome. *Damn instincts.* I smiled at the English swear word. Drakconese didn't have the same kind of swearing as English, and I quite loved their profanity. Besides, each time I swore, Seth and Caleb laughed, which made me laugh. I loved my mate-brothers as much as the ones who shared my blood.

I pushed off the wall to leave when I paused, soul throbbing. All of the raucous noise of the cheering crowd vanished as my entire being focused on one thing. A thin creature huddled near the door one of the fighters had come out of. His black hair was shaved to basically nothing, and his bones poked out of his dirty skin, but that wasn't what caught my attention—he was human.

Supposedly, no humans had come from Earth besides Seth. Caleb had been a spirit at the time, so he didn't count, not really.

How could this human be here?

Without thinking, I went to him. His brown eyes with round pupils narrowed at my approach. He crossed his bony arms over his chest, but his shoulders hunched and he curled in on himself as if he was expecting trouble. He was a couple of increments shorter than I was, but stars, he was thin. From Seth's physique, I knew this wasn't how he was supposed to look.

"Hello," I said in English. Caleb had mentioned there were many languages on his planet, and he spoke but one. I took a chance that this human spoke the same one my mate-brothers did.

The man's eyes widened. "You speak English?"

"I do. Why are you here?"

He licked his cracked lips with his pink tongue, and oddly enough, I liked it. He replied, "Agk owns me. I clean."

"How did you get here?"

"What do you mean? There's a lot of us here."

My soul froze. "What?"

"Some prince married a human. Shouldn't you know that? You're drakcol."

My youngest brother *had* mated a human. Kalvoxrencol and Seth were not often in public, but their mating was well known. Humans must have become prime products, like cats. So many cats had been stolen from Earth and sold on the black market, reproducing faster than anyone thought possible. As such, the ban on owning them had been lifted, though it was illegal to buy one from Earth now.

I grabbed his arm, my fingers easily meeting, and glanced around. I couldn't leave this human here. It wasn't safe, and he needed to tell Hallonnixmin what was happening so my eldest brother could address the Cohort, who would then fix this. The Drakcol Empire had to help these humans. It was a matter of honor. We had to fix the mistake we had unknowingly caused.

"What the hell are you doing?" He tried to rip his arm from my grasp, but I was significantly stronger than him. I felt horrible for touching him without permission, but the present situation required it of me. My tail curled about his ankle naturally, which made me pause momentarily as questions formed in my mind. I forced the thoughts away and continued to the closest door.

The human continued to protest, growing louder, so I pushed him against the wall and covered his mouth. He had lenses over his eyes, one of which was cracked, but I saw the panic rush into the brown depths. He thrashed under me with muffled screams.

"I'm not going to hurt you," I whispered in his ear. My mind scrambled to find the right words in English. "We must leave. Stay quiet, please."

Muffled words came from beneath my palm, but I didn't remove my hand; I couldn't risk him drawing attention to where we hid. I peered around, searching for a guard, or better, yet a well-marked exit. Nothing presented itself, except for where I had come in, and a couple of big garganlics guarded the main door with their four arms crossed over their muscular chests and their four eyes flicking over the crowd. Getting past them with this tiny human, especially with him struggling, was impossible.

Something wet and soft licked my palm, and I jerked back. His pink tongue slid back into his mouth, and oddly enough, I wanted to press my lips against his and feel the softness of his tongue on mine. I froze. What was going on with me?

Humans did not interest me.

"I can't leave," he said.

"Why?"

He lifted his arm, and I noticed a sizable lump under his pinkish gold skin. Dermal implant. That was unfortunate. I inspected the bump, running my thumb over it. His skin was soft, extremely soft. By the Crystal's light, he was so soft against my scales. I forced my attention away from the feel and to the pressing issue.

Because his skin was as soft as it was, cutting him open with my claws to extract the implant would be easy enough, but it would hurt—not to mention he would lose his translator. That wasn't much of a problem, because I spoke English and NAID on my shuttle was perfectly capable of translating if the need arose.

"I can take it out," I said, extending my claws.

The human pressed further into the wall. "How do I know you're not worse than Agk?"

"I'm trying to help you."

"So you say. People say a lot of shit."

Shit. Ah, humans. It was amusing but now wasn't the time. I had to get this human away. I could inform Hallonnixmin without the human, but the Cohort was more likely to act and believe me with him present. Not to mention, Seth and Caleb would never forgive me if I left him behind, and I would never forgive myself. Everything in me rebelled against the very thought of abandoning him. He needed to stay right beside me until he was safe.

"Please," I tried again.

"Fuck off."

I blinked, then remembered it was a swear. He was *not* asking me to masturbate. These humans. Their profanity was so colorful.

My eyes darted back to the two garganlics by the door. I wished I had the time to reassure him of my good intentions, but I didn't. I was going to have to do something unfortunate and I doubted he was going to like it, but I had to save him. This human would thank me in the end, I was sure of it.

I smiled in reassurance, and the human recoiled further, his pupils blown wide while the pulse in his neck throbbed wildly.

"I am so sorry." I covered his mouth and dragged him toward one of the shadowed corridors further away from the door and the massive guards. He fought against me, kicking my shins, but I didn't release him. He viciously bit me, and I grunted, but I held on. When I found a private space, I pinned him to the wall. My tail coiled around his wrist to keep his arm flat against the wall.

"Let me go, you *bastard*."

I didn't remember what the last word meant, but it was a swear, and my translator supplied: child of an unmated mother. "I offer you my deepest and sincerest apologies, but I have to rescue you, even over your protests."

"You fucker."

With a grimace, I dragged a claw over his soft skin. He cried out, which made my soul cringe. I didn't want to hurt him. I truly didn't, but I had to help him. The human kept crying, tears coursing down his cheeks, and I glanced at the door multiple times. Someone was going to hear. I covered his mouth, and he sobbed beneath me, thrashing as much as possible in my tight hold.

Red blood coated my fingers and dripped to the filthy floor. When the slice was large enough, I inserted my claws as delicately as possible, but the thin human released a muffled scream.

"I'm so sorry," I whispered against his ear and pulled the implant out; it fell to the floor with a tink. The human panted, shaking. I ripped the base of my tunic and wrapped his arm as I apologized over and over again, hoping he would forgive me.

He sagged, colliding with my chest, eyes closed and body limp. My arms caught him, supporting his weight with ease.

Had I hurt him more than I thought? What if I'd nicked something important? I knew nothing of human anatomy. I'd never needed to before this moment. Why hadn't I studied? I should've anticipated this. Somehow.

I lifted him, and he was far too light. I would have to feed him. Soon. I pressed my ear to his narrow chest. His soul beat steadily, and his breath came out without any rattle. The blood on the makeshift bandage wasn't growing either.

Pain must have stolen his consciousness.

"Don't worry, human. I'll make sure you're safe, alright? I'll even take you back to Earth if I can." I snuggled him close to my chest, tucking his face in the crook of my neck, his warm breath rushing over my scales. I would keep this little human safe if it was the very last thing I did.

Now how to get out of here?

With him securely in my arms, I went back to the door that led to the ring and peered outside. One of the fights had concluded moments ago, and a good portion of the crowd was filtering out.

This was our chance—our one chance. I set him on his feet, but the human crumpled. I caught him well before he touched the ground.

Well, that wouldn't work.

Keeping an arm around his waist, a wing hugging him, and his face turned to my neck, I walked out as confidently as possible, dragging the limp human beside me. My soul pounded, but I remained relaxed. All I needed was confidence. Everyone believed confidence. Act like you belonged, and people assumed the same.

I exited, and no one said anything. The guards didn't even notice us.

The moment the building was out of sight, I swept the human into my arms and rushed to my shuttle with my precious treasure.

Chapter 4

IF THIS IS A RESCUE, I DON'T LIKE IT.

Bartholomew

I woke to the floor vibrating beneath me. The sensation sent an ice shard right to my heart, and I froze, unable to move. For a moment, I smelled the stench of too many bodies crammed together, heard the sobs and cries of terror, and felt the overwhelming dread that I was going to die. That this was it—my last moment alive.

My arm throbbed in time with my rapid pulse, drawing my attention from the uncomfortable memories. I took a deep breath, trying to force myself to move, but my limbs were locked in place as a sense of helplessness filled me. I was stuck. Once again, I was stuck and going somewhere else. I tried to take deep breaths, but my lungs didn't want to cooperate and my pulse hammered in my ears, drowning out the vibration.

A pulsing throb went through my arm, and I focused on that. The pain. It was so clear and real. No shadows. No guilt hiding beneath the memories. No panic. Just my body telling me I'd been injured. Straightforward.

I drew in a huge gulp of air, then held it before releasing it. I did it again and again, then one more time. Slowly, my pulse settled, and I shifted. Moving was possible. First things first, I checked my arm. A jagged white cloth stained with red was wrapped around my arm. Red. Blood. I blinked, trying to collect my scattered thoughts.

What had actually happened, and where the fuck was I?

The cabin around me didn't say much. I was on the sole bed in the room. The walls were metal, though far nicer than anything I'd seen on Xome, and there were plenty of panels that looked like they popped open for storage. Besides the recessed lighting and a small monitor, there wasn't anything else.

All of a sudden it hit me like a ton of bricks. That fucker. The purple drakcol had cut me with his claws and kidnapped me. He'd fucking abducted me. Twice now I'd been taken by aliens. Why couldn't people stop kidnapping me?

One second, I was on the reasonably comfortable bed, and the next I was in a heap on the floor, groaning. The ship lurched again, sending me sliding across the floor and into the wall, making me yelp. I scrambled to my feet, tangling in the silky blanket, and smacked into the wall; blood coursed over my lips and tears rushed to my eyes. Swearing, I gingerly pressed my fingers against my nostrils to stem the tide from what I guessed was a broken nose.

What the hell was happening?

I slid again, hitting the bed, though the mattress cushioned the blow. I forced myself to my feet and scrambled to the doorway.

Crashing into the walls, I rushed down a tight corridor that opened into a cockpit. The white-haired drakcol was at the controls. He peered back at me, his deep green eyes wide while his slit pupils were narrowed.

"Ah, human, you're awake."

"What the hell is going on?" I asked, voice calm, as the ship squealed and lurched again.

"We're under attack."

"No shit." I could've figured that out myself. I slammed into the wall again, my shoulder screaming from the impact. Where the hell were the stabilizers?

The shuttle jerked, and I staggered, hands landing on the alien's shoulders to catch myself. He didn't even react, and his fingers continued flying over the controls.

"Who's attacking us?" There was no way Agk was coming after me. He didn't care enough. I was a product to be used and thrown away—nothing more, nothing less.

Vince. God, I'd left him behind. I had to go back for him.

The drakcol pushed me toward the stool beside him. "Xoi. They are after this ship or me. I'm not sure which, and they didn't bother to tell me when I politely asked."

"Why would they want you?" I asked, then paused, finally recognizing him. "You're that racer."

The drakcol gave me a wide smile that made me frown. He blinked like it was unbelievable that someone didn't like his smile. The ship jolted, and he pressed buttons faster.

"Dontilvynsan," he said, and at first I thought it was his name, but another drakcol appeared on the monitor.

The behemoth with black scales and purple hair stared at my drakcol. "What's going on?"

"I'm under attack."

The ship groaned, and I swore. I was getting rescued by a maniac, and I was going to die because of it. Not starvation. Not being sold to a restaurant. Not exposure. Not being ripped apart in the fighting ring. No, I was going to die because some drakcol decided to "save" me, then mounted a piss-poor rescue.

I was past the point of caring, though fear did zing through me at my imminent demise. Besides, wasn't this exactly what I deserved?

All that I truly regretted was leaving Vince. He would never know what had happened to me, and I couldn't imagine Agk being kind about one of his slaves wandering off. What would he do to Vince?

"Where?" the new drakcol demanded, voice deep.

"Sent you my coordinates."

"Why are you in Xionian space? You should not be there."

"I found a human," my kidnapper said.

"What?"

But there was no time to answer. A purple vortex appeared in front of us.

My kidnapper shouted, "They opened a slipstream. I can't veer out of the way."

"I will come for you, Serlotminden," he said. "We will always come for you. You must hold on. Promise me."

"I promise," Serlotminden replied right before we went through the vortex and everything went dark.

The ship stretched and creaked. I couldn't scream. I couldn't breathe. I couldn't move. Everything was happening and nothing was happening, then I released a huge breath as space returned to normal.

"Slipstream. Not comfortable," Serlotminden said. "My first time." His fingers tapped on the buttons and screens, then he yanked on a yoke. "I have no idea where we are, but we need to leave. Now. Because the other ship is right behind us."

"You need to take me back. I did not ask to be saved."

"We can't go back."

"I left Vince."

"Vince?" he asked with a growl.

"Another human."

He didn't respond, because the ship lurched as our pursuers continued to attack. I grunted, struggling to stay seated. The stool didn't have a back for some weird reason, making it difficult to stay on, but it did have arms that I clung to like a cat confronted with water.

The ship veered as Serlotminden did his best to flee the xoi who were hell-bent on pursuing us.

"Why do they want you?" I asked.

"I'm a prince, and this is a very nice shuttle. Newest model. My brothers gave it to me."

"So they plan to ransom you back?"

"Maybe. Or this is simple theft."

"Perfect," I said.

Speaking wasn't possible any longer, because the ship kept jolting and bumping from the barrage. One of Serlotminden's hands flew over the controls as the ship moved in a nonsensical pattern while the other controlled the yoke with practiced motions. I kept falling out of the seat, even as I braced against the console in front of me, trying to stay on.

Suddenly, everything went red, and a blue silhouette of a drakcol said in a monotone voice, "Engine failure is imminent. Shields are at ten percent."

Serlotminden glanced at me, and I recognized the expression. We were going to die. I sighed, terrified and yet oddly relieved. I was tired and the weight of everything I'd done was like rocks strapped to my back. Finally, it was over. I didn't have to carry anything any longer. I didn't have to hear the screams anymore.

He angled the nose of the ship toward a planet, sending us into a death spiral as flames licked the metal. "I'm going to try to set us down."

"My name is Bartholomew."

"What?"

"If we are going to die, I want you to know it. I don't want to die alone." I met his gaze. "I'm Bartholomew Reginald."

"Serlotminden."

The ship shrieked as we spiraled to a no doubt fiery death.

Chapter 5

WE CRASH LANDED AND ARE STRANDED.

Serlotminden

Cold air surrounded me, sending a shiver down my spine. I hated the cold—drakcol were meant for warm weather. I forced my eyes open with a loud groan to assess the damage. Attempting to land while under attack with failing stabilizers and shields was probably not my smartest plan, but what else was I supposed to do?

The front screen of my shuttle was shattered; snow and rocks covered the console and the open section. We'd crashed hard, but I was alive. I hadn't expected that.

I tried to stand, but my stomach spasmed, making my vision waver and whiting out my thoughts. My hand went to my gut and met wet warmth. A piece of metal was sticking out of me, and green blood oozed around the shaft, not fast enough to worry me, but it needed to be taken care of. And soon.

Alive, but injured.

"Barth…" I trailed off. What was his name? He was nowhere in my line of sight. Where was he? Was he alright? A whine ripped out of my lips when I tried to turn. I had to find him. The small human was mine to protect. I'd taken him, and in all honor, I couldn't abandon him. Gritting my teeth, I shifted enough to see the entire cockpit.

The human was crumpled on his side, not moving.

"No." I tried to drag myself to his still form. *Please be alive.* "No, please no." Fiery agony lanced my stomach from my pathetic attempts to crawl in his direction. "Human. Bartholomew. Please. No. Open your eyes. Don't leave me alone here. Please."

He took a jagged breath, then coughed several times in quick succession before rolling toward me. His lenses were gone, and his brown eyes were unfocused. My position and the darkness didn't allow me to see much—only the emergency lights were on—but he didn't appear harmed.

I stretched a hand toward him. "Are you alright? Are you well? Fine?" Which was the right word? I couldn't remember. Why didn't I remember?

"No," he said, sounding perfectly fine. "We crashed."

I coughed, pain shredding my stomach as my abdominal muscles clenched. "We did," I forced out, shivering.

Bartholomew appeared above me, and I stared at him. His skin was darker than Seth's by a shade or two, but still so pinky-white, and his hair was black, though it was so short that it was barely visible. His thin lips were pulled into a frown and his long nose was perfectly straight, though swollen. Why was it swollen, and why did he have blood covering his lips?

"Are you okay?" he asked.

"No. I got stabbed. My ship tried to murder me," I teased to make him laugh. I was fairly certain I'd pulled the joke off. I was very good at English.

He sighed, pinching the bridge of his nose, then yanked away. "Fuck."

"That is quite sudden, and I'm too injured," I said, shivering.

"You're not funny," he said blandly, pressing his pointer finger to his nostrils.

"Seth and Caleb think I am."

"Good for them." He disappeared across the cockpit, patting the debris.

"Careful." He could cut himself on pieces of jagged metal or shards from the screen, and I didn't like the idea of him being hurt more than he already was. I needed to check the cut on his arm, as well as find out why there was blood on his lips. Any injury could get infected.

Ignoring me, he asked, "Are they how you know English?"

"Seth and Caleb taught me, as well as Edith, but she's not human. My youngest brother mated Seth first, then my other younger brother mated Caleb."

"Hmm," he said. "So they're why I'm here."

"How?"

"Some xoi abducted us because humans are a commodity."

There was no way for Kalvoxrencol to have known that mating Seth would result in other humans being abducted. Also, they were soulmates; he'd had no choice once the Crystal revealed Seth, though my little brother would feel guilty. So would Seth.

"Found them." Bartholomew held up his lenses, more cracked than before, and shoved them on. He returned to my side and bent to inspect the wound on my stomach. "Do you heal fast?"

"Faster than what?" I didn't understand. People healed as they healed without treatment.

"Fast enough that this won't kill you."

"No."

"So what do I do?"

"You're going to help me?" I'd taken him without permission, crashed, and now, was injured and he was going to help me?

He scrubbed his shorn hair, and I wondered how it would feel under my scales. Was it pokey? Soft? Stars, I wanted to know. Would he let me touch it? Maybe. I shook my head. My thoughts were jumping about more than usual. Blood loss or shock was affecting me; I couldn't say which or if either.

"We're stuck here," he said evenly. "If you die, I'm even more *screwed* than I currently am. I'm not going to cut off my nose to spite my face."

I had no idea what "screwed" meant or why he would chop off his own nose—it was a perfectly lovely nose as far as noses went—but I understood he was helping me. I pointed to the back of the shuttle. "Can you check if the cabin is whole?"

Bartholomew struggled to his feet and disappeared from view. The moment he left my sight, I had an immediate urge to follow him or call him back. I didn't like him being out of my range of vision.

What if something happened? What if he hurt himself? What if he left and I was all alone?

"It's fine," he called. "Though it's dark. I can't see much."

The emergency lighting must be failing. That was not good.

"There's a lantern you can take back there," I said.

When Bartholomew returned, I gestured to a panel, telling him how to open it and how to turn the light on. After he'd finagled it open, he disappeared again, and once again, the same urge to call him back surfaced. My tail writhed and wiggled with agitation. He needed to stay within sight. That would fix everything. I was sure of it.

When he returned, I asked, "Can you help me to the cabin? I need to get out of the cold. So do you. You're too small."

He lifted an eyebrow.

"What?" He was. Bartholomew had nothing to keep him warm.

Without a word, he hooked his thin arms under my armpits and tried to drag me, but I barely shifted. I was too heavy, and he was too slight. This wasn't going to work. Bartholomew would never be able to manage my weight. With no other option, I tried to force myself to my feet, but I shook and my vision twisted before whiting out with the ripping agony.

"I'm too..." I tried to think of a word, but I was panting and my brain refused to work.

"Big. Muscular. Much of an asshole?"

"The last one is a swear for a butt hole. Why would I be too much of one? Or are you saying mine is large? I do not understand." My eyes closed as I shivered.

Something cool touched my cheek, and I opened my eyes. Bartholomew grabbed my chin, forcing me to look at him, and my soul throbbed. His brown eyes were flecked with bits of gold and green. They were a jungle I wanted to explore. Maybe then I would understand this calm human. And I wanted to. I wanted to understand him, to know him, and I couldn't say why.

"Stay awake," he ordered. "You dragged me here without my permission, and I need you to stay awake. I'm not doing this alone. Do you understand?"

"I do," I replied thickly. Why did I enjoy looking at him? It was nice. But more than that, I liked him looking at me. But that made sense. I was attractive. It was reasonable that he'd stare at me.

He vanished, and I instantly called for him. "Bartholomew!"

"Calm down," he said. "God, you're excitable."

Bartholomew returned with a blanket from the cabin. He tied it under my arms, then yanked with a grunt. My armpits immediately protested the abuse, and fiery-hot claws raked over my stomach, stealing a whimper from my lips, but I moved. He dragged and dragged, swearing under his breath, and I fought to stay conscious with the pain ripping me apart. He didn't stop, not even to take a breath, until we were in the cabin.

I pointed at the button on the wall, shaking so violently I didn't know if Bartholomew saw what I was gesturing to. He found it with ease and pushed it, but the door didn't close—it didn't even budge. That wasn't good. We needed to conserve heat; an open space didn't help with that. It was too cold for me, which meant it was far too cold for my small human.

My eyes closed, but the insistent fingers returned, and I forced myself to look at him.

"Don't worry about it," he said, stroking my cheek. "I'll find a way to block it." Bartholomew pulled the pad from the bed closer, then dragged me onto it. Panting, he untied the blanket and draped it over my legs. "Do you have a *first-aid kit*?"

"A what?" I understood all of the words, but not what they meant together.

He frowned, and a divot appeared between his eyebrows. I wanted to kiss the mark away. *Wait. What?*

"Medicine?" Bartholomew asked. "I need to do something about the wound."

I gestured to the panel on the wall.

He popped it and pulled out a metal container. "This?"

"Yes."

When he settled next to me, I removed a laser surgical tool, claspers, injectors, and two vials. I knew how to treat small injuries; I'd been trained to do basic medical care. I had to be able to take care of myself in case one of my long-haul races went wrong. Some lasted over six months with no other shuttles, stations, or planets nearby.

I had no way of knowing if the piece of metal had nicked anything important, like my bowels or one of my organs. If it had, I would bleed out when we removed the shaft, but I couldn't leave it in either.

"I'm going to need your help," I said.

"Tell me what to do."

I pulled out an injector and filled it with antibiotics, then another one with a blood inducer to help my body replace the blood I'd lost. "Press this into the side of my neck."

Bartholomew took it from me and pressed it against my scales without hesitation. I grimaced when the needle stabbed me and the liquid burned going in. "Rub the site, please."

His long fingers circled the puncture and kept up the even pressure until I said, "Next one on the other side, and do the same thing."

He leaned over me, arm brushing my chest and pushed the injector against my scales. I winced. Bartholomew squeezed my hand, and I returned the pressure as I breathed and he massaged the injection site. The pain would vanish soon enough.

After a few moments, the burning dimmed, but I didn't let him go. His hand in mine was nice. I had seen Kalvoxrencol and Zoltil-voxfyn hold their mates' hands—it was a human thing. I slid my fingers through his, pressing our palms together.

What did it mean? Neither of my mate-brothers had exactly explained it, and I never cared to ask, as humans didn't interest me in that way.

"Vince likes me to hold his hand when he's in pain as well."

I frowned, releasing him with a growl building in my chest. "I need you to pull the metal out."

"That's not a good idea."

"Do it," I snapped. Who was this Vince? Then I recalled the other human he'd mentioned. Why did he feel the need to talk about the other human right now? I was the one holding his hand. I was the one he was looking at.

"Fine. Die if you want."

He yanked the shaft out mercilessly, and I was unable to suppress the yelp that escaped my lips. I grabbed the claspers and ripped out the broken scales near the gash, whimpering with each pull. Blood gushed out of the wound, non-stop. My fingers shook and my vision spun until I couldn't see straight. I dropped the clasper, shaking.

"No," Bartholomew said, grabbing my chin. My eyes opened. I hadn't even realized I closed them. "What do I do?"

My fingers fumbled on the laser. He seized it from me and pushed the buttons until the tip glowed bright blue. I tried to point to the bleeding wound, but my vision was tunneling and my hearing was turning into static. Bartholomew slowly dragged the laser over the gash, and the mottled skin knitted together, making me cry from the intense burning.

I fought to stay awake for as long as possible, but the pain dragged me away.

Chapter 6

SO IT'S FUCKING COLD.

Bartholomew

After I cleaned the blood off my face, I started to dig through every panel to search for anything useful. I found plenty of rations and water cubes, so we wouldn't starve or die of thirst as long as someone found us in a reasonable amount of time. From the passionate way the big drakcol had talked, I assumed he and Serlotminden were in a relationship. He would come searching; I wasn't too concerned about that. It was more about whether we were in a place that could be found.

That thought sent a tremor down my spine and a needle to my heart.

What if we were somewhere that no one could find us? What if Serlotminden died, and I was here alone? What if—I viciously cut that train of thought off.

Spiraling into a pit of fear didn't help anyone, least of all me. Logically, I had to remain calm to stay alive as well as help Serlotminden.

Being freaked out about what *might* happen wouldn't help anyone. Survival had to be my main focus. Surviving so I was alive to return to Vince, because *he* deserved to be saved.

With great difficulty, I closed my eyes and breathed.

Once my pulse slowed, I popped open another panel and found several blankets, which was good because it was balls-cold in here, and who knew how cold outside. I covered Serlotminden in a heap of blankets, then kept searching. I needed to make some sort of tent because staying warm was going to be priority number one. My jumpsuit was thin, and Serlotminden was in a high-collared sleeveless shirt and pants—neither offered much warmth.

After more searching, I found a tarp made of a plastic-like material. It should work. The plastic would help contain our heat, and it was big. I unrolled the sheet to make a tent and saw an image of Serlotminden winking on it as well as a place for ties. It was a flag. Nice to know.

The end result, with several pieces of wreckage and ties I'd found, was a fort-esque tent, like I'd made as a kid with my moms and sisters. A sudden twinge in my chest started at the thought of them, and I pushed it away. Now wasn't the time to dwell on them. I had to stay focused.

I pushed all the remaining blankets, pillows, and even his clothes into the tent before joining Serlotminden. It was already warmer than the rest of the cabin.

Settling under the blankets with him, I cuddled close. There was no point in being shy. I didn't want to freeze, and I doubted he did either, not that he was awake to ask. Snuggling for warmth wasn't a new concept for me. When the weather turned cold on Xome, Vince and I had often shared a single cot for warmth because Agk had never given us a blanket or warmed our cell, saying it was unneeded. I scoffed. Agk was a sack of shit.

I curled against Serlotminden, draping an arm over his waist. The scent of musky rain wafted off him and made me take another deep inhale. Fuck, he smelled good. I was sure I smelled like B.O. and death had a baby, but bathing was a luxury I didn't often get. My smell was what it was.

I lay there, watching his chest rise and fall with each breath. If he died, I had no idea what I would do. Panic began to creep in. I tried to push it away, but it didn't want to go. I had successfully remained focused on surviving when I was moving. Now that I was still... I started to shake, fisting Serlotminden's shirt.

My thoughts flipped to Vince. Alone. God. He wasn't going to know what happened to me. Agk might punish him for me leaving, or sell him. I hoped not. The first thing I was going to do when we got rescued was go back for him. I would never leave Vince behind.

I burrowed under the blanket, hiding like that usually calmed me, and rubbed against Serlotminden's arm, soothed by the scritch of his scales. I took deep breaths to force the fear away, but it danced under my skin like ants.

What was I going to do?

Serlotminden had to survive. That big drakcol would come for him, and we would get out of here. Together. No other option was acceptable. This stupid ice and snow would not kill me. I had lived through too much to die here. I needed a chance to make up for my mistakes. I had to save Vince, who deserved to be rescued.

A tremor went up my spine, but I forced myself to still. I did not want to think about anything. Survival was all that mattered, and that was what I would focus on. I took several deep breaths to calm myself, but my pulse kept racing.

I slammed my eyes closed and pressed against Serlotminden, relishing the warmth emanating from him. First sleep. I had nothing else to do, and oblivion would be a welcome relief. When he woke up, we'd figure out the next step to fixing this horrid rescue attempt.

Serlotminden

My stomach ached and my head throbbed in time with my soul, making me groan, but I was warm. That was an unexpected surprise, and someone was pressed against my side, another nice surprise. My tail was curled around them, and I pulled the thin form closer, nuzzling the spiky hair. Bartholomew. My eyes popped open, taking in my flag and the blankets surrounding me.

He'd created a shelter for us.

Bartholomew was curled against my side with his head on my shoulder and his arm slung over my waist. His bones were poking out beneath the threadbare jumpsuit; he was severely underweight. Something I needed to remedy shortly. He was covered in dirt and the stench of sweat mixed with smoke clung to him, but he was alive. He was here.

My rescue hadn't gone well, but we were alive.

While aching, my stomach would heal.

I was going to have to protect this human until we reached safety. I might even be able to convince Dontilvynsan or another captain to make the six-month journey to Earth. That was if my brothers found me. I had no doubts they would search—they would never stop—but I didn't know how far we'd traveled in the slipstream.

It was possible Bartholomew and I were in uncharted space, making it near impossible for anyone to find us. If that was the case, I would protect him for the rest of his life.

I cradled him close, and my tail coiled up his leg, holding him securely. I liked the feel of him in my embrace. He fit. It was odd. No one had ever fit beside me. I'd always felt the urge to leave right after fucking, once the intimacy had vanished. Not that this huddle for warmth was romantic, let alone a post-fuck snuggle, but still, I had no urge to move. I had no words to express why, and perhaps it didn't matter. Bartholomew fit against me. It didn't have to make sense.

He shifted, and I tightened my hold, unwilling to let him go. If he fit, he needed to remain. Right here. That was only logical.

Bartholomew opened his eyes and his expression was completely blank. Caleb bounced around as much as possible in his body, and Seth was always fidgeting or turning red. Both were so expressive, but this tiny human showed no emotion.

Humans, of course, came in as many personality types as us, but I'd expected him to be similar to my mate-brothers.

"You're alive," he said calmly in an even, smooth voice.

"I am."

"Good." He closed his eyes and remained against me. Even he knew where he fit. It *was* logical.

"You made a..." I trailed off. I didn't know the English word for what he'd made.

Thankfully, he understood. "Tent. It's a tent. A shit one at that."

Shit. I believed that meant bad and poop. Humans. Their words doubled or tripled in meaning. I loved it. "It is a fine tent. It's keeping us warm."

He grunted.

I wanted to hear his voice. "How did you know how to create a tent?"

"My mom. She used to take me, my other mom, and my sisters *camping* every summer. None of us really wanted to go, but we had to. She finally stopped making us when I became a *teenager*."

"Camping" and "teenager" were a mystery, leading me to believe that Seth, Caleb, and Edith had lied about my near fluency, but I understood enough. "You have sisters?"

"Two."

"I have four brothers and one cousin who is like a brother."

Bartholomew grunted again.

"Three of my brothers are mated."

"So you said. They're married to humans."

"Two of them are." I turned my head toward him, my chin brushing his bristly hair. "Kalvoxrencol mated Seth, and Zoltilvoxfyn mated Caleb. Though Caleb had been dead, so he's not exactly a human anymore."

"What?"

Grinning, I told him the story of Zoltilvoxfyn and Caleb, and how Caleb came to be in a drakcol body. Bartholomew listened, bobbing his head occasionally in the human way that meant agreement. Although to me, it seemed like he was conceding to my dominance. Humans. Odd things. So adorable, though. I had the urge to squish him, much like I did Seth.

Once I finished, I told him of Kalvoxrencol and Seth, because why not? "They were bound by the Crystal."

His forehead crinkled in the cutest way. "The Crystal?"

How did I explain the Crystal that our people revered? I didn't know if I had the words. "It linked Kalvoxrencol and Seth together as soulmates." When Bartholomew didn't say anything, I continued, "We have different types of mates: bound and chosen. Chosen is when we pick our mates. The mate bond forms naturally between people. Bound is when the Crystal reveals your soulmate and ties you to them. You are physically linked and can speak mind to mind."

"Your brother can read Seth's thoughts?"

"Yes, sort of. It's complicated."

"That's not something I would like. No privacy."

I'd never thought of it that way. I had never dreamed of having a soulmate, but mind-speak had never bothered me either. "Mates are important to drakcol," I said. "Kalvoxrencol would never infringe on Seth's privacy. They love each other."

He grunted, not looking even remotely interested.

"We only have one mate ever. If our mate dies or rejects us, we usually die. We'll fade away. Drakcol can't live without their mates.

Seth is the most important thing to Kalvoxrencol, as Caleb is to Zoltilvoxfyn. Both of them are well cared for. I promise."

"Did I say otherwise?"

His voice was impossibly smooth, sliding down my spine like water. Wanting to hear more and to change the subject, I asked, "Are your sisters mated?"

"No."

My little human didn't speak much. "Tell me of them."

"Why?"

"So I can learn more about you."

Bartholomew grunted. He did that quite frequently. "We need to figure out what to do. I assume that drakcol you spoke to will come for us."

"Dontilvynsan, and yes."

"We have a decent amount of rations and water."

"But it will not last long, depending where we landed," I remarked.

"Do you know where we are?"

"We were attacked before I had a chance to study the star coordinates. I will have to try and get the computer working."

"Can you?"

I honestly had no idea. NAID wasn't something I frequently worked with. I maintained my ship, but I wasn't an engineer who knew the intricacies. "I will try."

He started to sit up, and I instinctively pulled him closer before relinquishing my grasp. I had no right to hold him. We hadn't discussed permissions. Bartholomew didn't have to accept my touch, even though I wanted to keep touching him. He was soft; it was nice. It was quite normal to like touching soft things. That was all. But we needed to talk, and soon, because it wasn't right for me to keep forcing my touch on him, though he didn't act upset.

"I have no idea where we landed," he said, "but now that you're awake, I'm going to check it out."

"No." I grabbed his hand to drag him closer to me, where it was safe. Animals or dangerous creatures might be outside. I didn't know what planet we'd crashed on. It was possibly inhabited. The local residents might not be friendly. They might take Bartholomew or hurt him, and I would be unable to protect him. Or he might leave me and never come back, and I would never know what happened to him.

Bartholomew shook me off. "I wasn't asking permission. You stole me when I didn't ask to be saved, then crashed. We need to know where we are. For all we know, we'll be stuck here for months and we're going to need food."

"You're right," I said, thoughts whirling. I had to keep him here. "We'll wait until I'm able to move, then we'll go together. It's safer."

He frowned at me, making that divot appear between his black eyebrows. Stars, it was cute.

"Let me get you some food." He slid over me with ease, and I struggled not to catch and snuggle him.

What was happening? I didn't understand. Never, not ever, had I felt this possessive of someone, certainly not someone I'd recently met. I desperately wished my brothers were here to talk to. They would help me work through whatever was going on, well after several rounds of well-meaning teasing, but they would let me talk it out or ask the right questions or blatantly tell me what was happening.

Perhaps humans had some sort of pheromone that made drakcol protective of them. That had to be it. I was reacting to him because of that. No other reason... Though Kalvoxrencol had never mentioned such pheromones, and he told us everything about humans. He was obsessed with researching human care; he did *have* a human mate to protect.

It must be because Bartholomew was small and helpless. Like a lost animal. I had to keep him safe and hold him close. He did fit beside me. Maybe we were meant to become great friends. That thought made me frown, and I didn't know why.

When Bartholomew slipped back in, he sat cross-legged beside me and handed me a simple nutrition bar. I accepted, my fingers brushing his. He was freezing, more than normal. He was too thin to be out in the cold for long. Watching him closely, I nibbled on the tasteless bar. It met our needs, but it was dusty on my tongue.

"I must say sorry about the food," I said. Bartholomew deserved the best, and this was hardly it, nor would this help him gain weight. How was I going to fatten him without supplies?

He lifted and lowered his shoulders, and my brain struggled to recall what it meant. I was so tired that my eyes started to close as I chewed. I fought it, needing to keep talking to him. We were going to be friends after all.

"It's fine," Bartholomew replied. "Better than what I normally get."

That simple comment sent a wave of anger crashing through me, waking me up. "That should not be true."

Bartholomew grunted and finished eating the bar, then popped a couple of hydration cubes in his mouth. The water would vanish long before the food, especially because humans required more than us drakcol. Humans were always dehydrated, from Kalvoxrencol's research. It was quite a problem. He had to constantly make sure Seth consumed enough water. Though I'd heard Seth blaming Kalvoxrencol for having to pee too often.

"Did you get enough water?" I asked, tail twitching. "You should drink another."

"I'm fine."

"You need more."

"We'll run out."

"Not a problem," I said. "When I have healed, I can melt some snow."

He wrapped his bony arms around his knees. "You know how to start a fire?"

I grinned, and his expression didn't change. Unusual. Most people were affected by my smile. I *had* won the Most Charming Smile award on Tamkolvanloknol for the last three cycles. I was an exceedingly popular racer because of my smile and aspect. That helped on my diplomatic assignments. Many species found me attractive.

Bartholomew was the exception apparently.

My soul throbbed. I didn't like the thought of that. Perhaps drakcol did not interest him anymore than humans interested me.

That didn't comfort me.

Letting it go, I answered, "I am fire." I lifted my hand and pushed up a single ember of the roiling wildfire in my gut. A flickering flame grew in my palm until it became a perfect sphere.

"You can create fire?"

"It is a rather boring gift," I admitted, wishing I didn't have to confess it to him, but Bartholomew deserved the truth. "All of my brothers have more exciting, not to mention rarer, inner fires. Mine is the most common, but it's the same gift as my mother, so I think that's rather nice. Also, in this situation, it's quite helpful.

"Every drakcol has an inner fire," I told him, even though he didn't ask or appear the slightest bit interested. "It develops in..." I trailed off. I couldn't think of the correct word. This was far harder without Edith, Caleb, or NAID to rely on to translate for me when needed. "When we grow."

"Hmm."

"Mine was boring when it appeared. I lit a bush on fire. Zoltilvox-fyn yelled at me for destroying the plant, then he sobbed. Kalvoxren-col had been so mad at me for making him cry. He's extremely protective of Zoltilvoxfyn."

"Ah."

Bartholomew wasn't talking at all, but he was nodding along or making encouraging noises. The longer I stared at him, the more I wanted to never look away. I could study the flecks of deep green and bits of gold in his eyes for the rest of my life and not be bored, which was new. I often got bored. Deep inside of me was an urge to run, play, fight, and never stop moving.

That urge wasn't present right now. Maybe it was the injury to my stomach, but perhaps not. The only other time I'd felt something similar was with my cousin Monqilcolnen. He could calm me with a glance, but he was the purest spiritual soul ever recorded.

Bartholomew didn't react to me staring at him; he simply watched me back. I smiled, and he didn't return the gesture.

"I'm a warrior soul," I said, hoping to impress him for some reason.

"Okay."

Not the reaction I was hoping for. Maybe he didn't understand. "The Crystal reveals our soul type. We get tested when we're little. Drakcol have four soul types: warrior, spiritual, seeker, and creator. I'm a warrior soul, and it's deep red."

"Ah."

"That means I'm a..." What was the word? "Full warrior. Warrior and seeker souls grow darker the more... of the soul they are. Seekers are blue." Stars, how did I explain that the purer the soul, the deeper the color was. "Spiritual souls, which are white, and creator souls, which are green, grow lighter."

"Interesting."

He didn't sound interested. I continued, "Warriors are very important to drakcol. The most important. I am an excellent one. I can and will protect you."

"I can keep myself safe."

My tail flicked. This wasn't going well. Bartholomew looked bored and unimpressed. I took his hand, and he didn't fight. I placed it over my thrumming soul, in the center of my chest. "I will keep you safe."

"Fine."

That was something. I smiled, and he didn't return it, but neither did he try and pull away from me. I kept staring at him, tracing the planes of his face. This human was special. I wasn't sure why, but I planned to find out.

"I'm thirty-one in standard or twenty-eight in Earthen age," I said.

"Hmm."

My tail twitched. "How old are you?"

"Twenty-four."

He wasn't that much younger than me, which relieved me for some reason.

When I could hold it off no longer and sleep started to claim me, I reached for him. Bartholomew came to my side without a word, and I hauled him close, settling him right next to me.

We would discuss permissions tomorrow. For now, he was perfect against me. By the Crystal's light, I'd never felt anything so wonderful. His head was tucked against my shoulder and his hand rested on my stomach, fingers trailing over me in lazy motions. I drifted off, warm and content.

Chapter 7

WE ARE NOT ALONE.

Bartholomew

After Serlotminden was deep asleep, I wiggled out of his hold and unwound his tail from my calf. He was a tactile person, always trying to touch me, but it didn't feel like he was creeping on me, more like he was reassuring himself that I was still here—that he wasn't alone. Vince had done that at times. He'd needed to hold my hand or pull me close to feel safe.

Tactile people needed to be touched. I got that, even if I didn't reciprocate the feeling.

I crawled over him and left the warmth of the tent, flicking the lantern back on—it shut itself off on a timer and I didn't know how to change it. Serlotminden probably did, but when he was last awake that hadn't been my main concern—making sure he ate had been.

The frigid temperature of the shuttle made me shiver as my breath rushed out in a foggy cloud. Fuck. It was mind-numbingly cold out here. The tent was probably not *that* warm, not that I had a thermometer, but it was a million times better than the rest of the cabin.

Snagging some of the clothes from the tent as well as a blanket, I tugged on a loose pair of pants over my thin jumpsuit. Serlotminden wasn't much taller than me, but he was far wider. He was exceedingly muscular, like he was intimately familiar with the gym. That had never been my scene, even prior to being abducted. I tied a piece of rope around my waist to keep them in place—the hole in the back for Serlotminden's tail worked perfectly as a belt loop—then wrapped the blanket around me.

I started to sort through more panels. The rations were in an insulated container, so I didn't worry about them freezing. There were circuit boards and tech parts that meant nothing to me, more clothes, these were jumpsuits, a couple of pillows, a bottle of thick liquid that smelled like Serlotminden's rainy fragrance, a bar of what I assumed was soap, and not much else. I shoved the pillows and clothes into the tent, then went to the cockpit.

The front window was broken inward from the crash. Snow and rocks blocked it. We weren't getting out that way. I had no idea what to do with the computer, so I left it alone.

The cargo bay was small, with a couple of locked crates in it. One was about the length of my arms, but the other came to my chest and was twice or maybe three times my width. They would have to wait until Serlotminden was awake, unless I planned to hit them with some of the larger pieces of debris in the hopes of breaking the locks.

That didn't seem smart. For all I knew, there were explosives or weapons inside that wouldn't appreciate being hit.

Ice and frost covered the metal walls and floor, but the bay door was easy to identify. I slammed the button closest to the hatch, assuming it opened the door, but nothing happened. There was no power anywhere in the ship—even the emergency lights in the cockpit had turned off—so I wasn't too surprised. Hopefully, it was that rather than snow blocking the entrance. If the latter was the case, no one would find us, and a horrible death awaited us.

Serlotminden would probably eat me. Maybe that was better than dying of thirst. At least I didn't have to worry about it at this exact moment. He wasn't doing anything physical until he healed. If I thought he was going to kill me... then I guessed I could do him in first.

I swallowed as screams and the thud of fists on metal echoed in my mind. Nope. That wasn't going to happen.

Whatever. It was what it was. Stressing about it right now didn't help anything.

My hands ran over the door. Maybe there was a manual override. That was a thing, right? I was working on sketchy knowledge from sci-fi shows and books and the limited access to technology I'd been allowed on Xome. A panel near the door popped open; a lever sat inside. I yanked on it with a loud groan. Shoulders screaming and arms trembling, I pulled and pulled and *fucking* pulled.

The bay door slowly creaked open. Wind gusted in and chunks of snow and ice tumbled inside, but the way was clear. Closing the door might be a problem, but it was the future me's problem. I wasn't going to worry about it at this exact moment.

Carefully, I climbed out, slipping on the frozen ground.

The shuttle had crashed into a cliff, and debris covered most of the ship, leaving the bay door clear. Anyone flying above wouldn't see us. I had no idea if Serlotminden's boyfriend would perceive our signature or whatever it was called because of the rocks; I truthfully didn't know how it worked. Cleaning the bodies and shit left behind from the fights hadn't given me much access to technology, so my knowledge was extremely limited.

Dark blue trees with dancing fronds like palm trees formed a jungle in the distance. The cliff behind us was tall enough I couldn't see the top, and it was a sheer drop, neither of which bothered me, but the car-sized nests sure as hell did. They were ginormous and formed from huge branches into spheres with gaping doors that had rough hides covering the entrances.

I hunched as a prey feeling swept through me, making me freeze like a deer caught in headlights.

What kind of animal even used a nest that size? Nothing I wanted to meet, as it most likely enjoyed skinny human. That would be a fitting end to the worst rescue in the history of rescues. Eaten by an alien bird.

My gaze roved over the nests, searching for any movement. There were no squawks, no cries, no creaks from the branches. I didn't see the flutter of wings or anything similar. In fact, there was no movement whatsoever, which was eerie.

Perhaps the nests were empty.

It was possible that whatever massive avians occupied the cliff had flown to warmer temperatures. That's what happened on Earth.

Why not here? Or the nests might be old and have been abandoned. There was no way to know.

I could stay here hunched like a rabbit or I could move forward. Nothing was threatening me, and the current danger was the cold. Forcing myself to breathe, I waited for my muscles to relax, then slowly stood. Tense, I crept away from the shuttle, shoulders curled against the cold.

Snow, snow, and more snow. I didn't see much else. It covered everything. The only signs of life were the trees, which moved independently without wind. I gave them a wide berth. For all I knew, they ate people. That was not how I planned to go.

My feet left a path back to the ship as I searched. For what? I didn't know. People? Civilization? A fully stocked spaceship to get Vince, then go home? I hoped so, though that was unlikely.

A growl sounded, and icy adrenaline raced through my veins. My limbs turned to steel and my thoughts sped in a hundred different directions. I tried to drop, but my muscles refused to respond as my heart thrashed against my ribs. Another low growl came from even closer, sending another jolt of white-hot terror through me. My foot slipped on the icy snow, and I crashed to the ground, muscles locked, but thankfully, a mound of snow hid my slight form.

A massive creature strode by. They were near eight feet tall with four arms, towering horns, and short light blue fur that was striped with icy gray streaks. The fur did nothing to hide the muscles upon muscles the alien was built with. They wore a vest decorated with bones and a fur loincloth. Their wide feet broke through the snow with little trouble as they held a wicked spear in their humongous, six-fingered grasp.

The alien had a flat nose like a cat, and they sniffed constantly. They had a heavy brow that hung over their deep set yellow eyes, which never stopped roving.

I stayed perfectly motionless and tried to take small breaths so as to not alert them to my presence. This alien was an unknown entity. They might be friendly, which would be nice, though unlikely in my limited experience with the universe. Clearly, they were a hunter. Whether that meant they were a solitary species or not, I had no idea.

The alien suddenly stopped not far from me, and a low rumble sounded in their broad chest. I stopped breathing and begged the universe, God, anything out there for this creature to not notice me. I did not want to be abducted for a third time.

After what felt like a thousand years, the alien stalked toward the trees.

When they vanished from sight, a huge gust of air rushed out of me—that had been too fucking close. I shakily got to my feet and ripped the blanket off, shivering in the freezing air, but I didn't care. A straight path of my footprints led to the shuttle. It couldn't remain. Bent over, I walked backward to obscure my earlier steps with the blanket. My fingers turned red, burning from the extended contact with the snow, and I shivered terribly; none of that mattered, though. I had to not lead a potential threat directly to us.

Kicking the ice and snow off the hatch door, I cleared the way as quickly as physically possible. Snot leaked from my nose, freezing to my face in streaks. I struggled to breathe and my limbs shook from exertion, but I refused to stop. When I stepped inside, I tried to grasp the lever, but my numb fingers wouldn't cooperate. I shoved them into my armpits, swearing at the sudden bite of cold.

Hopping, I said, "Warm up. Just warm up. For the love of god, warm up."

I tried again and managed to curl my fingers around the lever. With a hard yank back, I groaned, "Close. Close. Close. Fucking close, damn you."

Painstakingly slow, the door shut with a resounding thud.

The blanket was caked in snow, so I shook it off and draped it over a crate. Who knew if it would dry? Was that a thing? I wasn't sure. I had zero experience with snow.

I shuffled out of my extra clothes, as they were covered in ice and I didn't want it to melt in the warmth of the tent, then crawled inside. Serlotminden was still asleep. I snuggled against him, trying to get as close as possible, moaning low in my throat. God. He was like a heater. I shoved my hands beneath him, digging them into his shirt and placing them right against his scales, and my digits burned from the searing heat of him.

He grunted. "You're cold."

My teeth clattered together too much for me to answer, so I didn't.

His arm came around me, holding me securely to his side while his tail coiled around my calf. "I have you..." His voice trailed off into a snarling noise that I didn't understand, but I doubted it was anything negative because it sounded soft.

I buried against his neck and breathed in his clean scent until my heart slowed to a normal pace. The heat from Serlotminden eventually permeated my limbs to the point I could uncurl and lie against him. I pulled my hands from beneath him, draping an arm over his waist. My fingers automatically traveled over his chest, the silky fabric of his shirt catching on my callouses.

We were not alone on this planet. Birds of some kind might inhabit the nests on the cliff. A huge alien lived near where we crashed. The trees moved independently. It was balls-cold. I had no idea how to find food.

We were fucked. I'd been better off with Vince at the fighting arena.

Even as I thought that, my muscles tightened and my breath sped up. A tremor traveled up my spine, and I clutched Serlotminden's shirt. No. I didn't want to go back. I never wanted to go back. *Please don't make me go back*, I thought desperately as a wail sounded in my mind and the searing fire from the incinerator scorched my arms.

Serlotminden tightened his hold on me, muttering unintelligibly under his breath. The sudden tension that had consumed me eked out, leaving me quite weightless. I wrapped my arms around him, feeling... oddly secure. I sighed. I hadn't felt safe in a very long time. It was idiotic to feel safe next to the alien that abducted me, even though he'd been trying to rescue me.

Nonetheless, the feeling persisted.

Pressing tightly to Serlotminden, I went to sleep, exhausted. The future would keep for a few hours.

Chapter 8

IS THAT A SMILE?

Serlotminden

"You did what?" I demanded, trying but not succeeding in keeping the growl from my voice. My tail curled around his ankle and up his calf; I needed to hold him to assure myself that Bartholomew was safe; that he was here with me. But he could not have been. The *damn* human might have been snatched away from me, and I would've never known what happened to him.

His expression remained blank as he replied, "I went outside. I spotted an alien. Big. Very big."

My hold on him tightened. "Did they hurt you?"

"No, they didn't even see me."

I wanted to haul him into my arms and settle him on top of me, but I was still struggling to sit up. There was also the matter of Bartholomew and I having not discussed permissions. He might not like being touched, even in a friendly manner. Strictly speaking, I shouldn't have my tail coiled around his leg, but I couldn't help myself. Why? I couldn't say. But I had gone through a considerable amount of trouble to get him, and I wasn't going to let someone take him from me.

The mere thought was enough to make a rumble form in my chest. No one would take him from me. No one.

"What are we going to do?" he asked, drawing me from my vicious thoughts.

I didn't know what we could do. It wasn't that shocking that this planet had inhabitants. If the people here were space-faring, it would benefit us greatly. "What did they look like exactly?"

As Bartholomew described the alien, I tried to wrack my brain. They weren't familiar to me, but there were many different species out there. From the description, though, I assumed this species was not space-faring. If they had been, they would have sensed an unauthorized ship breaching their atmosphere and come searching for the culprit.

"It wasn't only the alien," he said.

My tail tightened around him as I practically barked, "What?"

"The cliff above us is covered in massive nests. I didn't see any animals or aliens, but whatever lives in them is humungous."

I loosened my hold, afraid of hurting him, and tried to breathe. So many potential threats in a very short time.

Once again, Bartholomew asked, "What do we do?"

"For now," I said, "we'll stay inside." When I was better, I would venture outside to make sure Bartholomew was safe where we were.

"The shuttle is almost completely buried by rocks," he said. "Is that going to be a problem for the drakcol that's coming for you?"

"The sensors should be able to find the ship, but I have to work on getting the..." How did I say emergency beacon in English? Seth, Caleb, and Edith had clearly been neglecting my vocabulary. "Finding sensor," I settled on, "working once I can sit up."

"The what?"

"The thing for them to find us because of the crash," I tried to explain.

"Do you mean a distress signal?"

"Maybe."

"In cases of emergency, ships put off distress signals so people can find them. At least in my world. And by ships, I mean ones that float on water. Though planes have black boxes that aren't actually black. I'm fairly certain they are bright orange so rescuers can find them in the debris."

I swallowed, tail squeezing his leg. Stars, I loved hearing him talk so much at one time. How did I get him to do it again? "That's the word."

"Distress signal, which is two words."

"Distress signal," I repeated several times until Bartholomew nodded.

"What about the xoi? Will they see the signal?"

I dragged the tip of my tail over the back of his calf. The simple touch was oddly calming. I wished I was touching his bare skin, though. My tail was incredibly sensitive, and I couldn't help but wonder how his soft skin would feel against my scales.

"Serlotminden," he said, touching my cheek.

I pressed into the touch, nuzzling him. I worked his palm up to my forehead, spreading my scent on him.

Bartholomew bent over me; his forehead crinkled in the cute way that it did. "Are you awake?"

"Yes," I replied. "You have a lovely name."

"Most think it's long or old fashioned."

"It's perfect."

Warmth rushed to his cheeks, and a grin spread over my lips. Blushing. I, not anyone else, had made Bartholomew pink up in the most attractive manner. I felt victorious, as if I'd won a race.

"It's actually Bartholomew Reginald Lucian Cavendish-Wallingford."

My mouth fell open at the length of his name. He had to be important, incredibly important to bear such a name. The length of a name denoted importance, at least for drakcol. Who was this human? Royalty? Seth and Caleb hadn't spoken much about the governing positions of their planet, and I'd never researched about Earth or humans, but this slight human must be among them, whoever the governing masses were.

"I told you. It's long."

"How did you come to have such a name?"

"When my moms married they *hyphenated* their last names. Do you even have last names?"

"No, but I understand. Seth and Caleb both have one." Though I didn't know what the word "hyphenated" meant, I wasn't going to interrupt him. He was talking, actually talking.

"My mom Charity's dad was named Bartholomew Reginald. It was important to her family. So when they adopted me, they named me Bartholomew Reginald, and my mom Isabella's dad's name was Lucien, so that became my middle name. It's not a big deal," he said with a shrug.

"It is. It's long."

The first smile I'd ever seen from Bartholomew appeared, and my soul pounded. I wanted to see that smile for the rest of my life. I never wanted him to stop. I traced his lips with my fingertip; they were incredibly soft. His smile faltered, but he didn't move away.

"Smile, please."

"I don't make myself smile when I don't feel like it."

"Then I'll have to make you smile often, Bartholomew."

"People call me Teddy."

I frowned in confusion. Humans gave each other nicknames, shortenings, endearments, and pet names with odd frequency. Drakcol might give a close family member, lover, or friend an endearment, but we didn't shorten names as humans often did. Rather, it was usually about the person's character or one of their interests.

Bartholomew's endearment seemed more in the drakcol way. It wasn't a shortening, and I was fairly certain teddy was also a word for a bear, which was a large furry creature. He didn't look particularly hairy or large to me, but I was unsure of what humans considered big or hairy. Drakcol didn't have hair anywhere but the tops of our heads, and almost all were tall as well as broad.

"I will never understand the human urge to destroy perfectly good names," I said.

He chuckled, and the sound made my soul pound. Bartholomew bent forward, almost touching me. "You don't have a nickname?"

"Seth and Caleb call me Mindy, and my brothers call me Speedy."

"I like Mindy."

I found, when he said it, I quite adored being called Mindy. "At least my endearment makes sense."

"What do you mean?"

"Mindy is a shortening, and Speedy was given to me because I run about or go at problems full speed. Your 'Teddy' is odd. You're not a bear."

"N-no, I'm not. This conversation has taken an odd turn, but alright. You're right I'm not a bear or a cub. Some might call me a *twink*, though, personally, I think I'm not cute enough."

Now I was very confused. What was a "twink," and why wasn't he cute enough to be one? Bartholomew was exceedingly cute. Humans gave children stuffed bears called teddies sometimes. Seth had already procured several for his and Kalvoxrencol's child. They were cute, I thought.

"Are twinks toys?" I asked.

Bartholomew gaped at me. "Some might like to be called toys. It depends on the individual, I suppose. I wouldn't, but that doesn't mean anything. But, so I can get some kind of grasp on this conversation, what in the hell have Seth and Caleb been teaching you exactly?"

I was even more confused. "Are you not called Teddy because of the cute bears?"

His eyebrows came together. "I think we are having two *very* different conversations."

"How did you get your endearment? Was it because of the furry toys?"

Bartholomew laughed, bending closer to the point his nose touched my chest. The joyous sound made me grin and my soul thrum. He was happy; even if it was because I'd said something stupid in his language, I'd made him happy. A warm sensation started in my soul and spread throughout my limbs. I had a desire—no, a need to make Bartholomew happy for as long as I could.

"Mindy, are you talking about teddy bears?"

"Yes."

"For future reference, 'bears' means something very different to gay guys."

My pulse spiked at the word gay. That I knew. It meant he was attracted to men or male-presenting people. Caleb had taught me that as well as other sexualities, like Seth being pansexual. Drakcol mostly didn't care about gender in regards to who they were sexually attracted to. Some of my people were solely attracted to a single gender, but that was uncommon.

But if he was gay, that meant Bartholomew could be attracted to me. I had no idea why that was so important, but it was. Exceedingly so.

"Teddy," he said, "is a common nickname for several names. Bartholomew isn't one of them, but my moms have called me Teddy since I was a kid. I'm not sure why."

I took his hand. "Humans are so cute. You more so than the rest."

Bartholomew grunted, but I wasn't deterred, because his cheeks had darkened. He was talking, and I didn't want to pass this moment up, even though I was exhausted again. We were going to be great friends... at least I thought so. That's why I was so protective and why Bartholomew fit.

Why else would he be so perfect?

"You should talk more," I said.

"Why?"

"I like it."

"So?" he replied.

He didn't have to talk, but I loved hearing Bartholomew's voice. It was so nice and smooth. My brain tried to find a reason why he needed to keep talking, and when I stumbled across one, I snatched it. "It will help me learn more English. This way there will be less confusion in the future."

"I suppose that's true. What do you want to talk about?"

The possibilities were endless because I needed to know everything about him. "Do you like my smile?" Something inside of me needed to know he thought I was attractive, for whatever reason. I gave him a wide grin.

His expression didn't change in the slightest. "You are an odd person."

My smile faltered, and I looked away, trying to rationalize the hurt prodding my chest. Bartholomew didn't have to like my smile, even if everyone else did.

A light touch made me turn back to him. Bartholomew refused to meet my gaze as he threaded our fingers together. "Odd isn't bad. Your smile is fine."

Fine wasn't what I desired, but it was better than nothing. I pulled our joined hands to my chest over my throbbing soul. "I think your smile is cute. Like a teddy bear, Teddy."

"Alright," he said, seemingly unaffected.

It was a start.

"Tell me more. I need to rest, and it will help me fall asleep."

"I thought you wanted to learn more English?"

"Sleep for now."

He lay beside me, head on my shoulder, and started to talk. "When I was twelve, I got lost in the woods, but not really. I knew where I was the entire time, and I wanted to watch the water in the river go by and observe the fish and bugs. My sisters were being too loud for me. But my moms didn't know where I was. They called every type of law enforcement to find me because both of them were convinced I'd been kidnapped or something.

"Anyway, they amassed a huge search party, and I wandered back, perfectly safe. I got in such trouble, after they stopped crying, and I remember, at the time, not understanding why they were so afraid. I'd been perfectly fine."

I chuckled, nuzzling him and inhaling his strong scent. Bartholomew needed a bath, but I quite liked the strong earthy scent coming off his skin.

"Don't disappear on me. I will search high and low for you, never giving up. Not ever," I promised, and I would. Nothing would keep me from Bartholomew.

Bartholomew grunted, but he began to stroke my chest and stomach as he started another story of him and his family when he was young. I closed my eyes, listening to the even timbre of his voice.

Chapter 9

THAT'S AN UNEXPECTED REACTION.

Bartholomew

I started awake, pulse pounding in my ears, sweat covering me, and bile creeping up my throat. My breath harsh, I shoved away from Serlotminden and sat up. My arms curled around my knees as I hugged them to my chest. I took a deep breath and tried to banish the nightmares of burnt bodies and sightless eyes chasing me, dragging me away, taking revenge, but every time I closed my eyes the ghosts were still there, haunting me.

I'd never used to dream on Xome, but here, I'd had nightmares every time I slept. Why now? Why couldn't the past stay where it belonged?

Probably because I deserved whatever punishment the universe doled out.

Something snaked around my forearm, and I yelped, falling over as I tried to get away. No. Please, no.

"Bartholomew. Teddy," a wonderfully deep voice said, and I released a long breath. I looked over, but the darkness of the tent didn't allow me to see anything. Mindy's tail tugged me closer, and I fell against his chest. "It's cold," he said, arms surrounding me. "Stay close."

My heart clogged my throat and a sudden wave of comfort crashed over me, making me feel so damn safe beside him. I laid an arm on his stomach and whispered, "Don't leave."

His chest rumbled in laughter. "Where would I go? Go back to sleep."

I hoped he was telling the truth, because I liked being right next to him.

"Are you sure about this?" I asked, chewing on my nail. He tugged my hand away from my mouth and held it to his chest, rubbing the back over his sternum where his heart vibrated. We'd been crash landed for three days at least by now, and the gesture had become normal. Mindy never stopped touching me. A tail around my ankle or wrist. Pulling me tight against him. Grabbing my hand. Perhaps drakcol were a physically affectionate species. I didn't really mind. He was warm, and it was cold even inside the tent. "I have to walk. I'm not going to rebuild my damaged muscles with the slight shifting I do to relieve myself."

God, I was thankful he hadn't needed my help with that. I would have. I wasn't a dick, but I didn't want to. "Alright."

"Help me, please."

"First, you need to put on warmer clothes, or more clothes I guess." I tugged on one of his pairs of pants over my jumpsuit, and his deep green eyes glowed as he watched, tail thrashing. I grabbed another pair that were soft and stretchy, like sweats and leggings had a baby. "Ready?"

"I like you in my clothes," he said in a deep voice as his tail slowly curled around my leg, coiling up my calf to tickle the back of my knee.

"Okay." That was odd, but whatever worked for him. "Ready to put on some more clothes?"

I pulled the pants over his ankles—feeding his tail in through the hole—then slid them up. When I reached his hips, he arched, and my mouth went bone dry while my cock twitched. He groaned and his face scrunched from the movement, and I had to breathe through a sudden wave of want.

What the actual fuck?

He was hurt and in pain, but Mindy's groan was turning me on. Me! I didn't get turned on very often. Sex and people rarely interested me. Romance, yes, though I hadn't indulged in that either. But when his lean hips lifted, it made my pulse skitter. In the past, my hand had been sufficient to meet my needs whenever the mood struck, but now, it was like something unfurled in my chest and stuck to my ribs. I wanted Serlotminden.

Of course, I wasn't attracted to someone reasonable. No, my cock was into an unavailable alien. Par for the course.

Teddy, I scolded myself, then shook my head. *Bartholomew Reginald, he is hurt and has a boyfriend. Calm the fuck down.* I took a deep breath. It would go away eventually. I would ignore my attraction to him until it vanished.

"Perfect," I forced out as I attempted to regain control of my traitorous body.

"Give me a moment," he said, tone laced with pain.

I moved before I'd even thought about it to stroke his cheek. Serlotminden leaned into my touch, pushing his nose against my palm, inhaling. He seemed to do that a lot—smelling me. Then he rubbed his forehead against my palm and wrist before smelling me again; he did that often too. It was weird, but I didn't say anything. It comforted him, and it didn't bother me.

"Take as much time as you need."

"How kind."

I smiled. Fuck, I'd smiled more in the last three days than I had in I don't know how long. Something about him brought it out. I'd also talked more than usual as well. I wasn't a talker, but whenever Mindy asked me a question, I had a hard time ignoring him.

After he'd relaxed, I placed his arms around my neck, then leaned back with him in my embrace. Mindy groaned, burying his face against my neck and making his silky hair tickle my cheek.

"Breathe," I told him.

Nose in the crook of my neck, Mindy practically huffed me as he held me with trembling arms. His nose and forehead rubbed against the column of my neck as well as my shoulder while jagged pants escaped his lips.

I smoothed a hand over his back to comfort him, but paused when I felt two lumps on his shoulder blades. I had no idea what they were, but they didn't matter at the moment. Easing the pain from his tense muscles was more important, so I stroked his back. He had to hurt. His stomach had been pierced by a sizable piece of metal. That would've kept me out of commission for far longer, if it hadn't killed me.

When his breathing calmed, I asked, "Did you want to lie back down?"

"No. Help me."

Part of me insisted he lie back and rest—I didn't like the idea of him in pain—but he was an adult; he was capable of deciding what was best for himself. I shifted out of his embrace to move to the tent opening and pulled it apart. Keeping a secure grip on him, I helped Serlotminden to his knees, then his feet.

Mindy sagged against me, and I hooked my arms around his waist to hold him steady. He trembled in my embrace and took heavy breaths, nose against my neck again. His long hair brushed my cheek, smelling marvelous. It had been a long time since I'd smelled anything this pleasant. Xome generally had the odor of smog, sewage, rotten food, and piss; the fighting ring hadn't been any better, and the stench of burning bodies never left me, not ever.

A memory surged from the depths of my mind. The mangled body of a reptile humanoid. Their arms had been ripped clean off, and their neck broken, head flopping. Blue blood coated them, sticky beneath my fingers. Me and Vince grunting and groaning as we threw them into the incinerator. The heat burning my hands, the sound of the roaring fire. The alien arching as they released a blood-curdling shriek that had lifted the hairs on my arms and stilled my heart.

Not dead. Not even close.

We'd tried to get them out, but Agk had slapped us away with a baton, the end crackling with electricity, which he always carried and slammed the incinerator door closed with a resounding thud, locking it with a bolt. His cold eyes set deep within his watermelon-head did not waver from us. The alien had failed and was of no use to him, like what would happen to us when we outlived our usefulness. The alien had not stopped screaming, throwing their body against the metal door, while me and Vince did nothing but listen to them burn to death.

"Bartholomew. Bartholomew."

I started.

Serlotminden was staring at me; his eyebrows drawn together. "Where did you go?"

"Nowhere," I lied, swallowing the rising bile. The alien's screams still sounded in my ears, but they were long dead—one ghost among the horde.

Serlotminden pressed his forehead against my cheek again and took another deep breath, then exhaled, his warm breath creating tingles in its wake. He whispered, lips brushing my skin, "I'm right here with you. Breathe."

He took another deep breath, and I inhaled along with him, sharing his air. His forehead rubbed along mine, and he breathed in a steady rhythm. In and out. In and out. The rush of warm air from his lips, the tickling of his hair, the musky rain scent that wafted off him, and the strength of his hold all eased the remaining tension from my body.

"I'm sorry," I said.

"For what?"

"I don't smell the best." Why was I apologizing? I hadn't made him huff me like a drug. He was doing that all by himself, but it was the one thing that came to mind after the potent memory.

Mindy took a deep inhale. "You smell marvelous."

He'd gone nose blind. That was the only explanation.

The masses on his back shifted, and his tail thrashed. I placed a hand on one of the lumps while my other stayed around his waist to support him. "Are you alright?"

"My wings. They need to stretch."

Wings? He had wings? "Do you need to take off your shirt?" My heart thumped at the thought. I liked that idea a lot—a shirtless Ser-lotminden. That sounded like an excellent plan. I should've thought of it sooner. If only we'd been stranded on a tropical planet instead of this icy wasteland.

"I have slits in the back of my shirt, but I need more room."

"Ah," I said. Too bad. "Then let's move to the cargo bay."

I closed the tent in an attempt to conserve the remaining warmth after grabbing the lantern and a couple of blankets. I wrapped one around me. The other was for Mindy after he stretched his wings. We were ready for a walk.

Chapter 10

AND WE'RE WALKING.

Bartholomew

I kept an arm around Serlotminden's waist and shuffled awkwardly toward the cargo bay. His steps were slight and his breath was harsh. He pressed against me, arm heavy on my shoulders. His far greater weight threatened to send me tumbling to the floor, but I gritted my teeth and managed, by some miracle, to stay upright.

"You can do it," I whispered, panting, and he paused in his step to rub his forehead against the top of my head. Heat rushed to my cheeks, and I had no idea why, nor did I know why he kept doing that.

I pushed my new awareness away. Mindy was the same idiot who'd kidnapped me against my will only a few days ago, though now thoughts of his smile, how he held me, how intently he listened to me, and his inquisitiveness invaded my mind. How in the space of ten minutes had my perspective of him changed? It made no sense.

It took more time than I would've guessed to make the short walk, but the longer we walked, the smaller his steps grew. When we reached the cargo bay, I set the lantern on a crate and shifted Serlotminden until he faced me, then tugged him against my chest, taking more of his weight, even though my arms were shaking.

"Let your wings out," I ordered.

Slowly, two wings burst from his back and stretched. They were the same shade of royal-purple as his scales; they each had a black talon on the bend and delicate scales along the top. They were massive, nearly stretching from wall to wall.

He groaned. "I needed that."

Unable to stop myself, I brushed one. The leathery texture slid under my fingertips, supple and smooth. Mindy pressed against me, bringing his wing closer, so I continued my exploration, tracing the membrane, the small veins, the scales, and the sharp talon.

"I like that," he said.

"Hmm." I kept petting him, enjoying the soft feel.

His wings enclosed me, and warmth seeped into my bones. I moaned before I could swallow it. God, he was so warm, like my own personal space heater, which on this balls-cold planet was a fucking miracle. I crossed my arms behind him to keep him where he was, and Serlotminden placed a hand on the small of my back, fingers stretched wide.

We stayed snuggled together while he occasionally stretched his wings, neither of us in a rush to move. It was cozy. One of my hands began to wander up his spine to explore the knobs and the expanse of his hard muscles, which contracted under my touch. Serlotminden nuzzled my cheek, and my pulse spiked.

How was this happening? It was like one of the romance books I so enjoyed where the hero suddenly liked his romantic interest. But that wasn't real. Then again... I hadn't believed in aliens two years ago either.

Eventually, he slid his wings back into his shirt, and I stretched the blanket over him. "There."

"Thank you."

I placed my arms around his waist again, palm flat against his back. "What's in the crates?"

"One has a couple of weapons, and the other has my racing..." He trailed off. "I don't know the word."

Probably racing junk. I nodded. "Junk."

"Junk?" The word sounded distorted but understandable.

"Yep."

"We can empty the bigger one and fill it with snow."

"And we would do this, why?" That sounded like a ton of work that I didn't want to do.

"I can melt it, so we can bathe."

"So I do smell."

"No." He pressed his nose against my neck and took a deep inhale, groaning. "You smell of something... I cannot say. I do not know the words."

"Foul."

"Is that bad?"

"Yes."

"Then no. You smell wonderful."

He was allowed his bizarre opinion. I wouldn't join him, but I wouldn't stop him either. "Instead of filling a crate with snow, we should do a bowl. Much more reasonable."

He grumbled something I didn't understand, and I didn't bother to question him. Mindy wouldn't be loading or melting snow any time soon. Besides, his focus should be on healing, then fixing the computer. We needed the beacon to be operational so his boyfriend could find us. I had to get back to Vince.

"Let's go back," I said. "You need to eat and rest."

"I have to check the cockpit."

"Tomorrow. Maybe."

"Teddy," he said, and something in my chest clenched at him using my nickname, but I forced it away. "I need to get it working."

"Not today," I repeated, holding him tighter. He melted into me and moaned, making me swallow. "You need to heal." He opened his mouth, probably to fight me, but I continued, "One thing at a time. First, you need to sleep so you can heal."

A smile spread over his features, and Mindy cupped my cheek, thumb running over my bottom lip. My heart stopped before speeding up. *That*, in my opinion, wasn't a friendly touch. He had a boyfriend, and he shouldn't be flirting with me. Though, was he? I didn't have any experience. I might be reading into the innocent touch now that I was randomly attracted to him.

"You take good care of me," he said.

"Someone has to manage this fiasco."

"I don't know that word."

"Mess," I reiterated. Mindy had made a mess of this rescue, not that he'd meant to. But we needed to be smart if we were going to survive this in one piece.

"I did make a mess, but you are here and you fit."

I blinked. I fit, where? I had no idea what he was talking about, so I said, "I suppose."

Mindy gave me a beaming smile, squeezing me close. "I knew you knew it. You fit."

Well, he was happy, but I had no idea what the fuck he was happy about.

Serlotminden

Bartholomew helped me lie down, and as I was catching my breath, he slipped out of the chilly tent. I reached for him, but he either ignored or didn't notice my grasping hand. I preferred when he stayed beside me. He fit, and he'd acknowledged it as well. We were on our way to being fantastic friends. Maybe even the closest ones ever.

Though thinking of Bartholomew as a friend bothered me for some reason.

My thoughts went back to the moments in the cargo bay. Bartholomew had been amazing to hold. The feel of his arms made me groan. And his scent? It was intoxicating, musky and strong with an earthen undertone that I wanted to roll in. He probably needed a bath, as I did, but, by the stars, I could not get enough of him.

At the thought of a bath, I fluffed the front of my shirt. I wanted to fill the entire crate with warm water for him to wash. My breath harshened at the thought of him scrubbing his skin while I watched. My cock twitched, starting to firm up.

That wasn't a friend response. I clearly needed to suppress my desire for physical company. I didn't want my Bartholomew to become uncomfortable with me.

The tent opened, and Bartholomew returned. He sat next to me and gave me a nutrition bar plus a couple of hydration cubes. My tail curled around his leg automatically; Bartholomew didn't even glance at me.

My tuft tickled his ankle, and he squirmed. I tightened my hold, unwilling to let him go, even though I should. We needed to have a conversation, but what if he didn't want what I needed? I *had* to touch him. A throbbing instinct deep inside me was comforted alone by his skin against my scales. But he was allowed to refuse me. I took a deep breath, strengthening my resolve. I would respect his boundaries, as impossible as that would be.

"I want to discuss permissions," I said.

"What?" he asked, popping a hydration cube in his mouth.

"Permissions."

"I don't understand."

"Drakcol discuss what touch is or is not allowed. It's for everyone. Friends, family, lovers."

He scooted closer to me, knees bumping my side, and hope flared in my soul. Perhaps he didn't mind the thought of touching me. I needed to feel his skin against my scales to reassure myself he was here and safe. Maybe he required the same from me?

"You've touched me plenty without permission."

"A mistake on my part," I confessed, wincing. I had taken without permission, and that was horribly wrong. "I must say sorry."

Bartholomew shrugged. "It's fine."

"Can I touch you?"

"How do you mean? Like..." His cheeks flushed.

It took me a moment to parse through his words. "Ah. I didn't mean fucking." Some friends fucked—I had several—but I didn't think he wanted to be fuck-friends.

He frowned, and my soul leaped. Did he want to? Did I want to? Humans had never inspired much arousal in me. Of course, both of the humans I'd met were mates of my younger brothers. Bartholomew wasn't. He was free. Very free and very cute and sweet and a little grumpy. Maybe I wouldn't mind being fuck-friends with him.

Vince.

The name stabbed me in the gut. He might have someone; someone he was committed to. Humans didn't mate once like drakcol did, but some did form lifelong relationships.

"Is this okay?" I asked, squeezing his ankle with my tail.

"It's fine."

I took his hand, pulling it to my chest, and my soul raced from the contact. "This?"

"Yes."

My mouth went dry. "What else is fine?"

"Well, we have to snuggle for warmth."

"True." We could do other things for warmth, and I was beginning to believe I would like such things. My cock twitched at the thought and desire raced through my veins. Yes, Bartholomew and I being fuck-friends would be very nice indeed.

"I don't really care. Vince likes to hold me too. He doesn't like being alone."

That human again. A growl started deep in my chest. I didn't like Bartholomew speaking of another person in that soft tone while I was the one in front of him.

I tightened my hold on him. "How can I touch you and when?"

"Detailed, aren't you?" he asked, but continued before I could speak. "Hugging, snuggling, touching me with your tail, or holding hands is fine. Honestly, I'm cool with whatever. Well, that's not true. Don't grab my ass or kiss me or anything like that. You said friends, right? Well, human friends don't do that usually, and I don't want to. You?"

"You can touch me however, wherever, and whenever you want," I said with complete sincerity. I wanted his fingers on me. I wanted to feel his much cooler skin on my scales. If he wanted to grab my butt, I was perfectly fine with that. I had a lovely butt, and had been told so by many of my past partners. It made sense if Bartholomew wanted to grope it. If he wanted to bite me... I ached for the feel of his teeth on my scales. I longed for his lips roving over me, telling me how much he liked me, how lovely he thought I was.

"That is a lot. Mindy, you have to have something you don't like?"

"If we are to remain friends, then you can touch me however. I like to be touched and to touch people. If we were discussing fucking, it would be different."

Bartholomew shrugged again. "Alright."

He shuffled out of his trousers—or rather my trousers. I swallowed, unable to rip my gaze from him. Was he going to get naked? Right after I'd brought up fucking? Why did I want to see his bare skin so badly?

"Your clothes are more comfortable—can I wear them?"

"Yes," I said, voice raspy. He most certainly could. I was fine with that. My clothes on his thin form made my soul pound. Bartholomew should always wear my clothes. That seemed logical. Why wouldn't he always wear my clothes? Covered in my scent. I let out a slow breath, unable to rip my gaze from him.

Snagging a shirt and the same trousers he'd taken off, he crawled out of the tent. My head fell onto the pillow. Why was Bartholomew changing outside? It was cold out there, and more importantly, I couldn't see him. After a moment, he clambered back in wearing a dark blue shirt and a pair of my black workout pants. He settled against me, curling close under the blanket.

I wrapped my arms around him, and he buried his head against me. I stroked his back, my fingers slipping into one of the wing slits on the shirt and brushing his smooth skin. I bit my lip to stifle a moan. By the Crystal's light, he was soft.

Bartholomew didn't say anything, so I continued to trace his prominent shoulder blades and the knobs of his spine. He was underweight, severely so. I had to make sure he ate enough. With his low weight and the cold, it would be a struggle to keep him warm.

I rubbed his bare, bony arm, claws dragging through the hair there. Drakcol didn't have much hair, but humans were different. I'd never seen one naked, so I didn't know the extent of how much hair he had, but Kalvoxrencol had painted Seth nude frequently—though my brother had mentioned humans varied in the amount of hair they grew. No matter. I loved the feel of the strands on my scales.

How had I gone my whole life without this?

"Stay close."

He grunted. "I'm not going anywhere."

My soul throbbed at his words. I didn't want him to leave me. Ever. Bartholomew needed to stay right here. With me. It was logical. He fit. We fit.

Chapter 11

FIGHTING BOREDOM IS A FULL-TIME JOB.

Bartholomew

I realized fairly quickly that Mindy didn't handle being injured well. The pain he handled fine; it was remaining in one place, not doing much, that he struggled with. His tail was always flicking, and he was constantly readjusting or snagging me close to rub his forehead on me. Apparently boredom and Serlotminden didn't get along, and after a couple of days in the cramped space with nowhere to go and nothing to do, he was a mass of antsy energy.

Giving him another nutrition bar, I sat next to him. He munched on the offering, mumbling under his breath. He was talking in his own language, but I was certain it was complaints. Mindy didn't enjoy the nutrition bars, but I didn't think they were so bad. Agk had fed us crap that was far worse. While mainly flavorless, they weren't chalk in my mouth and they didn't taste like dirt. All bonuses.

The second he finished, he dragged me to his side, arms loosely wound around my waist. I didn't even react; it was too normal now. Like if he hadn't grabbed me, I would've been more freaked out. The second Mindy stopped being cuddly, I would know he was dying.

"I'm bored," Mindy cried.

I shoved the rest of my bar into my mouth, then took a single water cube to wash it down before licking my chapped lips. "Okay."

"Bartholomew," he moaned from deep in his throat.

He really shouldn't call my name like that; it did things to me—uncomfortable things.

"We should do something," he said.

"Like what?"

Serlotminden wasn't well enough to sit in the cockpit and work. He'd tried, but I'd rejected that plan almost instantly because he'd been wincing and gasping. He needed to heal. Hell, he barely made it to the cargo bay and back when we took our daily walk to help strengthen his muscles and stretch his wings.

"I don't know. Something."

I fought a sigh. He was like a giant kid who needed to be entertained. I didn't really mind, but I didn't know what we were supposed to do. It wasn't like I had a phone to whip out for him to play on. God, a phone with numerous games would be beyond helpful right now. It would entertain him for hours upon hours.

When I started to turn around, he grumbled, his arms tightening around me. I tapped on one. "Let me go."

Instantly, he released me.

I shifted, facing him, and started to gather him close. Serlotminden pressed into my hold, not fighting as I helped him sit up. His
nose found its way to the crook of my neck, as it often did, and I
didn't bother to react. He liked smelling me; it was what it was.

Once he was seated and no longer panting, I leaned back. "Let's
play a game."

Mindy perked up, tail wriggling. "A game?"

I grabbed his hands and turned them, palm up, then I placed my
own hands above his. He cocked his head, hair tumbling over his
broad shoulder. He moved to grab me, and I slapped his palms.

Mindy blinked, expression showing his hurt.

"The point is for you to slap the top of my hands, not enough to
hurt, before I pull away. It's easy," I said.

He stared at me like I was speaking nonsense, but he moved to tap
my hands, and I jerked away.

"You have to be faster than that," I teased.

Serlotminden grinned, and my own smile threatened to grow. His
smiles were infectious. It was hard for me to resist him. He was a
magnet that drew me in; I couldn't help it, and if I was honest, I
didn't want to. I enjoyed being close to him, and I adored being the
one who put that smile on his face. It was addicting.

He moved faster this time, but I still pulled away, but not by
much. He was quicker than me—I was sure of it—but he was either
too injured or, more likely, too afraid of hurting me.

Our hands returned to in between us, and we started again. He
moved so fast that I didn't have a chance to draw away, allowing him
to smack my knuckles.

He smirked. "I got you."

"You did. My turn." We switched positions, but no matter how many times I tried, Mindy was too quick. He always got away, cackling like an evil witch in a cartoon and making me smile.

When he couldn't sit any longer, I helped him lie down and settled beside him because he reached for me immediately.

"What should we do now?" he asked, fingers tracing my spine.

"Maybe you can take a nap?" I suggested. Serlotminden needed more sleep to heal.

He tightened his arms around me. "I want to spend time with you."

"Okay." Whatever worked. It was his choice.

"Do you have any other games?"

We could play *I Spy*, but there wasn't really much around us, and I had zero interest in teaching him *20 Questions*. If he learned that, I would never get him to stop, and I didn't feel like answering tons of questions right now.

"No," I replied. "Do you?"

"Most Drakcon games are more physical than I can do at the moment."

I frowned. "'Drakcon?' I thought you were a drakcol."

"I am. Drakcon is..." He paused. "I am unsure of how to explain it in English. We use it as something belonging to our culture. Drakcon technology, Drakcon books, Drakcon games. Things like that."

"Ah."

Serlotminden asked, "So no games?"

"No," I replied. "You could tell me a story."

"Or you can tell me one."

I frowned, but in his defense, Mindy wasn't fluent in English and he was hurt; I was supposed to be entertaining him, not the other way around.

"When I was a kid, my mom Charity started calling me 'Ferdinand.'"

"Why? What does it mean?"

"I have no idea what the name means, but there's a book called The *Story of Ferdinand* that she used to read to me, and she said I was like that bull."

"What's a bull?"

"A big, horned animal. Fuzzy. Fierce. Some people make them fight, which I don't agree with." Fuck, I wasn't describing this well, especially without getting into animal rights issues.

"Why?"

"It's complicated. Anyway, in the story, there's a bull who doesn't play or fight with the others, but sits and smells the flowers."

"You like flowers? My brother Zoltilvoxfyn likes flowers. Sometimes we call him 'Bloom.'"

"Interesting, and yes, I like flowers, but that's not the point. The point was he was calm and liked to enjoy the slowness of life. That was me, even as a child. I was calm and liked to watch everything around me, so she called me Ferdinand. My other mom, Isabella, thought it was adorable. They called me that for a long time, as well as calling me Teddy."

Mindy lifted my chin. "Are you like that even now? Calm and enjoying life?"

"I'm calm. It's who I am. But I haven't enjoyed life in a while." What was there to enjoy? I'd tried to do things for Vince's sake. He'd needed hope; I hadn't. I, for the most part, had been fine with dying. Hell, it was probably what I deserved. My stomach churned as the scent of burning flesh and frantic screams haunted me.

"I will change that, Bartholomew. I will make sure you are happy and that you can sit and smell the flowers. I promise. You will be calm and happy one day. I will make sure of it."

I swallowed at the emotions creeping up my spine and settling behind my eyes. I didn't know if I believed him, but part of me wanted to. I wanted to believe that whatever he promised was better than what I'd left behind, that I was truly safe, and that the past wasn't unbreakable chains dragging me down. But doubts lingered. I feared Serlotminden would get tired of me, or that he would learn about what I'd done and hate me for it, or that he'd forget all about me and this odd friendship we'd made when we were rescued. If that happened, I would never save Vince and I would never be safe again.

What I wouldn't give to feel safe enough to simply watch the life around me and smell the flowers.

Serlotminden

Bartholomew had fallen asleep against my side in the middle of another story about when his family had gone to the woods again. I already knew from his first story that he had two younger sisters and two mothers.

In this one, I'd learned how much he loved them. His moms were deeply in love, and his younger sisters drove him mad, though he was fiercely protective of them. He'd also mentioned that he didn't live near them. Why? I wasn't sure, but I didn't think it was for negative reasons. He spoke too fondly of them for it to be bad. Though, even before he'd been abducted, he hadn't seen them in cycles.

It was impossible to imagine going cycles without seeing my parents, brothers, and cousin. Bartholomew's family didn't even know what had become of him and that he was alive. While I wished there was some way to tell them, I loathed the idea of being separated from him. Bartholomew was my friend, and I wanted the best thing for him, which was obviously staying right beside me. I would take care of him far better than anyone else.

But was it enough? Or once we were rescued, would he return to Earth? Would he abandon me?

I trailed my fingers over his face, lingering on his lips. Every once in a while, they quirked in amusement. He wasn't very expressive, my Bartholomew, but then again, life had been far too unkind to him of late. He needed more moments to exist and observe the world, and I planned to give it to him.

Well, as soon as I recovered.

He grunted, throwing a leg over mine, and I slid a hand lower, resting right above the slight swell of his butt, to hold him close to me. I took a deep inhale and grinned when I scented myself on him. But it wasn't enough. My instincts demanded more.

I rubbed my scent onto him, and it soothed the remaining tension from my body. His hand slid down my chest, lying over the injury to my gut. His light touch sent shards of glass through me, and I bit back a hiss of pain, teeth catching on my lip ring. I moved his hand over my soul, interlacing our fingers.

The feel of his palm against mine made me groan. I understood why humans and my brothers did this with their mates. It was nice. I lifted his hand and rested it against my mouth, enjoying the smoothness of his skin against the sensitive scales of my lips.

I wanted to kiss his knuckles, to trace the prominent bumps with my lips and then with my tongue. That was not allowed. To avoid the almost overwhelming temptation, I pulled his hand away, lowering it to my chest, right over my racing soul.

Kissing his knuckles was not enough. Not even close. My lips needed to press right against his. His breath on me, his tongue touching mine, and any noise he made mine to swallow. I craved it; I needed it, and I didn't understand why.

We were friends. Weren't we?

Perhaps I was in need of physical comfort? But Bartholomew didn't want that. I drew his palm back to my mouth, unable to help myself. This, whatever this was, felt stronger than anything I'd ever experienced before. It was disconcerting. Of course, I'd never rescued anyone like this before. He was mine to take care of.

My thoughts latched onto the word 'mine.' I liked it. A lot.

Taking a deep inhale of Bartholomew's earthy fragrance, I wished my brothers were here to talk to. They would help me through whatever was going on. Of course, if they were here, I would be competing for Bartholomew's attention, which I did not like the thought of.

Perhaps it was best we were alone. Once we were rescued, I would know how to keep his attention fixed on me. Completely and totally on me, where it belonged. I smiled, gathering him close, and fell asleep with his form pressed against my side.

Chapter 12

APPARENTLY, SUNLIGHT IS NECESSARY.

Bartholomew

"I need sun," Serlotminden whined—an honest-to-god wheedling whine.

It had been a full-time job keeping him entertained, and he couldn't lie on the floor of the cockpit or sit for long enough to work. I also worried about the sharp shards of screen and creaking rocks hurting him. When I told him no, he'd listened, which shocked me, but that meant he was bored.

"Is it life or death?" I asked, forcing a nutrition block into his hand.

He muttered darkly under his breath in his language, hauling me closer to his side, but he started to eat. "Drakcol *need* sun. Don't humans?"

Vitamin D was a thing, and I was probably in desperate need, but I hadn't been sweating what vitamins I needed or not. It was safe to assume I was deficient on pretty much everything.

I shrugged with a grunt.

"If I can't work on the beacon, I want to go outside."

"Have you forgotten the huge nests that could be dangerous and the massive alien?"

"I haven't."

"Then we should stay inside."

His bottom lip slipped out into a pout, and I rolled my eyes, though I started to soften. Mindy was working some kind of magic on me that I didn't understand, but it was sure as hell effective.

He said, "I have recovered enough to defend you. Besides, I promised to keep you safe."

I scoffed. I remembered, but that didn't mean placing ourselves in unnecessary risk.

Mindy nuzzled me, chuckling. "You like to worry about me, my Teddy."

"Someone has to," I muttered.

He grinned against my arm, and my mouth went dry at the feel of his lips on my skin. I viciously reminded myself of his relationship with the other drakcol. I refused to become enamored of Serlotminden.

And why him? Why now? I much preferred not being attracted to anyone, barring my celebrity and book crushes. No one would ever convince me that Jenson Ackles wasn't one of the sexiest men alive, though I couldn't say with certainty if I would've let him fuck me if he'd asked. I more liked the *idea* of people, romance, and sex than the reality. No one had ever interested me before now.

Which begged the question, again, why Serlotminden?

"Please," he pleaded like I had the final say, which I didn't. Mindy could do as he pleased. He was an adult, and he knew more of this universe than I did. Who was I to tell him no? Though the urge to keep Mindy safe didn't relent. I'd stood beside Vince when he needed it, sometimes shielding him from the consequences of his temper, and I felt the need to do the same with Mindy.

Of course, you didn't stop Agk or save anyone besides yourself, my brain viciously reminded me.

"Fine," I said, pushing my dark thoughts away, "but we need to stay by the shuttle."

"We? I'm going to go by myself."

I turned enough to see him. "There is no chance in hell you are going outside without me, Serlotminden. *We* are going or *we* are staying. What's it going to be?"

Serlotminden dropped his head to my shoulder, rubbing again. God, he did that a lot, and it sent waves of awareness through me, making my stomach swoop. After a moment, he said, "We will go and stay right next to the shuttle. You won't wander far, Bartholomew, right? I need to keep you safe. You're my friend and responsibility."

I ruffled his hair, and Mindy groaned.

"I get it," I said. "Let's go."

With my help, Mindy got to his feet, though he released a pained moan that made me wince.

I stroked his back, soothing his tense muscles. "Breathe, Mindy."

He huffed against my neck, and the urge to apologize for my smell swelled again, but I swallowed it. Serlotminden didn't care, and it wasn't my fault. I continued to run my hand over his spine, ignoring his twitching wings. Once he'd relaxed, we went to the cargo bay and opened the door.

Even colder air rushed in, which seemed impossible, but I shivered violently. Thankfully, the sun was shining brightly, glinting off the clean snow. Mindy grinned and dragged me out the door with an exuberant shout. The snow crust broke under our weight, sending cold shards into my ankles, but I didn't mind. It was nice to be outside.

Mindy let me go and stretched his arms above his head. His wings broke free of his shirt and sprawled. "I needed this."

I hugged myself, wincing in the bright light. "Do drakcol truly need sun?"

"Yes," he replied. "When we are babies, we have to spend a lot of time outside in the sun. Light, plants, and fresh air are important to our health."

"Then we need to make sure you get enough sunlight."

He cast a beaming smile at me before he began to explore the area in shuffling steps, scanning it with some type of technology. Probably a good idea. We needed to make sure the cliff was stable and not going to crush us. Not too worried, I took a seat on the cargo bay door, keeping the blanket tucked around me.

Serlotminden walked back and forth, peering at the massive nests. I didn't think anything about it until his wings flicked.

"Don't even fucking think about it," I said. "There might be hibernating birds or something in them. Let's not disturb anything."

"They could be a threat to you, and my sensor is not working. There is something in the ground or air interfering with my technology." His tail thrashed in what I assumed was agitation.

"Think about it. Right now, we are fine. Don't poke the bear."

"I thought bears meant something different to gay people?"

"Either way, let's not poke them, since they both growl."

However, he continued to inspect the nests. I wasn't going to be able to make him stay on the ground, even though I was fairly certain that flying would hurt his stomach.

A strong gust of wind blew over me, eliciting a shiver, and Mindy whipped in my direction. When I shivered again, he took a single step toward me. I frowned for all of one second, then I realized I *did* have the power to keep Mindy earthbound. I stared directly at him and stated, "I'm cold."

In a blink of an eye, he was moving toward me, arms extended. "Why didn't you tell me, my Teddy?" As he walked, Mindy limped, favoring his injured side, and panted in sharp bursts. Serlotminden wasn't doing as well as he acted.

He slipped behind me, legs cradling mine and arms about my waist. His wings came around me as he snuggled me close. I swallowed a groan at the warmth coming off him. I'd been cold, but I hadn't realized exactly how cold—practically freezing.

"You should have told me sooner," he said.

"Why?"

"You're mine to take care of."

"Because you rescued me?" I asked, my voice thick.

Serlotminden readjusted behind me. "You are my responsibility. I took you, and now I get to keep you."

"For how long?"

"Until you're safe." Mindy rested his chin on my shoulder, his long earring tickling me. "We fit, remember? We're friends, right?"

"Yeah," I replied. "Friends." *Because that's what I'm feeling toward him*, I thought sarcastically.

Serlotminden

I huddled close to Bartholomew, trying to steal the chill from his frozen body. He didn't generate enough heat to stay warm in this extreme weather. I should've realized he was cold earlier instead of studying the nests. My instincts had been demanding I inspect the nests nearest to us to keep Bartholomew safe, especially since my sensor didn't work well in this environment. I refused to allow any threat close to him. But how had I even contemplated leaving him alone? Something could've come and taken him, or he could've gotten too cold.

Humans were a considerable amount of work to care for. I now understood why Kalvoxrencol was always panicking about Seth.

I dragged my nose over the column of Bartholomew's neck, and he trembled. Still cold. *Hell it*. I grinned at my thoughts. I did love swearing; maybe it would make him smile like it did my mate-brothers.

He leaned into my embrace. "It's pretty here, when I'm not freezing and nothing is threatening me."

This planet was fairly decent for somewhere snowy. I wasn't fond of snow, but the blueish-green sky, the jungle in the distance, and the faraway jagged mountains all did have a certain charm, if I was forced to acknowledge it. I would enjoy this place far more if this was a pleasure trip. A warm bed, good food, a smiling Bartholomew—that I would love.

Bartholomew released a long breath and settled even further into my embrace. Once again, I was filled with a sense of perfection. He fit. I had no other way to word it. He was perfect. I pressed my mouth against the nape of his neck and breathed.

As his scent filled my lungs, fire sparked along my nerves. Groaning, I bit his neck, tongue flicking his sweet skin. Bartholomew jerked in my embrace, stiffening. I stilled, soul thrashing. What was I doing?

"Uh, Mindy?" His voice was calm, but I felt the tension in his muscles. "Did you bite me?"

I had, but why? Not a single word broke through the static of shock, not even an affirmative, which I owed him. I *had* bitten him.

"So we need to add that to our permissions," Teddy remarked.

My breath sharpened. Had he liked me biting him? Did I like it? My cock twitched, and I breathed through my arousal. If I got an erection, Bartholomew would feel it, and I didn't want that. We were friends... right? I thought so. Friends who did not fuck.

"Human friends don't bite each other. Or at least my friends don't, so I'd appreciate you not biting me again," he said without a hint of distress.

How was he calm? I was fighting against my body because of how amazing he felt in my embrace. Shouldn't he have experienced something similar? Anything? A hard shard of ice prodded my soul. Bartholomew felt nothing for me. Why did that hurt as bad as it did?

"I understand," I forced out.

He relaxed against me, returning to watch the scenery around us. "I'm not mad."

"Thank you."

I stared at the place where I'd bitten him. It had the slightest tinge of redness. An instinct rose from the depths of my being and demanded I lick the pain away and clean the spot, even though it wasn't a true injury.

"Drakcol lick wounds."

"Um, I'm going to need more context, Mindy."

I brushed a thumb over the redness, wishing it was my tongue. "We have a primal need to clean the injuries of those we care about."

"It doesn't hurt," he replied.

"That's good."

"Does that mean you want me to lick your stomach?"

My soul thrashed against my ribs, threatening to break free. An image of Bartholomew sprawled half on top of me as he bathed my injury flitted through my mind, and I growled. I very much liked the thought of that.

"I don't want to, Mindy," he muttered. "We are friends and all, but humans don't do that."

"I understand," I said, but disappointment filled me. I craved his tongue on me, badly.

"You need to rest."

I hid my face against him. "Not yet, please. I-I-I want to hold you."

"Alright."

I didn't understand my own feelings, but this, right here, was perfect. I nuzzled him, and Bartholomew continued to hold my hand, his thumb sliding over my knuckles in perfect distraction.

Chapter 13

BATHING CAN BE AWKWARD.

Bartholomew

It had been a few days, I thought, since Mindy had bitten me. The days were starting to blur together, and we didn't exactly have access to a clock. We slept when we were tired and were awake when we chose to be.

He'd acted the same, though he kept staring at me like he was trying to figure something out. I'd tried to act the same, but I still felt the press of his lip ring into my skin, his teeth against my neck, and the way his scaled tongue had dragged over me. Even just remembering sent shocks down my spine.

I liked it, and that was not going to work.

Serlotminden had started to recover faster. We went outside frequently, no further than directly around the shuttle, and he was now working on the computer to get the distress signal operational. As soon as it was, his drakcol boyfriend would hopefully find us.

Today, I'd left Mindy in the cockpit. As I was useless in that regard, I made other plans. What I wanted was to get clean, to wash away the stench of Xome and all that happened there. In reality, all I could do was scrub off the layers of grime coating me and get rid of the pungent odor that was making my own eyes water.

I opened the bay door and peered around for any threat. I hadn't mentioned my plan to Mindy or he would've come with me, but I was fine. The nests hadn't presented any threat yet, nor had the huge alien come near our crash site. Also, even with the looming threats, I *needed* a bath. I couldn't remember the last time I'd been properly clean. Probably not since I'd gotten abducted. Agk had sometimes given us water to wash, but it was a little more than a wet rag to scrape off the worst gunk.

This wasn't much better, but Serlotminden had a bar of soap and what I assumed was shampoo. Pushing my glasses up my nose, I filled a curved piece of hull with snow and dragged it back to our cabin. I would have to pull the water back out, but I didn't want to strip naked in the cargo bay. It took three trips to bring the bowl-shaped pieces of wreckage I'd found before I was satisfied. I didn't know how much water the snow would give us after Mindy melted it, but I needed enough for both of us. If I wanted to get clean, so would he.

Done, I closed the bay door. I didn't want the cold, let alone something alive, wandering inside.

I went to the cockpit, figuring enough time had passed. Mindy didn't pay attention to his own needs, and what he needed was to rest. He hadn't completely recovered yet, and I was determined to keep him as healthy as possible.

Serlotminden was fiddling with several panels, which were alive with light and strange symbols I assumed were his language. He'd made progress, apparently. His huge-ass boyfriend would find us sooner rather than later.

My jaw tightened at the thought. I should be excited about a proper rescue and being finally able to retrieve Vince, but the thought of that drakcol and Serlotminden made my stomach sour. I didn't fucking like it, even though I had no reason to. His and the other drakcol's relationship was none of my business.

We were friends—Serlotminden had said so enough times.

Hands fisted, I shifted to his side. I wrapped my arms around him, wanting to touch him, which was a first for me. But I liked the feel of him in my hold—sue me. Mindy leaned back into my embrace, and I pushed my frozen nose against the nape of his neck, making a shiver go down his spine.

"It's cold, and you need to rest," I said.

"You are quite shove-y."

"Pushy," I corrected, though it probably didn't matter; I understood him and that was all that counted. "And I'm making sure you don't hurt yourself."

"I don't mind. I like it. You take care of me like I take care of you. It makes sense."

"Come on. Besides, I have some snow for you to melt."

"My specialty." He stilled. Serlotminden turned around, hand clutching his injured stomach. "You went outside."

I shrugged.

"Bartholomew," he growled. "It's dangerous."

"I went to get snow. Nothing else. I'm fine."

"I would have gone with you," he said, dragging me between his spread legs and holding me against his chest.

I draped my arms over his shoulders. "You would've insisted on hauling the snow and hurt yourself." Mindy started to protest, but I covered his mouth. "Don't deny it."

His lips pursed against my palm, and my mouth went bone dry as I recalled the feel of his tongue on me. My hand slowly slid down, and he chased my touch before snagging my hand.

"Please don't do it again," he said. "I'm scared of something happening to you."

"I will be careful."

Serlotminden frowned, chest rumbling.

"Fine, I won't go outside without you. Happy?"

Mindy yanked me flush against him, our hips slotted together. "Now I am."

Heat swarmed my cheeks. I wiggled out of his hold. "Come on."

We returned to the cabin, and he went right to the bowls of snow. He could literally create fire with his mind. I hardly believed it, but I sure as hell wasn't going to question it. I needed to get clean, badly. He pressed his hand against the metal, and flames burned in his palm, turning the metal red from the heat. I kept a close watch on him to make sure Serlotminden didn't overtax himself. It wasn't worth a bath, as much as I wanted one.

When his breath turned harsh, I gripped his arm. "That's enough."

"I'm fine."

"I don't want you to hurt yourself. Please."

His resolve crumbled right before my eyes. "I don't want to worry you."

"Then sit." I had to help him, but he settled onto a stool I'd dragged in earlier. "You're going to need help bathing." He couldn't do this by himself, and my fingers tingled at the thought of touching him.

"You don't mind?"

"No." I really *really* didn't. I mentally slapped myself. *Don't be creepy.* He was taken and injured. Just because he was hot, it did not give me permission to ogle him.

I carefully peeled off his shirt and set it aside. I would dig out fresh clothes for him to wear after he was clean. With the hot water, I wet one of the towels I'd found and wiped his chest. He was formed with tight muscles and hard scales. The injury at the side exposed his mottled white and gold skin. New royal-purple scales, small ones, had started to regrow. After some time, they would probably cover the injury.

Back, wings, arms, and face, I washed him with the soapy towel before cleaning the soap off. I glanced at his pants. "Should I?"

"Sure," he replied, voice tight, as his tail thrashed, nearly smacking me. I helped him stand before undoing the ties on his pants. Thank god, he was wearing briefs. I didn't need to see what he was packing. I tried to focus on my task as I cleaned his legs, feet, and tail. Serlotminden took short breaths, his hands fisted on his thick thighs, while I scrubbed his tail. The closer I got to his firm ass, the harsher his breath became.

I had to be hurting him. He must have damaged something in the crash. Fuck. There was nothing I could do about that. Literally nothing.

Once he was clean, I said, "Let's get you dressed."

I fished out a clean pair of underwear, pants, socks, and shirt. He was shivering violently from the cold, but he was clean, except for his hair. I held up his briefs, looking anywhere but him.

Serlotminden took the black briefs from me. I heard some shuffling mixed with pained grunts. I tried to keep my gaze averted, but I couldn't when he released a high-pitched whine. I shifted to help him and froze. A taut ass topped by his tail and two perfect dimples greeted me. *Fuck me*. My fingers twitched, longing to touch him. My thumbs would slot into those dimples; I was sure of it, and I wanted to try.

He struggled to pull his briefs on and bent over, letting me see his large dick and his heavy balls. The crown of his cock was triangular shaped and wide. The entire thing was covered in delicate scales. He was thick, even without being erect. Much bigger than me or any other humans' I'd seen.

I ripped my gaze away before he caught me staring. Warmth burned my stomach, and my heart pounded in an uneven rhythm. Why him? Seriously, why him? And why now? I was twenty-four years old, and he was the first person who I actually knew that I was sexually attracted to.

I'd known I was demisexual for almost as long as I'd known I was gay, and I'd had many close friendships, none closer than Vince, and nothing. No one had done it for me, and I hadn't stressed about it. If I'd never had sex or fallen in love, I was still me, and that was more than enough. Besides, I loved the messy yet perfect romances that I found in the pages of my books.

But now, Serlotminden had charmed me with his smiles and enthusiasm, and I had formed a connection to him. One I'd never had with another living soul. Of course, this life-or-death situation had assisted. But I couldn't fight the desire he'd ignited.

It was fucking annoying.

When he was done, I helped him pull on his other clothes, trying to look at him as little as physically possible. He kept ducking his head, like he was trying to catch my eye, but I wouldn't let him. I needed to get a hold of myself first.

"Do you want me to wash your hair?" I asked.

"No. Tired."

Nodding, I snagged the edge of the tent and helped Serlotminden to his feet. Arms hooked under his, I directed him to the mattress, and he grunted, panting, as he settled. I brushed his long white hair behind his tapered ear, touching the gold piercings that went down to the long dangly earrings that practically kissed his shoulders. Unable to stop my fingers, I cupped his cheek, and he leaned into me.

"Are you alright?" I asked.

"Yes."

I didn't know if I believed him, because tension pulled his shoulders tight and a deep divot resided between his eyebrows, but I let it go. He was an adult. Serlotminden could take care of himself. Whether he lied about if he was fine or not wasn't my problem. Though I would keep an eye on him. Someone had to and his boyfriend wasn't here.

Shaking it off, I slipped from the tent to start my own bath while I tried to banish any remembrance of his body.

Chapter 14

DON'T LOOK.

Serlotminden

It had taken everything within me not to react to Bartholomew's gentle touch as he'd washed me. Stars above and by the Crystal's light, when he'd scrubbed my tail, getting closer and closer to the sensitive base, I barely suppressed the urge to moan and drag him against me before rubbing all over him. I'd wanted the softness of his skin on my scales. I wanted to force my tongue between his plump lips and taste him.

I made myself take a deep breath to slow the rapid beat of my soul. I was attracted to Bartholomew. I couldn't deny it. I could, but it was pointless because my cock had started to harden at the thought of him. Stars, when he'd taken off my trousers... If I hadn't been injured, I might've tried to gather him close and request his permissions so we could fuck or at least taste each other.

How was this happening? Humans had never been of interest to me. They were too short and soft. This human was different, though. He was near my own height; he was soft, but it wasn't the same with Bartholomew. I liked how he melted against me and how smooth his skin was against my scales. But we were friends. Nothing more.

But we could be friends who fucked, if Bartholomew was amenable. He hadn't acted interested, but maybe if he saw me in a more attractive light, he would desire my body. I hadn't been clean or put together before now. It would take time; that was it. Who wasn't attracted to me? No one. Everyone liked me. After he started to be attracted to me, we'd discuss permissions and be fuck-friends.

With a smile, I grabbed the edge of the tent and pulled it back a crack to talk to him. I needed to know he was there, but more accurately, I had to confirm what I was feeling. That this whole situation hadn't been a fluke brought on by him touching me.

My mouth dropped, and the words died in my throat. Bartholomew was shirtless. His ribs and the knobs on his spine stuck out through his skin. He slid his trousers off, and all thought fell from my mind so fast that all I did was gape. His butt was small and flat—thin like the rest of him—but he was so lovely. He cleaned his legs, which had black hair scattered over them, with a cloth and shivered in the cold. He didn't turn around so his cock remained hidden from my sight, and I was disappointed. I wanted to see it; I wanted to see all of him. Stars, or *damn* as the humans said, I really wanted to.

I needed to look away. I didn't have his permission to see him like this. I had to stop watching. It wasn't right. My hand didn't so much as twitch to drop the fabric, even when I tried; my tail thrashed and my cock hardened in desire. He kneeled on his shirt and bent toward the bowl of water, giving me an excellent view of his butt and his sack covered in black hair.

My breath turned harsh as I squeezed the tent, claws making holes in the flag.

He yanked on clean clothes, my clothes. They looked perfect on him, even though they were large and he had to tie the trousers up so they stayed on. Bartholomew turned toward the tent and started. My mouth opened, but nothing came out besides breathless moans filled with desperate need. I'd been caught watching, inappropriately so. I'd ignored all decency and permissions, taking what I desired. He was going to be mad, rightly so. I was furious with myself. Instinct and desire didn't excuse what I'd done. I tried to apologize, but all that came out was a strangled groan.

Bartholomew didn't say anything as he brushed past me and climbed inside the tent.

I tried to breathe through my arousal, but my cock was hard and obvious under the blanket; it was impossible to hide, so I didn't bother trying. Bartholomew lay with his back to me and curled into a ball.

Guilt shredded me like a claw to the gut. "My apologies."

Bartholomew lifted and lowered his shoulders.

I stretched to touch him, but I pulled back at the last moment. Bartholomew had consented to my touch, but he might not now. Consent could always be revoked. I wouldn't break his trust or force myself on him when he wasn't desiring of me. Instead of pulling him close, I stared up at the tent and scolded myself viciously.

Bartholomew

I held my burning cheeks. Serlotminden had watched me bathe and had gotten turned on. My own dick was hard as a rock at the thought of him staring at me. I wanted to turn around and press against him, but I didn't. I'd never been with anyone. I knew what to do, but I had no practical experience. What if I did it wrong? Or what if he wasn't actually interested?

Both were possible, and I didn't want to be rejected. Besides, he had a boyfriend, though they might not be exclusive or perhaps they had an open relationship.

Before I was abducted by aliens, I'd been my normal quiet self. I'd had friends, but the thought of dating and sex was something that made me squirm. Also, I'd never felt a pressing need to fuck. I liked jerking off, but my hand had been sufficient to meet my sex drive's needs. Now, apparently that wasn't enough. Though, actually, I hadn't had a chance to jerk off in months. Vince and me living in close quarters made that difficult, and most of the time, I'd been too exhausted to masturbate. Here? Literally no privacy.

Mindy had changed everything. I wanted him, but I sure as hell couldn't have him. At least, I didn't think so.

The urge to move closer to Serlotminden and bury myself beneath the warmth of his scales flooded me, but he had someone. The current situation was driving him to his attraction. Lust, that was the reason.

And I had no idea if I liked him or not. I mean, I probably did. We definitely had a connection, but this situation was fraught with tension and problems. There was the very real chance I was latching onto him because he'd saved me and we were stuck together.

"Mindy," I started.

"I am sorry, Bartholomew."

"It's fine, but in future maybe don't look at me when I'm naked?"

"If that's what you want."

I frowned, peeking at him, but in the muted light of the tent, I couldn't see his expression and he was staring directly above him. I asked, "Are drakcol comfortable with nudity?"

"Somewhat. We are not as comfortable as some species who've done away with clothes, but group bathing in hot springs is common enough."

"I've never been to a hot spring."

"I will take you when we go home."

The word home shot a bolt of longing through me. We had very different ideas of where home was. "I would like that."

"Then I promise to take you to a hot spring." Mindy took a deep breath. "I am sorry I watched you without permission. I intended to speak to you and I don't like when you're out of my sight, but I should've closed the tent when I realized you were naked and unaware of my presence."

"It's fine. Add it to the permissions, I guess."

His tail curled around my wrist, tugging me. "It's cold."

A smile fought my control at him repeating the same words I'd given him days ago. I shifted until I was pressed against his side. I took one deep inhale, and my eyes fluttered closed at his rich rain scent.

"You're warm," I said.

"Then stay beside me so you're never cold again."

Chapter 15

WE ARE JUST FRIENDS.

Serlotminden

I sat in the cockpit fiddling with the computer. This wasn't my strong suit, but I could hardly expect Bartholomew to assist me. *Bartholomew*. Stars above. I'd had to leave the tent lest I roll over and press myself against him. I'd wanted to nuzzle him, to scent mark him, so he smelled of me and me alone. There was no one near us, but I needed everyone to know this human was under my protection.

In my entire life, I'd never felt anything like this. Not once. What was happening to me? I didn't hate it, but I couldn't say if I liked it either. It was unnerving to be so protective of him so suddenly. I didn't understand it.

So I'd fled the warmth of the tent and turned to the computer. Getting the distress signal working so my brothers could find us was the first priority. Of course, the xoi might pick up the signal, but I hoped since they hadn't shown up yet, they assumed we were dead.

My brothers would not. They'd never stop searching for me—no matter how long it took.

It was late, not that it mattered. We didn't follow the sun to mark our days, but Bartholomew hadn't been asleep long. Even with my blunder in the bath, he hadn't changed—he was his usual calm self, forgiving me with ease. Why hadn't he been flustered? He'd seen me mostly naked, and I'd seen him.

Shouldn't it mean something?

Apparently, my little human only felt friendship for me, which was perfectly fine. Why wouldn't it be? We were friends. Just friends. I snarled under my breath, practically hitting the console as I attempted to get it to work. It showed my system, but it was not responding to my touch. Frustrated, I took a deep breath.

This wasn't working. I desired Bartholomew, badly, and it was clouding my thoughts. My cock began to harden, and I groaned. I peeked over my shoulder at the darkened corridor; it was empty. Undoing my ties, I shuffled my trousers to my knees and pulled my cock out of my undershorts. It was hard and the tapered tip was leaking with pre-seed.

I gripped the base of my shaft and pulled. A low moan broke out of me. It was drier than I liked, but stars, it was nice. Rubbing my crown on my palm, I bit off a rough keen of pleasure. I looked over my shoulder again. I couldn't be as loud as I normally was; Bartholomew might hear me.

Bartholomew. Oh, Bartholomew.

Soft moans came out of my lips as I pumped my cock and brushed the tip with the pad of my thumb. I needed to think of something else, but my brain refused to move from him. The little quirk of his lips. His breathy laugh. His soft skin. His deep brown eyes. His small butt. How he cared for me. How he ordered me around. Images of him on top of me, ordering me to moan, to please him, to beg filtered through my thoughts.

I cried, hips arching to fuck my tight grasp. I slipped one of my hands under my shirt to tweak a nipple, and I whimpered, hips rutting into my palm.

"Bartholomew," I breathed. "Teddy, please."

His lovely aspect appeared in my mind, and he smiled.

I grunted, hips canting faster.

"My Bartholomew," I moaned as I chased my pleasure. I spread my legs as far as my undershorts and trousers allowed to pull on my balls in the hopes of prolonging this. I wasn't ready yet; though at the same time, this wasn't what I needed.

I craved Bartholomew, but not his body alone. I didn't want to simply fuck him. I needed to feel close to him, to see him smile, to feel him hold me tight, and to hear him cry my name.

Covering my mouth, I pumped faster and faster, picturing Bartholomew with me, groaning in my ear in his smooth voice. Pleasure burned down my spine as everything tightened. A muffled moan tore out of me at the same moment white ropes of seed splattered my hand and chest.

Panting, I shivered in the chill, coated in my release. That hadn't been the plan, but *shit it all*, that was amazing. Still, as powerful as my release had been, it wasn't enough. I needed Bartholomew to fill the void of intimacy.

With the corner of the blanket, I cleaned myself and yanked up my trousers.

Somewhat calmer, I started to work on the computer again. My claws clacked over the cracked, blinking screen. Nothing was working. I'd managed to return power to the cockpit, but not much else. I wasn't an engineer. I maintained my racing shuttle, but rewiring or fixing a shattered computer was well beyond my expertise. But now was the time to learn. Bartholomew needed me, and I refused to let him down.

I sorted through the bin of extra parts I had, none of which were exactly what I needed, then popped open the panel and got to work. I might have to cannibalize other parts of the ship, but none of that mattered. We could survive as we were, but not indefinitely. The distress signal and NAID were the priorities. If I got NAID operational, it could guide me through fixing the necessary systems, like lights or environmentals.

Time passed as I ripped and replaced and rewired. My movements were mechanical, and my thoughts were completely focused on the task in front of me. Nothing else. The cold, my feelings, my fear, and my worry all vanished.

"Mindy," a steady voice said from the doorway.

I jerked, smacking my head into the console above me. "*Hell everything,*" I swore in English and clutched my forehead. A laugh sounded, and I stilled, soul pounding. Bartholomew leaned against the door jamb, arms crossed, as he chuckled. He was in nothing but my clothes, which hung off his thin frame. He didn't even have a blanket to ward off the chill.

"What?" Why wasn't he more covered? He was too underweight to withstand the cold.

"You need to rest."

His favorite words. I shifted, groaning in pain. My stomach clenched. It was healing slowly. Uncomfortably slowly. Bartholomew was at my side in an instant, helping me. My arms instinctively wrapped around him, gathering him close. He didn't fight my hold; instead, he pulled me flush against him. I took a deep inhale of his earthy scent and fought a groan. My imaginations from my earlier release returned with a vengeance.

I wanted my thoughts to be true.

"Why are you awake?" he asked.

"I need to get the distress signal and NAID fixed."

"Who? Your ship?"

"No, the computer. NAID stands for..." I trailed off, trying to remember the right words in English—Network of Artificial Intelligence for Drakcol. I pursed my lips. Seth and Caleb had never taught me, as far as I remembered. "It's intelligent, but not aware, like we are. Though there is a NAID, Edith, who's a person like us. But NAID is..."

"I get it. It's the main computer."

I smiled. He was so smart.

Bartholomew frowned. "You're still healing. You should be resting."

"Why are you awake?" I locked my hands behind the small of his back. He did love to worry about me. That meant something, right?

"You weren't there."

Warmth contrary to the frigid cold suffused me. I pressed against his neck to breathe in the earthy fragrance that belonged to him alone. I wanted to bathe in that smell. He was so perfect.

"Go back to bed," I said, shifting back or else I was going to try to kiss him, and I was still unsure of what was going on between us. More importantly, kissing was something he'd explicitly stated he didn't want. I would never violate his trust again. Not ever. Fuck-friends had to wait until he desired me as I did him. For now, we were the best of friends. I smiled. I liked that, sort of. Something inside of me demanded that wasn't enough. Not near enough.

He tightened his grip on me, refusing to let me move far from him. "I'm cold."

Guilt surfaced with a vengeance. Bartholomew didn't radiate as much heat as I did. Humans were naturally cooler than drakcol, according to Kalvoxrencol. My youngest brother loved to tell us facts about humans; now, I was grateful for his obsession. If I wasn't in the tent and beneath the blankets with Bartholomew, he had a harder time staying warm.

"Come." I directed him back to the cabin, keeping him by my side. He helped me lie down before cuddling against me and putting his cold feet on top of mine. I fought a hiss at the icy feel of his toes. The socks had done nothing to ward off the chill from the ship's metal floors. I rolled to my side, biting my lip against the pain that stabbed my side, and wrapped my arms around him to haul him close.

Bartholomew groaned and tucked his hands beneath the hem of my shirt. His fingers spread out over my back, making me swallow.

The cold temperature of his skin wasn't enough to dampen my desire for him, but I forced it aside.

We were friends.

For friends, though, I was having to remind myself of that fact very frequently, which wasn't normal.

And there was Vince.

How Bartholomew spoke of him was different. He didn't speak of much unless I forced him to, but he'd mentioned his resolve to get Vince back without prompting. Pain spiked in my chest. I didn't want him to love someone else, which was ridiculous.

I nuzzled him; the spiky texture of his hair scraped against my scales, making me groan. Bartholomew released a long breath of air and tucked one of his legs between mine, slotting us together.

"Are you warm now?" I kept scent marking him, and with each nuzzle, I relaxed as my scent subtly mixed with his.

"Yes," he said, breath tickling me.

"Good."

His grip tightened on my back. "Did you get the distress signal working?"

"Not yet. But don't worry, Dontilvynsan will find us," I said. Bartholomew squeezed me, and I winced. "You're hurting me."

He started, immediately loosening his hold. I couldn't make out his expression in the darkness of the cabin, but he sounded upset when he said, "I didn't mean to. Are you alright?" His fingers slid to my injured side. I fought a whine as he connected with the bare skin. It was so sensitive. I was grateful that the scales were growing back.

Caleb, who was my younger brother's mate and was now in a drakcol body, had several old injuries where the scales hadn't re-grown, and he had to be careful. Zoltilvoxfyn was always making sure his skin was covered or out of extreme weather as well as oiling it to keep it moisturized. We were not meant to be without scales, so any exposed skin required more care and was easily damaged.

"Mindy?" he asked, fingers tracing the injury and sending sparks of awareness through me that settled in my cock.

"I'm alright." That was a blatant lie. I wasn't alright, not even close. Bartholomew was changing something within me that I didn't understand, and it scared me.

"That Dontil... person, are you sure he'll come?"

"Dontilvynsan," I corrected. "And he will always come for me."

"I see."

His voice was harsher than usual and his jaw clenched while his fingers gripped me. I didn't understand why he would be upset. He'd never been mad in front of me before, even with my blunders. My brother coming was a good thing. I stroked his spine, feeling each and every knob.

"I will not leave you behind. I promise. We're friends, and even if we weren't, I wouldn't leave you."

He grunted in response, and I frowned, my hand stopping right above the small swell of his butt.

Bartholomew took a deep breath and rubbed his nose on my neck, and I swallowed. It had to be unintentional, but he was touch-ing one of my scent glands. If he moved his hand up on my side,

Bartholomew would touch another one. I liked it immensely. He should do it more often.

He said, drawing me out of my random thoughts, "Then I'll have to go find Vince, or at least, figure how to get back to him."

Fire grew in my stomach. Vince. I swallowed the anger. "I will take you."

"Will you?"

"Xome is dangerous. You cannot go alone."

Bartholomew chuckled, and the sound made my soul jump. "I might be safer without you. You attract a lot of attention."

There was truth in that statement, but I refused to allow anyone else to take him. I needed to spend as much time as I had with him. "We will bring guards and Dontilvynsan with us to find your Vince."

He grunted. "If he has to come."

We fell silent as his fingers continued to run over me and I continued to breathe in his scent, all the while fighting against my burgeoning desire. If my cock hardened, he would feel it, and the atmosphere would turn awkward.

"How did you meet Vince?"

"We were abducted at the same time."

I cursed my idiocy. Of course that was how they met. How else would two humans have met across the universe?

"We were both bought by Agk at the auction. We've been together for two years now."

Two cycles. How did I compete against such a timeframe and such a relationship? The answer was: I could not. Bartholomew would never be interested in me. My soul thrashed against my ribs, and my instincts demanded I never allow him to leave my side. I forced it away. I didn't have to compete. Friends didn't compete for another friend's affection. That didn't stop the growl vibrating low in my gut.

"We've been through a lot," he said. I wanted him to stop speaking of Vince, and yet a craving so deep it shook my soul swept through me to hear his voice, to learn more about him. "We met on the ship."

"What was it like?"

He pressed against me, and a tremor went through him. I slipped a hand under his shirt to stroke his bare skin. The contact seemed to soothe him because he relaxed beneath my touch.

Bartholomew said, "Horrible. At least a hundred of us were shoved into the hold. No water. No food. No place to sit. No bathroom."

My fingers tightened on him, but I forced myself to relax or else my claws would puncture his soft skin.

"We were offloaded and shoved into a large cage. They made us strip and sprayed us with cold water and some kind of foam that burned my skin." He shook his head as he took a deep breath. "Vince stayed beside me, holding my hand. He wouldn't let me go. No matter what. That's why Agk bought us. He wanted two people, and he liked that we got along. Easier to shove us in the same cell."

"I'm sorry." The words felt too small in light of what he'd experienced. "It should have never happened. I will do everything within my power to make sure it doesn't happen to anyone else. I know that doesn't change what has been done, but it's all I have."

I felt his lips press against the underside of my jaw, and it took everything I had not to roll on top of him and capture his mouth before demanding he give me his permissions. I was sure the "kiss" had been accidental, nothing more than his lips moving against me, but stars, it made my soul skitter.

"It's enough for me."

Heat filled every fiber of my being. "I will keep you safe."

Bartholomew

My eyes snapped open, and I looked around frantically, then breathed a sigh of relief. Rubbing the sweat off my forehead, I took deep, shuddering gasps as I tried to slow the pounding of my heart. Nightmares had never plagued me on Xome, but here it was an almost nightly thing and I didn't know why. Tonight, there had been hordes of burnt bodies chasing me, screaming at me, blaming me.

I covered my mouth to stifle a cry so as to not wake Serlotminden.

Warmth suddenly surrounded me, and I yelped, pushing away. The force held firm and a deep voice rumbled, "Are you well, Teddy?"

"Mindy," I sighed.

He nestled close to me, head on my shoulder and tail around my calf. Mindy sounded half-asleep as he asked, "What's wrong?"

"Nothing."

Grumbling low in his chest, he replied, "Then sleep. I am here, and you are safe beside me."

I clutched his arm, swallowing a sudden rush of emotion. I felt safe, but was it true? And more importantly, did I deserve to feel safe after everything I'd done?

Chapter 16

IT LIVES.

Bartholomew

Morning, if I could even call it that, came quickly, especially with the interruptions last night. When Serlotminden moved away from me, I groaned, holding on tight and trying to burrow against his chest. He froze, then relaxed against me. His hand pushed under my shirt and stroked the small of my back, lingering on the band of my trousers.

"Good morning," he said.

I gripped him, face tucked basically into his armpit. "No."

Serlotminden chuckled. "Yes."

"No." I was warm. I was comfortable. I felt secure next to him. I didn't want to move. We had absolutely nothing to do. Why couldn't we stay here?

His lips rested against my head, so light I barely felt them. It couldn't be called a kiss in any way, but my pulse skyrocketed. I'd kissed him yesterday, in the heat of the moment, but I didn't expect him to reciprocate, because I'd told him not to kiss me.

Mindy had done all manner of odd things—abduct me, nuzzle me, smell me, bite me, watch me bathe—but he hadn't ever crossed a clear boundary I'd set. When I didn't pull away and, instead, pressed closer, he kept his mouth right where it was.

After a moment or two, he laughed, and the sound made me smile. Serlotminden was adorable. There was truly no other way to describe him. His smile, his laugh, his energy—all of it was so precious. He was a magnet that drew me to him with every breath.

"I have to work on the distress signal."

"No," I said again. He could keep kissing me. Though maybe lower? I'd be alright with that. I mentally slapped myself. He had a boyfriend. That Dontilvynsan. Drakcol were simply physically affectionate.

"Come." Mindy moved despite my protests and opened the tent, flooding it with cold air. I shivered, biting out several choice swears, but I sat and drew the blankets tighter around me.

After we both pissed, we ate nutrition bars and a couple of the hydration cubes. I wasn't drinking enough water. Not even close. My throat was dry and my head ached, but there wasn't enough for me to drink more. Mindy would have to melt snow soon. We hadn't used all of the snow for washing, but I was nervous to drink it unless we boiled it. I had no idea what was in the alien snow or what germs clung to the makeshift bowls. I didn't want to be shitting my pants all night.

With my arm around his waist, I helped him to the cockpit. I wasn't going to leave today. I didn't need to. Serlotminden refused to let me explore, and if I was honest, I didn't want to. The strange alien and the nests scared me. I'd rather stay beside Mindy, inside our shuttle. Together.

I took a seat on one of the stools as he got to work. I watched his fingers move over the panels, then the exposed wires. I had no idea what he was doing, but I wasn't paying attention to the actual work. I was focused on him. The way his long fingers moved. The way his forehead crinkled. The way he muttered under his breath.

At the slightest sign of pain or exhaustion, I would force him to stop. I wouldn't let Serlotminden be hurt. Not ever.

He grunted under the console. "Can you see anything?"

"What am I looking for?"

"Anything."

The monitor was lit up, but I didn't see anything. No words like before. Of course, I had no idea what the hell I was looking for. "Nothing."

He released several snaps in his language, and I crouched to put a comforting hand on his leg. He stilled. I almost pulled away, but his tail coiled around my ankle, keeping me close.

"You'll figure it out. Calm down." I trailed my fingers over his calf, tightening my hold.

Serlotminden took a deep breath and started again. I sat next to him, holding him while his tail held me. The screen remained blank, a large crack through the center. I didn't know what I wanted. Did I want his boyfriend, Dontilvynsan, to find us? That would allow me to save Vince, which I needed to do, but I might lose Serlotminden as a result.

I scoffed. I wouldn't lose him. I did not *have* him. I would never have him, and I needed to accept that.

A blip appeared on the monitor, and I jerked, then shook his knee. "I saw something."

He jolted up, smacking his head on the console.

"Don't hurt yourself," I said; he needed to be more careful.

Mindy slid out from underneath, and I wrapped my arms and the blanket around him as he leaned over the monitor. I rested my chin on his shoulder to watch his fingers skitter over the screen and push button after button.

The screen was full of a language I didn't understand, but Serlotminden seemed to know what he was doing, though he was tense beneath me. I tightened my hold around him, and he leaned back, practically melting into my chest.

"So?" I asked.

"The ship is destroyed."

"I could have told you that."

"None of the sensors are operational, so I don't know what's out there. I might get the lights to work, but not environmentals or NAID."

No more lanterns—that would be nice. "The distress signal?"

He grinned, setting my pulse racing. "It's operational."

Mixed emotions stampeded through my chest. Relief? Worry? Anger? Possessiveness? I didn't know exactly, but they were overwhelming.

I pressed against Serlotminden and breathed him in as I tried to calm down. Whatever happened would happen. I couldn't control Serlotminden returning to his boyfriend after this, and I'd be able to get Vince, then we would get the fuck out of here, as long as someone took us to Earth. What if we couldn't return home? How in the hell were Vince and I going to survive? The universe was a mean place, and I didn't know much of it.

"I will protect you," he said. "No need to be tense. We'll be fine."

Sure, but what would happen when he left? He'd take me off this icy rock and probably help me retrieve Vince, but what then? He wouldn't put his life on hold for me or take me back to Earth, if that was even a possibility. So what did the future hold?

"You should work on the lights," I finally said.

"You're right. After this, we'll get some sun."

I grunted in acknowledgement. If he needed sun, then he was going to get sun. Nothing, not my worry, not my fear, not my anger, not anything, would keep me from taking care of Serlotminden.

Chapter 17

PLAYING... I THINK.

Bartholomew

I sat on the bay door, like usual, and Serlotminden walked the perimeter around the shuttle, scoping the area out. The day was warmer than I was used to, so maybe the planet was moving out of winter? Though that might spell the end of the empty nests, which would suck, majorly. I pushed the thought away, refusing to panic about it.

Mindy held out his hands, grinning. His white hair hung around his muscular frame like snow, and his purple scales shone in the direct sunlight. He was fucking gorgeous, but I didn't feel any inclination to move from my semi-warm place.

"Teddy," he whined, and I sighed.

I was going to have to move, wasn't I? His eyes grew larger as his tail wiggled, hand out, waiting.

With a groan, I forged through the snow toward him, but before I even got close, he crouched, growling. My pulse kicked up, and I paused, fear trickling down my spine like icy fingers. "Mindy?"

He rushed in my direction, and I didn't move, locked in place as my thoughts clouded in numbing panic. He crashed into me at full speed and knocked me into the snow. His arms came around me, keeping me from hitting the ground too hard. Serlotminden snarled against my throat, and I flinched. This was it. He was going to eat me. He'd had enough of nutrition squares and decided human was tastier.

"Teddy," he said, cocking his head. "Why didn't you run?"

"Why would I run?"

"So I can chase you."

The fear eked away. "You're *playing* with me."

"Of course. What did you think I was doing?"

Killing me. I wasn't going to say that, though; it might hurt his feelings. I shrugged.

Serlotminden rolled off me with a wince, and I helped him to his feet, moving to his shirt to check his wound, but he stopped me. "This time, my Teddy, run." He backed away from me before I had a chance to stop him.

"Are you sure this isn't going to hurt you?" I called after him. It seemed like it had, so why did he want to play again?

He didn't answer, crouching, and released a low warning sound. His tail thrashed and his wings spread, making my pulse pick up. My joints locked. I knew he was playing, but his aggressive act was triggering my flight or fight response, or rather my freeze response.

"Run," Mindy yelled. "Play with me."

It's play. It's play. It's play, I repeated over and over again. Mindy wouldn't actually hurt me. I forced myself forward and took off. My muscles burned almost instantly, and my lungs struggled to get enough oxygen. I hadn't exercised that much, and I was in desperate need of more food and water. Still, I forged on.

I heard growling behind me, and I lurched to the side. Serlotminden slid past me with a startled yelp. I laughed, heart pounding. "Close, but not close enough," I teased and took off in the direction of the shuttle.

Mindy snarled, and his feet crunched on the snow behind me. I pushed my screaming legs to move even faster. Running on snow was harder than I thought. Trying to escape him, I turned around as quickly as possible and ran in a different direction. Mindy easily corrected, following me.

Suddenly, a weight collided with my back and my face was pressed into the cold snow. I kicked and thrashed to get free, but he was too damn heavy. Rough hands forced me to turn over, and Mindy hovered above me, releasing low growls. My stomach dropped and a wave of want rushed through me.

Shit. This had been a bad idea.

I lay there, panting, beneath him, and I liked it. A lot.

Serlotminden

I stared at Bartholomew, who lay passive beneath me. Everything in me demanded I mold my lips to his and claim him for myself. I fought against the instinct, trying to reason with myself, but arguments of friendship and fitting fell away. All I was left with was the truth.

Bartholomew started to writhe beneath me, fighting me. He hit me, but not hard enough for me to think he intended to harm me. He was playing the game. He struggled, trying to escape, but there was none. I wouldn't allow it. I would never allow it.

I grabbed his wrists and trapped them above him. Bartholomew arched beneath me to throw me off, but I was too heavy. I transferred his wrists to one hand and bent to growl against his throat, and Bartholomew stilled.

"I caught you," I whispered against his ear.

"You did."

"I plan to keep you." This was my truth. I could not believe I hadn't understood what my instincts were demanding. I'd been scent marking him, claiming him, calling him mine. I'd been a fool. This human was mine, and I had no intention of letting him go. I wanted Bartholomew as my mate, and I planned to woo him until he realized what I had—we belonged together.

He didn't respond, staring at me, mouth open and breaths heavy. We stayed there in the snow, me growling against his neck and Bartholomew's chest heaving for what felt like an eternity.

When he shivered, I asked, "Are you cold?"

"Yes."

"Then I need to get you inside, next to me."

Red rushed to his cheeks, and something primal inside of me rumbled in pleasure. My mate might be a challenge to court, but I would succeed because this human was the only person I'd ever care about. He was mine, and that was that.

I started to help him stand, but my healing wound pulled, making me wince. Bartholomew was next to me in a flash, frozen hands on my side, rucking up my shirt to see the injury. My soul stalled when his cold fingers brushed my skin. I couldn't help but pull away; the skin was too sensitive.

Hurt flashed on my mate's face for a single moment before his blank expression returned. I bit my lip, teeth catching on my lip ring. Fiddling with his lenses, I gave him a soft smile. His aspect didn't change. I cupped his cheek and drew Bartholomew closer to me, settling his head on my shoulder.

"My skin is sensitive, my Teddy. Extreme temperatures are difficult for it," I tried to explain, smoothing his spiky hair.

"I'm sorry," he replied.

"Don't." I gripped the nape of his neck to keep him tight against me. "You didn't know." Reluctantly, I pulled back. "Let's go inside."

I took his hand in mine, marveling at the slimness of his fingers and how he perfectly fit within my grasp. How hadn't I noticed this earlier? I wanted to keep him against me all the time. The urge to claim him, kiss him, and rub my scent all over him persisted, but I respected his boundaries. Hopefully, in time, he would desire me how I did him, and not for a flash of lust, but for forever.

When we stepped inside, I ushered Bartholomew to the tent. He needed to warm up. While I preferred to warm him another way, I settled for gathering the blankets around him. "You need to eat."

He shrugged.

I shoved a nutrition bar at him, and when he was eating it, I grabbed one for myself, forcing myself to swallow the dry, flavorless bar before washing it down with a cube of water. I gave a couple of the cubes to Bartholomew and smoothed a hand over his head.

It seemed ridiculous that I cared so much about him all of a sudden. Well, it wasn't sudden. I'd cared about Bartholomew since the first time I'd seen him, but this was different. He was mine. How could I want someone for the rest of my life and not be in love? I liked Bartholomew, but I wasn't in love with him yet.

I'd always assumed when I discovered the one I wished to spend my life with, I would love them first. My youngest brother Kalvoxrencol hadn't loved his mate Seth at first, but he'd sought the Crystal for his mate. That was different. I wasn't sure about Zoltilvoxfyn and Caleb, but Hallonnixmin had fallen deeply in love with Gilvaxtin before they became mates.

But Bartholomew was my mate—I knew it—and yet I wasn't in love. It would happen—I knew that—but it hadn't happened yet.

It didn't matter. I liked Bartholomew and had every intention of keeping him. Besides, once we drakcol started to perceive someone as our mate, the bond formed and we were unable to desire another. We mated once, whether bound or chosen.

Bartholomew rubbed his temples, and I frowned.

"Are you alright?" I asked.

"I have a headache."

I shifted him closer until he was practically on my lap. "Will you be alright?"

"I'm fine." He licked his chapped lips and swallowed.

I forced him to look at me, tilting his chin up. "Bartholomew..." I didn't know what I was trying to ask, but he did not appear well.

"I'm dehydrated," he commented.

Panic coursed through my veins so rapidly it felt as if I'd been filled with fire. "What?"

"I haven't been drinking enough water, but it's fine."

It was not fine. It was not fine at all. Kalvoxrencol had told me several times of a human's need to drink copious amounts of water. Not enough and... Well, I didn't know what happened, but my younger brother had made it sound dire.

I shoved more hydration cubes at him.

"Mindy, I'm f—"

I didn't let him finish, popping one into his mouth. The feel of his lips on my fingers was enough to make my stomach curl, but I ignored it, far more concerned about Bartholomew's health. As soon as he swallowed, I pushed another into his mouth, tail thrashing. Unable to stop myself, I dragged him onto my lap, scent marking him.

"Another." I pushed the cube to his lips.

"Mindy, there's not enough."

"I can melt snow."

"I can't drink it unless it's been boiled. It might make me sick."

Stars, humans were fragile. I tugged him even closer, soul racing. I could lose my little mate so easily. "I can boil it."

"I don't want you to strain yourself."

I rested my mouth against his temple, not using any pressure. I would not kiss him, but the need to touch him pulsed with an intensity that refused to be denied. "I'm recovering perfectly fine, my Teddy. You need to drink more."

He frowned.

"You must tell me what you require, Bartholomew. I'm not familiar with every human need, so you have to tell me. Please. I have to keep you safe. Do you understand?"

His mouth was so achingly close to mine that I felt his breath on me when he said, "Fine."

Bartholomew took the other cube, then tucked against me. I cupped the back of his head, keeping his slight form tight against mine. Steadily, he warmed as I gave him a few more hydration cubes. Tomorrow, I planned to melt some snow for him to drink and for us to bathe. I would give my mate whatever I had, even if there wasn't much here.

He released a long breath. "Don't work on the ship without me."

"I won't if you don't want me to."

"I'm cold, and you need to heal."

I smiled, resting my lips on his spiky hair. My mate cared about me. He had Vince, but we would work out. I knew it. It only made sense.

Bartholomew

Mindy shoved another water cube at me, and I took it without fighting. There was no point. He was freaking out, and if I didn't drink the water, he would panic even worse. I was worried about running out and Serlotminden stressing himself to boil water for me, but at the same time, I was dehydrated and needed it.

His hand trailed over my back, a finger slipping into the slit of my shirt. I closed my eyes at the feel of his warm scales against my skin.

"How much water do you require?" Serlotminden asked.

"I don't know." I very much doubted he understood what ounces were. Besides, who actually drank the amount of water they were supposed to? If I did, I'd be peeing every other second.

"Bartholomew, please." His grasp tightened on me. "I need to know. I have to take care of you. Humans are so soft."

I peeked at him, frowning. "What?"

He poked my cheek. "So soft."

"I'm not weak," I said, shifting out of his lap.

Mindy reached for me, and I shoved him away.

"I'm not weak," I repeated, my voice deepening. "I survived, damn you."

"I don't mean that."

"It was not easy, but I fucking survived." Tremors wracked me. Smoke and blood filled my nose. The sound of flesh smacking flesh as a crowd screamed resounded in my ears. The small cell. The burning hot incinerator. The sharp zap as Agk prodded me with his baton. I clutched the front of my shirt, unable to stop shaking.

"I survived," I repeated. I had, right? A reptilian shriek ripped through my mind as Agk slammed the door of the incinerator closed, locking it with a dull clang. "I survived," I groaned, rocking. "I survived."

Warmth enfolded me, but I was blind to my surroundings. All I saw was blood, fire, and pain. Warm lips brushed my ear, and I flinched.

"Bartholomew, I'm right here. You're here. You're safe."

I shuddered.

He gathered me close until I was on his lap again. Serlotminden pressed his lips against my forehead, the metal of his piercing pressing into my skin. "I'm right here."

I fisted the front of his shirt, breathing in his scent, and forced it out, "I am not weak."

"I know, Bartholomew. I did not mean that." He lifted my chin until our eyes met. "You are mine to take care of."

I grunted, unable to form words.

He tucked me against him, tail coiled around my ankle.

I was straddling his thick thighs, and I didn't care or even react. I was trying to hold it together, but I couldn't. I shivered, memories flooding me. Serlotminden pressed his mouth against my temple and rocked me. I wrapped my arms around him, pressing closer, almost as if I was trying to claw my way inside of him.

"Can you tell me?" he asked.

"What?"

"Where did you go? What happened?"

"No." I wasn't ready to talk about it. At least not yet.

"If you ever do, I will listen. I'm not leaving you, Bartholomew. Not ever. You're safe."

I didn't respond, fingers digging into him to the point that it must be painful, but he didn't say anything.

Chapter 18

ROCKS ARE ROCKS, RIGHT?

Bartholomew

"Are you sure about this?" I asked.

I didn't know how much time had passed since we'd crash landed and Mindy had gotten hurt, but it hadn't been that long. Thankfully, Mindy was doing much better than I would've been if I'd been stabbed in the gut. I'd have been down and out, but he moved around with ease and told me he felt almost normal. Drakcol had to heal faster than humans did.

Maybe it was all the running. We had been *playing* every day. Mindy loved to chase and tackle me into the snow. I was getting faster and stronger. I was able to avoid him longer each time; the trick was changing directions quickly and taking advantage of when he got distracted, which happened often. Though no matter what I did, I ended up in the snow with Serlotminden on top of me.

He would pin me, then growl against my throat. It had gotten harder and harder to not react. Mindy also seemed equally unwilling to move off me. He always pressed his mouth against my neck, keeping it there without using any pressure. Only when I shivered or he worried about me drinking water did he slide off me.

Mindy had been melting and boiling water for me easily enough as well. After his freak out about me being dehydrated—he'd seriously acted like I was about to die—he'd made sure I had plenty of water. Maybe his dramatic as fuck reaction had something to do with his own biology. Perhaps dehydration was more dangerous to drakcol. If it was, I needed to watch how much Serlotminden was drinking; he didn't always take care of himself.

"I'll be fine," he said, tightening the blanket before checking the blaster he'd removed from the smaller crate in the cargo bay.

"We'll be fine," I corrected, and he frowned, tail writhing. He was welcome to try and leave me behind, but I'd follow him. If Mindy didn't want me to go out by myself, then he wasn't either. So if he planned to go, I was going with him.

I cocked an eyebrow and crossed my arms, silently challenging him to be a dick about this.

He snagged me, tucking me against his chest. I fought the sudden leap in my pulse. In the last couple of days, Mindy had gotten even more physically affectionate, if that was possible. I hadn't remarked on it, because I liked it. Touch had never been important to me, even as a kid, but it was different with him. I liked the feel of his scales on my skin, the warmth that radiated off him, and how I fit within his embrace.

This, regardless of my wild attraction to him, would go nowhere. Serlotminden was taken, and it was fine. We were friends, as he'd reiterated many, *many* times. Fuck him.

"Fine," he said, thumb brushing the edge of my jaw and resting right in front of my ear lobe. Mindy smiled, head lowering, and my stomach dropped. God, was he going to kiss me? Did I want him to? I almost snorted. Of course I did. I silently urged him to keep coming closer and closer until his lips were on mine.

He stopped, not touching me but close. His breath rushed over my skin as he said, "I will find you something tasty to eat."

I grunted. He was the one that was getting tired of the nutritional bars. I didn't think they were that bad. They were way better than the chalk Agk had fed me and Vince.

Serlotminden straightened, making me frown, and ran his fingers over my cheeks. He seemed fascinated with my beard—if you could call the patchy growth that. I'd never been able to grow a proper beard or mustache, so I usually shaved it. That wasn't an option at the moment. But it didn't matter that there wasn't much hair, he loved touching and rubbing his fingers over it. The hair on my head was also growing again, which he played with all the time.

"I would rather you stay here," he said in a low voice, his tail curling around my leg.

His prehensile tail was a curiosity to me. I loved him holding me, dragging the length over my skin, and tickling me with it. But I couldn't help but wonder how it might feel wrapped around my dick. Could he do that? How would the scales and warmth feel? I shook the thought away. My attraction to Serlotminden was getting out of control.

Being this interested in sex was unusual, for me at least, but I admitted it was more than that. I craved a closeness with him along with sex. I wasn't going to get either, so I needed to calm the fuck down.

"I'm coming."

Mindy stared at me, and I crossed my arms, daring him to argue. I could be stubborn when I wanted to be. I wasn't being left behind. We were going together or not at all. Besides, he'd agreed to me coming.

"Please stay close to me, my Teddy. I wouldn't survive something happening to you."

That was oddly dramatic. Sure, he liked me, but if I died that didn't mean he'd stop breathing. Me? I would have a much harder time, because I couldn't fix anything on the shuttle or melt water or find food when I eventually needed it.

I grunted again. That seemed to be enough for him, because he moved in front of me and pulled the lever, opening the hatch.

The day was clear, and the area looked the same as yesterday. I automatically peered at the ginormous nests. I was ready to duck or haul ass back to the shuttle if I saw even a flash of feathers. Though in reality, I'd probably freeze like a deer in headlights, and Serlotminden would have to drag me inside. Hopefully, those car-sized nests would be completely empty and nothing would happen.

But winter might be ending, and they might come back. Perish the thought.

Our feet sank into the snow as we moved across the landscape. It took maybe a couple dozen steps before I was panting and covered in sweat. My heart pounded, and my lungs burned. I was still weak, despite Mindy's insistence I "play" with him on almost a daily basis, and tramping through the snow was hard work.

He grabbed my elbow, and his tail coiled around my leg. "You should go back."

"I'm fine," I panted. If he thought I was going to leave him out here alone, he was a fool. I wasn't going to sit on the hatch door like normal while he was off hunting... at least not the first time.

The trees grew closer and closer. Their icy blue fronds moved without any wind. Independently moving plants were in no way a good thing, but Mindy didn't act bothered. Maybe moving plants was normal to him. Who knew what was out there in the universe? Not me. But they freaked me out, and I didn't want to go near them—something Serlotminden didn't agree with, because he led us straight toward them.

When we got closer, I noticed the trees weren't solid blue. They had gray stripes, like that four-armed alien I'd seen. A few bushes with wiry branches grew around the tree trunks. It was warmer beneath the trees, like a hot spring or something moved underground. The snow disappeared, leaving brown dirt with a purple tinge to it. What kind of nitrates had to be in the soil to make it purple?

Dead fronds, small leaves from the wiry bushes, and strips of dried bark littered the ground.

Mindy snatched a long piece of bark, picking at it with his claws. "This will burn well."

"We have to catch something first."

He grinned at me, showing off his canines. "I will catch something. I will provide for you."

I didn't need him to catch something, nor did I actually care, but he'd insisted. I kept an eye on the trees as we moved further into the jungle, attempting to move as quietly as possible, but that was hard. My feet found bark and twigs like no one's business.

A rushing sound reached my ears, and my pulse skyrocketed. I knew what that was—I would know that sound anywhere. I darted forward.

"Bartholomew," Mindy called after me, but I ignored him, bolting toward the low rushing. I broke through the trees, heedless of the branches scraping at my face and arms, and spotted a river of clear water.

The river cut through the trees, disappearing from sight. Tall trees and thick underbrush abutted the riverbank. There were a few clear spaces, letting me see the purple-brown dirt and rocks that looked like... normal gray rocks. I guessed rocks were rocks everywhere.

A quick peek around didn't reveal any animals, but they had to be around here somewhere. I'd been camping and watched enough documentaries to know animals flocked to water. I crept closer, avoiding the larger gray-spotted rocks, and peered into the clear water. No fish swam beneath the surface, but that didn't mean something horrible wasn't lurking nearby, searching for a meal. All I saw, though, was a rocky bottom.

Steam came off the river in waves. With a quick tap of the water to test its temperature, I found it was hot, like bathwater hot. I groaned.

God, I was desperate to slip in and get clean. To actually get clean. Maybe Mindy had had the right of it coming out here to explore.

Arms snagged me close, and Serlotminden's mouth pressed against my neck. "Be careful."

"It's warm."

"And it might be dangerous."

"Worrywart."

"I have no idea what that means."

Apparently Caleb and Seth hadn't taught him everything. "You're panicking more than needed."

He turned me around and palmed my cheeks. "I have to protect you."

He was so close. It would take barely any effort to close the distance between us, to press my lips to his, but I'd never done that. When I was a teen, I'd figured out I was demisexual. Now that I'd found someone I liked, I was hella interested. My experience was lacking, though I was willing to try. How badly could I mess up?

Moving toward him, heart in my throat, I was about to kiss him when I stopped. Dontilvynsan. His boyfriend. I couldn't do that to Mindy. He'd been nothing but nice to me, and he didn't deserve me changing the dynamic. Besides, he'd called me his friend so many damn times, and I'd said no kissing during the permissions conversation.

"I don't need you to protect me," I commented.

"You might not," he replied, "but that doesn't mean I'm not going to. You are mine to keep safe."

I grunted. If he wanted to, I wasn't going to stop him. I turned back to the water, and Mindy hooked his arms around my waist, resting his chin on my shoulder.

He took a deep inhale. "You smell so *damn* good."

I chuckled at the swear. He put so much emphasis on the word it was oddly forced. He sounded like a little kid swearing.

"Seth and Caleb laugh at me when I swear too," he pouted.

I cupped the back of his head, my fingers tangling in his hair. Mindy tucked against my neck, and I continued to brush the silky strands. The water rushed by, the air was warm with the stink of sulfur, and far off birds serenaded us. It was nice. Existing like this. How long had passed since I'd breathed and watched the world, enjoying the quiet?

There was a low rumble, but I ignored it, too comfortable to move. Mindy didn't react either, other than to tug me even closer. I leaned my head to the side, letting him press his face even tighter into me. Why was this so nice? We weren't doing anything, but it was comforting in a way I had a hard time articulating.

The rumble continued, and something bumped my leg, making me glance at whatever it was. My heart stopped, freezing me into place.

That was not a rock.

What I had assumed to be large gray-and-black-spotted rocks were in fact crab-like creatures. It was butting against my calf, black claws as thick as my forearm. Two distended eyes as well as two antennas peeked out from under the hard shell. Its long legs were arched near the top of the shell like a spider.

It seemed to be investigating more than anything, and I hoped to fucking god it didn't want to eat me. The rock-crab kept bumping into me, and it was joined by more and more of them.

Mindy hadn't noticed, and I was struggling to get the words out. I tried to force my voice to work or my hands to pat Mindy. Something. Anything. We needed to move. Now.

Serlotminden is in fucking danger, I screamed at myself, but still, I didn't move as I watched the growing horde of nightmares.

My breath whooshed out of me when I was yanked back. Wings came around me, and Mindy snarled. The rock-crabs released squeaks—actual fucking squeaks—and flattened to their rock form, though some scuttled into the river with loud splashes.

His arms remained like two iron bars around my waist as he continued to threaten them, I assumed, in his language. When none of the crabs moved for a few seconds, Mindy turned me around, then began nuzzling my cheek and neck.

Tremors wracked his body, muscles tense. His tail ran the length of my leg and his wings surrounded me in warmth. "Are you well—safe—alright?" He growled. "I cannot think of the right word." Mindy rubbed his forehead on my temple and grabbed my hand, shoving it under his shirt, then dragged it over his side.

He was freaking out. Like really freaking out. More than lack of water freaking out.

"Speak to me, Bartholomew," he demanded. "Please. I must hear your voice."

"They didn't hurt me."

Serlotminden sagged, releasing garbled words, then said in English, "Why didn't you tell me or pull away?" When I didn't say anything, he looked directly at me. "Bartholomew?"

How did I tell him that when I panicked, I froze? That was literally the worst thing in a situation like this—stuck on an unknown planet that was probably hostile. I couldn't get the words out, so I shrugged.

"Oh, my Teddy, you are far more work than I thought."

Pain flared in my gut. I yanked out of his embrace. "Sorry."

I started to turn toward the crabs, who remained motionless, but Mindy grabbed me, keeping me close. "I like work."

"Seriously?"

He cocked his head. "I am serious."

I took a deep breath. This was not his first language. He came from a very different culture. Getting mad was petty when I doubted he'd meant it badly. I met his confused gaze. "What you said was insulting. I don't want to be hard work for you. It makes it seem like you're mad that you have to take care of me, which you don't. I can take care of myself."

"No," Mindy shouted, making the crabs scuttle even further away. "No, my Teddy, I like caring for you. I love it. Humans are delicate, though. Like flowers. You need so much."

Every man wanted to hear he was a delicate flower. He sure knew how to rev my engine.

"But I will take care of your delicate self," Mindy said with a bright smile.

Yeah, this was getting worse.

"I don't need you to," I commented.

"As you have said before, but I need to. I have to. You are mine to keep safe. My flower."

"I don't like being called that," I said calmly. His expression fell, and I felt like an asshole. "But you can, I guess."

Serlotminden beamed. "My Flower. Pretty and delicate. Like that... bull. He liked to smell the flowers. I like to smell you."

I felt heat rush to my cheeks, then spread to my neck, and I grunted, refusing to acknowledge that maybe I didn't hate it as much as I'd thought.

Chapter 19

MEET-CUTE AT FIRST TACKLE.

Bartholomew

Eventually, I wriggled out of Serlotminden's hold to inspect the crabs. He grabbed me, tugging me back.

"No, they'll hurt you."

Mindy was worried about me—to an extreme level. I didn't know what to think about it, but it was probably how drakcol were. Or maybe it was him. He'd been protective of me since the beginning.

"They don't seem aggressive," I commented, successfully freeing myself from Mindy's arms. I crept closer and crouched. The rock-crab shook slightly. I patted it, and oddly enough, it began to calm. Slowly, it unfolded, and I swallowed my immediate rising terror. The creature looked like a crab, a rock, and a spider had a baby. I choked back the urge to scream and met the crab's distended eyes.

It studied me for several long seconds before ambling to the river. The other rock-crabs followed suit until the bank was free of them.

I stood with a slight smile. "See?"

Serlotminden held out an insistent hand for me. I shook my head, but interlaced our fingers. He was being ridiculous, but this was a stressful situation, so he was allowed a certain amount of leeway. Besides, at the end of the day, I quite enjoyed how overprotective he was. It made me feel safe... and cared for.

We continued to explore the riverbank in search of something to eat. My gaze kept moving to the waving fronds on the trees. The icy blue leaves never stopped moving. Something about the writhing movement captured my attention and made my stomach churn.

The world disappeared around me as a memory surged. The fight ring back on Xome. The creaky benches. The metal rivet floor around the dirt ring. The rancid smell of death, piss, sweat, and puke. Vince was holding my hand in a vice grip as two people fought in the center. One was a massive garganlic who worked as a guard for Agk. The other was a slight human male that had been brought by his owner.

My eyes had closed, but nothing blocked the screams or the coppery scent of blood as the guard played with the human like a cat played with a bug. On and on the fight continued until the crowd released a disappointed cry. I peeked, and the human was flat on the ground, thrashing as his mouth opened and closed, but nothing but blood came out.

His movements grew more frantic like he was suffocating. No one stepped forward to help him. Vince and I clutched each other, unable to look away, as Agk called for bets on how long the human would last. It felt like an eternity, but I doubted it was more than a minute or two.

When he was dead, Vince and I dragged him to the incinerator. Neither of us said a word—we didn't know his name, let alone anything about him. What might we have said? He was a human who had been alive, but then was dead.

We burned him to ash along with all the others. All the others who haunted me, asking why I was alive when they weren't. I didn't know. I had stood passive and watched them die. I probably deserved to be ash while they breathed.

"Bartholomew. Bartholomew."

I jerked. Serlotminden was staring at me. I responded, "Yeah?"

"Are you alright? You didn't answer me. My Flower, are you ill? Cold? What is wrong?"

I breathed through the past and filled my thoughts instead with him—his smile, his petrichor scent, his radiating warmth. "I was thinking about the past. I'm fine."

His worried expression didn't change.

"You worry too much about me."

"Not so."

"Yes, so."

I continued along the river, hugging myself as I avoided the sharp brambles. He followed behind me, getting further away than before, but not enough to concern me. Mindy was searching for something for us to eat, but I don't know what he was expecting—a deer to wander by and let itself be shot? We weren't exactly being quiet. Traps or snares would work better, not that I'd made either before.

My mother Charity had tried to teach me—she was big into camping and hunting—but I drew the line at killing animals.

Though apparently not sentient people.

Brutally, I shoved the thought away and moved further from the river, looking at the trees and bushes for berries or fruit. That seemed easier. As long as we saw animals eating them, we'd probably be fine. Or maybe Serlotminden had a device that could tell if it was poisonous?

One second I was standing, and the next I was on the ground. My back and hips throbbed as lights flashed behind my eyes. Blood filled my mouth and my chin hurt terribly. Serlotminden yelled my name before breaking off into his rough language.

Something huge was on top of me, squeezing the air out of me. I wanted to thrash, but I was stuck in place by the massive weight. I tried to inhale, but nothing came in. Black dots filled my vision, and my lungs screamed for air, but they weren't able to inflate.

There was a lot of yelling. Whatever was on me was snarling too; I felt their body vibrating. The thing was covered in light fur and dense muscles, and they were warm, warmer than Mindy.

My head whooshed while a crackling static filled my ears. I was going to pass out. It was coming. If I didn't get to breathe soon, I'd faint, and there was no way in hell that was going to happen. Serlotminden might need me. My panic was strong, though, and it was freezing my muscles in place and filling my mind with fluff. Even if I wasn't crushed by the ginormous thing on me, I wasn't sure if I'd actually be able to move.

Finally, the weight lifted off me, and I took in a sputtering breath before coughing.

God, nothing had ever felt better.

As suddenly as I was knocked to the ground, I was lifted up. An alien, the one I'd spotted earlier, or one of the same species, held me in their arms before tossing me over a broad shoulder, letting me see their toned ass covered in a fur loincloth. So I was captured again. How the fuck had this happened?

Serlotminden snapped in his language, and the alien screamed right back. I didn't think they understood each other, but I was pretty certain they were threatening each other. Mindy was probably brandishing his blaster while the other alien was lifting their club.

The other alien gripped my ass, and I scoffed. *Are you fucking kidding me?* Was I giving off an air for people to touch me? I wasn't even that attractive, especially right now. I was scruffy, skinny, and dirty. But most of all, I was done. Done with everything.

The panic that normally froze my muscles vanished under waves of anger and frustration and most of all rage. I rammed my elbow into the alien's ear. He screeched, and I fell. The air whooshed out of my lungs when I crashed into the ground, the hit reverberating through my bones. My back throbbed, and my hips weren't that happy with me either. Serlotminden rushed toward me, but the alien lifted a massive club, swinging it. Mindy dodged, skidding backward, before lifting his blaster and calling my name.

I crawled on the ground toward Mindy, but the alien swiveled in front of me, barring the way. When he reached for me, I tried to slap him away, but terror filled every cell. This alien was going to take me, and who knew what would happen then. My breath sped up and sweat trickled down my spine as my thoughts clouded into a tangled mess.

An orange beam smacked into a tree, making me jolt and sending bark raining down. Serlotminden. He was still fighting for me. He would always fight for me. Of that I was certain.

The alien whipped in Mindy's direction and crouched, as if he was about to attack.

I tried to breathe, move, or do something, but panic and pain twined. My spine and hips throbbed, my chin burned, and every movement sent shards of glass through my veins.

The alien launched at Mindy. They were at least a foot, maybe even close to two feet taller, and they were muscle on top of muscle with four fucking arms, but Mindy held his own, clawing and punching the other alien. He kneed the furry alien in their stomach, making them huff. The alien smacked Serlotminden in the side and drew a shriek from Mindy.

His injury. *No*. I forced myself to my feet, ignoring the pain in my back. I froze. *No, not this time*. Fear was normal, but Mindy needed help. I refused to be passive again. I refused to watch anymore when I was able to do something to help.

Move, Bartholomew Reginald, I ordered. *Now!*

Mindy cried again, and I snagged the club from the ground, the weight making my arms and shoulders scream, but it didn't touch me. All I focused on was that this alien intended to hurt *my* Serlotminden, then take me.

Never again. I was not getting fucking abducted again.

I swung the club like a bat and hit the alien in the back. The shock went up my arm, but I refused to focus on the pain and hit them again. Serlotminden kicked the alien off, scrambling to me.

Blue blood escaped from the alien's wounds, but they growled at Serlotminden, who flared his wings and returned the favor. I lifted the club, unable to think or hear or process anything by the all-consuming fear that I was going to be taken once again. My shoulders shrieked, and I swore I felt a popping tear, but in my panic, I didn't feel any pain.

I stepped in front of Mindy. "Mine, fucker. Back off."

I tried to lift the weapon again, but my fingers gave out, and it crashed to the ground. Burning began to rip through my awareness, sending tears to my eyes and making my breath jagged.

The alien stared at me, not approaching, then glanced at Mindy. They said something in a soft rumble and held out one of their hands.

An invitation.

Serlotminden yelled in his language as his tail thrashed, nearly smacking into me, and he hooked an arm around my waist, which drew a gasp from me. He instantly released his hold.

Panting, I said, "No. I don't want you."

The alien grumbled, upset, though their gaze kept flicking to Serlotminden as they proffered a hand, beckoning. It was almost like they were trying to warn me away from Mindy. We took a step back, and the alien followed, tense. They weren't going to let me go. How did I tell him I was safe? That I wanted to stay with Mindy.

An idea formed, but I didn't think it was a good one or fair to either of us. In fact, it was an asshole move. Mindy was taken. There had to be another option, but my brain struggled to conjure one. I was in horrid pain, exhausted, and terrified. This was all I had.

"I think they're worried you're going to hurt me."

"They are the one who hurt you," Serlotminden barked. "I should shoot them." But he hadn't, because I truly thought he didn't want to kill another sentient creature, which this alien definitely was. Mindy had morals. The thought hurt, and yet comforted me at the same time.

"I have an idea."

"What?"

"Do you trust me?"

"Yes," he replied without hesitation.

I turned around, clamped onto the back of his neck, and crushed my lips to his.

Chapter 20

IF I THOUGHT I WAS ATTRACTED TO HIM BEFORE...

Serlotminden

His lips were soft on mine. So perfectly soft. I fought to keep my arms from wrapping around him, so as to not hurt him again and keep my sight trained on the threat, but I couldn't stop my movement anymore than it was possible to stop the tide. I gathered him close and returned the kiss. He moaned into my mouth, fisting my hair. The threat of the other person disappeared. The humidity, the rotten smell, the ache in my side, and everything else faded besides the feel of Bartholomew.

I kissed his mouth open, and my tongue darted out, meeting the silk of his. I groaned and delved in as deep as possible and gripped his hips, yanking him flush to me. More. I needed more. He tasted so good. He felt so good.

Bartholomew returned my kiss with equal fervor, though his lips were clumsy and his tongue tentative. One of his hands was locked around my hair, while the other cupped my cheek. He pressed against me, like he was trying to get as close as possible, and his hips started to rock against my thigh, though I didn't feel his hardness yet.

The kiss grew wet and desperate as I sucked on his tongue, then nibbled on his lips, tugging on the bottom one, which dragged a startled gasp from Bartholomew. *Mine.* Bartholomew was mine. I was never going to let him go. I'd fight anyone and give up everything to keep him.

A growl startled me; I remembered we had an audience, a very dangerous audience. Enclosing Bartholomew in my wings, I snarled at the threat. "My mate," I said in Drakconese. "You cannot have him."

Bartholomew shook in my arms, nose pressed into the crook of my neck. I stroked his back, even though I shouldn't. He was hurt. How much? I didn't know. I lifted the blaster and aimed it at the stranger. I did not wish to harm them or worse kill them, but I refused to allow this person to take my mate.

The four-armed person watched me for several moments before they took a single step back. I allowed them to slowly walk away. When they disappeared from view, I swept Bartholomew into my arms and ordered, "Hold on."

I raced to the edge of the woods, ignoring the stabbing in my side. The moment we breached the trees, I spread my wings and took to the sky, racing to the shuttle. Bartholomew shivered from the cold or pain or fear—I wasn't sure which—and I needed to get him inside, away from any threat.

Landing near the shuttle, I carried him in. I set him down and yanked the door closed. Without speaking, I picked him up again and took him to our cabin. Bartholomew made no noise the entire time. Was he hurt? How badly? Or was he angry with me?

The kiss had been a necessity to force the stranger away. The intensity had not been. He hadn't wanted me to kiss him, and while he'd initiated it, I had pushed the intensity, overwhelmed by the feel of him. Perhaps I'd gone too far. I shouldn't have, but I was unable to resist him.

I put him in the tent and crawled inside to join him. I wanted to press my lips against his and continue what that kiss had wrought inside me, but I didn't. I would never hurt Bartholomew. Ever. No matter if he chose Vince over me, I would respect his boundaries, even if it killed me, which it would.

Drakcol didn't often survive the rejection or loss of their mate, and I could not live without Bartholomew.

"Are you injured?" I asked, hands fisted on my thighs.

He stared blankly at me like he didn't understand.

"Bartholomew?"

He did not answer. He lay on the mat, not speaking, eyes distant and muscles tense.

Gently, I nudged his cheek with the back of my finger. "Please. I need to know that you aren't hurt."

Bartholomew flinched, and I dragged my finger away. He said, "My shoulders."

"Shoulders?" Had the other person scratched him?

"Back."

That made sense. He'd been knocked to the ground. His chin was cut and flecked with red blood.

"My elbows."

Once again, that confused me. "Can I see you?"

He didn't answer. Was he in shock?

"Can I see?" My eyes flicked to the cut on his chin once again. I needed to lick that clean. I *needed* it. My instincts demanded I bathe the injury. "Flower, can I lick your chin?"

He blinked, not responding.

I had explained this to him before about the instinct to clean wounds. "Please. I need to."

Jerkily, he nodded.

I leaned over him, my hair surrounding us like a curtain, which made this moment feel even more private like we were the only two people in the universe. Bartholomew reached up to cup my cheeks, and I had to fight the urge to place my lips on his. Until he allowed me to, I wouldn't kiss him again. I pressed my lips against the wound on his chin, and he gasped. I licked the cut and the metallic sting of his blood played on my tongue. His kiss had tasted like this. Had he cut his tongue?

I swallowed the instinct to investigate. Instead, I focused on slowly licking his chin, dragging my tongue over the length of the cut, cleaning any grit out of the wound. Bartholomew moaned, his hold tightening. My cock twitched and began to harden at the quiet sound of my mate.

Harder, I dragged my tongue over the injury, making him cry out, "Mindy."

"Yes?" I whispered against his chin. I licked him again. "What, my perfect Flower?"

Bartholomew didn't respond.

I bathed the entire area, then leaned back, satisfied. The rough skin would heal in time. "Can I see the rest of you? I need to know how hurt you are."

"A-are you going to lick me?"

Stars, I'd give anything to suck his cock and drink his seed, but that wasn't what he meant. I answered, "I will clean all your injuries."

His breath turned even more jagged.

"I need this, Flower." I kept my focus on him, but I was desperate to see if he was hard like I was. Maybe this could become something else, after I secured his permissions. Though if he was too hurt to fuck, I could please him.

After a second, Bartholomew nodded.

I moved downward, letting my hair drag over him. Bartholomew shivered, and I grinned. He lay utterly still beneath me, except for his heaving chest. One glance at his groin made my soul throb. My mate was hard and pressing against his black trousers.

I rucked up the borrowed shirt he wore and carefully pulled it off. My arousal flagged. His arms had light scratches from the bushes or from falling, his elbows were raw, and I saw bruises all over his sides. I lifted one arm and began to clean it, paying particular attention to his elbows. Bartholomew winced and gasped occasionally, but I was careful to not cause him more pain.

When his arms were clean, I rolled him over and wanted to weep. His shoulders were swollen, and his back was coated in bruises that were steadily darkening. "My Flower," I whispered, running my fingers over him, not using any pressure. My purple scales appeared even darker next to his skin, and my claws looked so dangerous in light of how delicate I'd learned he was.

"I'm okay," he replied, voice shaky.

My fingers drifted to the band at the top of his trousers, dipping underneath. He gasped. "You are hurt here too. Can I remove them?"

"I'll be naked."

"Yes." I tried to swallow the pleased groan. I needed him naked and against me, safe and warm.

He pressed his face into the blanket beneath him and nodded.

I pulled his trousers off, removing his socks and shoes on the way, leaving him bare. He was beautiful. His butt was covered in bruises, much like the rest of him, but my eyes caught on his dark hair. I brushed my fingers over one cheek, and he shuddered. I wanted to lift his hips and bury my face against him to taste his hole.

Ignoring the urge, I searched for cuts to clean. I spotted a small one beneath one of the dimples at the base of his spine. Bartholomew moaned, hips arching, but the pleasure-filled noise turned into a pained grunt.

"Don't move," I ordered. "I will take care of you."

Every cut was thoroughly cleaned until Bartholomew was trembling beneath me. He was moaning, hips moving a bit. I licked his shoulder blades over the darkest bruises.

"Flower, I need you to roll over."

He shook his head, cheeks and the tips of his ears red.

I chuckled. Bartholomew was shy about his arousal. "You don't have to hide it," I said. "I don't care." I loved it. I loved the fact that my touch was driving him to this. I bent and licked his spine, letting my hair dragged over his sensitive skin. He moaned louder, but still not loud enough for me. I licked and cleaned each bruise as his hips gently rocked.

When I reached the swell of his butt, I licked one cheek, and Bartholomew released a jagged cry of my name as his muscles tensed and his hips stuttered.

He was coming... and calling for me as he did. My cock grew even harder. It was beyond attractive that I'd made him release with such little stimulation. I licked his other cheek as Bartholomew moaned into the blanket beneath him.

He sagged, relaxing, his breath harsh.

My fingers twitched; I was burning with the urge to stroke myself off and release my seed on his back, but he was injured, and that was more important than any pleasure. "Can you roll over now that you are..." The word escaped me, or perhaps I never learned it. I'd never really discussed sex English with either of my mate-brothers. I settled with, "Satisfied?"

Bartholomew's cheeks darkened. "N-no."

"But you're hurt."

"No, Serlotminden."

A claw ripped my gut at his angry tone. Had I messed up? Had I forced him to release when he did not wish for it?

"Can you leave for a minute?"

"What?"

"Leave, Mindy," Bartholomew snapped, and I jerked back. He'd never talked to me like that before. Not once. Never had he gotten angry like that.

"Alright, Flower," I said, voice barely audible, and I climbed out of the tent, my soul as cold as ice and shame filled me. I must have made a mistake again.

Bartholomew

Embarrassment ripped through me. I'd fucking come from Mindy licking me, and not even anywhere exciting. I'd been so turned on from being naked with him, and I came. Who the fuck came from that? What was he going to think? We were friends. But who licked their friend's ass? This had to be more.

My cum had soaked the blanket beneath me, making my raging embarrassment even worse. Carefully, I rolled over. My hips protested, and my back and butt joined in. I was a mass of bruises. My shoulders both felt stiff and swollen. I hoped to god I hadn't ripped anything like a tendon, but I didn't know.

Focusing, I cleaned myself with the soiled blanket, balled it up, and chucked it into the corner. Dragging on a pair of pants and a shirt, I moved to the edge of the mattress and curled up.

After several minutes, Mindy asked, "Can I come back in? You need water."

I grunted.

Mindy crawled in, and I curled up even tighter. I fucking came in front of him with basically no touch. I hadn't wanted our first time to be like that. Though had that even been our first time? We weren't together.

I heard rustling before I felt the warmth of him behind me. "You need to drink water, Flower."

I didn't move. I was too mortified. Logically, I knew there was zero reason to be embarrassed. Premature ejaculation happened, supposedly. I'd always masturbated alone, so it hadn't been my worry until this exact second.

When I continued to be quiet, he lay behind me and rested an arm over my waist. "Let me hold you."

Some part of me screamed to reject his touch, but I didn't. Instead I leaned back, and Mindy gathered me close. He nuzzled the nape of my neck. "What did I do wrong?"

I didn't answer, because he hadn't done anything wrong. It had been all me.

His tail coiled around my leg. "Next time, I will take care of you myself."

Pardon? Did he mean what I thought he did?

Serlotminden didn't continue, and I didn't ask.

Chapter 21

SO AWKWARD HAS A WHOLE NEW LEVEL. AWESOME.

Bartholomew

Two days had passed since the kiss and licking session as well as my subsequent accidental finish, and we hadn't left the shuttle once. I was leery about the possibility of the four-armed alien being out there, and Mindy probably was as well. Eventually, though, we'd have to go outside for water, food, and sunlight.

Also, the desperate need for space might drive us outside.

A palpable tension pulled between us anytime we were in the same room, which was often because this ship was the size of a fucking thimble. We couldn't get away from each other. Neither of us talked much, my usual, but even Mindy was quiet. We seemed to be dancing around each other.

At night he held me close because we had to cuddle for warmth, but otherwise he'd stopped touching me. Had I bothered him with... what happened? Mindy had said it didn't matter, but he might've lied.

As we were both avoiding each other as much as possible, Serlotminden spent most of his time in the cockpit, checking on the signal and working on who the hell knows what. I stayed in the tent. My shoulders ached; both were swollen and tender. The club had been too heavy for me to carry, let alone swing, and now, I was terrified I'd ripped something. I could move my arms, but they were stiff. I wouldn't be able to move if I'd torn something truly important. Right? Honestly, I had no idea.

My back, hips, and ass were bruised to hell, not to mention my skinned chin and elbows. But I was alive. So that counted for something. Alive was great, and fine was fantastic, which I was.

Well... I wasn't exactly fine.

The fucking kiss played through my mind on a loop, never leaving my thoughts. It had been good. That was the understatement of a lifetime. It had been perfect, revolutionary, searing. I couldn't stop thinking about it. Were kisses supposed to be like that? I had no frame of reference, so I wasn't sure.

Beneath the memory, my emotions rolled. I didn't understand them. At times I was sad. Serlotminden could never be with me. Then I was angry. Why did the kiss have to be *that* good if he was with someone else? Other emotions shifted through me, but they were harder to understand. One was impossibly soft and gentle, and scared the shit out of me, so I left it alone.

Instead of dealing with anything, I curled into a ball and did nothing. I tried to stay calm and logically think through the situation. The kiss had been marvelous, but it had been my first, so all of them might be like that. There was nothing to freak out about. The orgasm had been intense, burning through me. It shocked me that I'd come with what little friction I'd received from the blanket and his scaled tongue bathing my injuries.

Why had that turned me on as much as it had?

I banished the thought with cruel efficiency. I couldn't afford to get an erection right now or cream my pants; Serlotminden might appear at any moment.

With a deep breath, I continued to rationalize my current situation. I'd get over this crush. People often had loads of crushes in their lifetime.

This, whatever this was, felt different than a simple crush, though. We held hands, snuggled, talked, laughed, and basically lived together. This was more, but I needed to not run away with my emotions.

Mindy was in a relationship. That wasn't his fault or mine. Though he did act single. Licking couldn't be a friend thing in his culture. That didn't seem possible. Maybe he and this Dontilvynsan were in an open relationship? That meant we could be more, right?

It probably depended on their relationship, but was I okay with that? I'd never given much thought to whether I'd like to be in an open relationship or not. Sex, love, all of that had been a hazy maybe-in-the-future problem. Now, the future had met my present, and I didn't know.

I liked Serlotminden. I would admit that. He was funny and sweet. He had this air about him that drew me in and made me want to stay next to him. I'd never met someone as magnetic as him. It was hella hot. Though I worried he didn't think things through. He was asking for trouble half of the time, but perhaps I thought about things too much.

Like right now. Perhaps going along with what I desired, if Mindy was open to it, was the best thing, but at the same time, I wanted to contemplate the consequences. If we did start something physical, how would I feel when he returned to his boyfriend? When he was with both of us or him alone?

I frowned as something stabbed my heart. Yeah, I didn't think I'd like that. Maybe open relationships weren't for me.

Also, did I deserve to be happy? Did I deserve to be with Mindy when so many others were dead while I'd stood by and done nothing?

Footsteps sounded on the metal floor moments before the tent swished open, flooding the dark space with light. I swallowed as pressure built in my chest. I hadn't spoken to him, and Mindy didn't deserve my silence, but I couldn't make myself say anything. Nerves, fear, self-loathing, and unnamed emotions strangled me.

I needed to be a fucking adult and have a real conversation with him. It wasn't that hard. *Open your mouth and fucking talk to him.*

He lay next to me, not touching. "I fixed the lights."

That explained why it was so much brighter. The lantern only illuminated so much.

"Bartholomew." The blankets shifted. "I'm sorry. I messed up."

No. He hadn't. I took a deep breath and tried to say something, but the words clogged in my throat.

"Tell me what I need to do to fix this."

Nothing, because he hadn't made a mistake. *Ask about Dontilvynsan*, I screamed at myself. We needed to talk about our boundaries, or permissions, as he called them. That was all. All I needed to do was be a goddamn adult and talk.

"Please. I will fix this. I will do whatever you need to fix this," Mindy said, practically begging.

Nothing came out. Literally nothing. How did I explain what I didn't understand? The unfounded anger that my first kiss had been so mind-numbingly perfect, and that it was with someone I had no future with. The hurt that he was with someone else when he didn't know I'd existed not that long ago. The soft hope that maybe he might choose me, which was completely unfair. The worry that I wasn't good enough or that I didn't deserve him.

I tightened my hold on my knees.

He moved as close to me as possible without touching me, but I felt the heat of him.

With a deep breath, I opened my mouth to calmly and logically discuss what we needed to do. "What about that Dontilvynsan?" I asked, voice harsh. Fuck. I hadn't meant to say that. This was not fair to Serlotminden. None of this was.

"What?"

"That drakcol guy you're dating. Did I say his name wrong? What would he think about what happened between us?" I silently swore. I was screwing this up.

A half-laugh escaped him, and he started to talk, but I wouldn't let him.

"I know I have no right to be mad, but I am," I said. "I understand we're friends, but... Shit, Mindy. I don't even know what to say. I don't think I want something just physical—not that you're offering. Maybe there's a cultural difference happening between us, but it feels like you've been coming on to me. But you and that Don—" I cut off, unwilling to say his name, then sighed, pinching the bridge of my nose. "I'm trying to figure everything out. I'm not mad at you. I'm just mad and embarrassed and frustrated with myself and that damn kiss."

"Bartholomew, look at me please." His beaming tone made me peek at him. He smiled so softly as his long hair hung around him like a cloud. He gently clasped my damaged chin, turning me all the way toward him. "Dontilvynsan and I are not courting."

"I heard what he said." God, I sounded like a jealous idiot, which I was. I was jealous of the drakcol that got to touch Serlotminden, who got to hear him laugh, to see him smile, or receive his concern.

"He's my older brother, my Flower. He's very protective of me. All of us, each of my brothers, are very protective of each other. They will stop at nothing to find me."

My pulse picked up. "What?"

"He's my older brother. Has that been bothering you?" He licked his lips, bending closer. "Is that why you were upset when you reached... happiness or satisfaction?"

I looked away, heat slamming my cheeks.

"I care about you, Bartholomew."

"You said we were friends." I hated the neediness in my voice.

"I didn't understand my feelings. What are your feelings?"

Hope burned in my gut. Maybe...

Serlotminden leaned over me, hair tickling my cheeks. "I will respect it if you don't like me, but my feelings are real. I care deeply about you, Teddy." He smiled, but it was sad. "You're not the only one who is jealous."

"What?"

"Vince. You and he are a couple."

My forehead crinkled. "No. We're friends. That's it. Why would you even think that?"

"Truly?"

"Yeah."

"You're unmated?"

I grunted. He certainly got to the point. "Yeah."

"I wish to place my claim," he said rapidly.

"What?"

He grinned. "I want to be your mate. I've been courting you in the hopes of us becoming mates."

My mouth dropped open. "Y-you...Wh-what?"

"I want to keep you, or you can keep me. I'm not sure of the words. I have been courting you." He grabbed my hand. "Like this. We have been dating," he said slowly like he was unsure that was the correct word. "We are together."

My thoughts went back over his insistence at taking care of me, how he held me, how he'd enjoyed my extreme concern over him. Had we been dating, and I hadn't realized it? How was that even possible?

"You don't know me," I said.

"Which is why I wish to court you. But I know enough."

"Serlotminden." Had he actually thought this through? I didn't want my heart broken.

He bent closer to me, hovering right over me. "You are perfect for me, and I will prove it if you let me."

The soft, warm emotion returned in full force. I liked Serlotminden. A lot. It could be more than like, if I allowed it. My heart pounded, but fear laced each beat. When he found out about what I'd done, would he be mad? Mindy wasn't one to watch others be hurt, be killed, and that was exactly what I'd done. If he changed his mind, I wouldn't get over the rejection. I wouldn't survive it, not intact. I'd never cared about anyone like this before, and Mindy was... Fuck, he was becoming my own goddamn soul.

Still, fear aside, hope remained, burning bright—hope that I deserved what he was offering. "I want to date you."

He beamed. "Thank you."

I shrugged, struggling to meet his earnest gaze.

Mindy dragged me into his arms, fingers slipping under my shirt. "I'm so happy. I will make you very happy, like me right now."

I gave a breathy chuckle. "Will you?"

"Once we discuss permissions, I will satisfy you, even if it's quick."

A cough burst from my lips as heat rushed into my cheeks. "Please stop talking about it. I came too fast."

Serlotminden frowned, lifting my chin. "I liked it."

"You did?"

"It was... I'm lacking the words, but it was beautiful. I liked that you enjoyed my touch that much."

I buried my face in his neck. "Hot. You thought it was hot."

"Your satisfaction was very hot," he said, and I blushed. If we were going to date, I was going to have to teach him better dirty talk.

Chapter 22

A REQUEST THAT I CAN'T REFUSE.

Serlotminden

Bartholomew refused to look at me, but he allowed me to hold him tight and one of his hands slid up and down my back. He wanted to court me. He liked me, or I assumed he did because he'd agreed to be with me. I'd convince him we were mates; I simply needed time. I knew it deep within me. The feeling had been building since I met him; I hadn't understood. Now that I did, I intended to keep him.

It was that simple.

He and Vince were nothing but friends, which eased the fear in my soul. It seemed he'd been as jealous as I was, but over Dontilvynsan. I swallowed a laugh. My older brother had almost cost me my mate. I would have to tell him about it when he rescued Bartholomew and me. Dontilvynsan would find it amusing.

I nuzzled Teddy, taking a deep inhale and only smelled myself and my mate. None of the alien's scent remained. I swallowed a growl at the thought of that other alien touching *my* Bartholomew. I wouldn't allow anyone to ever harm him again.

He released a long breath, tickling my scales. An urge to place my lips on his almost overwhelmed me. Bartholomew had tasted so good and felt so right against me, and I needed to experience it again.

We hadn't discussed altering our current permissions, so no kissing, no grabbing his butt, or biting him, let alone sex. I desired all of it. But I would wait until he was comfortable with me and us before requesting more.

I wrapped my tail around his calf and covered him with one of my wings, though the tent was tight. "Are you still sore?"

"Yeah."

I needed to see the bruises, and not because I wanted to see Bartholomew without his clothes on, though that would be pleasant, but rather to make sure he was healing correctly and to clean them again. Instincts thrummed inside of me to bathe every hurt inflicted on him.

"Are they healing?"

"Yes," he said. "You worry."

"You're mine to protect."

He swallowed.

I didn't press the issue. Humans had different ideas of mating than we did. I knew this from my two younger brothers and their mates. Nonetheless, he was mine. But no matter the logic, the overpowering need to see the injuries wouldn't abate. "Can I see them?"

He lifted an eyebrow. "See or lick them?"

"Both."

Bartholomew sighed. "I know you have this... need to clean them, but I don't think I want you to do it again."

Hurt clawed me. "Was it wrong?"

Red filled his cheeks and spread to the tips of his round ears.

"Teddy?"

"It'll turn me on."

"Turn on?" He wasn't a piece of equipment, nor did he have an on and off switch.

"Make me hard," he said, eyes anywhere but me.

"I don't understand."

Grunting, he grabbed my hand and placed it on his cock, which twitched beneath me. "I will get hard, turned on, aroused."

My breath turned fast as I cupped him through his trousers—my trousers. My mate was in my clothes. Why was that so attractive? I met his gaze. "I wouldn't mind that."

Slowly, Bartholomew pulled me away. "I'm not ready yet."

"I will wait, my Flower."

He grunted, settling against me.

"What do you like to do?" I dragged my claws over his spiky hair. It was slowly growing. I couldn't wait until his hair was long enough for me to play with.

"What?"

"You said I didn't know you, so let me know you."

Bartholomew glared at me, and I grinned, biting my lip and playing with the ring. I wanted to hear his voice. I was desperate for him. With a long breath, he started. Not all of his words made sense, but he talked and talked until his eyes started to flutter closed.

He shook it off and started to talk again about going to the woods with his mothers and sisters—something they used to do often—but his voice trailed off again as his eyes closed. His breath turned even in sleep, and I readjusted until my face was right next to his, allowing me to feel his warm breath on my scales.

"I will take good care of you, Mate. I promise. I will make sure you want for nothing, so you'll stay right beside me. I will give you no reason to stray or go home," I whispered in Drakconese. "I will be whatever you need, so stay with me. Please don't abandon me."

He didn't answer, and his breath rushed over my cheeks.

Heat grew in my gut at the memory of his soft lips on mine. My cock twitched and then swelled in my trousers. I needed him. I rubbed the bulge, tempted to stroke myself off, but I refused to leave Bartholomew. I shoved my desire away. Bartholomew wasn't ready or desiring of my physical love, so I'd wait for as long as he needed, even if that was forever.

Bartholomew

Serlotminden pushed a warm bowl of water toward me with a wide smile. I didn't think I'd understood what I was agreeing to when I accepted his claim. He'd gotten excessively caring over my slightest need. He'd melt water for me to drink before I even woke up. He was constantly tying a blanket around me. His touch was so soft whenever he grabbed me. The last few days had consisted of him following me and trying to provide anything I needed, even though we were on a derelict shuttle.

His care was getting excessive, and I liked it. A lot.

He also asked constantly about my injuries, to the point of even neglecting his own. Mindy didn't seem to care he'd been stabbed not that long ago, though he did like whenever I fussed over him. He'd practically preen.

I smiled at the warm water. "Thanks."

"Of course, my Flower."

He stepped into the tent and pulled it closed to allow me some privacy. Since he'd fixed the lights, it was nice and bright. He hadn't managed to restore the environmental controls, so it was balls-cold, but light was better than nothing. I stripped and cleaned myself. Bathing was something I absolutely enjoyed now. So every couple of days, Mindy heated enough water for me to get clean.

My hair was slowly growing, but it wasn't even close to how I used to wear it or even curling yet. As I scrubbed my scalp, I wondered what he'd think of my curls. Would he like them? Play with them? Did it matter?

I scoffed. Of course, it mattered. I liked playing with his hair, and I wanted him to like mine.

Finished, I pulled on some of the last of the clean clothes. We were going to have to do laundry.

"Can I come out?" Mindy asked.

"I'm decent."

He crawled out of the tent and moved right by me, holding me, and inhaled deeply. Yeah, he still huffed me, even more so now. Serlotminden's chest vibrated against my back, and he rubbed his forehead on the nape of my neck.

"My turn," he said against my ear, "but you do not have to leave."

I snorted and went into the tent.

"You could've at least acted like you wanted to stay," he complained. "I am hot as *fuck*."

Laughter slipped out. Mindy was good at that—making me laugh. I poked my head out. "Would you feel better if I ogled you?"

Serlotminden crouched and bent over me, making his long hair tickle me. "I don't know what that means... ogled. But I would like you to watch me."

"You think I will fall for you if I see you naked?"

"I am attractive."

No shame. Literally none. I chuckled. He made me... happy. I'd never had someone who pulled me out of my brain and made me laugh so easily. He leaned closer, and for a second, I thought he might kiss me again, but he didn't. Mindy merely hovered over me, tail twitching.

"Will you stay?"

That felt like a loaded question. If I said yes, what was I agreeing to? Though if I said no, I'd hurt his feelings. "It's awkward."

"Why?"

"Because."

"I do not understand, but it's fine." He grinned. "How about I take you on a date? That is a thing, correct? Kalvoxrencol has talked of the dates he takes Seth on. Zoltilvoxfyn also takes Caleb on dates, though he is not as vocal." He looked around like someone might overhear us. "But they fuck in public. Like Zoltilvoxfyn's greenhouse. Caleb likes the risk of being caught. At least, that's what

Kalvoxrencol says. Seth caught Caleb and Zoltilvoxfyn, and it made him... turn red? I forget the right word."

"Blush?"

"Blush," he repeated.

The more I learned about Seth and Caleb, the more I wanted to meet them. They were humans who'd made their lives in space. Maybe I could do the same? I pushed the thought away. We were stuck here for who knows how long. The point was moot.

"I've caught them as well. They were fucking in their quarters with the door open. Worry not, Flower. That is not something I enjoy."

"Good to know," I replied. Not something we needed to worry about at the moment, but nice to know all the same, I supposed.

He beamed, then his smile faltered. "But if you like it, I can try."

"No." I might have no experience, but I didn't care for the idea of other people watching or finding me and Mindy fucking.

"Then we won't."

"What would we do on this date?" I asked, changing the subject. We'd done everything even slightly interesting on the ship.

"If I think of something fun, will you date me?"

My lips pursed. "Sure."

He moved even closer, leaving a hair between us. I felt his breath on my skin as he said, "Thank you."

I grunted, embarrassed, and went back into the tent. I listened to the sound of him bathing and tried not to think about him naked. I'd seen him before, and fuck, he was pretty. Though, my thoughts veered to the way he smiled, how he played with his lip ring when he was nervous, how he made me laugh, his tail that never seemed to stop moving, how he raced about, and the way his voice rumbled.

A few minutes later, he came inside, shivering as he dried his long hair. I slithered under the nest of the blankets and held out my arms. "Come here before you freeze."

Mindy didn't need to be told twice. He snuggled against me before I had a chance to react. I settled on his chest, listening to the thrum that must belong to his heart. I closed my eyes when his cold fingers started to stroke my back.

This was nice. Just this. Just us.

"Did you think of something fun?" I asked.

"We should venture outside again."

"What about the other alien? I don't really feel like getting attacked again."

"Trust me to protect you."

I snorted. "There is a difference between trust and asking for trouble. He was huge."

"We cannot remain in here forever. We will need water and food. We'll have to venture out eventually." He lifted my chin. "I will never let you be in danger. Not ever."

That I believed. He was too protective of me to allow something to hurt me. "Fine."

Serlotminden grinned. "Let's go swimming."

"Tomorrow?"

"Yes."

My first date. Unbelievable that it took an abduction, a desolate planet, and a hot alien to make me want one.

Chapter 23

SO DRAKCOL ARE LIKE CATS.

Bartholomew

I traced the ring in Mindy's bottom lip. He had several piercings, like the studs going to the tip of his ear, and the long gold chains in his lobes. I liked them. It had never been a thing for me before this—that I was aware of—but I liked Serlotminden's.

He bit my thumb, making me jump. "Your touch is... good. Distracting. I want a stronger word, but I don't know one."

"Why do you even speak English? Don't drakcol have translators?"

"We do," he said, claws scraping the back of my head. "I like to learn different languages myself. I feel like with every one I learn, my thoughts change a bit. I am a diplomat for my people. Not being reliant on technology has been helpful more than once."

"Hmm." I groaned, throwing a leg over his.

"Do you speak any other languages?"

"No. I mean, I took Spanish in high school, but I don't remember most of it."

"Spanish?" he said slowly, trying out the word.

"It's a requirement to learn another language in school, but most people don't remember them."

"That's sad."

It kind of was.

"You're not a... I don't know the word in English," Mindy said, "but you're not one people."

How did I explain this in a way that he would understand? "We're all human," I finally said. "The same species, but we have unique and diverse ethnicities, languages, and cultures."

"Interesting. It is like the barbarus and the tarmarus of Barus."

"I'm not sure."

"They are the same species," Mindy said. "Same biology, but tarmarus are all gray and white and live underground. Most Barusians and Tarusians don't associate."

"That might be the same, but I'm not sure." It was hard to agree when I didn't really understand what he was saying.

"Would you want to learn another language?"

I ran my fingers through his long hair, the strands wet and cold. "Sure. If you're the one to teach me."

"I want to. I want everything."

A sudden wave of emotions crashed over me, and I burrowed against him to hide.

His fingers worked gentle circles over my back, and I relaxed, loving when he slipped into the slits at the back of my shirt to touch bare skin. We stayed silent like that for quite some time. We had nothing to do. Mindy kept stroking my back, and I played with the fabric of his shirt, both of us lost in our thoughts.

"Talk to me," I said as I repositioned against him.

Mindy's hand flattened on my lower back, holding me securely. "About?"

"I told you things about me. I want to know you." If we really were dating, and I wanted that so badly it was an ache at this point, I needed to get to know him more.

"My brothers call me Speedy or..." a long garbled growl sounded, "in my language. I told you that already. I was given that endearment by my eldest brother, Hallonnixmin. I don't remember when he started calling me that, but Dontilvynsan likes to tell the story, occasionally."

I frowned at his older brother's name, still irrationally jealous.

He laughed. "Don't be mad. You are mine, and he is my brother."

"Did I say anything?"

Laughing again, he rested his lips against my scalp and breathed. "You are my flower."

I blushed. I shouldn't have liked that, but I did. It was annoying. "Finish the story."

"When I was young and full of energy," he started, and I scoffed. Mindy was still bursting with energy. He ignored my noise and continued, "I chased Hallonnixmin, who is five years older than me, all the time. He got annoyed with me always running back and forth, tripping over everything, until one day he called me Speedy. It was not a compliment. Now, it's different. We are very close. But the endearment remains."

"Hmm."

"Are you close with your family? You seem to be when you talk about them."

"I am. We don't live close to each other, though." I sighed, thinking of the last time I'd talked to my moms.

"What?"

"I fought with my moms the night before..." I couldn't finish that thought, because my stomach churned and fear turned to ice in my veins. "They wanted me to move back to my hometown, and I didn't. The last thing we ever did was fight. I hung up on them. I was frustrated they weren't listening to me. It seems so trivial now."

He didn't say anything and rubbed my back, one of his fingers slipping into the wing slits in my shirt again.

"Maybe when I go back, I can apologize." If I went back. I didn't know if that was possible. Did I even want to go back with the horde of ghosts following me? But maybe Earth would be better? I'd get some separation.

Serlotminden tightened his hold until it was on the edge of painful, and he rubbed his forehead on me, almost frantically. His tail strangled my calf as he groaned and grabbed one of my hands, pushing it under his shirt.

I frowned. He'd done that before. I tentatively stroked his side, and he relaxed under my touch. I asked, "Why do you do that?"

"What?"

"Nuzzle me."

His expression turned distinctly uncomfortable, which made me realize the answer was probably weird, by my standards at least. I didn't fight his tight hold or wiggle my leg away from his tail and continued to rub his side in an effort to calm him.

"I'm scent marking you."

"Like a cat?"

"Cats do that? Seth has not mentioned that about his Lucy."

Seth had a cat? No. I refused to be distracted. "Why are you scent marking me?"

"I'm desperate for you to smell like me. I have scent glands in my forehead, on the sides of my neck, and my sides."

"Ah." That explained him shoving my hand under his shirt. It was a claiming thing. Like cats. I wasn't sure how I felt, but I guessed it was instinct. We were dating, so I guessed he was feeling possessive. I could be creeped out or let it go. I decided on the latter. It was easier, and what did it hurt if I smelled like him?

"What was it like to grow up with so many brothers?"

I felt him relax at the question. I stroked his side, lightly tracing his injury, and felt him calm even further. A powerful feeling swelled in my gut. *I* was the one who made him relax. Me. It was nice. Weird, but nice.

"It was interesting. I don't know what to say. I've never known anything else. I'm the middle brother, and sometimes, I feel left out."

"How so?"

"Hallonnixmin and Dontilvynsan as well as our cousin Monqil-colnen are inseparable. Zoltilvoxfyn and Kalvoxrencol are the same. I move between them. We all get along together, but…"

I gripped his side. "You were left out."

"No. Never. But I know all of my brothers are closer to another sibling than they are to me. I love them, they love me, and we are all close."

I hated the thought of his family hurting him, even by accident. Serlotminden was the best person I'd ever met. He'd kidnapped me because he was trying to save me. He'd taken care of me. He'd made me laugh. He definitely didn't think things through, but he was the sweetest person I'd ever known.

No words came to mind, so I kissed the underside of his jaw and continued to stroke his side. If I couldn't find anything to say, then I could at least provide comfort.

Chapter 24

PERMISSIONS.

Serlotminden

I hadn't been able to sleep. I was too excited for our outing to the river. Bartholomew let me hold him all night as he slept, and I relished the feel of him in my arms. He was near my height, and much slimmer than me, for now, but I adored the way he fit so perfectly against me. A couple of times he whimpered or cried out in his sleep, and I'd soothed the tension away while whispering that I was there. I didn't know what nightmares plagued him, but after a moment or two, he'd fallen back to sleep.

When I started to shift away, Bartholomew released a long breath and gripped me tighter. While I didn't wish to move, I needed to prepare for our date. I snuck out of his embrace, or tried to. He held my shirt, forehead crinkling. I kissed the wrinkles. He was so cute—or as my mate-brothers would say, so *fucking* cute. I almost laughed, but I stifled it, as to not wake Bartholomew. Gently, I tugged his hands away and slipped out from beneath him.

The instant I escaped the tent, I closed it, trying to trap enough heat for Bartholomew to stay warm and to keep the light off him. I grabbed a comb and brushed my hair. I wished it was possible to shave the side of my head or pick more attractive clothes, but I didn't have access to any of that.

Normally, when I prepared for an outing, I dressed nicely, coordinating my jewelry, and made sure I was perfect. That wasn't an option right now, and this was different than anything I'd ever done before. I was courting someone—and not anyone—I was courting my mate. I wanted to look beautiful for him. Well, more beautiful. I was always lovely.

When I cleaned and prepared myself as much as possible, I returned to the tent and waited for him to awaken, watching his lids flutter with his dreams. Drool dripped out of the corner of his mouth and raucous snores escaped him, cheek pillowed on his palm. He gave a loud snort, and my soul clenched.

He was so cute. How had I survived before him? Was this what my brothers felt? If it was, I understood their complete and utter fascination with their mates. Though Seth, Caleb, and Gilvaxtin would never be as cute as Bartholomew. No one could be. It was impossible.

I shifted as close as possible to my mate, knees brushing his side. Bartholomew rolled toward me, reaching. Unable to resist, I tucked myself beside him. He grabbed the front of my shirt and pulled me flush against him. I rested my lips on the top of his head, but I didn't use any pressure. We still hadn't discussed further permissions and if he was alright with me kissing or biting him or having sex or anything more. My tail curled around his ankle, and I petted his back, my fingers slipping into the wing slits to brush his skin.

He awoke with a grunt, then a groan as he wiped his spit-drenched hand on my fresh shirt, but I didn't mind. His eyes lifted to mine and he jerked. "What the fuck?"

I would love to fuck him, but that wasn't going to happen right now. I grinned. "Good morning, my Bartholomew." I wanted to call him my mate, but that might scare him.

"Yeah," he said shortly, rolling over.

Sudden pain pricked me at the rejection. I shook it off. Bartholomew needed to get to know me better. He would accept me in the end. I was his mate. That's all there was to it. I didn't need the Crystal to tell me where my soul resided. He had it, and I planned to have his in return.

I snuggled behind him and inhaled deeply. Stars above, he smelled amazing. Like sunlight kissing grass or something more poetic. I wanted to bathe in his fragrance and rub it all over me, so everyone knew I belonged to him. I wanted our scents to mingle, and they did to some extent because we slept in such close proximity, but not enough. Never enough. Every drakcol needed to be able to scent me on him and him on me.

Bartholomew reached back, and I froze. Was he going to push me away? Why would he? But this was so new and fragile. *Please, don't*, I silently begged. *Please don't reject me*. His fingers enclosed my wrist and drew me closer. I groaned, dragging my nose against the nape of his neck.

"Bartholomew," I breathed. How had I lived without him? I didn't understand it. My life before made no sense. I should've been searching for him or known he was waiting, but I'd never even suspected a human was for me, but now that I had, I refused to let him go.

He interlaced our fingers. Bartholomew's palm was cool against mine, with rough calluses that scraped against my scales, making me shiver.

"We should eat before our date," he said.

"Yes." I was not going to disagree with him. Whatever he desired he could have as long as he remained against me.

"I suppose it doesn't matter what time we go, as long as it's not dark. It'll be cold outside either way, though."

"Probably." He was perfect in my arms. I breathed in his scent like I could imprint it onto my lungs.

"The water will most likely be warm whenever."

"Yes." How was he this perfect? It seemed impossible. No one was this perfect, but somehow Bartholomew was.

"We're not swimming naked, but we might want to bring a towel or something to dry off with, and more briefs."

"Sure." Could I kiss his neck? Would he mind? I wanted to bite him. I wanted to nibble on his soft skin. Kalvoxrencol had told me human skin marked when kissed and sucked on. Well, Seth's did. Did Bartholomew? I wanted to see it.

"I mean we can swim naked."

"If you like." I would bet my entire inheritance, all my properties, and even my racing shuttle that he tasted good. I salivated at the thought. Did his release taste good? Kalvoxrencol didn't mind Seth's or so he'd said. I swallowed a groan. I wanted to suck my Teddy.

"It's not like you haven't seen me naked."

"True." I would make him feel good if he allowed me. I had plenty of experience. I would make sure to obliterate any memory of previous lovers. No one would compare to me.

"Mindy," Bartholomew said, startling me. "You're not paying attention."

"I am," I lied. How was I supposed to focus when he was this distracting?

"I offered to swim naked, and you didn't say anything."

My stomach swooped. Naked?

"Either you don't like me as much as you say or you aren't paying attention."

My mind latched onto one word—naked. "I want to swim naked," I said, forcing him onto his back. I hovered over him, panting. "Let's do that. That sounds fun."

He laughed, and I'd never heard a better sound in my life. Slowly, he was softening, and that meant he might possibly care for me. I didn't need much. I could work with basically nothing. I was charming, attractive, a racer, and a prince. I was awesome enough that with a little time I could win him. I had to. There was no other choice.

Until then, I planned to treasure each and every laugh. Though even if we were together for a hundred cycles, I doubted that would ever change; he was too precious.

Bartholomew palmed my cheeks. "Now you're listening."

"I'm sorry," I whispered, fighting the urge to press my lips against him. "I should have been listening. Every word you say is important."

Bartholomew flushed as he dropped his hands. "Not really."

"It is, and I am sorry."

"It's fine."

I could feel him pulling away from me emotionally. I did not understand it. Sometimes he would open up, and then jerk away, disappearing. I wished we had discussed permissions. If I was allowed to, I would press gentle kisses along his eyes, cheekbones, chin, and anywhere else I could reach until every trace of tension left his expression. I felt that such touches would help build intimacy between us, which might stop him from hiding from me.

But I couldn't do that. Yet. I would prove my worth as a mate to him, and Bartholomew would choose me, then I would have the right to care for him however he needed and chose.

"Let's eat," I said, trying to get my mate to speak again. "I must feed you."

The slightest smile tugged at the corner of his mouth, and like that I felt him return. Bartholomew was hard to understand at times, but I would. I would know all about him.

I cupped his check, thumb brushing his skin. A smile grew at the feel of his hair on his cheeks. I'd never seen Seth with hair on his face, but I loved Bartholomew's. I lowered, rubbing my cheek against his and groaned loudly.

Bartholomew stiffened beneath me. I almost moved back, but his hands clamped onto my lower back, keeping me in place. Nuzzling his neck and cheek, I breathed in his fragrance and moaned. My mate jerked beneath me, his breath harshening.

"Bartholomew," I whined.

"What?" he asked, breath jagged.

"Can I kiss you?" I craved his soft tongue curling around mine in tentative movements. The most precious pink bloomed on my mate's cheeks. I dragged my nose over the color. He was beyond lovely. "Little Flower," I cooed.

He cupped my cheeks, pulling me away, and my gut fell. But he didn't push me aside. Instead, he drew me to his lips and lightly kissed me. A groan from deep within me ripped out of my mouth at the small touch. I'd never felt anything like it, ever.

I pressed closer, shoving my hips into his as I kissed him, licking and nibbling. Bartholomew gasped, and I dove into his warm mouth, swiping at his tongue. His legs hooked over mine, and he returned each of my touches with his own. His silky tongue slid over mine as he grunted.

Withdrawing, I tried to lure Bartholomew into my mouth, and he chased me, investigating. His touch was hesitant, but I moaned at the feel of him, grinding my hips into his.

Bartholomew jolted and something hardened beneath me, making me grin against my mate's mouth. I wanted to keep rutting into him until he found release, but I stopped. One, we hadn't discussed it, and two, he was so upset the last time he finished early.

Pulling my mouth away from his, making Bartholomew complain, I began to kiss his face, tracing his soft skin. He panted beneath me, cock hard and hips canting.

"Mindy."

I licked his scabbed chin. It was healing; all of them were. Well, the ones that weren't hidden by his clothes. Bartholomew had refused my desire to bathe the injures again, so I hadn't confirmed the healing with my own eyes. I cleaned his chin before moving to his neck, licking and sucking on the delicate skin. One of his hands buried in my hair as his hips rutted into mine. I moaned from the friction on my cock, but it wasn't enough to distract me from my assault on his neck. I had to leave my mark on him. No one might be here with us, but everyone needed to know this human was mine.

My Flower cried out, fisting my hair to the point of pain while the other clutched at my hip. He ground against me, moaning. I sucked and licked, biting, at his neck, but I did not grind into him. We hadn't discussed it, but I was perfectly fine with my mate taking his pleasure.

"Yes, Flower," I said against his neck. My hands went to his hips to help him rub against me. "That's it. Take what you need."

"Mindy. Fuck." A low whine came out of his lips as wet warmth bloomed, and I smirked. My mate was very sensitive, and he clearly enjoyed my touch.

He panted, limp beneath me.

I pulled back, admiring the deep purple mark on his neck as well as the blissed expression on his face. Bartholomew's eyes were heavy and his muscles relaxed. I kissed him again, and he returned it, movements lazy and sated.

"That was beautiful." I adored the fact that I brought my mate such satisfaction so easily.

The color returned to his cheeks, and he looked away from me.

"Did I do something wrong?"

Bartholomew took a deep breath. "No. I'm... I'm embarrassed."

"Why?" I cocked my head. He stayed silent for a few moments, and I didn't rush him.

Teddy eventually said, "I came so fast."

"And?"

"You didn't even touch me."

"And?"

"It's embarrassing."

"Why? It's hot, remember?" That was the right word, wasn't it?

He smiled, and my soul soared. "You liked it."

"I do." I kissed him again. "Can we discuss permissions again now that we are courting?"

"Yes."

I beamed, and Bartholomew traced my lips. I nipped at his fingers, and he grunted but didn't pull away. Kissing the digits, I asked, "Can I kiss you?"

"You are."

"But when can I kiss you and where? Can I bite you? Can I touch your butt? Do you want to fuck? And if you do, what do you like or not like? What touch do you like?" I asked, tail wiggling. "I want to know. No, I need to know."

His eyes didn't meet mine, staring at the tent. I waited, tail thrashing. His release was soaking the front of his trousers and mine, and I was still hard. I wanted to have our permissions established so perhaps I could also come, preferably in his mouth, but I wished for a release with my mate, regardless of how.

"You can kiss me," he told me. "You can bite me. I like it, shockingly. You can touch my butt, but don't kiss or bite it yet. I... I need more time." Bartholomew's cheeks darkened. "The same with sex. I know I've... we've—" He paused to take a breath. "I'm not ready."

I kissed his cheek. "That's fine."

"You?"

"I want you to kiss and touch me, Flower. I love my hair played with and I love my tail and wings played with. I'm not fond of pain, but I doubt your teeth can do much damage to me, so feel free to bite. I want to get to know you and hear your voice, so please don't pull away from me." I nuzzled his cheek. "I want you. Not your body, though I do love it, but you. I want to know you. Please don't hide or lie to me. Especially tell me if you need something. I need to care for you."

He nodded against me.

I pursed my lips as I tried to think of things I didn't want. It was hard when Bartholomew was so distracting and my body craved him on a cellular level, but I had to be honest with my mate. "I'm not fond of my feet being played with or kissed. I like..." What was the human word? Caleb, Seth, and Edith had truly neglected sex terminology lessons. "Before sex fun."

"Foreplay?"

"Perhaps. I also like being brought to close to pleasure, then denied, then teased again and again without my satisfaction."

"You like being edged," Bartholomew said.

Fucking permissions weren't needed right now, and there was more, but we could wait. "We can discuss sex permissions later."

"So what else do you not like?"

"Being left alone."

His forehead crinkled. "What?"

"I'm often alone with my races or my diplomatic missions, and I don't like it. I get lonely. I don't like being ignored or forgotten. Not that you have to be with me all the time, but—" I broke off, trying to think of the words I needed. "Being left behind hurts. I often feel as if my brothers are leaving me behind or I am leaving them. I don't like it. I love racing and my work, but I don't like being forgotten."

"Do they forget you?"

"Not intentionally. But they're busy."

He drew my lips to his, gently kissing me. "I will never forget you, Mindy. I won't leave you behind."

"Thank you." I nuzzled him, breathing in our mixed scent as well as his spend. It was a heady fragrance. I licked the mark I'd left. "We should clean you, then eat, and go on our date."

The color returned to his cheeks, and I laughed. While I didn't understand his embarrassment, it was adorable.

Chapter 25

A FIRST DATE TO REMEMBER.

Bartholomew

We were completely silent as we went to the river, and the silence didn't bother me, neither did my early climax, well, after we'd talked. Serlotminden had liked it, though I wished our... intimacy, I guessed, had lasted longer. But whatever.

No, what was stressing me out was going to the river when there was an unfriendly alien. God, it was so stupid, but I had a hard time saying no to Serlotminden, especially when he gave me a puppy-dog smile that made me want to kiss and smack him at the same time.

The moment we stepped under the trees, I tugged the blanket off and folded it over my arm. I stayed close to Serlotminden's side as we walked. I wanted to drag him back to the shuttle where that four-armed alien was unable to hurt him or me, but that would make him sad.

Fuck. Emotions sucked. Romance sucked. Why anyone wanted this was a mystery to me. Why *I* wanted this was a mystery. I liked

Serlotminden. I liked his smile. I liked his laugh. I liked his touch. I liked how he raced about. I liked how his mind worked.

I supposed that was answer enough.

The river gurgled peacefully as steam came off the water in waves. Serlotminden scoured the edge, tail flicking. The crab-rocks were nowhere in sight. They had been freaky as hell, but I didn't think they'd hurt us.

He pulled out a type of scanner with limited range that I'd seen him use before. Mindy growled. "The scanner doesn't work well, but from what I can see, the temperature and microbes in the water are safe for me. We shouldn't drink it. It might make us sick, though more likely you. Maybe if I boiled it. I'm not sure. And I'm not certain if the water is safe for you. Seth is mostly compatible with our environment." He stared at me, teeth playing with his lip ring.

"I'll be fine." I started to pull the hem of my shirt up, and he froze, tail thrashing. He was nothing if not obvious. He'd seen me naked before. He'd licked me all over, for the most part. Thinking of his tongue had me blushing, so I forcefully shoved the memory away.

I wasn't going to give him a show, nor was there much to see underneath. I was skinny as hell. The nutrition bars kept me alive, but they didn't help me gain any weight. There was also the fact that Agk had barely fed me or Vince, and I'd given some of my food to Vince. He'd needed it, and I hated the thought of him being hungry.

God. Vince. I hoped he was alright. Safe. As safe as possible in the situation I'd left him in.

Without ceremony, I stripped my clothes off, leaving the briefs where they were. Serlotminden watched with burning eyes. His gaze lingered on my swollen shoulders and elbows as well as the bruises decorating my back. He reached for me but hesitated.

"You can touch me," I said in a low voice as my dick began to perk up. I fought it; I did not want to pitch a tent in these tight briefs. "You won't hurt me. No licking, though."

What world had I stumbled into that I needed to specify that my boyfriend couldn't lick me?

My mind froze on the word boyfriend. Mindy was my boyfriend. I smiled, but fear ticked in my chest like a doomsday clock. If Mindy lost interest in me, it would hurt like nothing I'd ever experienced before. But more than that, if someone hurt him, I wouldn't handle it well.

My mouth went bone dry. Someone could hurt him. That alien or... my mind ripped back to the fighting ring. The strong smell of piss and fear that soaked the walls. Me and Vince huddling close. The smacking of flesh as the two aliens in the ring fought. Neither of them wanted to, but collars on their necks forced them to obey or they would deliver painful shocks.

Vince had gripped my hand tightly as people shouted and called out their bets. If Agk had gotten tired of us... that was our fate. To be beaten until we stopped breathing.

Fingers traced my back, and I practically leaped out of my skin.

"Flower, did I hurt you?"

Pulse pounding in my ears, I tried to force the past away. "No."

He kissed my neck. "Where were you?"

My first instinct was to lie, but Serlotminden had asked me for the truth. He wouldn't force me to speak of it, and yet... he deserved it, even if it terrified me. I whispered, "Before."

"Before what?"

"Before you saved me."

Mindy kissed my neck again. "Do you want to talk about it?"

"No." If I opened my mouth, I feared everything would spill out and I'd never stop. What would he think if I told him everything?

"When we get home, you can speak to a doctor if you'd like."

I didn't respond. Home meant different things to us, and I wasn't sure if we'd ever leave this place.

Carefully, he traced the bruises. It didn't hurt, but the feel of his scales dragging over my skin formed goosebumps on my arms and sent tingles of electricity racing under my skin. My breath turned harsh when he moved to stand behind me, his fingers sliding over my sides and up my stomach. One brushed the edge of my belly button, and I jumped, panting.

"You're still hurt. Your shoulders are swollen." He pressed a kiss to each one.

"I'll be alright." My voice was sandpaper. My thoughts whirled as he continued to caress me. Every inch of me was alive in a way I'd never felt as he stroked and touched me. The cold air was nonexistent in the face of the warmth of Serlotminden. He bent lower and his breath rushed over my neck as his thumbs rested on the dimples at the base of my spine.

His lips ghosted over my skin at the nape of my neck, and I leaned my head to the side to give him more space. Serlotminden kept his touch whisper-soft as he pressed kiss after kiss against my neck. He kept a hold of my hips, but he did not grip or squeeze me; he simply held me securely.

I melted.

I pressed against him and moaned when his scaled tongue touched the sensitive skin behind my ear. A whimper, a fucking whimper, ripped out of my mouth as he sucked on my earlobe, scraping me with his sharp canines.

"Serlotminden," I said, breathless.

"Teddy?" He kissed the nape of my neck again.

I was going crazy. If he didn't stop, I was going to turn around and mash my lips to his. If that happened, this date would probably go a very different way, even though I'd told him no sex. But I could not move away.

No. I'd already decided to wait, and I needed it. I needed more time.

I pulled away, and he instantly let me go.

"Bartholomew?" The question was obvious in his voice.

I did not answer, shaking. I eased into the warm water. My joints practically groaned at the feel. How long had it been since I soaked? I couldn't remember. I sank in, staying near the bank so the water wouldn't sweep me away.

Serlotminden entered beside me in nothing but his briefs. He was as beautiful as ever—all lean muscles and purple scales. He hissed when his side hit the water and jerked back up.

"Are you alright?" I asked, getting to my own feet.

"My skin is sensitive, and my scales haven't regrown yet." He sat on the edge, not looking at me, and took deep breaths.

God, I was such a tease, but I was unsure of what I wanted. I would get there; first though, I needed to know him better.

I ducked under the water and scrubbed my scalp. When I burst back out, I crouched low enough for my shoulders to be submerged. I released a long sigh at the warm water. I stretched and groaned—the heat was starting to relax my swollen joints.

Mindy scooted closer and held out the bottle of shampoo. "I can wash your hair."

How was he this nice? Like really? I wanted to say yes, but I took the bottle from him with a slight smile. "I can do it."

Serlotminden bit his lip, playing with the gold ring.

Turning away from him, I scrubbed my short hair, then dunked underwater again. When I surfaced, sputtering, he presented the bar of soap, which I accepted, trying not to make eye contact.

Not that he had the same problem. Serlotminden watched me the entire time, tail wriggling beneath the water.

From the corner of my eye, I peeked at him, unable to keep my gaze off him for long. He was a magnet, and I was helpless against him. Serlotminden grunted, holding his side as he tried to angle his body correctly to get his hair wet. When that didn't work, he started bringing water to the top of his head, which wasn't doing much better.

Since we couldn't actually swim, and I'd made it weird, though really because I wanted an excuse to touch him, I offered, "I can wash your hair."

He grinned. "I'm not going to say no."

It was awkward to get him low enough while keeping his injured side out of the water. We managed with him leaning on one elbow and on his knees. He lowered enough for me to get his hair nice and wet before lifting him out. Starting at the roots, I worked my fingers over his scalp in slow circles. He moaned beneath my touch, making my dick stiffen.

"Bartholomew," he cried. "Yes, that's so good. Flower, right there."

I swallowed.

"*Ungh*," Serlotminden groaned. "Don't stop. Please, don't stop."

Seriously? I was a fucking virgin, but I knew sex noises when I heard them. He *had* to know what he was doing. It was no accident. When he practically screamed my name, I hardened completely, cock throbbing in the water. Mindy was shameless, and yet, I wasn't annoyed, at least not completely, just horny.

I thoroughly washed his hair as I tried to ignore my needy cock and his lewd noises. When I was finished, I rinsed the shampoo off, then helped him sit back. The water dripped down his dark purple scales as he stared at me with his deep green eyes. I took a jagged breath.

"Thank you, Teddy."

I nodded, strangled.

Serlotminden smiled. "You are amazing."

I shrugged.

He grabbed my hips and lifted me onto his lap. His hard cock pressed into mine, and I gasped.

Serlotminden kissed the corner of my mouth. "Don't fear. I won't do anything."

I grunted, shivering in the air. His wings spread out, glistening with drops of water, and surrounded me. Warmth seeped into me and banished the chill. "I'm not trying to tease you."

"You're not, Flower." He kissed my cheek. "You're not ready. Yes, I'm... hard." He paused, and I nodded so he knew it was the right word. "I'm hard because I'm attracted to you and enjoy your touch. It's not teasing. Besides—" He grinned. "I like to be teased."

I flushed.

Serlotminden tightened his hold around me, and I pressed against him. We hadn't gone swimming, and it had gotten awkward at times, but this was a great first date.

Chapter 26

YOU THINK THAT IS CUTE?

Serlotminden

I didn't want to leave the river, because Bartholomew was sitting so prettily on my lap and I adored it, but I didn't want him to grow cold. So we emerged from the warm water, and I carefully dried him off. He tensed, making me stall in my movements. Did he not like it? I enjoyed taking care of him, but that didn't mean he liked me doing it.

"Can I take care of you?"

His mouth opened, then paused, clearing his throat. "How did you mean?"

"Like this." I started to dry him again. "I need to take care of you."

"Fine."

Grinning, I dried him off, but I kept my pressure soft so as not to cause him pain. Bartholomew was covered in bruises. They had turned a sickly yellow in places, but my mate had assured me he was fine, and I'd chosen to believe him.

When I moved behind Teddy, his breath sharpened and his head bowed. Taking advantage of the bare skin, I bit the back of his neck, and he gasped. I bathed the same spot in case it had hurt, and Bartholomew groaned low in his throat.

"Flower, you need to change. I don't mind assisting you."

Bartholomew leveled me a glare, which made me smile, and he stepped away. He stripped right in front of me, taking the wet undershorts off without hesitation. My soul pounded in need at the sight of him completely bare. He yanked on a dry pair of undershorts, pulling them over his flat butt.

"Change, Mindy, and stop staring at my ass."

"Hard to do, but as you wish." I removed my wet undershorts and tugged on dry clothes.

"Let me," Bartholomew said, turning my back toward him. His fingers slid through my wet hair, making me groan loudly, and he started to braid it. "I like taking care of you too."

"That's because you fit."

He chuckled. "Explain this 'fitting.'"

I frowned. "You fit." How else was there to phrase it? "When I hold you or we spend time together, you fit."

"I guess I do."

"You do," I assured him. He was my mate; of course he fit.

Once we were dressed, I started toward the shuttle, keeping my eyes on the surroundings for the other alien. I refused to let the threat of them steal any enjoyment of time with my mate, but I'd never risk Bartholomew. Not ever.

The jungle was silent, and we made it out of the tree line without incident. I tucked the blanket around my mate, brushing the skin of his neck. Bartholomew shivered, and I grinned.

"Come on, Flower. I want to take a nap with you."

He let out a long breath, but he didn't fight my hold.

We trudged across the snow to the cliff. The nests appeared empty, but I hadn't investigated them. My mate had stopped me the first time I'd tried. In retrospect, I agreed that poking around nests that might have sleeping creatures was probably not wise. Nonetheless, I kept watch on them, but truthfully, I wasn't concerned.

Leaning over, I nuzzled my mate and took a deep inhale of his earthy perfume. Stars, he was certainly my flower. I kissed him, and Bartholomew squirmed. I chuckled, straightening, and continued to the shuttle. A nap curled around my mate sounded extremely nice.

Bartholomew came to an abrupt stop.

"Flower?"

He pointed, and my gaze traveled in the direction he indicated. A creature lay in the snow—not moving. It wasn't large enough to cause concern; not to mention there was a good chance that whatever it was, it was dead. But my mate was stricken and trembling.

"I'll check." I motioned for him to remain where he was. My mate had enough things troubling him that he didn't need anything else to clutter his thoughts. Carefully, I stepped closer to the blob, patting the blaster on my hip. The animal was covered in white fur, and had six long legs like the crustacean creatures from the river, but this one did not have a rock shell. It was soft and pudgy with floppy ears. It had a curly tail that wiggled and a snout that snorted at my approach.

When I crouched in front of the creature, its beady red eyes opened and it let out a pitiful whine. One of its legs was broken, pointing in the wrong direction.

"Poor thing," I muttered. I would need to end its suffering. Normally, I'd bundle the creature and take it to the closest medbay, but we didn't have that here, and I refused to allow it to suffer.

Someone grabbed my forearm, and I looked at Bartholomew, who stared at the small creature. "It's hurt," he said.

"Yes."

"Can we help it?" he asked, expression expectant.

Stars, how did I say no? And if I did, would he forgive me? The poor animal was suffering, though. Was it right to leave it in pain? "I don't know how."

Bartholomew crept closer to the creature, and it opened its eyes once again With a single finger, he stroked its snout, and its tiny tail wiggled. He smiled—a full smile—and petted it again. The creature tried to move closer, but it couldn't. A pained whine sounded, and my mate frowned, scooting closer to the injured animal.

"I think its leg is broken," he said. "We can help it, right?"

"We can try." I might not know how, but I'd do everything possible to save this small animal for my mate.

He smiled again softly, petting the creature. "It's so cute."

Cute? It was cross-eyed and had floppy-ears and snaggle teeth. What was cute? I was cute. This was... odd... ugly... not cute.

Teddy started to take off his blanket, but I stalled him. My mate was far too thin to manage in the cold. I whipped mine off and helped bundle the rather docile creature. I carried it in the crook of my arm and tugged Bartholomew along as I tried to puzzle through how Bartholomew found this creature cute. It seemed impossible. If he thought the animal was cute, then did he think I was? I fought a frown. I refused to be jealous over an animal. I snagged my mate close and stepped into our current home.

Bartholomew

I made a nest for the creature I'd christened Pookie. She was the ugliest thing I'd ever seen, but she was so ugly it was cute. She looked like a rabbit in size and shape, with beady eyes and long ears, but she had long legs like a spider that crowded her body, though each one had small paws—complete with pink toe beans. Her front teeth stuck out and were jagged and her tongue was long and forked. Her piggy nose and tail completed the ugly-cute picture.

Pookie was an odd thing, but I liked her.

Every time I petted her, Pookie's small tail wiggled, and she pressed closer. I kissed the space between her floppy ears, and Mindy frowned. I rolled my eyes. He was so easy to read. He wanted to be the center of attention. Whether that was with everyone or me alone, I didn't know. Selfishly, I hoped it was the latter.

Pookie whined, her one crooked leg trembling.

"I'm going to hold her, and you can straighten her leg," I said.

"She might bite you. Let me hold her."

"No," I replied. "Trust me. Please."

"Flower..."

"Mindy, come on. I can do this."

Worry drove his eyebrows together, but he said, "Fine."

I gathered Pookie to me, making soothing noises while she whimpered. Mindy gently grabbed her leg and pulled. A sickening snap sounded, and Pookie screeched but didn't attack. Mindy quickly wrapped her leg with a couple of pieces of metal he'd salvaged to keep it straight, and I kept petting her in an attempt to calm her.

"Are you well?" he asked me.

"Perfectly fine."

He brushed his strong fingers over Pookie's long ears, and she thumped her tail. His lips quirked. "It seems we have acquired a pet."

I booped her snout. "I've always wanted one."

"I love pets," Mindy said loudly, shifting to my side to hug me. "We'll take good care of her."

"We will."

Mindy kissed my cheek before bounding off. He got water for her and more blankets, shoving a couple of our shirts in her nest so she got used to our smell. He kept talking and talking about Pookie and what we should do and how we'd be like a small family. She'd fallen asleep almost instantly after we set her leg, but I leaned against the cold metal to watch him.

My heart pounded as warmth filled my stomach. Serlotminden was so adorable. He put his whole heart into everything he did. Giving everything. I hugged myself, watching him dart around to provide Pookie whatever she might need. Was this why? No one had ever touched my heart like this, and was it because I needed someone like Mindy? Someone who loved so fully? I wasn't sure, but I liked him now and I didn't ever want to stop.

When my eyes started to flutter close, Mindy gathered me into his arms. I made a grunt of protest, but he kissed me and put me into the tent.

"What about Pookie?" I asked, already half asleep.

"She's fine. I promise." He settled beside me and drew me close. I shifted on top of him, sprawling, cheek on his chest. Mindy covered us with some blankets, but I pulled it over my head, burrowing against him. I preferred to be completely covered. I felt safer. Hidden. I didn't know.

"Am I too heavy?"

"No, Flower. You're perfect."

Serlotminden

My mate was fast asleep on top of me, his weight not near enough to bother me, which worried me. He was far too thin; he needed to gain more weight. A snort came from the other side of the tent, and I smiled. It wasn't only Bartholomew anymore. Pookie, as he called her, would need food as well. My mate was attached to her, and I had to do the absolute best to care for her.

I dragged my hand over his back and smiled. This was so nice. "Flower, I will take care of you. I promise. I will find a way to provide, even here."

He grunted, fisting my shirt.

The movement made my smile broaden. Bartholomew was slowly getting more and more comfortable with me. It was only a matter of time until he trusted me entirely. I was sure of it.

Chapter 27

COURTING GIFTS.

Bartholomew

I felt like an Old West housewife, or an Old West wife, I guessed. All of them were housewives, weren't they? I wasn't really sure. Whatever. It didn't matter. I snapped the wet briefs and draped them over the strand of wire Serlotminden had strung between two makeshift poles.

The day felt warmer than usual; whether that was true or not was anyone's guess, but we'd opened the door and decided to do laundry. Or rather, I'd decided to do laundry, and Serlotminden had insisted on hunting, alone. He'd made several good points about being faster and quieter by himself. In the end, I'd agreed. He was determined to provide, and nothing was going to stop him. With a kiss, he'd left.

Handwashing clothes sucked ass. I hated it. At one point, I'd simply stomped on the clothes in the sudsy water. Everything was dirty, though, and we didn't know how long it would be before his brothers came for us. I wasn't even sure how long we'd been gone. The days had blurred together, and we'd settled in, hence the laundry.

Pookie was sleeping in her nest, perfectly content. She drank the water we'd provided, and nibbled on the nutrition bar without any enthusiasm. I had no idea what she ate. Spiders ate bugs, rabbits ate vegetables, and pigs ate everything, so what did Pookie eat? Mindy hadn't been sure either. We would have to try a variety until we found out what she liked.

Another reason why Mindy had gone hunting. The nutrition bars were running low, and we had to eat. Water wasn't an issue, with the ice everywhere and Serlotminden's ability to create fire. I even had warm water for washing the clothes.

Food was the problem.

The four-armed alien hadn't returned, and we had no way of knowing if there were others like him out there, though I assumed so.

I didn't want anything to happen to Serlotminden. I liked him. A lot. Since our slightly awkward date, he'd treated me even nicer than before. Always giving me water or food; always dragging his claws over my prickly scalp; always snuggling me close; always... taking care of me.

I shook a pair of pants out and stretched them over the line. I needed to hurry and wash some of the blankets. I wasn't going to do them all. What if they didn't dry in time? Did things dry in freezing weather? Mindy had said it would be fine. I wasn't so sure. But no matter. I wasn't washing all of the blankets, just in case. We'd freeze without something. I planned on doing them in stages.

I held the jumpsuit that Agk had made me wear. The water slid down my arm, dripping into the tub. I hated it. I hated even the sight of the worn brown cloth. With as much force as I could muster, I chucked it; the skinsuit hit the snow with a satisfying slap. I'd wasted energy washing it. I wasn't going to wear it ever again. I'd keep wearing Serlotminden's clothes. Besides, he liked me in his clothes, if the heated looks he gave me were evidence.

Finished, I went to our tent, gave Pookie a pat, and snagged some of the blankets and shoved them into the soapy water. Stomping on them, I tried to take all of my frustrations out on them. Sleeping next to Serlotminden was torture. Every night, I snuggled right beside him or on top of him. It was so warm and comfortable, but it was starting to not be enough. The urge to explore his body, taste him, kiss him, and never stop kept growing.

God, I wanted him to fuck me so bad that it was an ache. The thought of him on top of me, his hair dragging along me, his breath jagged with pleasure. My pulse picked up as a tantalizing curl of want gathered in my stomach.

Crunching reached my ears, and I jerked. Serlotminden came toward me, panting. He held a bird about the size of a turkey, but it was bright red and covered in fur, not feathers. Its beak was curved with a deadly point on the end, and its talons were easily as long as my middle finger.

"Did it hurt you?" I asked.

"No."

"Good," I grunted.

Serlotminden came to my side and took a deep inhale, which made me blush. I shoved my glasses up my nose, ignoring the steam on the cracked lenses.

"For you, my Flower," he said, holding out the dead bird. "I can and will provide for you."

My caveman. Be still my beating heart. "Thanks."

That was enough for him. Serlotminden planted a kiss on my cheek and raced away. He cleaned the bird with the laser scalpel that was in the med kit. I had no idea how to do that, so I was happy to stand aside and keep washing the blankets while he dealt with the blood and guts.

Besides, I'd had enough blood and guts for a lifetime. I didn't need any more. My mouth went dry as my pulse sped up. I shook my head, trying to focus on the warm water. I didn't want to think about what had happened. Not again. But the memories surfaced without prompting. Blood pouring out of my nose as Agk hit me again with the baton. Vince screaming in the background. The sharp pain of the xoi hitting me in the ribs.

A squeal shattered the silence, and I jolted. Pookie scrambled out of the shuttle, one of her six legs lifted. Her snout wiggled as she took deep inhales. I patted her with wet fingers when she walked by, moving toward Serlotminden. Shaking off the past, I continued stomping on the blankets.

"Pookie," he called. "My adorable daughter."

I swallowed a laugh. I'd mentioned this morning that humans often called their pets their kids. Mindy had asked if it was the same with cats as with other animals, and I told him yes. He had then proceeded to tell me all about the house gods us humans worshiped, and one in particular, Lucy who belonged to Seth.

Yeah, someone had lied.

Apparently, Seth or Caleb had told the drakcol that humans worshiped cats, and they believed it. How far the lie extended, I wasn't sure, but I had no intention of correcting their misunderstanding. Instead, I'd nodded along and corroborated that humans worshiped cats. Because why not?

Serlotminden petted her, but she ignored him, focusing on the pile of organs. A frenzied squeal came out of her before she leaped onto the pile, eating. My stomach churned as blood splattered her white fur and the organs squished between her teeth.

"We found what she likes to eat," Mindy said with a broad smile, patting her back.

I swallowed the surging bile and turned back to the blankets.

When Pookie finished, she started back to her nest, limping, but Mindy snagged her. With a wet cloth, he cleaned her fur of blood while she wiggled, legs thrashing to get away. When he released her, she snorted at him and scrambled back to the hold.

"She doesn't like baths," Mindy commented, and I chuckled. "Flower," he groaned, nuzzling me. I flushed. He caught my chin to mold his lips against mine, and I moaned at the soft touch. Serlotminden didn't press for more as he gently kissed me, nibbling on my lips. Much too soon, he pulled back and brushed my cheek with the back of his finger, then bounded away.

Before long, Serlotminden had a blazing fire going and was roasting pieces of meat on it. Fat dripped, sizzling on the hot flames.

The tantalizing aroma wafted in my direction, and I abandoned the laundry. The blankets were done, and fuck it all, my stomach was grumbling. I hadn't had fresh food in years, not since before I'd left Earth.

I wandered toward the fire, practically drooling. Serlotminden held his arms open in invitation, and I didn't hesitate for a single moment. He tugged me close and nuzzled my head and neck. I rolled my eyes but didn't move away, because he needed it. Scent marking relaxed him, and it didn't hurt me in the slightest. When I sagged against his broad chest, his tail coiled around me in a gesture that was becoming familiar. That was another thing that calmed him, holding me, and it calmed me too, oddly enough.

The meat continued to cook over the flames as we stood next to the warm fire. My focus kept returning to the empty nests time and time again. Where were the creatures who lived in them? Maybe the rockslide from when we crashed into the cliff had scared them. That was possible. But would they return? I hoped not. I forced myself to stop looking at them because why worry about something that might never come to pass?

"We need to cook the meat thoroughly to make sure it's safe," Mindy said against my neck, huffing me like usual.

No matter what we did, we could get sick. It wouldn't be a fun night if we spent it puking... or shitting. But cooking the meat thoroughly wasn't a bad idea. Even dry and overcooked, it would taste better than anything I'd eaten recently.

After a while, Serlotminden shifted back, but he kept his tail around my ankle. He pulled the meat off the flames and took a nibble. "It tastes fine."

I doubted he could taste deadly meat, though I was sure he'd scanned the bird before bringing it back. He gave me a large piece, and I shoved some in my mouth. A groan ripped out of my lips as I chewed frantically, stomach rumbling. It tasted closer to beef than chicken, but it was greasy and amazing. My fingers couldn't force meat into my mouth fast enough. I breathed out, tongue burning from the heat, but I didn't care.

More. I needed more.

When I finished my chunk, Serlotminden handed me another. I ate it with a gusto. I tried to slow down so I wouldn't choke, but I couldn't. It was so damn good, and I was so hungry. I ate until there was nothing left, then I leaned back against Serlotminden, stomach bulging.

Laughing, Mindy nuzzled my neck and placed a hand on my gut. "I will feed you well, my Mate."

I stilled. He'd never called me that before. Not once. My heart pounded. What did it mean precisely? And if it meant what I thought, did he mean it?

Serlotminden

I snuggled against my mate, utterly satisfied. The blankets smelled fresh, but soon they would smell like him, which was better. Bartholomew was fed. I'd called him mate, and he hadn't panicked, but he didn't return the sentiment. Nonetheless, I would continue bringing him gifts to show him I could care for him as he deserved, even here.

He was mine, and I would give him everything.

Bartholomew gripped me, and I held him back, pressing my nose against his skin. How did anyone smell this good? I groaned against his neck, and his breath sharpened, which made me smile. He liked when I made noise. I'd discovered that at the river. He always reacted when I moaned and groaned in pleasure. That boded well for us later. I wasn't quiet when I fucked.

My lips found his skin, tracing over his neck. I licked a light bruise, and groaned at the taste of him. My Flower was lovely beyond compare. I continued to nuzzle and kiss Bartholomew as I held him tight within my embrace.

A long breath came out of his lips as he shuffled out of my arms, curling into a ball. Pain stabbed my soul. My mate did this sometimes. He pulled away instead of turning toward me. Why? I needed to know.

I followed. This could not remain. He liked me. He did. I knew it. I gently rolled him, and he refused to look at me, so I grasped his chin. "Why do you pull away, Mate?"

"Do you mean that?"

"What?"

"The mate thing."

I brushed his cheek. "I told you I was going to claim you. I'm going to care about you for the rest of my life."

"You can't know that."

"I can." I could and would care about him for the rest of my life. Drakcol could take multiple sex partners, but we had one mate. Some sought the Crystal to find their perfect soulmate, like my younger brother Kalvoxrencol. Others, like me and my elder brother Hallonnixmin, met the person we wanted for the rest of our lives, choosing for ourselves.

I'd chosen Bartholomew. He was my mate. I would never desire anyone else, ever. Whether he chose me back or not, Bartholomew held my soul. I was willing to give him my one chance because he was special. I'd never felt this way before, and I was willing to stake my life on this feeling.

Most drakcol did not outlive their mates or survive when they were rejected, which was why we guarded our emotions, but I hadn't bothered. Bartholomew was meant for me.

Besides, it was only a matter of time before he chose to stay with me for the rest of his life. I was attractive, successful, and perfect for him. Why wouldn't he keep me? He wouldn't abandon me. I was sure of it.

"You can't know that, Serlotminden," he repeated.

I cupped his cheek. "I can and do. I will always want you. I am never going to leave you. Trust me."

His wide eyes stared at me. "Do you promise?"

"Yes." Easiest promise of my life.

Bartholomew grunted, rolling to his side.

Once again. Why did he do that?

I settled behind him, my knees against his, his butt cradled against my hips, and I kissed his neck, making his pulse jump beneath my lips.

"Mate, speak to me. I do not understand."

His muscles tightened, and I surrounded him more, sliding my wings out from the back of my shirt so one draped over him. Bartholomew was completely enclosed in my embrace. Safe.

"I have you, and that will never change," I said.

"Okay."

I frowned. Maybe he needed more reassurance? "You are amazing."

He grunted.

"You are. You are caring. You always make sure I'm resting and not doing something foolish. You have an amazing laugh, and you always make me happy. You're so smart and clever. You're gorgeous. You are my perfect match in every way." I did not need the Crystal to tell me who I belonged with. Bartholomew was my mate. He was it.

Bartholomew rolled over in my embrace. One of his legs slid between mine. I cupped his cheeks, running my fingers over the sparse hair. My soul pounded in need. He was mine, and I was his.

"Don't hide from me, please," I said in a low voice. "I like all of you."

"I'm not hiding. I promise."

"Then what are you doing?"

He frowned.

"What?"

"I'm worried."

"Why?" What did he have to worry about? I was here.

"I'm worried you'll change your mind about wanting me."

I laughed, kissing his cheek. "Trust me. I am yours. No one else's. Not now. Not ever."

"Do you promise? No matter what I say or have done?"

My lips pursed in thought. "There is nothing that would change how I feel."

Bartholomew snuggled against me. "Alright."

I beamed. Had I proven my worth? I hoped so, because I didn't want to live without him.

Chapter 28

THE PAST CAN BE UNPLEASANT.

Serlotminden

A scream tore through the air, and I bolted upright. Bartholomew had rolled away from me in his sleep, and he was writhing on the blankets, sweat covering his exposed skin. Pookie was screeching outside the tent. My wings threatened to flare as I searched for the threat in the darkness, but there was nothing besides us.

"It's alright, Pookie," I called out and slid over to Bartholomew, pulling him into my arms. He thrashed, screaming. I rolled on top of my mate, pinning him to the blankets, so he couldn't hurt himself.

"Flower, I'm right here. You're safe." My lips traced gentle kisses over his skin. "I'm here, Mate."

He jerked beneath me, panting.

I nuzzled his cheek. "It's alright."

Bartholomew gripped my back, securing me to him. "Mindy."

"Flower."

Panting, he held me even tighter. "Mindy."

"I'm right here. You're safe."

He took deep breaths and squeezed me.

I tried not to put all of my weight on him, as I was significantly heavier than my thin mate, but it was difficult with how tight he held me. I kissed his cheek, and Bartholomew turned, catching my mouth with his. I groaned at the softness of his lips. His legs hooked around me and his fingers buried into my hair. Bartholomew tentatively licked my lips, and I opened for him without hesitation.

His silky tongue slid along mine, and I moaned into his mouth. He swallowed the sound and pressed closer. My tongue twined with his as we slowly kissed. My hands wandered his frame, and Bartholomew arched beneath me.

My cock started to thicken. I drew back, my breath harsh. I needed my mate, but he wasn't ready. And I was far more concerned about why he'd awoken screaming.

Bartholomew chased my lips, and I stayed out of reach. He asked, "What?"

I licked his neck, and he jolted with a moan. I nipped him, then replied, "Why were you screaming, Flower?"

He turned away, burrowing against me.

Not tonight. I didn't wish to force the issue, but I needed to know how to help. I'd noticed that he had nightmares frequently, but this was the first time he'd woken up screaming. I hooked my fingers under his chin, making him look at me. In the darkness, I couldn't see much. The lights were on a low setting, so it wasn't pitch black, but still, there wasn't enough to truly see him.

"Please, Teddy. What's going on?"

A long gust of air escaped from his lips and rushed over my scales, making my cock twitch in desire, which I ignored. He repositioned beneath me and froze. "You seem to be interested in doing something other than talking."

I bit his neck. "I wish to fuck, but I want to know what's wrong more."

"I have bad dreams."

"About?"

"About what happened on Xome."

I snuggled my mate close, squishing him with my weight, but he didn't seem to mind, because he held me as tight as I did him. "I'm here."

"I know, Honey."

I paused at the endearment. Honey was a sweet, sticky substance created by a certain type of insect. As Caleb had explained, mates often had pet names or endearments for each other, as we did. And if humans called you something sweet-related, it was good.

My lips trailed over him, trying to ease the tension from him. "Tell me."

His hand slid under my shirt to stroke my back and side. When he touched my scent gland, I bit back a groan. It felt so good. My hips canted into him as my lips found his neck. I bit and sucked. No. I jerked back. I refused to be distracted.

"Bartholomew."

He sighed. "What if you don't like me afterwards?"

I met his gaze. "I will always be here."

"Promise," he ordered.

I was more than happy to comply. "I promise."

However, he hesitated.

"No matter what, Bartholomew, I won't leave you."

"Even if I did something unforgivable?"

"Even then." I brushed his cheek. "Nothing will keep me from your side."

Bartholomew took a deep breath, closing his eyes. "Agk's was... horrible. Vince and I cleaned the mess left behind from the fights. The trash, vomit, spilled drinks, blood, and the bodies. We would put them in the incinerator." He fell silent, and I brushed my thumb over his cheek. Bartholomew looked straight at me. "They weren't always dead."

My gut fell. "Oh, Mate."

The words spilled from his mouth of the first time Vince and he had burned a living being alive, and the others that followed. More of the humans and other beings they'd watched die. Tears poured down his cheeks as he shook beneath me. The starvation, the loneliness, the threat of being sold, and the regular abuse from Agk.

More and more came from my mate as he told me of the horrors that had happened to him, and more and more I had the urge to return to Xome and rip Agk to shreds. That xoi had hurt my mate and many others; he deserved to die, and I'd be more than happy to assist with that.

When Bartholomew fell silent, shaking beneath me, I kissed his neck. "Oh, Flower." I wanted to apologize, but that wasn't enough. It would never be enough.

"I killed them. More than one. I killed them. It was me or them, and I killed them. I stood by and let people die or pushed them along. I was the one who locked the door every single time so Vince wouldn't be tainted by murder. I did it time and time again. No matter their tears, no matter how much they begged, no matter how sick it made me. I can still hear the thud the bolt made and the screams," he said, crying. "You wouldn't have done that. You would have fought. I killed them all, and I feel so damn guilty. Ghosts haunt me, Mindy. Every second of every day. I don't know why I'm alive and they're not."

"You did not kill them," I said, grabbing his chin.

"I did," he sobbed, shaking. "Now you hate me, and you should. I didn't deserve saving, Mindy. You should have left me behind."

"No, Mate. No, to all of it. It was not your fault, I still care about you, and you most certainly deserved to be rescued. You survived, Bartholomew. Agk killed them. He bought them and made them fight. He made you burn them. If you had said no, you would've died. It was not your fault."

"I killed them."

My words alone wouldn't absolve him of the guilt he carried, but I repeated, "No, Bartholomew. You survived, and that is not your fault."

"I wish I didn't."

"Oh, my Mate." I kissed his cheek. "I'm glad you survived. I'm glad you are right here in my arms."

"Even with the ghosts haunting me?"

While I doubted any ghosts truly followed my mate—and when my brothers found us, I could have Zoltilvoxfyn check—I didn't care if hundreds stalked him. I said, "Even then."

His arms wrapped around me as he burrowed into me. "Do you still want me?"

"I will always want you. That will never change." His past would never turn me from his side. Bartholomew had survived, and I was grateful for it, though I wished he'd never had this happen to him. "I will never leave you. Not ever."

"Stay here," he muttered, voice heavy. "Right here."

"I will. Sleep, my Mate. I will guard you."

It did not take long for his breath to even into a steady rhythm. I was still on top of Bartholomew and his legs were loosely hooked over the backs of my knees. His warm breath rushed over my scales, and I swallowed a moan at the tingles it created. I took a deep inhale of his earthy scent.

"Oh, my Mate," I whispered, lips brushing his skin. "I will keep you safe. I will make sure life is easy and slow, so you can smell the flowers. I promise."

He grunted.

With a soft smile, I started to lift myself off him, but Bartholomew gripped my shirt in tight fists, muttering. I rested my weight on him again, and he quieted, grasp loosening. Grinning, I nuzzled him to spread even more of my scent. Bartholomew liked me—it was obvious in how he took great care of me—but it was more than that. He needed me; his clinging proved it.

"Don't worry, Flower. I will never leave." My lips trailed over the sparse hair on his cheeks and chin. I loved it. I hoped when we were rescued that he wouldn't get rid of it. My tongue ran along the line of his jaw, and Bartholomew grunted, his legs tightening around me.

Warmth bloomed in my stomach and spread to my limbs, flooding me. My soul skittered as I stared at Bartholomew beneath me. Mine. He was mine. That was something I knew, but this new all-consuming heat was something else; something far softer and much more potent.

Pressing my lips against his temple, I groaned. "Bartholomew, I love you. I love you so much."

He grunted.

I smiled at the snore that escaped him. I would tell my adorable mate how I felt and soon, but for now, I would bask in his presence.

Chapter 29

COLD CONFRONTATIONS.

Bartholomew

"What have I done?" I whispered the second I woke up. Mindy was passed out beneath me, but I distinctly remembered him being on top of me when I fell asleep *after* I'd told him everything. Literally everything.

Panic coursed through my veins as my pulse pounded in my chest. I'd told him everything and had just fallen asleep like I didn't have a fucking care in the world. I had lots and lots of cares. Why had I said anything, let alone passed out afterward?

Yes, Serlotminden had said he was fine, but how could he be? I'd confessed to *murdering* people. No one normal would be fine with what I'd done. Either he was lying or he was insane. I was guessing the former.

Slowly, I slid off Mindy's chest, and he groaned, tail squeezing my calf. "Flower," he said, half-asleep.

I cupped his cheek, dragging a thumb over his scales. He took a deep breath, giving me a goofy smile as he fell back into a deep sleep. His tail released me, flopping to the mattress, and I wiggled out from beneath the mound of blankets. Trembling, I shoved on my glasses, tugged on my shoes, and crawled out of the tent.

Pookie immediately stood and snorted in welcome. I absent-mindedly patted her, my thoughts circling on my conversation with Mindy. Why? A little nightmare, and I'd confessed everything like a scared kid? I should've kept my mouth shut. He didn't need to know what had happened on Xome. How could he possibly look at me the same way, when I would never see myself in the same light again?

The shuttle was too confining for all of the emotions clogging my head. I needed out. I needed air. I needed to not look around and see metal.

Shaking, I yanked the cargo bay door open and stepped into the freezing cold. A gust of wind blew over me, making the blanket flare and raising goosebumps on my arms. Ominous clouds hung in the sky, approaching with every second that passed, and my breath came out in a frozen cloud with each breath.

I ignored the growing storm and the frigid air. They both seemed far away in contrast to the icy storm coiling inside of me. I'd told him everything. My eyes closed and I sank to the snow, wrapping my arms around my knees. Mindy should have left me on Xome. I should not be here.

Screams echoed in my mind, followed by a resounding thud of the bolt. I had closed it each time to protect Vince. I, not he, had killed all of them. I had stood there and let them die, even as he stared at me.

Tears froze to my cheeks as the wind picked up, howling.

Something cold nosed my elbow.

"No, Pookie," I said.

She snorted, grabbing the blanket with her teeth, and tugged.

"No, Pookie," I cried. "Just go back to Mindy."

Pookie crawled onto my lap, wiggling and shaking. I tried to hold her, but she refused to sit still and kept attempting to direct me toward the shuttle. The wind gusted and a snowflake landed on my nose, making me jolt. I looked up; the clouds had swelled in the short time and the temperature had continued to drop to the point I felt frozen where I sat.

Terror filled my limbs, locking me in place, at what I could only describe as buckets of snow falling so fast it almost appeared like a white wave coming toward me. It wasn't possible. It couldn't snow that fast. It couldn't.

I tried to move, but my body refused to budge. My thoughts clouded and a sense of complete helplessness filled me as I stared in horror at the incoming snow.

"Bartholomew!" Serlotminden's voice sliced through the air. He snagged me and Pookie, who was squealing, and raced inside. My arms wrapped around his neck, holding him tight. I was going to lose him, wasn't I? I deserved it and so much worse. I almost heard the ghosts in the back of my mind agreeing with me.

He set me down and cupped my cheeks, ignoring Pookie who was skittering around, squealing. "Are you well?"

I shook my head.

His eyes widened and Mindy started to frantically pat me. "Where? Where are you injured, Mate?"

"Why did you save me?"

"What?"

"Why the hell did you save me?" I demanded. "I didn't ask to be saved."

"I don't understand. Was I to leave you in the snow?"

I didn't know how to respond, so I shook my head again.

Serlotminden pointed to the door that didn't completely muffle the sound of the raging wind and asked in a cracked voice, "Did you try to harm yourself? Why would you do that?"

"You shouldn't have saved me. I don't deserve it."

"Answer me, Bartholomew." He grabbed my biceps, tears gathering in his eyes. "Did you try to harm yourself?"

"No."

"Then why were you outside in that storm?" When I didn't respond, his grip tightened. "Talk to me. I need you to speak. Why? Why would you risk yourself?"

"I told you everything."

"What?"

"I told you everything."

"We talked about this last night." Serlotminden pulled me into a tight hug. "I'm right here. I will always be right here."

But he wouldn't be. It wasn't possible. I shoved him back. "Stop lying."

"I'm not."

"You are," I snapped, breaking. Tears coursed down my cheeks and shivers wracked my body. "You are lying. You have to be. You can't be fine with it. I killed people, Serlotminden. I killed so many people. Their burnt bodies and their screams will never stop haunting me." I gripped the front of my shirt over my heart. "I hear them demanding why they're dead and I'm still here. How can you be alright with that?"

Mindy tried to reach for me, but I slapped his hands away. He said, "It wasn't your fault."

"It was." It was my fault. I could have said no. I could have fought. I could have not locked the damn bolt, but I had every damn time, to save my own skin. They were dead, and I was alive. The stench of burning flesh filled my nose and the low bangs mixed with screams filled my ears. My stomach climbed my throat, and I swallowed, trying to keep it down, but it refused to be contained. I dropped to my knees. Bile burned my throat and tears dripped down my nose.

A hand rubbed my back, and I didn't have the strength to force Serlotminden away. Shivering, I kneeled on the freezing floor, unable to move. Gentle kisses rained down on the nape of my neck and soft hands stroked my arms, sending tremors down my spine. Slowly, Mindy settled me on his lap, tucking my head against his shoulder. Pookie pressed against me with loud snorts.

"It wasn't your fault," he whispered. "You are not to blame."

"Then why do I feel so guilty?"

"Because you survived." He dragged his claws over the back of my head. "I'm not a professional, Flower, but you survived something horrific and it left wounds behind. You need to heal."

Tears slid down my cheeks, and Mindy brushed them away.

"I wish I had the power to take away your guilt, but I don't." Serlotminden lifted my chin. "What I can tell you is: I will never leave you." I tried to shake my head, but he didn't let me. "So please don't leave me, Mate. Please. I need you."

I closed my eyes. I felt beyond guilty for what I did on Xome, but I could try to let it go, couldn't I? I didn't know.

"Please, Teddy. My Flower."

"I don't know how to move on," I warbled.

"It has not been that long, even though it feels as if it has. You need time. Time to heal. Time to feel safe. Time to think. And you don't have to do any of it alone."

I kissed his palm, sniffling. "Don't leave."

"I won't."

"I'm sorry," I whispered, tears dripping down my cheeks. I wasn't sure if I was apologizing for going outside at the beginning of a snow storm or for slamming that bolt closed back on Xome.

"I know."

I hugged him tight, and Serlotminden simply held me in his strong embrace as I wept.

Serlotminden

"Do you think we'll get snowed in?" Bartholomew asked quietly.

My eyes closed at the sound of his voice. I had carried him back to the tent after he'd calmed some, but my mate had not spoken since. I'd been worried he'd fallen back into the spiraling guilt that had nearly taken him from me earlier. While he hadn't been intending to harm himself, Bartholomew could've easily been lost to the snow.

"I don't know," I replied.

He grunted, fingers running over Pookie's back. She was snuggled with us in the tent. I pulled Bartholomew even closer, wing draping over him. I wished I had some idea how to help him, but I didn't. He needed something that I couldn't provide. Only Bartholomew had the ability to forgive himself for what happened, and I didn't know how to make him understand what had happened wasn't even slightly his fault.

I pressed a kiss to the back of his head, and Teddy released a long breath. "I am sorry."

"You don't need to apologize," I said.

"I scared you."

"You did," I answered. Seeing him in the snow with a whiteout coming had terrified me to my core. "But you were scared too."

He glanced over his shoulder at me.

I gently rolled him onto his back and held his perfect face, I said, "You thought I'd leave."

"I didn't see how you could still like me after everything."

I pressed a soft kiss to his lips. "I will never not want you, Flower. I love you."

Tears gathered in his eyes again.

"No, I didn't mean to make you cry again."

Bartholomew chuckled wetly. "Not all tears are sad, Mindy."

He captured my mouth, and I opened for my mate, moaning. I would never tire of the feel of his lips on mine, his tongue twining with mine, and the feel of his skin against my scales. He gripped my back and pulled me on top of him to hook his legs around mine as we slowly kissed, simply connecting to one another.

"I love you," I whispered to Bartholomew, and he groaned, claiming my mouth again. After a few moments he pulled away, and we lay in each other's embrace while listening to the wind howling outside.

Chapter 30

I'M READY... AND YOU'RE SHOCKED.

Bartholomew

Serlotminden returned as he always did with some kind of animal. The days after the snow storm had passed with him hunting and bringing dead animals back to me and Pookie with a wide grin. He was a fucking caveman, and Mindy loved it and so did I. He hadn't treated me any different after I'd broken and told him everything. If anything, he was kinder, and he certainly touched me more, not like he was expecting anything, more like he couldn't help himself.

I was... I don't even know, trying to work through what I did on Xome. Often, I stared at Mindy and expected him to suddenly change, to hate me, to never want to look at me again. But he didn't. He kept loving me. Though no matter how much Serlotminden said I had no reason to blame myself, I still felt guilty as hell and memories haunted me, dragging me into the past at the oddest times. Nightmares also plagued me with some frequency, but every time I woke up screaming, Mindy was there, kissing me and soothing me back to sleep.

Maybe Mindy was right. I needed time to process what happened. At least, I hoped he was. I hoped there was a future without the past hanging over me like a cloud.

Huddling near the fire with Pookie by my side, I watched as he carefully roasted the bird. Serlotminden had brought other animals, fruits, and root vegetables back to our makeshift home, but the beefy birds were my favorite, which he knew. He was always extra pleased when he managed to catch one, usually boasting about his skills, smug as hell.

I was finally eating enough that I'd started to fill out. My ribs weren't as visible, and my arms weren't as bony. It would be a while before I wasn't underweight, but I was certainly looking better than I had in a very long time. Serlotminden, though, had lost weight. Not enough to worry me, but enough for me to notice his looser clothes.

My teeth sank into my lip as I stared at his sculpted ass. He was as gorgeous as ever. It didn't matter what he was doing, I loved watching him. His laugh was so contagious that it almost always brought a smile to my face.

He was good. So perfectly good.

I looked up and flushed. Serlotminden was smirking at me. He wiggled his hips, and my cheeks burned. He laughed, head going back. "You are so cute."

I frowned, but I wasn't actually annoyed. With every touch, look, and word, it made me desire him more. Snuggling against him was enough to perk up my dick. I wanted him. Bad. Which was new for me. Desiring the concept of romance or sex with someone and desiring someone *I* actually knew were two very different things. The first I'd experienced before; the latter, this was the first time.

Crossing my arms, I decided to be direct. He was straightforward; I could be as well. "I want to fuck."

Serlotminden fell backward into the snow, ass planting on the ground. "What?"

"Fuck. I want you to fuck me," I said again in case he hadn't heard me the first time.

His mouth dropped open.

"I've never been with anyone before. You're the first person I've ever kissed, so we'll have to go slow. I know you need permissions or whatever. I don't know exactly what those entail, because I don't really know what I like or not. I mean, I've jerked off, and know what I like in that regard, but I haven't had anal sex or played with toys or even my fingers. I'd never been interested before. Sex wasn't really much of a need for me."

He continued to gape at me.

"I want you inside me, though. I need it. So, yeah, I want you to fuck me. Maybe tonight. If you want. We could do it now, but I'm hungry and that smells good."

If he didn't close his mouth soon, his tongue was going to freeze. He seemed incapable of speech as he stared at me. Hurt pricked my chest like needles. Did he not desire me now that I was offering myself?

"Is that a no?" I asked. "We don't have to if you don't want to."

"No," he said in a rush, scrambling over to me. "I mean, yes. I mean..." He grabbed my cheeks and kissed me. His lips were hard against mine, frantic in their movement. I brushed his sides, dislodging Pookie who was snuggled against my hip and she snorted. She skittered toward the roasting bird, even though she'd eaten the entrails already.

"I want to," Mindy gasped against my lips. "I want to so badly."

I pulled him closer until he straddled my lap, but he supported most of his weight on his knees. Cold emanated from the ground under the blanket, but the fire warmed the backs of my hands and he warmed my chest. I gripped his hips, lips moving over his. His tongue flicked out, and I opened for him. He slid his scaled tongue over mine, making me moan. He sucked on my bottom lip, biting me, before pillaging my mouth.

My cock hardened and pressed against him; it was not alone. The hard length of Serlotminden pushed into my stomach. I groaned, trying to gather him even closer. I wanted him so bad. He rocked, giving both of our dicks much needed friction. It was good, but not even close to enough. More. Fuck, I needed more. So much more.

"Mindy," I breathed. "I need you."

"You have me. I will never leave you. Not ever. Not if the stars cease to shine or even if the sun extinguishes. I am yours, now and forever. No force will ever tear me from your side."

I groaned.

Food could wait, except my stomach chose that moment to growl. He chuckled against my lips, making me grin. He pulled back, humor dancing in his green eyes. "You did say you were hungry."

"I am, but I'm also fucking desperate for you."

He nuzzled my neck as he took deep breaths, huffing me as usual. "Let's eat first. Then maybe nap. Tonight, we'll fuck."

I opened my mouth to protest, but my stomach grumbled again. Serlotminden was never going to let me be hungry. He was too concerned about how thin I was. Relenting, I kissed his ear and nibbled on the gold studs until I reached the tapered point, which I bit. He moaned. Hmm. *That* was something I'd need to investigate later.

"Fine." I peeked at Pookie and snapped, "Stop!"

She paused, legs scrunched like she was about to leap onto the flames. Her pig nose wiggled and her forked tongue flicked out.

"Pookie," I warned.

"Come here, Daughter," Mindy called in a cajoling voice.

Pookie cocked her head, eyes going two different directions. I swore she was the ugliest, cutest thing I'd ever seen. Mindy called her again, and she looked at the roasting bird one more time before crawling over to us. She snuggled against my side and Mindy stroked one of her long ears.

"She's fine now," he said.

Kissing his neck, I buried my face in the crook and snuggled him close.

Serlotminden stayed on my lap until he was sure the bird was done, then he got up and gave me most of it, though he did give Pookie a big chunk. I tried to give him some back, but he refused.

He said, "I like feeding you."

"I don't like you losing weight."

"I like you not being as starved." He kissed my cheek. "I am fine. I promise."

I ate, but I did manage to give Serlotminden more. Afterward, he tugged me into the cabin and we curled up together. How was I this happy or content? I sure as hell didn't deserve it, nor did it make sense. Perhaps I didn't have to deserve Mindy and maybe it didn't have to make sense. We just were, and I never wanted that to change.

Chapter 31

WHO NEEDS TO NAP? NOT ME.

Bartholomew

"You need to sleep," Serlotminden muttered, brushing my cheek with the back of his finger.

I leaned into his feather-light touch that sent tingles racing down my spine.

"Sleep," he whispered. His hands explored me, and I returned the favor, dragging my fingers over him. I adored the light scritch from the edge of his scales against my skin.

I lingered on his smiling lips. "Are you that happy?"

"I am incredibly happy. I have always desired this and have never found it."

"This?"

"My mate."

I shook my head, but I didn't contradict him. I couldn't imagine my life without him, even though it had been such a short time. Somehow, someway Serlotminden had become indispensable to me.

My fingertips trailed over his full lips, playing with the golden ring. He nipped at my fingers, and I grinned. He licked one, sucking on the tip before kissing it with a gentle smile. Serlotminden was so beautiful. Before him, I'd never have thought purple scales, wings, and a tail were attractive, but he was the most attractive person I had ever seen. He was as lovely inside as he was outside, and he was mine.

I didn't deserve him with... everything that had tainted me, but I sure as hell wanted him and I planned on keeping him. I refused to allow my past to separate me from Serlotminden.

I kissed him, forcing his lips apart to delve into his hot mouth. His scaled tongue brushed mine and he moaned. I swallowed his pleasure and pushed him onto his back, straddling him. I yanked my shirt off, and his breath harshened as his cock started to firm beneath me.

"I thought we were going to nap?" he asked.

I scoffed. He'd wanted that. *I* wanted him to fuck me within an inch of my life. My mouth returned to his, my hands framing his face. Mindy groaned into me, and I slipped my tongue into his mouth, slowly tangling it around his. His taste, the feel of his scales, the heat of him—it all made me press closer.

I needed more.

Serlotminden pulled back, and I chased his lips. "No."

"We need to talk."

I was hard and desperate for him. "Now?"

"We need to discuss permissions."

"Anything you want is fine," I grunted, capturing his lips again.

He moaned into me as I attacked him. His arms gathered me close. "Teddy," he groaned. "Oh, my Mate."

I slipped my broken glasses off, tucking them somewhere safe before claiming his lips again. I had to have Mindy. Now.

Breaking away, he said, breathless, "We must actually talk."

I sighed. I wasn't going to get out of this, and if he needed it, I had to give it to him. I shifted back and rested my chin on his chest. "Talk," I ordered.

Mindy laughed. "What do you like?"

"I don't know. I've never done this. You're my first. I've never wanted anyone besides you."

He squeezed me. "Bartholomew."

"It's the truth," I said with a shrug. I wasn't embarrassed about my virginity; everyone was ready when they were ready and who fucking cared about the timing?

"So you don't know."

"Nope." I *had* mentioned that. "Can we figure it out together?"

"I want to." He slid his hands up my back, creating tingles. I pressed closer and captured his mouth. I was too impatient to wait, so I kissed his lips open and swiped my tongue over his. I sucked on his tongue as my hips rocked.

"Bartholomew," he said. "I have things I need to say, but I don't have the words."

"I trust you."

"Thank you."

I kissed his cheek. "Trust me. I'm learning, Mindy, so if you don't like something, tell me."

"I do trust you. We will have more speech later."

Fine by me. I needed to feel him against my skin. Frantically, I yanked at his shirt. Serlotminden leaned up, allowing me to rip it off. I threw it behind me. My fingers traced the ridges around his scales over his taut muscles. When I brushed the small scales covering his injury, he arched and moaned loudly, calling my name in a scream.

Movements unhurried, I pressed gentle kisses over his ear before taking the pierced tip in my mouth and sucked, curious. He bucked under me as desperate sounds escaped his lips. I sucked harder, and he grew louder. I teased the tip with my tongue to make him cry out, and he did. Licking and sucking, I played with him.

"Flower," he practically screamed, gripping my back.

God, he was so loud. I loved it.

My lips trailed over the column of his neck, licking tentatively at his pulse point. He groaned, "Yes, Mate."

Nerves slid down my spine and settled in my stomach, forming a roiling unease. God, I had no idea what I was doing. I was horny and wanted him so fucking bad, but I'd never done this.

What if I made a mistake?

I shook the nerves off; he'd tell me if I did something he didn't like. I slid off my pants, making Mindy whimper, then pulled off his, leaving him bare. I tasted as I explored every inch of his chest. I'd never been able to do this before, and I wanted to enjoy it, even if I was slightly terrified. Serlotminden clutched my back as he groaned with every touch. I reached his nipples and sucked one of the nubs into my mouth.

He arched. "Bartholomew. Mate."

I laved my tongue over him, sucking.

"Perfect. Like that. Just like that. You're doing so good."

I continued to work one nipple in my mouth while I pinched and rubbed the other. Serlotminden scraped his claws over my scalp, though he didn't hurt me. I sucked hard and pulled back with a pop, glancing at him.

His eyes were wide and his mouth was open, panting. He cupped my cheeks, rubbing his thumbs over me before drifting down my sides, skating over my hot skin. "You are doing amazing."

Encouraged, I moved to his other nipple to give it the same treatment. After working the nipple, I moved downward, licking and kissing, but I froze near his cock. I'd never done this. I'd seen blowjobs in porn, but that was different.

"I don't know what to do," I confessed, not meeting his gaze.

Serlotminden caught my chin. "You don't have to."

"I want to, but I don't know what to do."

His thumb rubbed my chin as he smiled at me. "Lick me."

A bead of pearly pre-cum oozed out of the slit on his tapered cockhead. He had no pubic hair, which shouldn't surprise me, but it did. He was much longer and wider than me, and his shaft was covered in delicate scales that I was desperate to trace with my tongue. Nervous, I gave it a tentative lick, swiping up the liquid. His groan matched my own. He tasted sweet. I licked and sucked on the tip for more, and Serlotminden rested a palm on my head to keep me in place. I stroked his heavy balls, and he arched, sending his cock further into my mouth and making me gag.

"Sorry," he panted. "It's so good."

I kissed his shaft, then looked at him. Mindy panted, thumb stroking my cheek. Encouraged, I continued kissing his shaft, loving the feel of his scales against my lips. How would they feel inside of me? Amazing, I imagined.

When I reached his hairless sack, I tentatively licked him, and Serlotminden moaned. I took one of his balls into my mouth, liking the weight and feel.

Serlotminden said, "Like that. Run your tongue over me, Mate."

I swirled my tongue around it before turning to the other. He panted, shaking. Either I was really good at this or he was really sensitive. I was leaning toward the latter. Serlotminden was easy to please. He moaned and whined, telling me how amazing I was—happy with my fumbling attempts. Each sound made my own cock throb. I was harder than I'd ever been.

I returned to his cock and sucked on the tip. Opening wide, I tried to take as much of him as possible, but I gagged, tears burning my eyes. I tried again, but when his crown hit the back of my throat, I gagged.

Serlotminden caught my chin before I attempted a third time, pulling me off him. "Don't try to take all of me. Take as much as you can and use your hands on the rest."

I flushed.

"Don't be embarrassed," he said, brushing my cheek. "I am very much enjoying this."

"Do you promise?"

"Yes."

My lips closed around his tip, and I sucked. He moaned, head falling back as he held me tight. I slid down until I felt the urge to gag, then I sucked up. Finding a rhythm with my hand, I worked his dick. His pre-cum was sweet on my tongue and his cries were music to my ears. His musky scent filled my nose. All of it made me moan. I loved the feel of him in my mouth. I loved that I was the one bringing him such pleasure.

All of sudden, Serlotminden pulled me off him.

"What? Did I do something wrong?"

"I don't want to... I don't know the word. I'm not done."

"You don't want to come yet."

He yanked me up and caught my mouth. He sucked and nibbled on my lips, rolling me over to pin me beneath his weight. Serlotminden broke away, breath harsh. He kissed my neck, sucking and biting. I groaned and dug my fingers into him.

When he pulled away, Serlotminden smirked. "I love when you mark."

"It's called a hickey."

"I like it." He kissed my chest, sucking as he went. I was going to be covered in hickies, but I couldn't bring myself to care. Each swipe of his tongue, each rush of warm air, each brush of his fingers made my arousal grow. Pre-cum leaked out of my cock, covering my stomach. I was as hard as a rock. It wouldn't take much to send me over the edge.

Serlotminden sucked on my nipples, pinching them. I groaned, biting my lip at the bolts of electricity. His tongue dragged over the nub, and I gripped the blanket, fighting against the urge to arch into him.

"Do you like that?"

I nodded.

"If you don't like something, tell me. I am not Dontilvynsan. I cannot read your mind. You don't know yet, and neither do I. We can find out, as long as you talk to me."

"What? Read minds?" I asked, breath harsh, but the question fled my thoughts when he gripped my hard shaft and pumped. A long groan ripped out of my lips, hips canting to chase the friction of his palm. Fuck. That was amazing. "Don't stop."

He chuckled against my skin, his breath warming my swollen nipple. "I won't, Mate. I shall make you... release better than ever before."

"Harder, come harder," I corrected, then scolded myself. Did that *really* matter?

Serlotminden kissed my stomach, tongue flicking my navel, which made me whimper. When he reached my hips, he rubbed my pubic hair. "I love this. All of this." His fingers carded through the hair before stroking my legs. "Are all humans like this?"

I wouldn't have thought about hair being an attractor for an alien, though I appreciated a hairy chest. "Sort of. Some people have more hair than others."

He rubbed me again, and I moaned when he brushed my shaft.

"Please," I begged. No doubt I'd feel embarrassed later about my needy tone, but I didn't care at the moment.

Mindy didn't deny me. He never did. His mouth enclosed my dick in wet heat. I gripped his hair; a strangled gasp came out of my lips, hips arching. I'd never felt anything like it. Serlotminden pinned my hips so I couldn't rut into him. His tongue swirled the tip, and I gasped at the pleasure. My orgasm built with alarming speed.

Serlotminden took my entire dick into his mouth, swallowing. The muscles of his throat contracted around my head, making me cry out. He moaned and the vibrations went up my shaft, and I shivered. He cupped my balls, teasing them, while he bobbed on my cock. I fisted his hair, hips trying to chase the heat of his mouth, but he held me securely. His fingers slid over the sensitive skin behind my balls and circled my rim with a knuckle.

"Serlotminden," I screamed at the sparks shooting up my spine.

He sucked off me, and I cried in protest. Serlotminden grabbed my legs and pushed them up and out, exposing me. I blushed, but I didn't fight the movement.

"Hold your legs," he ordered.

I clasped behind my knees, keeping myself open for him. Serlotminden settled between my legs, pulled my cheeks further apart, and licked my ass. I jerked at the sensation of his rough tongue scraping me.

"Are you alright?" he asked.

"Don't stop."

He nipped my cheek, making me start, then attacked my hole. I could not stop the animalistic cries ripping from my throat. Every brush of his tongue, every nibble, and every suck sent tingles up my spine and stole my thoughts. My cock bucked and throbbed with need as pre-cum leaked all over my stomach. His name slipped from my lips as I begged him. For what? I had no idea. But god, I hoped he gave it to me. When his tongue slipped inside, I screamed, trying to impale myself on him.

"Honey," I cried, letting go of one of my legs to fist his hair. "Don't stop. Please."

He didn't. He continued to fuck me with his tongue, and I rocked against him as much as I could in this position.

Serlotminden pulled away, and I panted, "No. Honey. No."

"You like that?"

I nodded, breath harsh. "Inside me. Now."

He looked at me over the length of my body. "I can't."

"No. Please."

"I want to, Mate, but I can't prepare you." He lifted his hand, showing me his claws. "You are more delicate inside than I am, according to my brother. I could hurt you. I'm large, and you are not experienced in this. Spit is not enough. We need... I don't know these words. Oil? Slick? Butter?"

"Lube."

"Lube," he repeated. "We need lube. My butt does not lube on its own, neither does yours."

I understood, but I needed him, and we had soap as well as water. We could make what we needed. Also I could prepare myself. I knew how, even if I'd never done it before. "Mindy," I started.

He kissed my inner thigh, interrupting me. "I will not hurt you. It would be uncomfortable to do more without what we need. Please, Flower. Please don't make me hurt you. I can't."

I frowned. I would never convince him otherwise, and I didn't want to stress Mindy out. I cupped his cheek. "We can wait."

He kissed my palm. "I will please you in other ways."

Serlotminden kneeled in between my legs. The head of his cock rubbed against my wet hole, and I moaned, lifting my hips to chase it. He slid his cock over my pucker a few more times before angling our hips and thrusting against my dick.

The friction of us rubbing together, plus the scrape of his scales, made me pant. I grabbed his cheeks and claimed his mouth in a fierce, possessive kiss. He was mine. No fucking ghosts of my past, no doubts of deserving, no fear of him leaving were going to keep him from me. We would have time later. We had all the time we needed. I would convince him to fuck me when this wasn't as new.

Lifting me, Serlotminden settled me on his lap. His tail wound around our cocks, squeezing them together. Our pre-cum, his much more than mine, mixed with our saliva and lubricated our shafts, allowing his tail to work us with ease. I groaned, enraptured by the sight of his tail sliding over our cocks like an erotic snake. The sight of my pale pink dick pressed against his royal purple one made me swallow.

I canted my hips, thrusting against him, and Mindy moaned. His hands went to my hips. "Yes, Teddy."

He arched into me, meeting my thrust. Moaning, I matched him, movement for movement, until we were fucking the tight hold of his tail. The scrape of the scales on his tail and cock plus the warmth of him had me grunting and groaning. Sweat dripped down my spine and everything tightened pleasurably.

My eyes closed at the intense pleasure. It was so damn good.

"Look at me, Teddy. Please. I need it," he pleaded. I met his gaze, and he smiled. "There you are. You and me. Just you and me forever." Mindy groaned as our dicks scraped against each other.

I whimpered, clutching his shoulders. "I'm close."

"Me too, Mate."

His tail worked our cocks in slow, tantalizing movements. It was driving me crazy. The scales were so smooth and silky against my cock, yet scratched me in the most perfect way. The sensation was intense. I wanted it faster and harder, but he seemed determined to draw it out. I writhed against him, moaning into his neck. I bit him, fucking into him faster, and he jumped under me.

"Sorry."

"Again," he demanded. "Harder."

I bit him again, harder, though not hard enough to hurt. He grunted, his tail continuing its unhurried pace jacking us off. I rocked, thrusting against him. I needed more. I nipped him again, and Serlotminden called out my name, tracing my back, but he didn't seem to get the memo.

Unable to take it anymore, I shoved his tail away and pumped our cocks, hard and fast, taking what I needed. My balls hugged the base of my shaft, and everything was painfully tight.

"Mate," he cried, gripping me tighter. His claws dimpled my skin, not drawing blood, but stinging in a way I quickly decided I loved. The slight pain added to the pleasure and made me moan. He tightened a tad more and said, "Keep going. You're doing so good."

I pumped and stroked us until I crashed over the edge with spurts of cum splattering my hand. I faltered, lost in a wave of bliss unlike anything I'd ever experienced. Serlotminden took over, wringing every ounce of pleasure from me while chasing his own release. He came with a growl as cum sputtered out of his tip, adding to the mess between us. My cock gave one last spurt, and I trembled in his embrace, sagging against him.

It took a bit for me to calm down; shivers wracked my body. Serlotminden settled me on top of him and ran his fingers over my back, making soothing noises. I'd never come so hard in my life. Not ever. Fuck, that was intense.

I smiled at him, and he traced my lips. I couldn't remember the last time I felt this happy, he was so good at filling my world with joy. I had no idea how he did it. Mindy was magic, and that magic had wrought foundational changes in my soul. This intense feeling could be post-orgasmic bliss, but I didn't think so. This was more. Serlotminden had done this.

The soft emotion that had scared me so badly unfurled in my chest, becoming a permanent bond tying me to him forever. I cupped his cheek. "I love you."

His mouth dropped open.

"Do you understand? I love you, Serlotminden."

A beaming, bright smile broke over his face. He crushed our mouths together. "I understand. I love you." Serlotminden rolled on top of me. "I love you. I love you."

I laughed as he kissed me over and over again.

Serlotminden

My mate was draped over me like a blanket, a beautiful one at that. He had finally fallen asleep after we'd come another time and cleaned ourselves. Slight shivers went up his spine, but I knew it wasn't from the cold, but from his strong releases. The tent was filled with the scent of salt, sweat, and seed. I breathed in it, groaning at the perfume.

Bartholomew was mine. He loved me as much as I loved him. My fingers trailed over his back, feeling the bones that were slowly disappearing. I was taking care of him as he deserved, and I would continue to do so.

We hadn't spoken of the future yet, but he would stay? He wouldn't leave me after this, right? He couldn't. He had been terrified of me leaving, so I had a hard time believing that he would abandon me instead.

Once we got Vince, Bartholomew and I would return to Tamkolvanloknol, though I didn't spend much time there. I went from race to race or diplomatic mission. Was that something he'd enjoy? It wasn't the most stable of lives, especially not if we wanted children. Another thing we hadn't discussed.

I squeezed him close as I tried to soothe the rapid pounding of my soul. I couldn't lose him.

He groaned, patting my chest. "What's wrong?"

"What?"

"You're hurting me."

I instantly loosened my grip. "My apologies."

"It's fine." He looked at me with blurry eyes. "What's wrong? Did you need another round?"

I didn't understand his meaning until he palmed my cock through my trousers. It gave a valiant attempt to rise, but it didn't. "No," I said. "I am happy."

"Then why are you awake? Do you need me to move? I'm probably squishing you."

I locked my arms around. "Don't move."

With a grunt, he snuggled closer, sliding until he was completely under the blanket and burrowed against my chest. "Sleep, Mindy."

The troubles would keep until later. We had plenty of time to talk. Right here and now with my mate was enough. With my arm around him, I forced myself to sleep.

Chapter 32

TOGETHER.

Serlotminden

I woke to a skittering, snuffling noise. Bartholomew was still draped over me, deep asleep. Carefully, I moved to the side, keeping my mate on top of me. He grunted, fisting my shirt. Teddy had insisted on us getting dressed before going to sleep. It *was* cold, but I'd wanted his bare skin against mine for the entirety of the night.

I cracked the tent open; the dimmed lights shouldn't wake Bartholomew, especially with him under the blanket, but it was enough to see by. Pookie was racing around. On the walls. That was new. I was unaware of her ability to climb walls, but she acted happy enough, so I assumed it was normal for her species. Her tongue was lolling and her spiral tail was wiggling. Her broken leg was still elevated, but I assumed it was healing well because she'd put weight on it every few steps.

She snorted and scuttled over to me. I opened the tent wider, and she climbed in, settling beside me and Bartholomew. I ran my fingers over her soft ears, and she snorted, snuffling the blankets, and curled her legs up, making her even smaller. Pookie's eyes closed, and she drifted off.

Here, at this moment, I was content. Bartholomew was on top of me, and Pookie was pressed against me. We were a small family, and I loved it. I'd desired this; I'd been jealous of Hallonnixmin and Gilvaxtin, then Kalvoxrencol and his mate, for quite some time. Now, I had what I'd always needed.

A hand joined mine on Pookie's back. Bartholomew's fingers twined with mine, and I smiled, drawing them to my lips to press gentle kisses to his knuckles. He peeked out from beneath the blankets, and I smiled.

"Good morning, Flower."

He grunted.

Ah, my Teddy, he was not much of a talker. He did speak more now that he knew me better, but I doubted he'd ever be chatty, even with me. But I was alright with that. I loved my mate as he was.

"Did you sleep well?" I asked. He hadn't woken with a nightmare last night, but that didn't mean he hadn't had one.

Another grunt.

Perhaps he was embarrassed about last night? I knew he'd enjoyed it, but in the light of day, or whatever we called this moment, perhaps he was struggling to find words. I tugged him up, making him squeak, then rolled on top of him.

Bartholomew's cheeks were flushed. I was right, embarrassed. I nuzzled his neck, my scent growing. "I love you."

His arms came around my back. "I love you too."

Heat suffused my gut and spread to my limbs. I rubbed and nuzzled him. My mate. My lovely mate. I had to claim him. Everyone needed to know this small human was mine, and I had no intention of sharing or letting him go.

He hooked his legs around the backs of my thighs. "What did you want to do today?"

"Spend it with you."

"You always spend it with me."

"Is that a problem?" I asked, giving him a bright smile.

"No," he answered, tracing my lips. "I want to spend every day with you."

I squeezed him. "I love you so much, Flower. I will take care of you and make you happy and love you and—"

He covered my mouth. "I understand."

"Good," I said, voice muffled. "You can teach me more human games or we can play in the snow."

"We could." He arched beneath me, grinding his cock into me. "Or…"

My tail thrashed under the blanket, and a squeal was my only warning before Pookie started attacking me. She didn't bite hard enough to hurt, but she certainly wanted to play. I wiggled my tail to the side, and she chased me. I laughed. I moved to the other side, and she chased. I burst into more laughter as I played with our daughter.

Bartholomew cupped my cheeks. "I love your laugh."

My soul thumped and my tail went still.

"I love your smile." He pressed a chaste kiss to the corner of my lips. "I love how you feel in my arms."

I started to pant, unable to look away from him. His expression was utterly serious, as usual, but I saw the warmth.

"I love how nice you are. I love how you care. I love how you race around. I love how you protect me. I love how you play with me. I love how you love me."

The backs of my eyes started to burn.

"I love your wide hands," he said, kissing my fingers. "I love your shoulders." He moved over my shoulders and to my butt. "I love your ass. Your tail. Your muscles. I love you, Honey. And it shocks me how much I do. I've never cared about someone like I do you. You're so fucking special, Serlotminden, and I'm so lucky you're mine."

A tear escaped, and he kissed it, tongue swiping me.

"I know I struggle to talk, and I don't want to hide from you. It's... All of this is difficult for me, especially because I don't feel like I deserve you." I opened my mouth to assure my mate that he did indeed belong with me, but he stopped me with a hand over my lips. "I know what you're going to say, and I'm just telling you what's going on." I offered him my throat in concession, and he smiled, stroking my neck. "I need you to know exactly how much I love you, and not because you tried to save me, not because you're pretty, even though you are. I love you because you are you." His cheeks were bright red. "Alright?"

Words were beyond me. I closed the space between us and claimed him. I licked his mouth open, then fucked it. Bartholomew grunted, rocking into me. His hard cock pressed into me, and I groaned. I craved him. I needed him. I wanted him. The potency of my desires stole my breath and filled my cock.

"Flower."

"Push Pookie out of the tent, then fuck me," he ordered.

I complied without question. Pookie squeaked in annoyance but scuttled out of the cabin. I closed the tent and focused on my mate. He bit his lip, and I licked him. He was still nervous about us. Fucking was new to him, but he had nothing to fear. We were meant for each other.

Bartholomew pulled me close, mouth on mine. We made quick work of our clothes, only separating when we had to. As soon as we were naked, I dragged my hands over him. He made impatient noises and reached for my cock, pumping it.

"Flower," I groaned, rutting into his grasp.

"I need you."

I rolled over so he was on top. Bartholomew stared at me, chewing on his lip again. I kissed his chin, enjoying the feel of his hair against my lips. I loved his beard so *damn* much. My tail slid up his leg and settled between his legs, tickling his pucker, then pressing against it. I slid it in leisurely circles over his tight hole.

"Fuck," he bit out, tilting his head back. I nipped the knot in his throat, then sucked to leave a dark mark behind.

My tuft moved over his balls, and he squirmed. "Mindy."

"Yes, Mate?" I asked as I kept torturing him with my tail.

"I need more."

I ran a hand down his back, cupping his butt. "Turn around."

"What?"

"Shift so your backside faces my face."

"You want to *sixty-nine*?"

I had no idea what the numbers meant in this context. "You'll suck me and fuck my mouth at the same time."

His breath turned harsh.

I moved to swat his butt, as he'd liked the bite of my claws, but stopped. He might not enjoy it. "Can I spank you?"

Bartholomew groaned, nodding.

I spanked him, then rubbed the same spot. Pre-seed leaked from his cock onto my stomach. "Turn, Flower. Unless you don't want to try this."

His cheeks pinked, and he shoved his butt back, asking. I spanked him again, harder, and my mate moaned, and more pre-seed leaked onto me. I gave him a couple more raps before massaging the cheeks and pulling them apart.

"I want to," he muttered against my lips.

"Then let me see your pretty butt."

Slowly, Bartholomew turned around, and I growled at the sight of him in front of me. His butt cheeks were pink from my slaps, and his cock was dripping all over my chest. I pulled his cheeks apart and licked my lips at the sight of his tight pucker that had black hair around it.

Unable to resist, I shoved my face into him and licked. I moaned at the taste of him. Perfect. He was perfect.

"Mindy. Fuck, that feels so damn good."

He moaned and writhed under my tongue, but I didn't stop, desperate. I arched beneath him, wiggling. I was hard and needy for his warm mouth on me. One of his hands circled the base of my shaft and pumped. I moaned against him.

"Scream for me," Bartholomew ordered right before he took my crown into his mouth, silky tongue circling my tip.

"Mate," I whined beneath him.

"Louder," he commanded, popping off my cock. "Louder, Mindy."

He sucked me back into his mouth, and the point of his tongue prodded my slit. I screamed, fingers digging into his thighs. "Bartholomew!"

He took me in as deep as he could and pumped the rest, groaning around me and sending vibrations up my shaft. My tail curled around his arm, and I buried my tongue in his hole, making him grunt. I wanted my mate to feel as good as I did.

I pulled out, and Bartholomew protested around my cock. I repositioned his hips to take his leaking cock into my mouth. I groaned at the bitter salt of his pre-seed. I licked and sucked, fighting my orgasm that was swelling too rapidly under my mate's insistent tongue. My balls were tight and my cock felt impossibly hard. Teddy made low grunts and desperate noises as he sucked me.

"Mate," I rasped. "Fuck me."

Bartholomew glanced back at me, panting. "I don't want to hurt you."

I nipped his butt. "You won't."

Taking his cock into my mouth, I urged his hips downward. Slowly, he filled my mouth, then withdrew. I moaned at the feel of him dragging over my tongue.

Bartholomew grunted, and his speed picked up until he was fucking my mouth in hard, fast strokes. "Honey. Fuck. You're so damn warm."

When he hit the back of my throat, I swallowed. Bartholomew whimpered. "Fuck. Fuck. Fuck. Holy fuck, Mindy." I swallowed again, the muscles of my throat contracting around the crown of his cock. He slid out and instantly pressed back in with a groan. "Honey. Shit. That feels so fucking good."

His thrusts grew faster and faster. Bartholomew had completely forgotten my cock as he chased his own pleasure, calling my name over and over again. I didn't mind. He was new at this, and I wanted him to feel good. Besides, I loved the feel of his silky cock sliding over the scales on my tongue and hearing his smooth voice screaming for me.

"I'm coming," he warned.

Warmth splashed over my tongue less than a breath later, and I swallowed his release, reveling in the taste. His hips thrust into my mouth, chasing his orgasm, until he sagged against me, panting.

I kissed his butt. My cock still craved attention, but I loved pleasing my mate more. "Did you like that?"

He didn't reply with more than a tired grunt. Bartholomew grabbed my cock and rubbed the tip on his cheek, making me bite my lip. Shudders wracked my body at the softness of his skin on the sensitive glans. My breath turned harsh, and my hips bucked.

"I want you to come on my face."

"Please, Flower," I begged. "Please." The thought of my seed covering his face made my soul thump and my cock twitch.

Bartholomew sucked on the tip, pumping my shaft. I screamed and writhed, hips canting. I was trying to keep from plunging into his throat, but it was hard. I wanted to chase the friction and warmth of his mouth. My mate kept working me in harsh jerks as his tongue flicked and laved over my tip.

"Louder," he demanded, and I complied, gripping his hips as I begged, cried, and whimpered beneath him.

My cock jerked, balls tight, and I panted, "Now. I'm..." I couldn't think of the word with the pleasure racing through me.

He sucked off me, hand shuttling up and down my shaft. "Come, Honey. I want to be dripping in it."

"Bartholomew," I shouted. My hips arched, and fire swept down my spine. Seed erupted from my tip. My hips canted as I gripped Bartholomew's thighs, riding out my orgasm. I whined, writhing beneath him before I gasped, letting him go. My claws had left little red marks behind. I licked them between my pants, shaking.

"Let me see," I demanded.

My mate turned around, and I growled at the sight of my seed covering him. I dragged him closer and licked his cheek.

Bartholomew moaned. "Yes, Honey. Fuck, yes."

The sweet taste of my release clung to my tongue and mixed with his bitter one that lingered in the back of my throat. I cleaned him, not swallowing, then pressed my lips against his to feed him my release. He grunted, but Bartholomew's tongue twined with mine. I forced all of it into his mouth, and he palmed my cheeks, keeping me close as he swallowed.

Breathing hard, he said, "We are going to do that again."

I laughed. "So you liked it?"

"A lot."

"All of it?" I needed to know.

"All of it."

I snuggled him close. "We'll try many things. I promise. After we return and I can better speak to you, we'll do many *many* things."

I held him and breathed in his scent as I allowed my soul to resume its normal pace. Bartholomew stroked my chest as he occasionally kissed me.

"Now what do you want to do today?" he asked.

I chuckled. "We should get clean, eat, drink some water, then maybe get some sun."

"Will you hold me outside?"

"What?"

"Can we sit together for a while? I want to watch the snow and the trees in the distance."

"Of course, we can." I was desperate to hold my mate and be with him as we observed the world. I promised him I'd let him smell the flowers, and now, he'd invited me to join him. In the future, I always wanted to sit beside him, providing him with a safe space to breathe and be.

Chapter 33

WHAT JUST HAPPENED?

Bartholomew

I sat with my back to Serlotminden in the tent, fiddling with some random wires and twisting them into a bracelet for my boyfriend because I had nothing else to do. Our icy home didn't offer much in the way of entertainment besides sitting around.

Pookie did offer some distraction. She enjoyed scuttling in dark corners and scaring the shit out of me or leaping onto Serlotminden from the ceiling and chasing his tail. She'd never hurt either of us, but she did like to play. Yesterday she'd escaped out of the hatch and caught an animal, bringing it back for us. Pookie had panted, tail thumping in obvious pride. I'd been horrified, but Mindy spent at least thirty minutes calling her smart, cute, and amazing, all the while petting her. Pookie had eaten every ounce of affection and come back for seconds.

Mindy had cleaned the dead animal, but the laser scalpel started to flicker and die. We used it a lot and hadn't recharged it, because we couldn't. He'd assured me he had the skills to make a knife with some bone from an animal or shrapnel from the shuttle, but still, I was concerned. We only had a couple of nutrition bars and a handful of water cubes left. Sure, Mindy was providing, but I liked having a back up.

What if there was another snow storm? What if it lasted longer and we were snowed in?

With ruthless efficiency, I shoved those thoughts into a drawer in my mind and locked it. I refused to let myself panic about something that might never come to pass. We were fine, and Mindy's brothers would rescue us soon.

Besides, Serlotminden was doing his utmost to distract me day in and day out. Usually with funny stories from his youth, language lessons, or mauling me. Currently, he trailed kisses over my shoulders, tongue flicking my skin. He'd found out how much he loved giving me hickeys, and now, it was his favorite pastime. It was getting ridiculous how many marks he'd left.

His tail tickled my ass as he kissed my neck. "Mate."

I rolled my eyes at his cajoling tone and continued making a bracelet. Since there was nothing to do, Serlotminden would much rather pass the time making out or fucking. The former, I didn't mind usually, but I also liked being able to breathe without him attached to my mouth. The latter, I wasn't always in the mood.

"I want to go on another date," he announced.

"Because our first one was so spectacular?" I teased, twisting a wire around a random stone.

He nipped my neck, making me laugh. "This time we could actually swim or..."

"Yes?"

"You can fuck me."

"What?" I asked, turning around and abandoning my project.

"I've been thinking."

"A bad sign."

Serlotminden hauled me onto his lap, making me straddle his muscular thighs, then bit my nose. "Silence, you."

I chuckled.

"I do not require as much preparation as you."

"Because you've had anal sex before."

"I have, but no. Drakcol do not need as much stretching as humans, at least according to Kalvoxrencol. I've never been with another human beside you."

"We don't have lube." That had been his whole argument with me. Though we did have soap. It would work fine. But I didn't see the need to go to the river. We could fuck right here.

"The water might be enough."

I frowned. So he still hadn't thought about the soap, and he planned for me to fuck him dry. Yeah, that was a no. "I don't want to hurt you."

"You won't. I need you inside me. I do not normally... What is the word?"

"Bottom?" I offered.

"Perhaps. I am usually the one who fucks."

"You top."

Serlotminden replied, "If that is the term. It seems Seth and Caleb were bad in my language classes."

"They didn't teach you proper sex terminology? How shocking."

He nipped my nose, probably understanding my teasing tone more than my words. "I want to try."

"We can wait."

"I don't want to. You cannot take me, but I can take you."

My lips pursed. Serlotminden had a bad habit of not thinking things through. I was worried if we tried and it hurt, he wouldn't tell me. Also, I didn't like the idea of being exposed in the river when there were unfriendly aliens around. In the shuttle, the door was closed and locked. It would be hard for someone to come in, and we'd hear them.

Not to mention, part of me had hoped our first time with penetrative sex would be a tad more... private? Romantic? I wasn't sure exactly what word I was searching for to name the emotion coursing through me, but I wanted Mindy and me to have an unforgettable experience.

"Please," he said. "I want to. I really want to. I need this, Flower. I need to feel connected to you."

Fuck. There was no way to say no when he was being this romantic. Still... "Why, Mindy? Why do you need it? We're already fucking."

"It feels more intimate to me. I want to be the same person." His brow furrowed and his tail thrashed as he fell silent. After a few moments, he said, "I want to feel your soul beat with mine. I need it."

Fisting his hair to pull him even closer to me, I said, our lips brushing, "You want to be one with me."

"I need it."

I wanted it too. Hell, I needed it. "Fine, but we're bringing soap because it can work as lube. I will not fuck you dry."

He grinned against me, pushing me onto my back and covering me. His lips found mine. The kiss was soft and unhurried, not leading anywhere, but my dick perked up.

All it needed was a smile, and it was raring to go. I'd never desired someone like I did him. It felt odd, yet nice. "And," I said, breaking away, "we are thoroughly checking the area for danger before we fuck."

"Alright."

I rubbed his cheeks with my thumbs, and he nuzzled my forehead like a needy cat, making me smile. He was so fucking cute. I hooked my legs around him to lock him against my body. "And I need a promise."

"Anything."

"If it hurts or is uncomfortable, you will tell me and we'll stop."

Serlotminden frowned.

"I knew it." I rolled on top of him, changing our position so I was sitting on him. "You were going to stay quiet."

"I want you."

"And I don't want to fucking hurt you. Sex is not worth it unless we are both enjoying it. Besides, penetrative sex is not everything, Mindy. We are perfect as we are right now."

A warm smile stretched over his lips. "I will tell you, and we will stop. I promise."

When his fingers trailed down my naked chest, following the trail of hair, I took a sharp inhale. He palmed my hardening shaft through my pants, and I groaned. Fuck. I ground my dick against him, chasing the friction.

"That's it, Mate. Take your pleasure. I want to see it."

I licked my lips. "If you want to go on a date today, you need to stop."

He kissed my neck. "Let's go, then."

We both got fully dressed before stepping into the chilly cabin. Pookie didn't even look up from her nest. She was curled into a tight ball, legs pressing into her body, asleep. Serlotminden slung his arms around my waist and he rested his chin on my shoulder. I'd never known someone as physically affectionate as him before, but I didn't mind. He only released me to grab the blaster, in case we came across trouble.

The air was nippy as usual, but I swore it was growing warmer. Winter was probably ending. I was ready for less snow and cold.

Serlotminden snagged me, swinging me around until I faced him. I pressed my lips against his, wrapping my arms around his neck to keep him close. I was so happy. It was stupid. It was unbelievable. It was undeserved, probably, maybe, I honestly didn't know. But god dammit, I was.

He escaped, racing away from me. His tail wiggled in anticipation.

"You're ridiculous."

My words didn't dampen his smile as he crouched, eyebrows lifting.

I held up a hand. "Don't. Don't you fucking dare."

With a growl, he launched at me, and I darted in the opposite direction. My pulse pounded in my ears. Anticipation flooded me. The first few times we'd done this, I'd panicked, but Mindy wasn't attacking, he was playing. This time promised to end in sex, and I was excited for it.

Running faster, legs burning, I bolted in the direction of the shuttle.

"Bartholomew," he screamed; the true terror in Serlotminden's voice made me freeze. I glanced over my shoulder and saw him rushing toward me, blaster drawn. Time seemed to slow as I looked forward.

A massive alien was flying straight at me. They had a humanoid appearance, huge sprawling wings, talons for feet, and were covered in black feathers. The owner of the nests.

I was locked in place as the alien flew toward me, talons spread wide. My heart pounded as they got closer and closer. I ordered myself to move, to fall to the ground, to do something, anything, but my knees were locked and I was stuck in place. Helplessness clouded my thoughts, making everything around me feel like a dream. Impossibly slow, the alien flew toward me, promising death, and with that promise the ghosts that haunted me screamed and a metallic thud of a bolt echoed in my thoughts.

Something smashed into my back, knocking the air from my lungs and me out of that clouded, dream space, and I crashed into the snow. The weight crushing me disappeared as a shriek rent the air, making my hair stand on end.

Rolling over, I shouted, "Serlotminden!"

The creature's talons were dug deep into Serlotminden's side as they struggled to fly away with him. I grabbed the blaster that had fallen to the snow, fumbling, and lifted it. My hand shook. My muscles started to freeze and terror flooded me. I'd never shot the blaster before. I hadn't needed to. I did not want to hit Mindy. I might kill him.

"Let him go!"

The alien didn't react, struggling to take him away.

They were hurting Mindy, *my* mate.

I lifted the blaster higher and pulled the trigger. An orange beam shot out of the muzzle and singed the alien's feathers. They dove. I scrambled to my feet, not giving myself even a second to think, and chased after them, yelling. Serlotminden did not make a sound, and he hung lifelessly from the alien's talons. I lifted the blaster again and shot. The beam hit the alien in the wing. They screeched and dropped Serlotminden, who crashed into the ground in a motionless heap.

I kept the blaster pointed at the alien, but they didn't attack again. Instead, they jerkily flew to the cliff, clinging to the nest as black blood dripped from their wing.

I slid to the snow next to Mindy, and a wide green puddle surrounded him, marking the snow.

"Serlotminden," I screamed, clutching his cold cheeks. "Honey, please."

His eyes fluttered open. "Bartholomew."

"Keep talking," I demanded as tears coursed down my cheeks, but he didn't. His eyes closed and didn't open again, no matter how much I cried.

The alien screeched, and I lifted the blaster. They hadn't left the cliff, staring at me. I wanted to kill them. They'd hurt Serlotminden. I'd never wanted to kill anyone before in my life, not even Agk, because I had seen too much death, but I wanted to kill this alien. They deserved to die. They deserved to feel the pain Serlotminden was experiencing. My finger shook on the trigger.

But if I shot and missed, it could cause a cave-in and block the shuttle. That would spell death for Mindy. I lowered the blaster, and the alien screeched again.

I could not leave Serlominden to grab anything to help me drag him, so I ripped the blanket around my shoulders off and tied it under his armpits. Keeping my eyes on the alien, who watched me, blood dripping from their wing, I dragged Serlotminden toward the shuttle.

I had to get him inside. Now.

With grunts and tears frozen on my cheeks, I hauled him inside painfully, agonizingly slow. I slammed the door closed, keeping us safe from any threat. Skittering came from behind me, and Pookie snorted, snuffling Mindy.

"Not now," I told her. "Please, Pookie."

She trailed me as I dragged him to the cabin and into the tent. I ripped off his shirt and pants. Blood leaked from the deep punctures in his abdomen and thigh. The alien's talons had gone straight through his scales. One had also pierced his old injury, and it was deep, leaking green blood everywhere.

I grabbed the medicine he'd first used and the laser scalpel. I tried to fill the needle with the medicine, but I didn't know how much to use or how it worked. It didn't draw like a human one, not that I had experience with that either.

I patted his cheek. "Serlotminden. Please, Honey. I don't know what to do. You need to tell me what to do."

His breathing was shallow.

"Do not do this to me. I cannot lose you. You promised! We're supposed to stay together. Damn it, Serlotminden. I need you. Do you fucking hear me? I need you!"

Serlotminden didn't open his eyes, and blood continued to stain the blankets under him.

Tears continuously slid down my cheeks as my hands shook. I fiddled and finally got the vial filled. I had no idea if I did the right amount, but I injected him, massaging the site for a few moments. I grabbed the tweezers and pulled the broken scales away like he had before while trying to apply pressure to the open wounds, but there were too many, too much blood, too much. Fuck, there was too much.

I flicked the laser, but it shuddered and clicked off. My heart stuttered.

"No. No." I flicked and flicked. It didn't come back on. Throwing it with a scream, I grabbed one of the blankets and shredded it. I wrapped the pieces around him like a makeshift bandage. Blood soaked them. It was not enough. Serlotminden was going to die.

A sob caught in my throat. "Please, don't leave me. I can't do this without you." I shook my head. "I don't want to do this without you, Honey."

Serlotminden did not respond. His breathing was shallow and wet as his scales grew cold.

He needed help, but there was no one here except me. Useless me.

Pookie nosed me, and I petted her, sobbing. He needed someone, anyone, but I had nothing.

That was not true.

The four-armed alien was around. Maybe he'd help if I somehow made him understand. I thought of the winged alien outside. It would be a risk. A huge one. Perhaps the four-armed alien had thought Serlotminden was one of the creatures from the cliff, and he'd been trying to protect me. Of course, he could've been trying to steal me for his own reasons.

My eyes went to Serlotminden. I would have to leave him, but he'd die if I did nothing.

I pressed a hard kiss to his forehead, taking a deep inhale of his fresh scent, though it was tainted with the tang of blood. "You are not allowed to die. I love you, and you love me. You have to stick around and let me make you laugh. We have to grow old together. I don't want any other future."

I grabbed Pookie and planted her on top of his chest. "Protect him. Don't move."

She grunted, laying down.

With one last glance, I left the safety of the shuttle to brave two different aliens. I would not freeze, I would not stop, and I would not fail. Serlotminden was counting on me.

Chapter 34

HELP.

Bartholomew

He will not die. He will not die, I repeated the mantra, never stopping. The last time I heard his voice would not be my name on his lips. He would not die trying to save me. Serlotminden and I would become cranky old men together. I refused to accept any other possibility.

I dashed through the woods, searching for the four-armed alien. The winged-creature hadn't been on the cliffs, from what I'd seen, and I hadn't tarried to search for them. I screamed for the four-armed alien, even though he didn't understand me. I hollered and shouted like the other animals living in the jungle weren't a threat. I didn't care. I needed help. Serlotminden needed help. If he didn't survive... I refused to contemplate it.

The jungle was completely quiet except for my broken voice. The fronds on the trees moved of their own accord, curling and stretching at will. No birds sang. No bushes rustled. There was nothing. Absolutely nothing.

The four-armed alien was gone. Serlotminden had no one but me, and I was failing him even as I tried to save him. I turned in the direction of the shuttle and ran back, lungs heaving after a few seconds. I couldn't leave him alone for long. He shouldn't be alone when... My heart stuttered as a sob clogged my throat, making it hard to breathe.

Serlotminden was going to die. I was going to watch the light vanish from his green eyes and his chest stop moving, like all the others. But unlike the ghosts who were chains dragging me down, I knew Serlotminden. I loved him. And yet, just like those I had seen die, I'd failed to save him. I'd failed to help him. I was going to outlive him. I didn't want to.

Blurry-eyed, I raced back. I needed to see Serlotminden. I needed to curl up against him. I needed to hold him.

Everything looked the same with the looming cliff and the monstrous nests, but it wasn't. Dread filled every step I took. What if Mindy was already gone? Tears slipped down my cheeks, but I brusquely wiped them away and continued forward. He needed me, and I refused to abandon him.

The bay door creaked open, and my steps echoed loudly on the metal floors. My heart was in my throat and my fingers trembled as I opened the tent. Pookie snorted in welcome, still on top of Mindy, but I paid her no attention, solely focused on the love of my life buried in a mound of blankets. He was utterly motionless.

"Honey," I whimpered, knees losing any power to hold me up. I crashed to the floor, sobbing. I crawled toward him. "Please, Mindy. No."

I burrowed under the blankets to lay a hand on his scales and paused.

Serlotminden's chest rose and fell, then rose and fell again.

Palpable relief rushed through me. I sagged, boneless. "Fuck." I'd never been so scared in my life. I curled against his side, hand on his chest and watched it move with his shallow breathing.

"I love you," I whispered. "I love you, Serlotminden. I don't deserve you, but please, Honey, let me keep you. Don't leave me. Stay right here with me, and I promise to make you happy, to make you feel loved, and to strive every day to deserve you."

His chest continued to rise and fall, but he did not open his eyes.

The rest of the day and night passed with me watching Mindy breathe. Each one I feared would be his last, but it never was. His wounds still bled and he would not awaken. If he did not get help soon, he was going to die. There was no other outcome. This wasn't something that he could recover from without assistance, which meant I had to go back out into the snow and brave the jungle once again.

Serlotminden needed help, and I had to find some.

When I was positive enough time had passed for the sun to have risen, I placed a kiss on his forehead and combed my fingers through his blood-stained hair. "I will be back, Honey, and you had better be here when I return."

I set Pookie on him again, and she curled up without complaint, but her eyes were more watchful than usual, almost as if she was guarding him. I pressed a kiss to her snout, and she snorted.

Taking a deep breath, I set off again. This time I was more careful and looked around for threats as I called for help, but it didn't matter. I saw nothing, not even the rock crabs next to the river. The jungle was utterly silent, yet I couldn't give up. Stopping meant surrendering. Stopping meant Serlotminden was going to die. Stopping meant I'd failed again.

I refused to fail. I had to save one person. I refused to have Serlotminden's ghost join all the others who haunted me.

A low roar broke the silence, and I whipped around, searching, but the dancing fronds didn't allow much to be seen of the sky. At a run, I broke through the trees, and the ground rumbled, shaking and shuddering beneath me.

"What the fuck?" I fell to the ground, knees stinging and palms burning from the impact. Was this an earthquake? A sliding crash sounded, and I jerked.

Rocks slid off the edge of the cliff and crashed into the ground.

"Serlotminden," I screamed, shoving to my feet. "No!" The shuttle. If it got buried, I'd never be able to dig him and Pookie out.

I started forward but skidded to a stop. A ship. There was a fucking ship. It had landed near where Serlotminden and I'd crashed. Was it the xoi? A different kind of alien? The shuttle was far nicer than those the xoi possessed, but who knew who this ship belonged to.

Fear burned under my skin, locking me in place as memories of being sold and all that came with it flooded my brain. Never again. I didn't want to live through that again. But Mindy... Someone was here. I had to move. Mindy needed help, and I didn't care who they were if they could help him. But I was too far away, and my body refused to respond as terror ran rampant through my thoughts, clouding my brain.

Figures were moving in the distance near the ship. They looked bigger than a xoi. Maybe his brothers were here?

"Move," I ordered myself. If his brothers were here, I needed to go with him. Mindy and I needed to be together. "Move, Bartholomew Reginald." With a snarl, I got to my feet. I refused to think about anything other than Serlotminden and plowed through the snow as fast as physically possible, but I felt like I was moving through molasses. I never seemed to get closer and the people moved faster and faster. A floating stretcher slid out of the shuttle, Serlotminden's white hair fluttering in the wind. Pookie was on his chest, arched, but not moving off him, and my heart clenched.

What if they hurt her?

"Wait," I screamed. "Wait, please!"

One of the people froze and looked around, but he didn't turn toward me. Even from this distance, I saw his long blue hair, broad frame, and tail. It had to be another drakcol, and even if it wasn't, I had to go wherever Serlotminden was. We belonged together. No matter what happened.

"Please," I shouted, charging through the snow; my thighs burned and the cold made me shake. I wasn't moving fast enough. I kept yelling, but the drakcol boarded the shuttle with Serlotminden.

Light flared from beneath the craft as it rose in the air. A gust knocked me over, sending me into the snow. I stared at the ship as it became smaller and smaller, leaving me behind.

I lay on the snow, unable to process what had happened. Someone had taken Mindy and Pookie, while I was stuck here.

A screech tore the air, and I forced myself to my feet. The winged alien was back. They circled, their movements jerky. I tried to stay calm as I lifted the blaster. The alien veered, and I raced to the shuttle. The door was closed, but I opened it and stepped inside, locking it behind me.

Everything was the exact same as before, but an emptiness hung in the air. I was alone. Serlotminden was gone. Pookie was gone. I went to the cabin. The tent had been knocked apart. Blood-covered blankets were strewn about.

Tears burned my eyes. He was gone, and I was alone.

Maybe this is what I deserve?

No. I couldn't think like that. Trying to bury my dark emotions, I took several deep breaths. I needed to focus or I was going to die. *Calm down and focus*, I ordered myself. *One thing at a time. Choose the most important task and move on from there.*

I resembled the tent and shoved everything not covered in blood back inside before crawling in. I hugged my knees to my chest as I forced myself to breathe in steady, deep breaths.

Not many water packs or nutrition bars remained. Serlotminden was not here to melt water or hunt. The tasks now fell to me. I could figure it out. It was cold. Even more so without his furnace-like body next to me, but I had to survive. Winter was ending. I'd be fine.

When Mindy got better, he would return for me. Serlotminden would not abandon me, right? He loved me as much as I loved him, right? I swallowed as doubts crawled out of the cracks in my mind. This was the perfect opportunity for him to get rid of me. What if he had been pretending this whole time? Using me?

"No."

I was being ridiculous. He hadn't lied or hidden anything. Mindy loved me, and he would come back. If he survived.

I buried my face against my knees, shaking. He had a better chance of living with whoever took him than with me. The xoi would heal Mindy if for no other reason than to ransom him back to his family. Same for another alien race. His brothers loved him and would make sure he received the best care. Serlotminden would be back, and I would be here waiting for him when he arrived.

Serlotminden

Voices surrounded me, but none were the calm, smooth one I wanted to hear. I pushed someone away, forcing my eyes open. A familiar face hovered over me and something inside my chest un-clenched.

"Pest," I groaned.

He relaxed, forehead dropping to mine. "Do not ever scare us like this again."

I patted the bed beside me, but it was empty. "Where is he?"

Another person appeared, one I vaguely knew. A doctor on Dontilvynsan's ship. "You've been hurt, Prince. I need you to stay calm."

The memories returned with a vengeance. The alien going for Bartholomew. The talons piecing my flesh. The agony. Bartholomew's broken expression above me.

I snarled, sitting up. Hands pushed me down. I growled, thrashing. My stomach stabbed in agony, but I didn't care. Where was *my* mate? My wings slid out and my tail slashed the air as I shoved the people surrounding me away.

"Where is he?" I demanded.

"Your pet is in your room," Kalvoxrencol said as he and Zoltilvoxfyn pinned me. "Seth took it."

Seth and Caleb hovered in the background, and Seth said, "It's fine. I wasn't terrified it was going to eat me or anything. It wasn't like I was holding a creature from my nightmares at all."

"It was scary as fuck. I refused to touch it," Caleb remarked.

I didn't pay any mind to them and kept searching. Bartholomew was nowhere to be seen.

"Where is he?" I roared.

"You were alone besides your pet," Kalvoxrencol said, forcing me down. He was stronger than I, and I'd never hated that fact until this moment. "Whatever attacked you was gone, Serlotminden. You're safe. Your pet is safe. Everything is fine."

My soul shattered and a void opened up within me. My mate. The alien must have taken him after I fell. Tears gathered in my eyes, and I arched, pain ripping through me.

Machines beeped rapidly while my soul thrashed against my ribs. I screamed, grief so powerful it stole my breath and tore me asunder. My mate was gone. Bartholomew.

"Serlotminden," voices called over and over again, but I couldn't focus on them. I had failed to protect my mate. He was gone.

"Stand back. I'm going to sedate him."

Something trickled through me, dimming my awareness. My brothers were all staring at me, but I looked at Seth. Perfectly human Seth.

"Where is he? Please. I need him."

Seth's mouth opened and his eyebrows drew together. "Mindy," he said, pushing Kalvoxrencol and Zoltilvoxfyn aside. "Who?"

My tongue stuck to the roof of my mouth, and my eyes closed. I fought it, but I couldn't resist the medication. Cool fingers touched me while someone asked, "Mindy, who? Who are you looking for?"

But I couldn't answer.

Chapter 35

TEAM HUMAN.

Bartholomew

Things could be better. Serlotminden had been gone for a long time, though I had no idea how long exactly. I was freezing. I couldn't warm up without Mindy. I was out of water and nutritional bars. I couldn't leave the shuttle, because the winged alien refused to budge. I always heard their talons scraping on the door, trying to figure out how to get inside, and then screeching outside. I'd tried to shoot them more than once, but the alien was smart, moving out of the way, and I wasn't skilled with a blaster.

I couldn't build a fire to melt snow, and I couldn't hunt. I was trapped.

I curled into a ball around the blanket that most smelled like Serlotminden. I was going to die. I knew it, but I couldn't bring myself to care. He was safe. Whether he came back or not, Serlotminden was safe and alive. I knew it. I refused to believe otherwise. Him living was enough. I inhaled the light scent on the blanket and curled into a tighter ball, freezing.

Serlotminden

I awoke with a growl. Physical pain throbbed through my body, but it was nothing to the grief drowning me. My mate. My perfect mate. Bartholomew was gone. A keening sound broke the silence, and it took me a moment to realize the noise came from me.

An arm wrapped around me and a tail coiled around mine, but I didn't want the comfort. My mate was gone. I tried to push the person away; I was unsuccessful.

"Speedy, I have you." Kalvoxrencol, my youngest brother.

The grief was unbearable. How had Zoltilvoxfyn lived through this when he thought Caleb was gone? An agonizing sob ripped from me. It was impossible.

"Where is he?" I demanded, even though I knew the answer. I couldn't stop the words from spilling out. I needed Bartholomew.

"Who?" Kalvoxrencol asked. "You were alone."

His response brought a new wave of grief. I'd been rescued, but they were too late for Bartholomew. My fault. It was my fault. If I hadn't insisted on going to the river, he would be tucked against me right now. Screams came from deep within me as I writhed. Kalvoxrencol tried to hold me still, but I kept thrashing.

"I'm going to have to sedate him again, Prince," the doctor said as she appeared. "He must be in shock from the attack."

I was not going to survive. It felt like my soul had been cleaved in half. Agony that had nothing to do with the injuries wracked my body. I could not breathe. I could not think. All I could do was feel his blinding absence beside me.

"Mindy." Seth leaned over me. Human Seth.

"Please," I begged him. He would know. He would help. He was human. "Please." I tried to grab him. "Please, Seth."

He shook his head, and Kalvoxrencol tightened his hold. Zoltilvoxfyn and Caleb appeared, but they could not take my focus from Seth. All I saw was Seth. Human Seth.

"Please. I need him," I begged as another sob ripped out of me. Kalvoxrencol held me securely, and Zoltilvoxfyn joined him next to me.

Seth's mouth fell open. "Oh my god." The doctor approached, and Seth ordered, "Wait."

"Seth, Serlotminden needs help," Kalvoxrencol said.

Seth bent until he was level with me. "Don said there was a human with you."

Tears poured out faster. My poor Bartholomew. He'd needed a better mate than I. I had failed him.

He bobbed his head. "He's your mate."

Kalvoxrencol drew in a sharp breath, and his arms tightened.

"I need him."

"We scanned the planet, but all the sensors came back with was your beacon. And we found you alone, Mindy," Seth said.

A loud, keening noise was my only response. Kalvoxrencol was joined by Zoltilvoxfyn and Caleb. They both held onto me, but Seth continued to stare at me.

"We found you in the shuttle," he said. "Inside. Bandaged."

"No."

Seth said, "I need you to think clearly. Did you see the human get hurt? This is important, Mindy. Did you see him get injured?"

Emotion clogged my throat, not allowing me to speak. My Bartholomew. My mate. Maybe. Maybe. Maybe. I needed the hope burning through me to be real.

Seth pulled out a touchstone. "Dontilvynsan. I need you to come to the medbay."

"What are you doing, Seth?" Zoltilvynsan asked.

"We need to find out what happened, and Mindy's not talking."

Caleb moved next to Seth. "Do you think..."

"It's a possibility. The sensors weren't able to pick up anything. Some techno-babble I didn't understand, and if not for the distress signal, we wouldn't have found Mindy. And when we did, Mindy was bandaged and inside the shuttle. If it was me, I would've gone looking for help for Kal. Any help. Why wouldn't this human do the same thing?"

I snagged Seth's hands, and Kalvoxrencol growled in warning, but I ignored him. My breath turned harsh as I tried to drag Seth closer. "Please. Please." I didn't even know why I was begging, but I couldn't help it. "Please."

The door opened, and Dontilvynsan staggered back. Zoltilvoxfyn immediately moved to his side. My surging emotions were probably too much for Dontilvynsan's inner fire, which allowed him to experience them with me, and as much as I wished to spare him, there was no controlling the twining agony and hope spiraling inside of me.

The closer Dontilvynsan came, the more his breathing harshened. When he reached the side of the bed, his pupils were blown wide and his nostrils were flared.

Seth stepped aside. "We need to know if he saw the human being injured and if he bandaged himself."

With a shaking hand, Dontilvynsan touched me, the contact allowing his gift to strengthen. I sobbed as the grief tore me in two. My mate. My perfect mate. But he might be alive. He could be waiting for me. I had to get him. Dontilvynsan ran his fingers through my hair, and waves of calm rushed into me, stealing the grief.

"I have you, Speedy. I will always have you. What is their name?" he asked.

Bartholomew. "Please," I begged, the calm cracking in my mind. The waves grew stronger as Dontilvynsan's face scrunched and his breath sharpened. He was taking my grief while he pushed calm into my mind.

"Bartholomew," he said.

"Yes."

"His mate?" Seth asked.

"Yes. Speedy thinks he's gone. An alien I don't recognize attacked them."

Arms tightened around me as Kalvoxrencol and Zoltilvoxfyn whispered comforting words. Dontilvynsan kept pushing soothing thoughts, but it only dimmed my pain, not erasing it.

"Mindy, when did you last see them?" Seth asked. "Think about it. Please."

My thoughts turned back. The kissing. The happiness. Laughing. I was running toward Bartholomew to play with him, then it turned to something else entirely. The pain. Landing in the snow. Bartholomew above me, then nothing.

Dontilvynsan panted, fingers tight on my cheek. "He last saw Bartholomew in the snow. Not in the shuttle."

"He could still be there," Seth said. "We have to go back."

"It's not our space. It's Maykian territory. We already violated it once," Zoltilvoxfyn said. "If we get caught..."

"It's a human and Mindy's mate. We have to," Seth said.

Caleb bobbed. "We have to. Team Human to the rescue."

"I need him," I cried, trying to get up, but pain shot through my abdomen. Kalvoxrencol and Zoltilvoxfyn held me fast while the doctor came closer. "I have to have him."

"I know," Seth said, bending closer. "Trust me, Mindy. I will never leave a human behind. Neither will Caleb. He followed me here, remember? If Bartholomew is there, we'll find him, even if we have to search the entire planet. I will go myself." Kalvoxrencol started to protest, but Seth continued over him, "He'll see a friendly face. A human one."

But what if Teddy was gone? How did someone learn to live without their soul? They didn't. They couldn't. It wasn't possible.

"I'll go too," Caleb said.

"No, you will not," Zoltilvoxfyn immediately said. "The cold is not good for you."

"Team Human to the rescue," Caleb shouted over his mate. "Led by our fearless leader, Seth."

"Me? Why am I the leader? You thought of it."

Caleb scoffed. "I'm a poor choice. Come on, Seth. Be serious."

The two humans continued to bicker, but my attention ripped from them when the doctor injected me with something. I lurched and gripped Dontilvynsan's biceps, his scales shiny.

"I have to get him," I said.

"The next time you wake, he will be here. Beside you. Trust us," Dontilvynsan whispered.

But our thoughts were too entwined; he was lying. Dontilvynsan didn't know if Bartholomew was alive or not. He had no idea if it was possible to bring my mate back to me. His hold on me shattered, and he broke away, panting. All of the grief came back, crashing over me. I tried to fight the medication as I struggled to a sitting position.

Kalvoxrencol held me fast, forehead against mine. "I will find him, Speedy. I promise. None of us will leave what is yours behind."

My tongue became heavy and my thoughts turned wispy. "Bartholomew," I breathed before I was whisked away.

Chapter 36

A PROPER RESCUE.

Bartholomew

I heard a creak, but I couldn't move. I wanted to, but I was so tired and cold. My limbs felt like a million pounds, my mouth was painfully dry, and my stomach was the size of a raisin. Voices echoed in the frozen air. Maybe the winged alien had finally broken inside? Hopefully, death would be quick.

Burying my nose in the blanket that contained the faintest tinge of Serlotminden's fragrance, I gave in to whatever was to come. The voices grew louder and louder. One voice I understood. The words. English. I didn't recognize who spoke, though. It wasn't Serlotminden.

The tent parted, and light blinded me through my eyelids. I couldn't even twitch.

"No. Oh god. Fuck. This poor kid. Mindy will never forgive us," the deep voice said.

I groaned. "Mindy."

A blurry figure hovered over me, leaning closer. A perfectly ordinary human with brown hair, brown eyes, white skin, and round face appeared. Human. I breathed, "Serlotminden?"

"Alive. Are you Bartholomew?"

"Teddy."

He smiled, drawing away, and I said in a rush, "Don't leave me. Please."

He swallowed, grabbing my hand. "I have you. You're safe, Teddy."

Other drakcol shifted closer. One was grayish-blue, another was black, and the last was light gray. I tried to shift back, but I couldn't do more than grunt as I slightly wiggled. Serlotminden. I wanted him. No one else.

"It's alright," the human said. "My name's Seth."

"Seth." Mindy had talked about him. He was the reason we humans had been taken in the first place, but I couldn't be mad at him. He'd come for me. He was saving me. Tears burned my eyes. "Thank you."

Seth rolled me onto a stretcher because I shied away when the drakcol came near me. Anytime Seth tried to let go of me, I reached for him; I didn't want him to leave. I didn't want to be alone again. I was so cold, and I hurt so bad.

He settled next to me in the shuttle, gripping my fingers. "Leader of Team Human, indeed."

The drakcol with gray scales laughed. "I told you." His voice was rough, but his words were in English, though severely garbled, almost like Serlotminden's. "I'm a horrible choice. You're naturally the best."

"Seriously, Caleb?"

He was Caleb—the human ghost in a drakcol body.

"Don was talking to the Maykian warship about violating their space again, and he declared you owned all the humans, so we had the right to come and retrieve Bartholomew."

"What?" Seth squeaked. "What did you just say?"

"'Owned' might be wrong. Maybe lead? Control? I don't remember. But he was arguing fairly hard, and I might or might not have given him some insider tips," Caleb said, grinning and snuggling into the black drakcol's side.

"Caleb," the black drakcol said with a chuckle.

Caleb continued, "Did you know that Maykians are super protective of families and have really strict protocols? So having you be the undisputed leader is a good thing. This way we won't die. Isn't that great?"

Seth sighed. "Fuck."

"I thought it was a pretty great idea. I wandered Maykian space back when I was dead for at least a year, maybe more. I know a lot. Like *a lot* a lot. Don seemed to like the plan, and we haven't been shot yet, so it's fantastic!"

"Caleb," Seth groaned.

My eyes closed as they bickered in English. I didn't exactly understand what was going on, but I knew one thing. I was going back to where I belonged. To my mate's side. That was all that mattered.

I blinked. Vines covered in flowers hung over me, intermixed with recessed lights. I took a sharp breath and promptly sneezed. My nose dripping and my eyes itching, I looked around. Where the hell was I? It was warm, wherever it was. That was an improvement, and the bed was soft—also nice.

A hand tightened on mine. Seth. "I've got you, Teddy. You're really cold and dehydrated and skinny. You look like hell." He flushed. "Not that it matters. Or doesn't matter. You're going to be fine. There's a great doctor here. He'll check you out."

"Serlotminden?" I asked, struggling to speak. I sneezed again, making my muscles ache. God, my eyes were on fire.

"I'm taking you to him right now."

The plants disappeared and were replaced by gray. Almost instantly, I spotted Serlotminden on a bed. My pulse skyrocketed. He was here. But he wasn't moving. Why wasn't he moving?

"Mindy," I shouted. I groaned when I tried to throw myself off the cot. I needed to touch him.

Seth gripped my shoulder. "Hold on."

"Serlotminden," I called. "Honey."

His deep green eyes snapped open and locked onto me. "Flower," he growled and launched forward. I tried to get to him as he clawed off the bed to reach me. The grayish-blue drakcol held him, and Serlotminden wordlessly yelled, tail thrashing.

"You're going to hurt yourself. Stop it, Speedy," the blue alien ordered.

"Hold on," Seth said while I struggled to escape his hold. Mindy roared, punching at the two drakcol keeping him on the bed. "For fuck's sake," Seth yelled. "Hold on for one fucking second."

He shoved the stretcher to Mindy's side. I didn't wait for help and crawled to him. Serlotminden seized me and dragged me closer. His breath was rough as he nuzzled me. "Bartholomew."

I held him tight. He was alive. He was alright. He was here.

Someone came close, tugging on me.

Serlotminden snarled, pushing the man away. "Do not touch my mate."

The blue and black aliens tried to pin Mindy, who was growling.

"Fuck it all," Seth said. "I swear you are all the most dramatic brothers I have ever met." He pushed the drakcol away and snagged Mindy's chin, which made me frown. "Teddy is hurt. He needs help, so shut the hell up."

"Bartholomew," Mindy said, focusing on me.

"I'm going to sedate both of them." A female drakcol with golden hair in a long braid approached. Another person, a human man who had dot tattoos on his face, agreed.

I tried to protest, needing to see Serlotminden more, but I was so tired.

Seth said, "We won't take you away from Mindy, but we need to treat you both without the drama. Or Mindy attacking someone."

Something pricked my arm, and my vision went weird, but Serlotminden was in front of me. I took a deep breath and relaxed against him. We were together.

Someone burst into the room. "Prince Consort Seth, you are needed immediately. The Maykians are threatening to destroy us."

"This is your fault, Caleb," Seth said, voice growing further away.

"It will be alright, Husband," another voice said. "I will protect you."

Caleb spoke, "Don't worry. I'll talk you through it. Everything will be fine. I mean, if they do kill us, it won't be so bad." When several people growled, he continued in a rush, "But they won't kill us. You'll be supreme leader in no time, Seth. I'm a great talker. Ask Fyn. It will be perfectly fine. I swear. I'm great at plans."

The door closed before I heard a response, but I didn't really care. My fingers were waving and doubled as I lifted my heavy arm to touch Mindy. He was here.

"Flower," he muttered, tail hooking around my ankle.

I breathed in his scent and let myself drift away.

Serlotminden

I rubbed Bartholomew's arm, relishing the feel of his skin against my scales. He was settled against me with several tubes in both of his arms. He was ill. Severe dehydration, multiple vitamin deficiencies, extremely underweight, slight tears to his shoulders and elbows that were already healing—he was lucky to be alive. The Amorian physician, Klars, had assured me that all Bartholomew needed was time to recover.

I was far more injured, though I was conscious, unlike my mate. Bartholomew hadn't reacted well to the sedative, but I'd been told by Klars that my mate would awaken eventually.

The creature who'd attacked me had had some kind of venom on their talons, making the wounds slow to heal. They kept reopening, even when sealed, and the venom was spreading. Doctor Muznim had done several things, but she was still trying to neutralize whatever was preventing me from healing. Hopefully, she would find an answer soon.

But I wasn't that concerned for myself. I needed my Bartholomew to awaken, badly. When I heard him call my name, it had dragged me out of my medicated sleep. Seeing him next to Seth and my brothers had been surreal and I'd needed to hold him, to assure myself he was actually here.

His earthen scent tickled my nose and soothed my stress. He was here beside me. He was safe. We were fine. I never wanted to feel the despair of not having him beside me again. I would do whatever was necessary to keep him. I could not lose him. Not to Earth. Not to death. Not to anything.

My lips trailed over his forehead. "Mate."

Kalvoxrencol laughed. "You are deep in love. Hallonnixmin and Gilvaxtin are going to be sorry to have missed this."

I scoffed. More like they would've enjoyed teasing me. When Dontilvynsan decided to search for me, he'd left Hallonnixmin and

Gilvaxtin in Monqilcolnen's care. Our cousin had escorted them home, much to their protests.

"You are no better. Where is Seth?"

"Probably feeding the nightmare pet you brought home, arguing with the Maykians who are calling him the Supreme Human of Earth, or watching our child."

"Does he ever look away from your kit?"

"No," he said, leaning back, wings resting on either side of him. "He can't. We have been gone longer than planned, and it worries him. I believe the doctors in charge of our child are happy about our delay, because Seth normally arrived in the morning at the nesting facility and only left when I dragged him away. Having him beside the baby's pod is... difficult for them."

I wondered if Bartholomew would be that clingy. We had not discussed children, but I wanted a child who looked exactly like him. A little baby with his deep brown eyes that had green and golden flecks. His black hair that I was desperate to see long. His smooth pink-golden skin. I took another deep breath of his fragrance as I rubbed on him to scent mark him.

"There were more humans?" Kalvoxrencol asked.

"That's what my mate says. His close friend was on Xome. I have to retrieve him."

Kalvoxrencol lifted an eyebrow. "Competition?"

"No," I said, brushing Bartholomew's arm. "Friend. Vince."

His brow crinkled.

"What?"

"I think I've heard that name before."

"Humans do share names, much like we do. Though," I said, grinning, "my mate has a much better name than yours."

Kalvoxrencol growled in warning, which I ignored.

"Bartholomew Reginald Lucian Cavendish-Wallingford," I said with pride. My mate was the best, obviously.

Mouth open, he blinked. "Is he royalty?"

"He says no, but I think he's lying."

"He must be with a name like that."

I laughed, and Bartholomew shifted against me. I kissed his forehead, holding him closer. "I have you, Flower. I'm right here."

He relaxed, still asleep.

Kalvoxrencol's tail twisted around mine. "I'm glad you found him."

"As am I. I can't imagine life without him."

"Please don't scare us again."

"Didn't like a taste of what you've done to us over the cycles?" I teased, regretting the words the instant they left my mouth.

He jerked back, expression shuttering.

I reached for him. "Pest."

"It's alright."

"'No," I said, hugging my littlest brother with one arm. "It's not. I didn't mean it. My apologies for scaring you."

Kalvoxrencol smiled, but it was tainted with sadness, and I felt so guilty. He had tried so hard to move on from his past mistakes, and I didn't want to be the one to remind him of them. I ruffled his hair, squeezing him. He slipped out of my grasp, and then the room. When the door slid closed, I promised myself to make it up to him.

My gaze went back to my mate, and my soul thrashed. Bartholomew was staring at me.

"Mate," I breathed.

He grinned, but his eyes turned wet.

I lifted his chin and kissed him. "No, please, don't cry."

Tears slid down his cheeks, and the sight shattered me.

I wiped them away. "I am here. I promise."

"I thought the last thing I would ever hear you say was my name," he sobbed.

"Never. I will never leave you."

"You'd better not."

Now was not the time, but I couldn't help but ask, "Are you going to leave me?"

He met my gaze. "Never."

"Do you mean that?"

"I'm not going to leave you."

I pressed my lips to his, keeping the movement gentle. We were both fragile. We would have time later to do more. Right now, I needed to be with my mate. To feel him beside me. To breathe the same air.

"I love you," I whispered.

"I love you too, Honey."

The translation was odd—sweet insect secretion—as was hearing his voice in my own language, but I recognized the endearment for what it was. I rubbed my nose against his and pressed as close to him as possible. My mate. My flower. My soul. We had survived, and I wouldn't let him go.

His hand slid to one of my bandages. "Are you alright?"

I opened my mouth to lie to him, but I stopped. I would wish for the truth if the situation was reversed, so, of course, he deserved the same from me. "No."

Bartholomew's eyes widened in worry. "Honey?"

"No, Flower." I groaned when I tried to roll toward him.

"Stop moving," he snapped, the anger a rare show for him.

"That alien did some damage to me, but Doctor Muznim is taking care of me."

He grabbed my chin. "You are not allowed to die."

I grinned. "I won't."

"Where's Pookie?"

"Our daughter is in my—our quarters. The doctor healed her leg, and Seth has been taking excellent care of her."

A long breath rushed out of his lips. "Thank god. I was scared someone might hurt her."

"She's safe." I nuzzled his head, and Bartholomew took a deep inhale. "We're safe. We're together. Everything is fine."

Chapter 37

I GUESS WE'RE LYING NOW.

Bartholomew

Caleb and Seth sat across from where I lay on the bed in the medbay. Serlotminden was asleep beside me, his head tucked against my neck, breath tickling me. I had an arm wrapped around him, securing him to me. The doctor, whose name I didn't recall, had given him three injections this morning. Three. Mindy had been sleeping excessively, and from the amount of times someone changed his bandages, I knew something was wrong. But no one had told me exactly what was going on.

I kissed the top of his head, then brushed the rough bracelet I'd made him. The silver wires mixed with shiny bits I'd found on the shuttle and a rock looked much nicer than I'd thought against his scales. After I'd woken up, I gave him the small gift, and he'd been so happy when I slid it on him, beaming and calling me talented, lovely, smart, and all manner of nice things. I finger-combed his hair, hoping he'd wake up soon so I could hear his perfect voice once more.

Refocusing on Caleb and Seth, I noted that nothing had changed. Seth was blushing; he hadn't spoken the entire time they'd been here. Caleb had continued to ramble about anything and everything, switching topics so fast that I struggled to follow at times; whereas, Seth stared at the floor. I wasn't even sure why they were here. One of Mindy's brothers usually remained in the medbay with us, but this was the first time I had been left alone with the other humans.

Though Caleb wasn't human anymore.

He was massive, even for a drakcol, who all appeared to be larger than humans. He had soft gray scales and short mahogany hair, a long face, and was generally attractive. A metal cane with a soft grip rested against his leg and his large hands waved as he spoke. His English was garbled but understandable. He *was* human, though not really.

"Anyway, I gave Seth the right words, so he is now the Supreme Human of Earth according to the Maykians," Caleb said.

"I can't believe you told them I claimed Earth," Seth muttered.

"Yeah, I might have given you some pretty words about honor and blood and a claim of utter truth, which means a lot to them, but it was for the best. Trust me."

Seth crossed his arms. "They think humans are descended from the lost Maykian tribe who went off to some unknown space."

"We might be," Caleb protested. He was met with a cocked eyebrow. Even I was fairly skeptical of that, and I didn't know much about the situation. "Okay," he relented. "Fine. That lie will probably bite us in the ass later, but hey, we're alive. They didn't shoot us out of the sky. All good things."

I gave a breathy chuckle. "True. I like not being dead."

"It really isn't so bad," Caleb mentioned, "but I'm for living as well. I want to stay next to Fyn, and living is the best way to do that."

My fingers buried in Mindy's hair, and he didn't react. "Well, it does seem like a more substantial lie than the cats."

Seth flushed, and Caleb laughed, then asked, "You heard about that?"

I nodded.

"It started as a joke," Seth muttered. "Caleb blew it out of proportion."

"You had it that humans had a cultural law that we couldn't move a sleeping cat no matter where they are, and that they're house gods we worship. I had to make it fancier. It only made sense, and it's funnier. Like adding shrines for the house gods with catnip, towers, toys, and beds, and, you know, naming towns after cats," Caleb said. "There are already several drakcol cities named after Lucy, not to mention other famous Earth cats."

"No one has figured it out?"

"Nope," Caleb said. "Drakcol have access to information from Earth, but very few have actually researched cats. Besides, it's taken on a life of its own. Though cats and cat videos are very popular. Besides, it's a harmless lie. Something for us."

I had zero qualms about keeping it a secret.

"Don't think about it in front of Don," Caleb warned. "He'll hear your thoughts."

Mindy had mentioned something about that. I glanced back at him, and he was deep asleep, his breath even against my neck and his tail was coiled around my ankle.

"When are we getting the other humans from Xome?" I had to save Vince, and whatever humans were left. Besides the fact that Vince was my closest friend, I needed to do one good deed to balance out my karmic debt. Maybe it would lessen my guilt? Probably not, but those humans deserved to be saved.

Seth smoothed his fancy blue tunic over his round gut. "Don is finishing removing all the debris from where you crashed, then we'll return to Coalition space."

"We need to get them," I said, voice growing louder. "I can't leave them behind."

"We're not going to," Caleb snapped, resting a hand on Seth, who'd flinched from my shout.

"I know this is my fault," Seth said, eyes on the floor. "Because I stayed with Kal. I will never leave any human behind, I swear it, but we can't rush in and steal them."

"Why not?"

"Because slavery and indentured servitude are legal on Xome, and they are not a part of the Coalition," Seth explained. "If we steal them, it could cause an intergalactic incident, if not a war. Don is already getting his ass chewed out by the Cohort for violating Maykian space, not once but twice, to rescue you and Mindy."

"So we leave them?" I demanded. I refused to leave Vince behind. I couldn't. I swallowed as panic rose and strangled me. I almost saw his face joining all the ghosts haunting me. I closed my eyes. I refused to let him down. I had to save one fucking person.

"No," Caleb said. "We told you we wouldn't. Seth and I, but mainly Seth, are requesting funds from the Cohort to buy all the humans back. Don will negotiate with whoever has them, and no matter the price, we will get them back."

"We'll get them," Seth said. "All of them."

"If we get the money." I hated the idea of having to buy Vince and the others, but if they could be freed, it was worth it.

Caleb laughed. "We'll get the money. The Cohort *loves* Seth. They'll give him whatever he wants. And this comes down to honor. They're honor-bound to rescue the rest of us humans. They brought Seth here, and now they have to clean up the mess."

"I will get them, Teddy," Seth said, finally meeting my eye. His voice was firm and allowed no argument. "I promise. I will protect everyone."

In that instant, I saw the reason why Caleb had nominated Seth the leader of Team Human.

I nodded, believing him.

Before he could respond, Seth yanked a glowing blue stone out of his pocket. "Babe, what's wrong? It is the baby?"

I heard nothing, but Seth sighed.

"I'll be there soon." He shoved the round stone back into his pocket. "The Cohort is ready for us."

Caleb carefully stood, using his cane for balance, but Seth didn't budge. Caleb flicked him with his tail. "Come on. I'll be there."

Seth still didn't react.

"Kal will be there," added Caleb.

Seth perked at that, standing.

"And you can show them pictures of the baby. The Cohort *loves* seeing the baby."

Seth smiled, head ducking.

"There we go." Caleb looked at me. "We'll be back, and I imagine one of Mindy's brothers will be along in a few minutes."

"Do I need to speak to this Cohort?" I asked. Dr. Klars, who appeared human but wasn't, had said I was allowed to leave the medbay, but I refused. Mindy would panic if he woke up and I wasn't here, not to mention I was nervous to leave him alone for even a few minutes. With Seth feeding Pookie, though he didn't seem happy about it, I hadn't had to leave.

"No," Seth answered. "If we need you, I will have someone get you, but you need to stay here with Mindy."

They gave me a quick goodbye and left.

I turned to Mindy, snuggling him. His breath remained even. The winged alien had clawed open his stomach and he had two punctures on his thigh; none of which were healing right.

"Come on, Honey. Make me smile, or tell me another story, or just talk to me. Please."

He stayed firmly asleep.

The drakcol doctor approached with yet another injection. Before she administered it, I stopped her. "Another? He's already had three."

"Bartholomew Reginald Lucian—"

"Bartholomew or Teddy," I interrupted.

"But," she started.

"Bartholomew or Teddy," I repeated. I was not listening to my full name every time a drakcol wished to address me.

She looked horribly disappointed, her eyes going down and her tail falling to the floor. "Bartholomew, Prince Serlotminden is not healing and he is bleeding heavily. His body cannot keep up. I am hoping the inducer will be enough, rather than a transfusion."

The doctor injected him in the side of the neck, but I waved her off when she was going to massage the site. I did it instead. Mindy was mine. It was my job to take care of him, not hers. Once I was done, I held him close and hoped his beautiful green eyes would open and meet my gaze.

They didn't.

"What's your name?" I asked.

"Muznim. I am female and I use the she and her pronouns. Prince Consort Seth informed me humans like to know exact pronouns, and I quite love the idea of telling people on introduction."

"What exactly is wrong with Mindy?" I asked.

Muznim pursed her lips, and her tail flicked. "The punctures are not closing. The toxin, perhaps a venom, on the alien's talons is spreading through his system, not allowing the blood to clot. We are searching for ways to combat this toxin, but so far, we have not made much progress."

"Do the Maykians have any idea?"

"No," she replied. "Planet 62, as they have designated the planet you two crashed on, is non-spacefaring. They have left it alone, not studying the species, except for passive scans."

"So what's next?"

"We keep testing." Muznim said, "I will do all I can to save Prince."

I nodded.

A few minutes later, the door opened and Zoltilvoxfyn, or Fyn as Seth and Caleb called him, came in. "Any change?"

"No," I replied shortly, tightening my hold on Mindy.

The smallest quirk tugged at his lips before it disappeared. "I will not take him from you. Speedy would want to remain right beside you, where he belongs."

Fyn might have tried, but he wouldn't have succeeded. I wasn't an aggressive person, but I sure as hell wasn't going to budge from Mindy's side.

"I am glad you're alive," Fyn said, resting an ankle on his opposite knee. "Serlotminden was bereft, and thankfully, only for a few days. That type of pain is indescribable."

"You've experienced that? I thought drakcol only mated once."

"We do. Caleb was a spirit first. He vanished from my side for over eight weeks. I thought he was gone," he replied, voice tight.

"I'm sorry."

"You have nothing to apologize for. You survived."

My fingers worked over Mindy's scalp. "It's his turn."

"Indeed."

"He can't become another person that I failed to save, another ghost haunting me," I muttered.

Fyn tilted his head and looked around. "There are no spirits."

"What?"

"You have no spirits around you, Bartholomew."

I did. I could see them even now—burned and broken, blaming me, demanding to know why I was alive when they were dead, begging me to save them.

Fyn stood. "Did Serlotminden explain inner fires?"

"Yeah, he makes fire with his mind."

With a slight quirk of his lips, Fyn brushed a lock of Mindy's hair. "He does, indeed. Mine is the ability to see spirits when they linger on this plane." Fyn met my gaze. "There are no spirits around you, Bartholomew."

I fought a clawing emotion in my gut, but words escaped my control. "Then why do I see them?"

"Perhaps you are having a health crisis?"

Chuckling, I closed my eyes. "I'm not sick or having a mental breakdown."

"Then why do you see spirits that are not there?"

"Because I'm the reason they're dead," I whispered. I didn't know why I was telling this virtual stranger everything. The words were slipping out without my permission.

"Guilt is powerful."

"You're not going to tell me it wasn't my fault?" I asked.

"I don't know what you did. Is it your fault?"

"Yes."

"Then I cannot absolve you of your guilt or spirits. Only you can do that, Bartholomew. You are the one holding them here. Not their anger, not their pain, not their malice. It is only you and your guilt. You have to let them go."

I confessed, "I don't know how."

"My mate-brother," Fyn said, "you have to forgive yourself."

That was something I didn't know if I could do. I was alive, and they were not. It wasn't right. Why was it me who'd survived?

Fyn returned to his seat. "I will help you if I can."

"Why would you help me? You don't even know me."

He gave me a slight smile. "Because someone I didn't know well helped me. Seth helped me and still stands beside me when I need him. I would like to do the same for you."

I held his gaze for several seconds before looking away. While I had a hard time believing I'd just spilled my guts to a stranger, I also felt a tad better, a bit lighter. Changing the subject, I asked, "What did the Cohort decide?"

"They had not come to an agreement when I left," Fyn answered. "We didn't wish to leave you or Serlotminden alone, so I came here. Seth has need of Kalvoxrencol, and Dontilvynsan is still in trouble, so many wished to chastise him. I was unneeded at the meeting, for Caleb shines well without me, and I was needed here."

I grunted again, and we fell silent. It was awkward between us, at least on my side, but I refused to let that stop me from caring for Mindy. My lips found his forehead again. He wouldn't leave me. The doctor would figure it out, and everything would be fine.

Klars appeared by my side. A congenial smile was on his lips. In the short time I'd known the Amorian doctor, he'd always been in a good mood. "Prince Zoltilvoxfyn, nice to see you."

Fyn tilted his head slightly to the side. Drakcol did that. I wasn't entirely sure why—acknowledgement, or concession maybe.

"How are you feeling?" Klars asked me.

I grunted.

"That is not a cognizant response, Bartholomew," he scolded like I was five. "Use your words."

I had several choice words for him, but I didn't say them. "I'm fine."

"I doubt that, but you are recovering," he commented. Klars added more fluids to the tubes connected to me, took a blood sample, then tutted about this or that. I didn't care what he did as long as he didn't try to make me leave. "You are going to need a high calorie diet to assist in gaining weight. I have made a slurry of nutrients for you."

The proffered tube of gray sludge didn't appear appetizing.

"I made three, and Seth informed me this one was the least vile," Klars said with a wide grin.

A snort came from Fyn's direction, but by the time I looked, he'd covered his mouth, hiding a smile most likely.

Accepting the tube, I figured it couldn't be any worse than other things I'd eaten over the years. Besides, I had to gain weight. It was what it was. I took a sip, and thanked god Seth had tasted the other two first. This one was horrible, the texture slimy and chunky at the same time. I forced myself to drink it all, the mixture landing heavily in my stomach.

When it was empty, I swallowed convulsively.

"Excellent," he said, putting the tube in a chute on the wall. "You will need to drink three of these a day in addition to your regular meals."

"The tubes?" I asked, lifting my arm.

"Will remain." He crossed his arms. "You need vitamins and you have to stay hydrated."

"Fine."

Klars gave me a smile before wandering to a monitor on the wall. An old woman—seemingly human—though blue in color, appeared on the screen. Her tower of curls bobbed and her multiple chins jiggled as they talked. The conversation was too low for me to hear all of it, but it sounded nutritional, probably devising more shakes for me.

"Are you alright?" Fyn asked.

"Yeah."

Fyn looked at his brother who was curled against me. "It's good Klars has a plan in place to help you before Serlotminden awakens. He'll worry less."

I chuckled, combing my fingers through his hair. "My Mindy does love to worry about me."

"It is a Drakcon quality. We care for our mates."

Mindy did indeed take care of me. His injuries were a testament to how much. He'd gotten hurt protecting me. "Now it's my turn to take care of him."

Chapter 38

STAY WITH ME.

Bartholomew

Mindy still hadn't awoken, and it was starting to worry me as well as his brothers. It wasn't just his unconscious state, though. The blood inducer was no longer working. Dr. Muznim had said she was doing everything possible, but I wanted to yell at her, though I refrained. It wasn't her fault. It was mine. Mindy wouldn't blame me if he was awake—I knew that. He'd laugh it off and say it was his responsibility to take care of me. However, the guilt remained.

His brothers had started donating, because apparently, real blood versus synthetic was better. Dontilvynsan and Zoltilvoxfyn were matches, though what those matches were I didn't know or care. As long as it worked.

No matter what the doctors said, I'd refused to move from his side. I'd learned fairly quickly that the drakcol catered to us humans. Seth had merely to say something, and people literally jumped to follow, tripping over themselves to help him first. It was similar for me, though drakcol didn't cater to me as they did Seth.

Caleb wasn't treated the same, which made me feel bad for him. He was human and not.

But knowing how much the drakcol catered to us, I was positive they wouldn't force me from Mindy's side. Besides, Seth had ordered all the doctors to leave me be, and that was that apparently.

Caleb had been right about the drakcol loving Seth.

With Seth watching Pookie, I didn't have to leave, though he didn't like taking care of her. Yesterday, he'd almost been in tears when he came into the medbay. Pookie had ambushed him in Mindy's room. She'd been playing, but it freaked him out.

Thankfully, Caleb had found it hilarious and agreed to feed her today.

We'd left Planet 62's orbit and were traveling to Xome. The Cohort had agreed to pay for the humans' return. Don was entering into negotiation for them before we even reached the planet. Soon Vince would be here, and I wanted him to meet Mindy. He'd tease me, incessantly, about how quickly I'd fallen for Serlotminden, and I was looking forward to them becoming friends.

If Mindy would wake up.

Kal, who was beside us, probably felt the same.

I smoothed a hand over Mindy's cheek, relishing his warmth. "Time to wake up, Honey. You have to meet Vince soon, and I want to see your gorgeous eyes."

He didn't react.

I was unsurprised.

Muznim came toward Mindy with a needle, and I tensed, tugging him closer. "What is that?"

"Seth negotiated with the Maykians for help. They, along with Edith, helped me create a serum we believe will neutralize the venom," she said.

I didn't know who the hell Edith was, but I was thankful for her and the Maykian's assistance. "But?" I asked. There was always a but, a risk, something.

"It might not."

I glanced at Kal, and his tail was flicking, but he didn't offer an opinion. I kissed Mindy's temple and said, "Fine."

She carefully unwound his bandages, and the wounds seeped blood. Carefully, she injected the edge of the worst wound on his side—right where the piece of shrapnel had stabbed him.

I swallowed my nerves and watched as she continued injecting around the talon punctures. I helped her move him to reach all of the injuries. When she was doing one on the back of his thigh, Mindy jolted.

"Honey?"

His muscles contracted and he began to flail.

Muznim pulled him away from me, and I tried to grab him, but Kal held out an arm to waylay me. "Let her help him."

I shoved him away, but Kal caught me around the waist as I fought to follow Serlotminden who was being moved across the medbay. Muznim and technicians swarmed him, taking him away from me.

"Mindy," I called.

"Bartholomew," Kal said. "Let her help him. Muznim is one of the best. We would never entrust our brother to anyone incompetent."

"Let go of me."

"My apologies, but I cannot. You need to let them take care of him." Kal held me close, keeping me back. "I know you want to be with him, and so do I, but let her do her job."

Mindy needed me. I had a hard time seeing him through the crowd, but what I did see of him was shaking as if he might be having a seizure. I fought Kal's iron grip on me, calling for Mindy.

Klars appeared in my line of vision and said in a soothing voice, "Muznim is one of the best, and if you do not calm yourself, I will sedate you." He lifted a full injector with a wide smile.

I frowned but ceased writhing, and Kal released me. He stood right beside me, chest heaving and tail thrashing. We both waited, eyes never leaving Serlotminden, for someone to come talk to us again.

It took an agonizingly long time before Muzmin returned. "He had an adverse reaction."

"No shit." I took a deep breath. "Is he alright?"

"We stabilized him, and the treatment does appear to be working."

Kal sagged. "Thank the Crystal. How long until he wakes?"

"I do not know."

"I need to tell my parents and my brothers. Are you well, Bartholomew?"

"As soon as they give him back to me, I will be, yeah."

He raised his eyebrows but didn't comment and left the medbay.

Muznim continued to monitor Serlotminden on the other side of the room, and a wall of technicians blocked me from seeing much of him. Eventually, she waved me over. Apparently, Mindy was staying on his new bed. More machines were attached to him, and his scales were shiny with sweat.

Placing a hand on him, I breathed. Fuck. That had been too close. I clambered onto the bed to lie next to him, snuggling against his side, and his tail coiled around my ankle, making me smile. I tilted his chin up and pressed a gentle kiss against his lips. We might not have discussed if he was comfortable with public affection or me kissing him in his sleep, but I knew Mindy wouldn't deny me something I needed. And I desperately needed to kiss him, to assure myself that he was right beside me.

Whispering against his lips, I said, "You fucking scared me. Please don't do it again."

Dr. Muznim returned, and I watched her with narrowed eyes. There was no fucking way she was doing anything else to him right now. She offered me her throat but didn't appear bothered by my glare.

"We need to stretch his wings."

"I will do it." Something about someone else touching Mindy right now was grating on my fractured nerves, even though it was logical for the professionals to take care of him.

Once again, she offered me her throat before assisting me in turning Mindy over—he was heavy. Once he was on his stomach, I gently grabbed his wing, and Muznim said, "By the talon and be very slow. If one opens, so will the other. It's a reflex."

Nodding, I hooked my fingers around his talon, careful of the point because it was exceedingly sharp, and pulled. His wing unfolded and the other followed. I kissed the closest one before hauling him practically on top of me. I tucked Serlotminden's head against my shoulder, breathing in his scent.

He would wake up soon; I knew it. I kept my arms around him, hand running over his back. My fingers felt every knob on his spine and the delicate scales between his wings. He was lovely. The sheet kept him from exposing himself to everyone, because, apparently, drakcol didn't believe in hospital gowns. Nope. Patients who needed full-time care remained all natural.

Time passed with me and Serlotminden alone, and it was kind of nice. I wished he was awake, but for the first time since we'd left the planet's surface, the two of us were alone. Mindy's brothers were always around—them or Seth and Caleb. I wasn't used to spending so much time with other people. For the last two years, the sole person I had spent any meaningful time with was Vince and then Mindy.

"You know," I told him, "since we are alone, if you were awake, we could make out."

"If you'd like."

My heart skipped a beat, then skyrocketed.

Bright green eyes met my gaze.

"Serlotminden."

"Greetings, Flower."

I planted my lips on his, giving him a chaste kiss. "Are you alright? Are you in any pain?"

"I missed you."

A wet chuckle escaped me. "You were asleep, Honey. How could you miss me?"

"I just did." Mindy closed his eyes, shifting closer to nuzzle me.

I tried to force away the tears that burned my eyes. He was alive. Everything was fine. "Mindy."

"Yes, my Mate?"

"Don't ever scare me again."

He laughed. "I will try my utmost not to."

"I love you."

"I love you as well."

I asked, "How are you feeling?"

"Tired, and my stomach hurts."

"That makes sense. You were caught by a giant bird and had your gut stabbed by talons."

"I am glad it was me instead of you."

I grunted. That wasn't a sentiment that I shared.

"Are you well?"

"Yeah."

"Truly?"

"Yes," I repeated, giving him a soft kiss. "Your brothers have been taking very good care of me."

Before I could say anything else, Dr. Muznim approached. "Prince, you are awake."

"Yes," he said, pulling me closer, his tail coiling up my calf. It appeared I wasn't the only one who didn't want to separate.

She checked his wounds and discussed treatment plans with him, but Mindy struggled to keep his eyes open during the conversation. As she was finishing, the door opened, and all of Mindy's family—well, the ones aboard—poured in. All of them were calling his name and pulling him close.

It was touching to see how much his family loved him, and yet, it was a painful reminder of my own. A sudden longing for my mothers and my two sisters rushed through me. It had been so long, and I doubted they had any idea what had happened to me. I shoved the thought away, tightening my hold on Mindy. I wasn't alone, and there was nothing that I could do about being taken from Earth.

Serlotminden tucked his hand under my shirt, brushing my bare skin as he chatted with his brothers, assuring them that he was well. I ignored everyone else and stared at the love of my life, tracing his face as it moved through his different expressions and reveling in the fact he was awake. Mindy was here, and we were together. That was the most important thing.

Serlotminden

It had been two days since I'd awoken again. The gashes I'd received were finally starting to heal, now that the toxin had been neutralized. Bartholomew hadn't left my side, except rarely to walk or move around the medbay—neither had my brothers. All of them, even Dontilvynsan, had remained in the medbay with me and Bartholomew as much as possible.

I had scared them, badly.

Between them, my mate-brothers, the doctors, my parents and Hallonnixmin pinging frequently, and even Edith popping in to tell me she was researching my further care, Bartholomew and I never had a moment alone. I needed to spend time with just him, and more than that, I was desperate to kiss him, which I hadn't done since right after I awoke. And that kiss, while lovely, had been far too short. I craved to thoroughly explore him and cover him in my scent.

But, as I looked at Kalvoxrencol and Zoltilvoxfyn who sat right beside the bed where I and Bartholomew were, I knew it was not going to happen.

Bartholomew was sitting beside me, and I had my head on his thigh. He ran his long fingers through my hair, making me groan in the back of my throat. It was good. So impossibly good.

I listened, not truly paying attention, to Pest and Bloom detailing how exactly they had found us. Instead, I focused on Bartholomew's fingers on my scalp. He contributed to the conversation, his voice even and perfectly lovely. I nuzzled him, scent marking him. My scent had faded from lack of marking him, and my instincts demanded that I claim him lest someone else steal him from me.

The mere thought was enough to make me growl, and I started nuzzling him more frantically.

Bartholomew cupped the back of head. "I'm right here," he whispered, then went back to finger-combing my hair.

"Speedy," Kalvoxrencol started, "are you well?"

"Yes." I was, mostly. I was simply jealous of a fictional person who might take my mate, which was foolish.

"I'm glad you found us," Bartholomew said. "Though Mindy was taking excellent care of me, barring the bird alien who gutted him."

I glared at him, and the smallest smile tugged on the left side of his mouth, which made me beam. My mate was teasing me. I kissed his thigh, wishing he wasn't wearing trousers.

"Princes," Klars said in his perpetually happy voice. "Teddy, it's time for your nutritional slurry."

I winced at the gray liquid in the polymer tube. I had tried it and nearly puked. How Bartholomew drank it without even wincing was a mystery. "Surely we can make it taste better?" I asked Klars.

"I have. This is the best so far. He needs to drink it, Prince."

When I opened my mouth to further protest, Bartholomew interrupted me by stroking my cheek. "It's fine."

Without hesitation, he drank the supplement; I shuddered. He was far stronger than I.

Head on his thigh, I glared at my brothers, who didn't look away from me. I fought the urge to tell him to leave. I normally adored being the center of attention, but right now, I hoped they'd leave so Bartholomew and I had some time alone.

"Done," he said.

"Excellent," Klars declared. "Now I need to take some blood."

I growled.

Bartholomew didn't care about Klars taking regular samples; I did. I hated the thought of him being in any pain whatsoever. My mate smoothed a hand over my back as he told Klars, "Fine."

Once the sample was taken, Klars said, "I will analyze it and return later. Though, from my estimations, you are recovering enough to be disconnected from the support machines."

Klars disappeared and the door opened; Zoltilvoxfyn smiled, alerting me to who it was. Caleb moved into my eyeline, and I blinked. Pookie was on Caleb's head like a hat. She snorted when she saw us, leaping off and sending him swaying, and landed on top of us.

Zoltilvoxfyn growled, but he caught a laughing Caleb before he could fall.

Pookie snorted, snout wiggling as she crawled all over us, sniffing. I planted a kiss on her, and she squealed. "Have Uncle Caleb and Seth been taking good care of my daughter?"

"Daughter?" Kalvoxrencol asked.

"Humans sometimes refer to pets as their children." For once, I got to educate Kalvoxrencol about humans.

He glanced at Caleb, who nodded enthusiastically. "We do."

"Even cats?" Zoltilvoxfyn asked. "I thought you worshiped them."

"Even cats," Caleb said.

Bartholomew ran his long fingers over Pookie, who pressed against him, her spiral tail wiggling. "She hasn't been any trouble, has she?"

Caleb sat on Zoltilvoxfyn's lap and replied, "Not for me. She's been stalking and play-attacking me when I visit her, which is cute. Oh, also, I turned the environmentals in your quarters way down, so it's cold in there. She seemed fine with it being warmer, but I was worried. Anyway, she freaked Seth out. She was on the wall above the door when he came in and launched at him."

I winced.

Kalvoxrencol crossed his arms, tail thrashing. "She terrified him. He doesn't like spiders, and your pet attacked him."

I put a protective hand on Pookie's back. "She didn't mean to."

"And we're not calling her a spider," Caleb said. "It's illegal to own spiders, so she is a rabbit-pig hybrid. Maybe throw in crab or something. You guys have those spider-crabs on your beach. We need to lean into the fur and mammal-ness of her so the Vveekian Authority doesn't take her."

Bartholomew looked at me, eyes wide. "She won't be taken from us, right?"

"Of course not, Mate."

He snuggled Pookie close, and I nuzzled his leg to soothe him. No one would take her from us. We were a family.

My brothers and Caleb continued to talk to Bartholomew, who cuddled a happy Pookie. I didn't pay any attention to their words, instead focusing on the solidity of my mate. He was here. Pookie was here. My family was here. Everything was fine.

Chapter 39

ALONE AT LAST.

Bartholomew

"Here we go," I said, supporting Serlotminden to his room on Don's ship.

Serlotminden and I were *finally* leaving the medbay. It had been a week or so—the days had sort of blurred together—since he'd woken up. Having a moment alone with him was a relief, not to mention having some breathing room without so many people buzzing around.

I helped settle him onto the backless couch, how comfortable, with a groan. He kept a hold of me, pulling me next to him. I glanced around, fiddling with my new glasses. Their computer had created new lenses for me, so I could finally see clearly. The apartment wasn't large, with only a living room and a single doorway, which led to a bedroom.

Racing stuff was everywhere, but it wasn't displayed. It was haphazardly scattered around. Pookie had made a nest with flags and racing suits. I didn't currently see her, which meant she was either in Mindy's bedroom or with Caleb—he was rather attached to her.

The temperature was frigid, as Caleb had warned; we were going to have to raise it for myself and Serlotminden. It was too cold for us. In time, we'd have to see if she tolerated a warmer temperature or if we needed to construct some kind of home for her. I wasn't sure, but we would provide the best possible home for Pookie.

Pressing a kiss to his bare shoulder, I asked, "Do you want to lie here or in the bedroom?"

"Bedroom."

I helped him to his feet again, swearing. He was fucking solid. We should've gone to the room first. I yanked the blanket back before helping him lie down. He whined in obvious pain.

Gently, I tucked his hair behind his tapered ear, tracing the studs and long earring down to his neck. "Are you sure you're ready to leave the medbay?"

"Yes." He was panting, which made me pretty sure he should still be there.

I didn't argue, and closed the door before adjusting the environmentals to raise the temperature. "Lean up, Honey," I said, tugging on his shirt.

Serlotminden complied, allowing me to get it off him. He bit his bottom lip. My eyes latched onto the gold ring and my cock twitched. God. It took nothing to set my heart racing. I forced my gaze away. It was wrong to get horny when my boyfriend was in pain.

His chest was leaner than it used to be, and there were healing punctures that were free of scales. The injuries were jagged white against his mottled skin. I hoped they would fade and his scales would return, but no matter what, he was as hot as hell.

Bending, I pressed a gentle kiss to one of the marks, tongue licking the rough skin. Serlotminden groaned and the front of his pants began to tent. I wasn't the only one who didn't need much encouragement. I trailed from one injury to the other, pressing my lips and tongue over them. With each brush, his breathing harshened and his cock swelled.

"These look uncomfortable," I teased, sliding my finger under the waistband of his pants. Since he'd been in the medbay, we hadn't been able to do anything intimate, not even kissing. His brothers had always been around, and it was sweet, but I was desperate for him. I wanted to touch him, and assure myself that Mindy was alright.

"Please."

My fingers made quick work of the ties. I slowly slid them down as Serlotminden lifted his hips. He hissed in pain, his tail whipping before it coiled around my arm.

"Don't hurt yourself," I ordered. "You are going to lie here and take it."

He laughed. "Yes, my Flower." "Good job," I joked.

I pressed a kiss to his cock still trapped in his briefs. Serlotminden moaned. I nuzzled the soft fabric, breathing in his musky scent as he cried beneath me. He was so loud, my Mindy, and I loved it. Every noise, every sharp breath, every movement. All of it. I feasted on it.

I pulled his briefs off, and his cock smacked into his taut stomach. Pre-cum beaded on the tip of his cock and made me lick my lips.

I was already anticipating the sweet taste. I bent and lapped it up, groaning. "Fuck, you taste so good."

"More," Serlotminden demanded, which made me smile.

Who was I to deny him? I dragged my nose over his shaft, breathing in his scent. I would never tire of it. Was it because of the mate thing between us or because it was Serlotminden?

I pressed open-mouthed kisses along his shaft, licking the ridges of his scales. I was desperate for him to be inside me, pounding my ass, but it would have to wait until he was better. I reached his heavy sack and took one of his balls into my mouth, sucking and circling it with my tongue. Serlotminden rested a hand on my head and released a lewd moan.

"Do you like that, Honey?"

"Please," he begged. Serlotminden was very good at begging.

I licked the seam between his balls, and he groaned, arching. His sound of pleasure changed to pain.

"Do not hurt yourself. I will take care of you."

He chewed on his lip.

When I was sure he wouldn't move, I kissed the tip of his weeping cock, relishing the sweet taste of him. I sucked the crown into my mouth, and he called my name, claws scraping on my scalp. I lapped at the slit, then circled the tapered crown, and his noises grew louder. I worked his shaft with my hands, wanting more pre-cum. Loosening my jaw, I took him as deep as I could, gagging. I tried to breathe through it but couldn't.

Serlotminden caught my chin. "Don't worry about it."

"I want to take all of you." He deepthroated me with ease, and I wanted to return the favor.

His thumb skated over my chin and bottom lip. "We can work on it later, then, but don't worry about it right now. I love your touch. I love everything you're doing. I love you."

Blushing, I took him in my mouth again as deep as was comfortable. I bobbed as I pumped the rest of him while my other hand played with his sack. I moaned at the feel of him in my mouth. I loved the stretch of my jaw, the weight of him on my tongue, and the sweet taste of him on my lips.

Feeling brave, I circled his rim with my finger, and his grip tightened on what hair I had.

"Mate. So perfect. Again. Please. Please."

My finger ran over his hole, keeping the pressure light. We didn't have lube right here for me to finger-fuck him, and I wasn't sure if he liked it. I sucked him, cheeks hollowing. Spit slid out of the corners of my mouth as I worked his cock, desperate for his release on my tongue. I tugged on his balls and circled his hole, making him scream.

"I'm coming," he warned, voice strangled.

I slid up, tongue prodding his slit. Serlotminden released an animalistic cry as his cock jerked. Warmth coated my tongue, and I swallowed the sweet, tangy liquid. Some dripped out of my mouth, even though I tried to keep all of it. I didn't want to waste any, but there was a lot.

He went boneless beneath me as he panted, fingers stroking my cheek. I licked up every drop, then slid up his chest, dragging my tongue over him. He shuddered. "Bartholomew."

"Honey." I was hard. So hard. I needed to come. I crushed my lips against his, and I forced my tongue into his mouth, swiping mine against his. Serlotminden gripped my hips. I jerked my cock with no skill or patience. I was desperate to come. "I want to come on you."

"Mate, yes."

My breath came out in short gasps against his lips as I pumped my cock. My orgasm built with intense speed before crashing over me. I moaned as ropes of cum splattered Serlotminden's chest. He kept hold of me as my hips canted, chasing my pleasure.

I crashed on the bed beside him. Fuck me. I swallowed at the sight of my white cum stark against his dark purple scales. Serlotminden dragged his fingers though it, then plunged them into his mouth, tasting me. I groaned. Why was that so hot? Fingers wet, he rubbed my cum over his scales, and I frowned.

"What are you doing?"

"I need to smell like you."

I laughed. "What?"

"I need to smell like you," he repeated in a matter-of-fact voice, smearing the substance around before lifting his fingers to his lips, cleaning my release off them with tantalizing licks.

I kissed his shoulder up to his neck. "You're lucky you're cute."

"That sounded like an insult."

My lips continued their journey up his neck to his ear. "Let me clean you up."

"No, I want it to stay for a bit."

If he wanted my spend to soak into him, I wasn't going to stop him, no matter how gross I thought it was or how hard it was going to be to get it off later if it dried. Snuggled against his side, I said, "When you're better, I will let you fuck me."

"I will have to recover quickly, then."

I grunted.

"We do need to have a more comprehensive permissions discussion."

That's right. I'd forgotten. Now that their ship's NAID, which I was pretty sure was an artificial intelligence of some kind, was translating for us, this conversation would be much easier. I looked at him, bracing myself. Mindy was very attractive, popular, and loved physical affection. Naturally, that led me to conclude he was very sexually active. I had zero problem with that. But I was fairly certain he had a lot of kinks and things he enjoyed. Which once again, I had zero problem with, but this conversation was going to be long, involved, and probably eye-opening for me.

"Alright, Honey, where's your sex dungeon and what exactly do you want to do to me?"

Serlotminden paused. "Humans have underground prisons for fucking?"

So their computer wasn't well-versed in sex terminology. Good to know. "No. I mean, we do have sex dungeons, but they're playrooms meant for fun."

"You desire one of these?"

"No." I pinched the bridge of my nose. "It was a joke."

"I like certain things."

And here we go, I thought.

"I like fucking, Bartholomew, a great deal, but it is more than fucking to me."

I moved so my chin was resting on him.

"For me, I need the connection. The intimacy of the act. It's about closeness for me. Even with... I believe you called it edging?" I nodded, and he continued, "It is about my partner seeing how close I am, then stopping, comforting me, and beginning again. I like feeling how close we are. And I need that with you. I need to feel close and connected to you."

"Okay," I said slowly. "What are you saying, Mindy? I'm fine with edging you. I'm fine with you edging me. Well, at least once. I've never done it to myself, so I'm not certain if I like it or not."

He smiled, but it was tense. "I am boring when it comes to fucking."

That I was not expecting.

"It has been something that has been brought to my attention more than once. I enjoyed spanking you because I was fairly certain you would like it. I wouldn't mind you tying me up, because I think you would like that as well."

I squirmed, cock twitching. The thought of Mindy tied to the bed and begging beneath me as I rode him made my mouth go dry. Yeah, I wanted to try that.

"But in general, I mostly wish to have sex that is slow and is about us connecting, which is why I talk to you. I also thought it might help your nervousness, but I like being emotionally close to you."

He bit his lip. "I'm not much for being fucked either. I don't hate the sensation, but sometimes I feel as if people are forgetting me or using me."

That was one of Mindy's big things. He enjoyed being the center of attention, but it was because he didn't want to be overlooked. The other times we'd had sex came to mind—his loud cries, his holding me close, his calling my name and seeking my gaze. It was more than that. He was always touching me, pulling me close, huffing me, and always needing me. Mindy craved connection, and sex was the ultimate form of connection.

"Sex is about intimacy for me; the rest is trappings," he said.

"I don't care if you're boring, Mindy. I don't. I want to try things, but it will always be about us being together, not the fucking alone. If you ever want me to fuck you," I whispered, "I won't forget you or use you. You are not a toy or a thing for pleasure. You are my boyfriend, my mate, my Serlotminden and I love you."

He beamed, then pressed his mouth to mine. I groaned into his kiss. Mindy said against my lips, "We'll try things. Lots of things. Whatever you want... as long as I don't hate doing it. I do have some limits."

"Which is good. I do too." I didn't know what they all were, but I sure as hell knew I had them. "I don't like blood."

"Me either."

Off to a great start. "I don't want you to put anything inside my dick." I'd read about sounding in a smut book once, and it freaked me the fuck out.

"I don't mind that, but we do not have to."

"I don't want to be punished or disciplined."

"I don't want to do that or have it done to me either."

"Good." I tried to sort through the random porn things I'd seen or read, but I was fairly vanilla all things considered. "I'm not super flexible."

"I am. You can fold or tie me into all sorts of positions."

"Good to know." Blanking, on what else to make off limits, I said, "I like you biting me." In response, he nipped my shoulder. "I like you spanking me, and I do want to tie you up."

"I'd like that."

I kissed his neck. "I like you teasing me with your tail."

He groaned.

Moving up, I licked his earlobe, and Mindy cried out. I smiled. "I love your noises and when you beg."

"Mate."

"I want to try shower sex."

"We can."

"I want to try floor sex."

"Easy. Very easy."

"I want you to fuck me from behind."

Serlotminden panted.

"I want you to fuck me against the wall while I cry and scream for you."

"Oh, Mate," he said, voice thick.

"I want to edge you until you're begging for release, then make you come so fucking hard."

His breath sharpened.

"I want to try everything."

"We can. Anything."

I kissed the cartilage to the tip of his ear, and he wiggled under me. I knew what he wanted, so I pressed a kiss to the tip, then gently tugged on the piercing. Mindy called my name and pulled me fully on top of him. I had to balance my weight on my knees to not hurt him. I licked the tip of his ear again, and his hands clamped onto my ass.

"But you know what I really want?" I asked, meeting his gaze.

"What, Flower?"

"You, Mindy. I want to spend my life with you. I want to see you get old. I want to hear you laugh. I want to be there when you cry. I want to hold your hand and know you're holding me back. I want to go to sleep, sated and safe, in your arms."

"Bartholomew," Serlotminden whined. "I love you."

His cock was hard again against me. I pumped him, keeping my eyes on his, and he whimpered. "Where's your lube, Honey?" I asked in a husky voice.

He pointed to the bedside table. I climbed off him to snag it. I peeked at his writhing tail, picturing it on my cock again. "Maybe we could..." I trailed off, gesturing to his tail.

Mindy said with a grin, "I want that as well." He reached for me, and I straddled him. "Lube my tail, Flower."

The lube was nice and slick, though it was cold. I rubbed it between my fingers before grabbing his tail and sliding along the length.

Serlotminden groaned, "Slowly. Go slow, my tail is very sensitive."

I hadn't known that. I made a mental note to explore it later. Right now, I was more interested in loving on Mindy. After I'd slicked his tail, I rubbed lube over our cocks and pumped them together. His tail curled around us, jerking us in slow movements. I bent over him and claimed his mouth.

The pace was slow and steady, but I didn't rush him. I gently thrusted my cock against his and into the tight clasp of his tail. Serlotminden groaned beneath me; I swallowed his pleasure and kept up my rhythm, determined to show him how much I loved him, how much I saw him, and how much we belonged together.

When my orgasm came, it wasn't mind-blowing, but it was potent, and most importantly, I felt so fucking connected to Serlotminden. His cum, my cum, our cum, indistinguishable, splattering our chests. His rough breath against my lips as he called my name. His tail eking every ounce of pleasure from us with steady movements. His warmth seeped into me and his scales scraped against me with every movement.

He held my cheeks. "I love you."

I kissed him and replied, "I love you too."

Chapter 40

EARTH IS A POSSIBILITY?

Bartholomew

After a few minutes, I stood and returned with a towel. Serlot-minden complained, but I cleaned him before tossing the soiled cloth aside. I stretched out against him, arm over his waist, and kissed his chest, nose wrinkling. He smelled like cum. He'd have to take a shower to get rid of it, but I wasn't going to worry about it at the moment.

My fingers trailed over him as I asked, "Will we be able to get Vince?"

"Dontilvynsan has assured me that he is close to ending the negotiations for Vince and the rest of the humans. I can go to the planet myself and retrieve him."

I bit his chest, his scales hard against my teeth. "Not alone. I will go with you."

"Of course. We belong together."

I hid a smile against his chest. "We should probably also bring a guard or your brothers."

"I doubt they will leave me alone, even if I requested it."

That I understood. "What happens after we get Vince? We haven't really talked about it. Are we going back to your planet? Where do you live?"

He stroked my back. "I live on my home planet, Tamkolvanlo-knol, but I'm not there often. I race shuttles and I'm a diplomat. I travel a good portion of the time."

Well, that would be interesting.

"But we don't have to," he said in a rush. "I can and will give it up for you."

My lips closed around his nipple, licking it, and he jerked before grunting in pain. I rested a hand on his stomach to keep him in place. "I don't want you to sacrifice anything for me. I don't mind traveling if I'm with you. It will be exciting. But I don't know if Vince will like doing that. Can he live on your planet?"

"Certainly, or we'll take him back to Earth."

I stiffened. Home. *Earth*. "We can go back?"

Serlotminden tensed, arm tight around me. Too late, I heard my words. *We*. I had promised to stay, but I hadn't realized Earth was a possibility; that seeing my family again was a possibility.

He gripped me so tight that his claws dimpled my skin. "You can go home. I will take you."

"Mindy," I started.

"I will, but I don't want to. I know it's not fair, but I need you, Bartholomew, forever. I can't breathe without you. The very thought of separating from you guts me." He took a deep breath. "But I will. There are things you have to know first. Your memory would be erased. You wouldn't know me or anything that happened while you were off Earth. I can't go with you. The Coalition won't allow it, and from what I understand of your planet, I wouldn't fit in."

If Serlotminden came to Earth, he'd have to hide. How could I do that to him? I couldn't. It wouldn't be right nor would I enjoy it. We could never be open together.

I stared at him, and he watched me with wide eyes as he took deep breaths. His hold remained like a vice around me and his tail was coiled about my leg. I kissed his chest. I'd promised him to stay. I loved him, and the thought of being apart from him... My mind refused to conjure it. My family probably thought I was dead at this point, anyway. Not that I missed them any less. I wanted my moms to meet Serlotminden—they would love him. Marie and Joy would tease me horribly about Mindy, but they'd like him too.

Rolling on top of him, I tried to put all my weight on my elbows and knees, so I didn't hurt him. His hands moved to my hips, gripping me and making it difficult to not squash him. I pressed my lips to his firmly in a claiming kiss that broke no argument of who he belonged to.

"You need to know something, Serlotminden."

"Yes?"

"I love you."

"I know that."

"I am never going to leave you. Do you understand? You are mine, and I'm keeping you."

A wide smile stretched over his lips. "Thank you."

I scoffed. "You say that now. Wait until I'm old and cranky, and you're desperate to get away."

"That will never happen."

I captured his mouth, sucking his tongue, but my thoughts went back to Earth. My family was there. My moms. My sisters. I was leaving them behind. How was that fair to them? They probably thought I was dead, but that didn't mean they wouldn't like to know I wasn't.

Serlotminden groaned against my mouth. I buried my fingers in his hair. How could I leave him? Attacking his mouth, I knew I couldn't. He was mine, and that was all there was to it.

Chapter 41

TEAM HUMAN: FIRST OFFICIAL MEETING

Bartholomew

I sat on the mossy floor, staring at Seth and Caleb who were on the couch, equally silent. Serlotminden had arranged for us to hang out, and I wasn't sure why. I mean, they both seemed nice from the limited amount of time I'd interacted with them, but that didn't mean we had to awkwardly stare at each other. Seth was sweating, his round face red, and he wore a thick black hoodie, which couldn't be helping. Caleb clutched his cane, wings out and tail wiggling.

"So you were dead," I said, then immediately wanted to smack myself. Who led with that? Apparently I did.

Caleb, thank god, didn't seem upset. "Yep. I died falling down a staircase, then wandered around, found Seth, got stuck in a body, and now I'm here. It's been a whirlwind. Well, a twenty-three-years-dead whirlwind, but sure."

"Sounds interesting." I glanced at Seth, who tugged on the front of his sweater. Caleb patted Seth's arm, and he smiled tensely. I asked Seth, "Kal took you?"

"This giant crystal showed we were soulmates, and he abducted me."

I nodded. Mindy had mentioned something about a crystal that tested people's soul types and also paired mates. I supposed at some point I would be soul tested, and I wasn't sure how I felt about it. On one hand, who the fuck cared what type of soul I had? On the other hand, it might be fun to know.

"It's sort of their religion," Caleb explained, banging his cane on the floor rapidly as his tail wiggled. "It's difficult to explain, but they revere the crystal. Big C crystal, FYI."

"Good to know."

"It can find soulmates and ties people together," he continued. "Like genetically." Caleb gestured to himself and Seth. "We're bound to Kal and Fyn. We can't be too far away from our mates. The Crystal linked us. The bond also allows us to speak telepathically, though that doesn't work with every species. Apparently, we're more compatible than most."

"Hmm." That was interesting. Invisible alien chains. Who knew? "Well," I said, changing the subject, "Mindy abducted me, trying to rescue me. It wasn't the best start for us."

Seth nodded again. He took a peek at the tablet next to him, and I felt like the worst host in the world. I was boring him. But then again, I knew very little about either of them.

"Don't worry," Caleb commented. "He's checking on the baby."

"You have a kid?" Caleb had mentioned a baby in the medbay, but I hadn't put two and two together that they were talking about Seth's baby.

"Not yet," Seth said with a soft smile. He slid off the couch and held out the tablet. A tube with green liquid on the display appeared. A tiny fish with legs twitched. Alien? Animal? I had no fucking clue.

"What am I looking at?"

He chuckled. "Mine and Kal's kid. They're still little."

My gaze whipped back to the fetus. "You and Kal, like genetically?"

"Yeah. Same-sex couples can have biological kids here."

"I was more questioning the inter-species thing," I remarked.

Seth flushed, and Caleb chuckled before commenting, "Some species are compatible to reproduce, and others are not. Humans and drakcol are extremely compatible."

"Humans and drakcol," I muttered, touching the screen while my heart pounded loud enough to drown out all the other sounds. It was possible for Serlotminden and me to have a baby if we wanted, which I did. I'd always wanted one. Adoption had always been the plan, and we could do that as well. But I wanted to look at a baby and see Mindy. We could do both, multiple times. I'd always hoped to have a large family. A vision of a horde of half-drakcol and full drakcol kids surrounding me and Mindy made my pulse quicken.

Fuck, I wanted that.

"Was it hard?" I asked.

"No," Seth replied. "They took samples of... you know."

I rolled my eyes. Semen. It was not a hard word.

"Then spliced them together. I don't know exactly how it works, but after some testing, we had a viable fetus within a couple of weeks."

"I want one." My fingers traced the screen.

"No," Caleb said with a dramatic flair. "Be like me and Fyn, the cool uncles."

"You can be a cool uncle to our kids," I remarked. I almost pictured a tiny baby with his purple scales and green eyes as well as my black curls. "I think we'll wait, though." Mindy and I hadn't been together very long, and I needed more time with him when it was us alone.

Seth shrugged. "There's no rush. Me and Kal have been together for three years. I didn't even want kids at first, but he did. Now," he took the tablet back, "I can't wait."

"You have a cat?" I asked, grasping for something to say.

"You'll never meet her," Caleb cautioned.

"Why not?"

Seth frowned at Caleb. "You're making me sound like a stingy asshole. Lucy's shy. She doesn't like new people. I'm not hiding her away."

"Ah."

"But you can get a cat if you want," he offered.

Cats were not my thing, and I was fairly certain Pookie would eat a cat. Not that I was going to tell Seth that. I glanced at Pookie, yet again. I'd had to turn up the heat in the living room so we didn't freeze, but we still didn't know if Pookie would be safe living at a higher temperature. So far she seemed fine, but I planned to keep a close eye on her. Currently, she was curled up in her nest, a beheaded plushie in between her front legs, and her snout twitched with her dreams.

Refocusing on Seth, I said, "That's cool."

Silence descended again.

"So we're the humans," I said.

"Team Human," Caleb announced, bouncing, then he froze with a grimace.

"You okay?"

"Yeah, I sometimes forget that this body doesn't like sudden movements. Yolkeltod, this body, was in an accident with his sister Tinlorray before me. Oh, Tinlorray. Shit. I forgot to message her. She's going to be worried and angry. I can't believe I forgot. We're sort of siblings. I mean my body is her brother. I'm not, but I am, you know."

That sounded very confusing, so I nodded along as Seth watched his baby, smiling. My life had suddenly gotten very odd.

"So Team Human?"

"Yep," Caleb said. "Seth's the leader."

"That makes sense."

"How?" Seth asked, dropping the tablet. "How? Explain it to me like I'm five. In what world am I a good choice?"

I chuckled, but Caleb replied, "You are. Besides, the Maykians think you're the supreme leader."

"Which is your fault."

"So? We're not dead. It's a win. Not dying is always a win. You have to agree with that."

"But lying has a bad habit of biting me in the ass, like the cats."

"I can't believe I'm allergic to Lucy. It's not fair. I want a cat, but the doctors and Fyn are concerned about me taking allergy meds all the time with my other health problems."

"I'm allergic to all this pollen," I remarked. Klars had given me an injection to help, and it did, but I still got sniffly and sneezed more than I liked. Damn plants everywhere.

"That does suck," Seth commented.

"But you have a pet," Caleb said. "I want one so bad, but after the cat incident, Fyn is worried. He likes to worry about me. A lot. I swear it's a favorite pastime for drakcol and their mates."

Seth nodded.

"Mindy does that too."

"Not shocking," Caleb said. "But I want a squishy pet, and Lucy doesn't like me, even if I could squish her."

"Pookie does."

Caleb grinned, and Seth's ruddy face lost all color; he peeked over his shoulder, but she hadn't moved from her nest.

"Do drakcol drink?" I asked, needing some kind of fortification, not to mention a subject change before Seth fled in terror. My world had altered so suddenly over the last couple years. First abducted, then sold, then kidnapped, then stranded, and now in an instant family. Drinking seemed like a good idea. Besides, friends did that, drinking and playing cards. "Do you have cards too?"

"Yes to both," Seth said. "You've got to try this drink."

Caleb laughed. "You asked for it."

I was probably about to get very drunk, but I didn't care. This was my new family, my brothers-in-law, and I wanted to get along with them. Though as Seth walked to the dispenser, talking, my thoughts went back to my moms and sisters. I missed them. When I was on Xome, I'd never thought about them, let alone missed them. Now, it was like I couldn't go two seconds without thinking about them.

What was wrong with me?

"Oh," Seth said, startling me. "You might have to touch the Crystal."

"For soul testing, right? But it's like a mate finder, isn't it? I already have Serlotminden."

Caleb laughed. "Mate finder? God, you're funny. No, remember it's their religion, and it's what stuck me in this body, by the way. And soul testing isn't done by touching the Crystal unless you're part of the royal family. Anyway, humans are special regarding the Crystal."

"What do you mean?"

"The Crystal can talk to us," Seth said, putting a pitcher of blood-red liquid and some cups down before grabbing a deck of playing cards and poker chips. "It doesn't talk to the drakcol, but it does to us."

A talking rock. This place got better and better. "So I have to touch it?"

"Probably," Seth said, pouring a drink. "You'll be soul tested for sure, either way."

"Don't worry," Caleb said. "The Ranks, they're the Crystal's priests and priestesses, are obsessed with Seth. They'll leave you alone."

Seth flushed. "They're not."

Caleb laughed. "They are. He's *chosen*."

My eyebrows lifted, and Seth's flush deepened. I wanted to poke his cheeks, but somehow I doubted he'd enjoy it, because, I don't know, he was a full grown man, but god, I had the urge.

"Stop telling people that," Seth said. "I was the first human to touch it. That's it."

"Technically," Caleb said, "but it doesn't matter. It likes you best. Because you're *chosen*."

Seth glared at him, and I swallowed a laugh. So, Team Human with an ex-human and a chosen one. Life had certainly gotten weird.

Serlotminden

"What do you mean he will have to touch it?" I demanded.

Dontilvynsan lifted his eyebrows, and Kalvoxrencol laughed. Zoltilvoxfyn repeated calmly, "The Ranks have already sent a request to have Bartholomew appeal to the Crystal."

"I am his mate," I growled. "I will not surrender him."

"No one is asking you to, Serlotminden," Dontilvynsan said. "They wish to see if the Crystal will speak to him as well."

"But if he appeals, it will show him his mate," I forced out, trying to stay calm as my tail flicked. "He is too old for a simple soul testing." Most drakcol were soul tested with a piece of crystal that connects to the true Crystal, but not us royals. We touched the actual Crystal in a ceremony when we were ten. "What if the Crystal shows him his soulmate and it is not me?"

"You don't know that will happen," Zoltilvoxfyn said.

"And you don't know it will not happen," I snapped. "He is mine."

"I'm with you," Kalvoxrencol said. "Though you won't be Crystal-bound mates."

"So?" I had no interest in that. Bartholomew was all I desired.

He didn't look offended in the slightest and smirked.

Annoyed, I said, "No matter what, they'll stalk Seth."

His smile disappeared.

The Ranks had hounded Seth because of his soul. He was the darkest red, therefore the purest, warrior soul in recorded history. Caleb was a blue seeker soul with a tinge of spiritual white, which was perfectly fine and average, but drakcol venerated warrior souls. The purest warrior soul, mixed with the Crystal calling him chosen, had made the Ranks nearly feral for him. Kalvoxrencol had kept the anxious, shy Seth away from them to the best of his ability.

"I'm on your side," he protested.

"My apologies," I replied. Everyone felt like a threat to me and mine at this exact moment.

Dontilvynsan commented, "You are very desperate to root your Bartholomew here. Binding him to Seth and Caleb. Trying to make us like him. I thought you would use the Crystal to force him to stay."

I looked at the floor, soul pounding and tail thrashing. Bartholomew had chosen me, but I sensed his hesitation. His expression when he'd learned he could return to Earth haunted me. The longing, the hope, the utter desire. He wished to go home, and I needed him to stay. I was asking him to remain with me and give up his life on Earth, to give up that longing, to give up his family.

"If he loves you, he will stay," Dontilvynsan said. "I know you love him. I have felt it. I have experienced your grief at the thought of him being gone, but you cannot force or trick him, Speedy. In the end, it is Bartholomew's choice."

Kalvoxrencol moved to my side and pulled me closer, his forehead resting on mine. "I know the urge. Trust me. I felt the same with Seth, wanting to tie him to me. But trust your Bartholomew. I didn't trust Seth for a very long time, and I almost lost him. Don't make the same mistake."

I pressed against my brother. "He told me he would stay, but I think he wants to go home with Vince."

"The human that was with him?" Dontilvynsan asked.

"Yes."

Kalvoxrencol hooked an arm around my waist, holding me, and I relished it. He hadn't used to be as affectionate with us as he was now. Seth had helped that. I wanted to see how Bartholomew and I would change and grow together. I loved him. I needed him. The thought of him abandoning me stole the very breath from my lungs.

"Talk to him," Zoltilvoxfyn advised. "And trust him. If he says he's going to stay, believe him."

My thoughts kept straying to my mate in our room. I needed to hold him to make sure he was alright; that he was here. I smiled and gave all the right answers, but I wasn't paying the slightest attention.

Dontilvynsan knew. Of course he knew. He stole my thoughts right from my brain. I hated his inner fire so *damn* much. The moment the thought entered my brain, guilt swamped me, and I peeked at my older brother. He gave me a gentle smile as his tail curled around mine. He never got mad about it. Not ever. All of us had hated his inner fire over the cycles, but he had never once spoken against it. No matter what we thought of it.

Dontilvynsan had always planned to join the navy, but when his inner fire presented itself, our parents had been nervous. He could push calm into people, but he could also push in every emotion or memory he'd stolen over the cycles. He had the potential to be turned into a lethal weapon.

Thankfully, Dontilvynsan's mind had turned toward science. He oversaw several science projects, including the most important—the Immortal Planet. Though I didn't know if the military had ever ordered him to do things he hadn't wanted to do. I'd never asked, and he never said.

After a bit, Caleb pinged Zoltilvoxfyn on his touchstone. Apparently, Seth was drunk. Caleb didn't drink, because of his health problems, but Seth enjoyed alcohol frequently with his close friends, Wyn and Urgg.

Kalvoxrencol and Zoltilvoxfyn rushed out, leaving me and Dontilvynsan alone.

Dontilvynsan patted my cheek. "Go see your mate. I'm sorry you didn't get to ask Pest all the sex questions you wanted to."

Kalvoxrencol was the only one of us who had intimate knowledge of human sex, and as a curiosity in the past, I'd bombarded him with questions about his sex life. Pest was more than happy to share. Now, I required more technical information; I didn't want to hurt my mate.

"I will ask him tomorrow."

"While Seth is vomiting?"

I chuckled. "Pest's little mate is something."

He kissed my temple, and I was a tad surprised. Dontilvynsan did not touch us often, because of his inner fire. "So is yours, and I shall like him as well as my other mate-siblings."

"Thank you." And I truly meant it. I hoped for Bartholomew to belong to my family. I knew he loved his own family, so I didn't want him to feel isolated from those most important to me. Also, as Dontilvynsan had noted, I was desperate for him to connect and place roots to keep him here.

"Talk to him," Dontilvynsan said, "and leave before Seth and Kalvoxrencol return. You don't want to watch him puke."

Very true. No one wanted that.

Chapter 42

HUSBANDS?

Serlotminden

When I returned to me and mine's quarters, the room was in chaos. Seth was clinging to Kalvoxrencol, laughing incoherently. Caleb was urging him on, all while Zoltilvoxfyn was attempting to stop him. My Bartholomew was smirking at the situation from where he leaned against the wall.

The sight of him was enough to stir my instincts. I rushed to my mate and kissed him. He started, and I pulled back. We hadn't discussed public affection. When we discussed permissions the first time, we had been alone. No one else to worry about. The second time, I'd forgotten.

Bartholomew pressed his lips against mine and hauled me flush against him. He squeezed my butt, and I groaned, licking his mouth. He opened without hesitation. My cock started to stiffen and pressed against his stomach as his tongue slowly danced with mine.

He chuckled, then nibbled on my bottom lip, teeth catching on my ring. "Kick everyone out so we can fuck."

I was tempted to use my feet to physically force everyone out of our quarters, even though I knew that wasn't what he meant. He slipped out of my arms and went to the bedroom.

"Out," I ordered everyone.

Caleb burst into laughter and slung his arms around Zoltilvoxfyn's waist. "They want *alone* time. What, oh, what will they be doing?"

Zoltilvoxfyn smiled at his mate, tail curling around his leg. His eyes dipped. "He seems quite excited. I could take a guess if you'd like, Little Soul."

Caleb laughed, clinging to my brother. "I like this game. We should play it more often."

I growled. Normally, I was entertained by their antics and joined in, but now, every moment away from Bartholomew felt like an eternity.

Kalvoxrencol was far too busy with a drunk Seth to add his own teasing remarks. Seth swayed and sputtered something about not being tired while my brother argued that he was indeed exhausted.

Zoltilvoxfyn raised his eyebrows, and I growled again, motioning to the door. Why weren't they leaving? Caleb gave an exaggerated yawn, and Zoltilvoxfyn smirked. They took their time to leave, dragging the moment out to irritate me. When they finally stepped into the doorway, Caleb grabbed Zoltilvoxfyn's butt, which made me huff. Caleb had a desire to publicly claim Zoltilvoxfyn, and he certainly did it frequently.

Kalvoxrencol stepped in front of me, blocking the sight; Seth was cradled in his arms, sleeping. "I left some things for you over there."

"What?"

"Protection for Bartholomew so you can prepare him, and the lubrication that I've found works the best."

My soul pounded at the thought of being intimate with my mate, but at the same time, I felt a tinge of embarrassment that my little brother had to help me with my sex life. While drakcol had no shame in regard to sex and my brothers and I were very open about our activities, I didn't enjoy Kalvoxrencol having to assist me. Yet I appreciated it.

"Thank you."

He nudged me with his tail. "Happy to help. Now, I need to get my husband to our quarters."

My gaze flicked to the gold band he wore. It was something humans did. Caleb didn't care for the tradition, so he had Zoltilvoxfyn hadn't exchanged rings, nor did they call each other husband. But perhaps Bartholomew wanted to. We could be husbands.

I grinned. I liked the thought of that. We would be mates and husbands—bound together even tighter.

Kalvoxrencol departed with his mate, and I collected the items he left behind before limping into my bedroom.

We hadn't fucked yet, and I yearned to be inside of Teddy so bad. Since my injury, we hadn't done more than sucking or frotting, because I was in too much pain. But in the last few days, I'd recovered enough that I was ready for more.

I froze in the doorway, soul leaping. Bartholomew was stretched out on the bed, naked. My cock swelled in a hurry, making me dizzy. I'd seen him without clothes many times, but each time burned me like it was the first.

He lifted his arms above his head and arched with a low groan. I chewed on my lip, my teeth catching on my piercing. He was so lovely. I had never seen anything more attractive than my naked mate, on my bed, waiting for me.

Bartholomew frowned. "I don't have my glasses on, so either you are stunned speechless or this is doing nothing for you and I'm making a fool of myself."

I sprang forward. "You are gorgeous." I crawled on top of him and captured his mouth. He grabbed my butt as he played with my lip ring, making me growl. My tail whipped and my wings sprawled. One of his hands moved tentatively over one cheek to the base of my spine where my tail began.

He grabbed it, and I moaned into his mouth. He caressed the delicate scales at the base, and I hissed, shards of pleasure racing up my spine. Bartholomew grinned and caught my lips again as he continued to play with my tail.

"I need you, Mate." My cock was hard and dripping pre-seed in my undershorts.

"Sounds good," he said against my lips, shoving my trousers down a tinge to caress the bare scales on my butt.

"I want to enter you."

"I figured that's what you meant." He whispered in my ear, his breath hot and tainted with alcohol, "I got ready for you while you kicked everyone out."

A moan ripped out of me, and I kissed his cheek before stripping off my trousers and undershorts. I straddled him and ripped my shirt off. His hands immediately roamed my chest, tracing my healing injuries, which made me whimper. My skin was so sensitive. He traced and explored my chest before reaching one of my nipples, rolling it between his fingers. I bit my lips, rocking against him to seek friction for my needy cock. In no time at all, something started to harden beneath me. I smirked. As much as I craved my mate, he desired me just as much, and there was something so attractive about that.

Bartholomew moaned, gripping my hips and dragging me harder onto him, so his cock slid against my perineum and balls. "Now," he ordered. "Now, Honey. I want you inside of me."

"Not yet. I must get you primed."

When he frowned, I kissed the cute divot between his eyebrows. Bartholomew protested as I shifted off him, but I didn't let it deter me. I had to take care of him to ensure I didn't injure him. I put everything I needed within reach. Staring at the neat line, I swallowed as nerves skittered down my spine.

What if I hurt him?

This was Bartholomew's first time, and my first time with a human. Humans were so fragile, and he was more so than normal. He was still underweight and slight, frail from his lack of nutrition. I didn't want to damage him.

Bartholomew reached for me, and I couldn't resist. He kissed me. His lips were soft on mine. Undemanding. Unhurried. He cupped my cheeks, thumbs sliding over me. "Stop worrying and fuck me."

I nuzzled his palm. "I'm scared of hurting you."

"You won't. I'll tell you if you do. I promise." When I didn't respond, Bartholomew arched and kissed my lips. "We don't have to, Honey. If you need more time, we can wait. Remember, it's only good if we both enjoy it."

I lay on top of him, and he held me tight. Bartholomew pressed gentle kisses to my ear, his tongue flicking out to play with my earrings. "I'm here," he whispered. "Sex or not. I'm here."

It wasn't that I didn't want to, but I was terrified of doing something wrong. I'd had a small taste of what life would be like without him, and I never wanted to go back. Also, my very cells revolted at the idea of causing my mate pain. I couldn't do that.

He rocked beneath me, and our cocks brushed, sending sensations through my limbs. I gasped, hips canting toward him instinctually. He ground against me, rubbing, chasing the perfect friction.

Bartholomew moaned. "Honey. Oh, fuck, that's nice. So nice. Don't stop."

I met him thrust for thrust, dragging our cocks against each other. I bit my lip, chest rumbling. Bartholomew trailed his fingers over my back and sides. When he hit my scent glands, I lurched, moaning. He smiled against my cheek.

"Right there, huh?"

"Yes, Flower. More. Please."

His fingers massaged the spots as we gently rutted against each other. Bartholomew planted kisses over my cheeks, eyes, and the tip of my nose. "You won't hurt me, Mindy. I need this and you. I want to feel you inside of me. I want to feel that connection with you. And I'm pretty sure you do as well."

"I love you so much."

"I know," Bartholomew said, catching my chin and forcing me to look at him. "I know, Honey."

He was so calm—he was always so calm, my Bartholomew, even now. I was terrified of injuring him, and he just wanted me.

I sealed a kiss to his lips, tracing them with my tongue. He arched beneath me and clutched my back, fingers raking over me. I groaned when his mouth opened and his tongue twisted around mine.

Every cry, moan, and whimper I uttered was swallowed by him while his hands dragged over me. My lips broke from his and moved to the column of his neck. I licked the tight tendons, nibbling. I loved leaving little marks all over him—subtle claims that he belonged to someone, to me. I sucked and bit as Bartholomew stroked my back and brushed his fingers through my long hair. Soft whispers of encouragement came from his lips and made me writhe with happiness.

My mate was taking care of me.

I nuzzled the hair on his chest. I loved it. We didn't have body hair, and I was fascinated with his. I dragged my nose through the strands. "You are so perfect."

Bartholomew chuckled. "I'm glad you think so."

I kissed the sparse hair, dragging my tongue over it, and savored the taste of him. My mate. Taking one of his nipples into my mouth, I sucked.

"Mindy," he called, breathless.

My tongue laved over the nub, and he grunted, hips arching. His cock wanted attention. I smiled, sucking on him softly. I made sure to take it slow. My mate had never been with someone else, and this was all new. This needed to be good for him. The best.

I brushed my fingers through the wetness gathering on his cock, spreading it before I pumped his shaft from base to tip. He whimpered. I shifted to his other nipple, giving it the same treatment as the first as I stroked him. My own cock was rock hard. My breath was rough and needy, but I was going to make this amazing. Bartholomew deserved the best, and I planned to give it to him.

I licked down his chest and stomach. My tongue circled his navel, and he gave a breathless moan. A line of hair went from right below his navel to the patch of hair above his cock and I dragged my tongue over it, but he didn't cry out. Curious. I went back up, kissing. Latching onto his navel, I licked and bit the skin.

His breath turned rougher the more I attacked it. Bartholomew fisted my hair, panting, and his hips canted, cock searching for friction. I grinned as I licked his navel. My mate cried out. I'd found something he liked—clearly a lot. I tucked that knowledge away for future use and continued to pay particular attention to it, licking, sucking, nuzzling, until he writhed.

"Honey," he said, not quite begging but close. His hips were bucking beneath me.

Dragging my tongue over the line of hair to his navel, I asked, "What?"

"Mindy. I need more."

And I was happy to provide him with that. I pressed gentle kisses to the sharp bones of his hips. "I will make you feel amazing."

Bartholomew panted and shakily brushed my hair behind my ear. "You always do." I opened my mouth to protest, but he covered my lips. "I mean it, Serlotminden. I have never been this happy in my life. Ever. I want to stay with you for the rest of my life. I want to have kids with you one day. I want to grow old looking into your eyes. I love you, Serlotminden."

Tears gathered. "Do you mean it?"

"I do."

I buried my face against his stomach. "I love you, Mate. I love you so much."

"I know. Now, make me feel good."

I laughed, kissing his navel, which elicited a shudder from my mate. "I will."

I lifted his legs, and Bartholomew flushed a dark red. It was adorable. I wanted to press kisses to the color, but my cock leaked steadily between my legs, needing to be buried deep inside of him. I forced his legs up higher and out, exposing the tight pucker of his hole. I swallowed as my cock twitched. The urge to plunge inside of him was so strong, but not yet. I refused to hurt him.

"Hold yourself open for me, Mate."

His hands gripped the backs of his thighs and his chest heaved. I could roll him over, but I wanted to see his face in case I hurt him or did something he didn't like. Also, I didn't enjoy fucking from behind as much. It was like my partner could forget about me, and I hated that thought. Bartholomew wiggled his butt, clearly trying to entice me.

I settled in between his legs and rubbed his ball sack with my nose, inhaling. I loved the wiry hair and the musky scent coming off him. I nuzzled him some more, making Bartholomew groan.

"Stop teasing me," he demanded.

I laughed. He often made me beg. I was fairly certain he liked it. Once he was comfortable, I could easily imagine him riding my cock and making me beg for release. Bartholomew might want to be fucked, but he definitely liked being in control.

I nuzzled him again, then nipped his inner thigh. "Be patient."

Bartholomew opened his mouth to protest, but I licked his hole, and his words turned to a strangled moan. I smirked. I swiped my tongue over and over his hole, relaxing it. He wiggled and moved as quiet noises escaped his lips. He wasn't loud like I was, but I didn't care. Every noise was like music to my ears.

I shifted back, and he protested, "No. Come back."

I kissed his leg. "Hold on, Mate." I grabbed the thin glove made of a strong polymer. Nerves gathered in my gut again. Kalvoxrencol would never hurt Seth or allow me to do something dangerous to Bartholomew. I put some lubrication on one of my fingers and circled it around his hole, making him whimper. I increased my pressure slowly, not wanting to injure him, but he was so tight.

"Exhale and push, Mate," I said. As he bore down, I pushed my finger inside of him. Bartholomew took a sharp inhale. I froze. "Did I hurt you?"

"I'm fine, Honey. It's just a different feeling."

I sucked the tip of his cock into my mouth and laved my tongue over it, prodding the slit for the bitter liquid of his pre-seed. Bartholomew moaned, canting toward my mouth. I sucked him, bobbing on his cock to distract from any possible discomfort. When he relaxed completely around me, I thrust my finger in and out of him, loosening the tight ring of muscle. I pressed another finger in, stretching him, and he jerked.

"Mate?"

"Give me a second."

"We can stop," I said, starting to pull out.

"No, I want this. Calm the fuck down. I'm not made of glass."

I blinked, pain prodding my soul from the sharp rebuke—something he almost never did.

"Shit. No, Mindy." He stroked my cheeks. "I'm sorry. I didn't mean to bite. I love you. I want this. I will tell you if it's too much. I promise."

I kissed his thumb. "My apologies. I'm scared of hurting you. I can't lose you again. You are the most important thing to me. I cannot live without you."

"You won't lose me," he said, rubbing my chin. "Stop worrying. Stop panicking. Just love me. Love me, Serlotminden. You are the only person I have ever desired. I only want you."

I kissed his inner thigh, then dragged my forehead over the skin to mark my mate with my scent.

I thrust my fingers in deeper, and he moaned. "God, right there."

"Here?" I asked, touching the same spot again.

"There."

I watched him in fascination as his eyes scrunched closed and his mouth hung open. I rubbed that spot, and he moaned. "*Ungh*, Mindy. Fuck, Mindy. That's so good."

I fucked him with my fingers nice and slow. Bartholomew kept calling my name, and I moved closer, unable to resist kissing him. His lips were harsh against mine. I swallowed his moans, tasting him. I pressed a third finger into him, and he winced. He took a single deep breath before he captured my mouth again.

The kiss grew wetter and hotter as I fucked him with my fingers, our tongues tangled, tasting, exploring. Finally, I slipped out of him, and Bartholomew protested, "No."

I chuckled. "Patience."

His response was a needy whine I quite enjoyed. I put a generous amount of lubricant on my cock. I guided his legs around my hips and hovered over him, rubbing my cock on his hole. His hips moved to chase me as I teased him.

I notched the crown of my cock to his hole. "Breathe, Mate."

I pushed. The muscles resisted my entry as Bartholomew winced. He was tight, even after everything. It took a couple breaths before the ring of muscles gave way and the tip slipped in. I groaned at the hot, tight sensation of his channel enveloping the crown of my cock. "Bartholomew, you're so tight."

He clutched my shoulders, panting.

"Are you alright?"

"Give me a second."

I kept my hips perfectly stationary and kissed his mouth open. I wanted to thrust into him, filling him, but I waited, loving on him. As he relaxed, I pushed in. I went slow, working my cock in and out of his hole until my hips were flush against him. I kissed his neck. "I'm inside you."

Bartholomew didn't answer. He groaned. It was a needy noise full of pleasure and demand for more, which I was more than happy to give him.

I pumped his cock until the tip glistened with pre-seed. Gently, I thrust in and out of him in long smooth strokes. Bartholomew had his arms wrapped around my neck and his legs held me close. My tail curled around his ankle, and my wings spread out wide, covering him, protecting him.

His harsh breath rushed over my lips, and his eyes stayed locked on mine. "Honey, it's so good."

I gave him a gentle kiss, panting. Every movement stoked my pleasure, building my orgasm. He was so tight and perfect. I'd never felt anything like it. Bartholomew rocked in time with me, making me plunge deeper inside of him.

"Yes," he called. "Right there, Honey. Right *fucking* there."

Gripping his butt, I angled to hit the spot that made him moan with every thrust. Bartholomew released a strangled cry; his eyes closed and his hands fisted in my hair. My moans twined his, mixing with the slick sound of my pounding into his hole and the slap of my scales onto his skin. His hole was clamping onto my cock, and he was holding me tight, screaming my name. I'd never felt so close to someone, and Bartholomew was not anyone—he was my mate.

I jerked his cock in time with my thrusts to increase his pleasure, and his grip tightened. His breath turned rough, making his chest heave. I licked a drop of sweat that slipped down his face, and a moan ripped out of me at the salty taste. I kissed his lips, panting.

"Flower," I breathed, and he grunted, eyes closed as he chased his pleasure. "Look at me, please," I begged.

His brown eyes popped open. "I'm right here, Mindy. Nowhere else. I'm with you. Just us." I thrust into him, and his legs squeezed me. "Oh, god," he cried. "Honey, I'm close."

Kissing his neck, I said, "Come with me."

He bit his lip, sweat dripping down his chest, as I continued to fuck him with powerful thrusts. I licked the beads, pumping his cock and pounding his hole, and all of sudden, his head arched back into the pillow, tendons of his neck tight, and a strangled cry ripped out his throat. Seed erupted from his cock, painting our stomachs while his hole clenched around me, and I fought my own release as I rocked into him, extending his pleasure, until I could hold back no longer. I slammed into his tight hole and my orgasm exploded. I bit his neck, hard, releasing a muffled shout.

My hips rocked in slow aftershocks as I panted against my mate. I licked the dark red mark on his neck. I hadn't broken the skin, but it had to have hurt. "Sorry, Mate. I bit you harder than I meant to."

He moaned, shaking.

I laughed, nuzzling his neck. When I began to soften inside of him, I snuggled as close as possible. I wanted to stay here, connected, but I knew I couldn't. Drakcol usually remained connected for quite some time before separating, but humans didn't, according to Kalvoxrencol—his Seth didn't enjoy it. I breathed in Bartholomew's scent, enjoying the closeness while I had it. He stroked my back, then traced my wings, pressing kisses to every part of me he could reach.

"That was amazing."

Happiness burned me. I nuzzled him one last time before withdrawing. Bartholomew winced when I started to pull out. "What?"

"Don't leave."

"I thought humans didn't do that."

"Stay for now. I like the feel," he whispered, a deep red.

I kissed the blush. He was so damn cute. Bartholomew. My perfect Bartholomew. I remained on top of him, sharing his air, until he kept wiggling. I had no idea if it was my cock buried in his hole or my weight. Either way, I couldn't remain. I slipped out, and my seed spilled out of him in an erotic display that I had to watch for a moment before laying beside him and draping an arm over his side as well as covering him with one of my wings.

Staring at him, I said, "I love you."

"I love you too."

I shifted until my forehead hit his. "Do you want to be husbands?"

"What?"

"Husbands. Kalvoxrencol and Seth are husbands. It's a human thing. Drakcol have mates, but humans have husbands, right?"

"You want to get married?"

The word translated odd. Mates. Bond. Unity. Property. But I was fairly positive it was the same thing as mates or similar enough, though humans did not mate for life as we did.

"I do."

"Well, I don't think there is an officiant in space."

Another word I didn't know, but NAID supplied the words priest and judge. While having NAID translate Bartholomew's words was lovely, it didn't fix everything. "Is that a no?" I asked, unable to keep the sadness from my voice. Being husbands did not matter in the end. We were mates. It shouldn't bother me, yet it did. I had to tie myself to Bartholomew, so everyone knew we belonged to each other.

He kissed me. "I want to be your husband."

I beamed. "I will buy you whatever ring you desire."

Bartholomew grunted and rolled on top of me. "Good." He kissed my neck as he rocked against me. His cock was hard again. "First, I want you to fuck me again."

If my smile grew any larger, my scales would shatter. "Happily."

Chapter 43

WAITING SUCKS ASS.

Bartholomew

There was no date yet for when we would retrieve Vince from Xome. I was anxious to get him immediately, because I knew exactly what he was suffering at the hands of Agk. If Agk had even kept him. I understood Seth's reasoning about not going in guns blazing and stealing them, even though that's what I wanted to do.

Vince and the rest of the humans needed saving, and I had to do it. I needed to be the one to do it, even though I couldn't really say I was doing much; at this point, it was all relying on Dontilvynsan's negotiating skills. Nonetheless, I'd never leave the other humans behind. But I didn't think Seth would either. He cared. He might not know them, but he cared, and he would use whatever power he had to save them. To save all of us that could be saved.

However, waiting for the green light was killing me. I paced a lot, which bothered Serlotminden, though he was doing his part to keep me distracted, usually with sex. I was more than fine with that.

I was currently on a high calorie diet as well as several nutritional supplements to help me gain weight, and more than that, become healthy again. My starvation and abuse on Xome had wreaked havoc on my body and mind. It was going to take time to heal, if I ever did. I wasn't certain if my mental wounds would ever heal, because ghosts continued to haunt me, telling me that I didn't deserve to breathe.

Mindy, now that the toxin had been neutralized, was healing in record time, at least by my standards. According to drakcol, it was rather typical.

A quiet moan came out of my lips when Serlotminden pressed kisses to my ass. He chuckled, then bit the fatty part on one cheek. I'd discovered that I loved to be bitten. Pain? No. Not my thing. Biting? Yes. Spanking? Yep. Really liked that. I also loved my belly button to be licked and sucked, and I had no idea why. I would've never thought of the belly button as an erogenous zone, but it somehow was on my body.

Mindy nipped and bit his way down my ass cheek, nuzzling as he went. He was obsessed with my hair, wherever it happened to be on my body. Currently, we were in a small war over my facial hair. It wasn't enough to be considered a beard or mustache, but Mindy loved the scruff and wanted it to remain. I wanted to shave it off, especially after Caleb had teased me about it.

Mindy pulled apart my cheeks and groaned. He kissed the crease to my gaping hole. "You are so beautiful."

I scoffed. He just liked seeing his cum leaking out of my ass. I gasped when his tongue swiped over me and he began to suck.

"What are you doing?" I asked, voice high-pitched.

Mindy dragged his scaled tongue over me, and I whimpered. Breath on my ass, he said, "Eating my seed out of your hole."

"Fuck," I ground out when his tongue delved inside of me. I fisted the sheets and felt my dick beginning to grow. "Fuck," I cried again as Mindy continued to eat me out.

It had only been a few days, but Mindy was definitely finding out what I liked and didn't like in regards to sex. I quickly decided I liked this. So did he, if his muffled cries and moans meant anything.

His breath rushed over my wet pucker, making me squirm, and Mindy nuzzled me. "I have you, Mate," he said. When I stilled, he asked, "Yes or no?"

He wanted to know whether I liked what he was doing or not. It had been a commonly repeated question of late, and I answered with ease, "Yes."

"Good. I like it too." Mindy didn't waste any time and delved back in.

Strangling the sheets, I gasped. I wasn't particularly loud when we had sex, but Mindy was trying his damndest to draw noise from me, and each time I got a bit louder. Though I had nothing on him—it sounded like I was murdering him whenever we fucked. It was a miracle security didn't break down our door on a regular basis.

Either our room was soundproof or people were used to his noise. That thought made me frown. Mindy had been with a lot of people before me, and I couldn't help but be jealous. More than that I was worried.

How did I compare to a horde of people I'd never met? Also, sex was rather new to me. Was Mindy going to get tired of my lack of experience?

Two fingers plunged into my ass, and I cried out, arching into him.

"That's it, Flower," he crooned. "Fuck yourself on my fingers."

Whimpering, I did. One of his fingers brushed my prostate, and I groaned, angling my hips upward to drive him in deeper.

"More," I ordered. Sometimes Mindy was far too gentle with me, and I had to demand what I wanted.

A third finger entered me, and I pushed back on them, head bowed, groaning. I was getting close, so damn close. My cock bounced in between my legs, untouched, but it didn't matter; Mindy's fingers were more than enough stimulation for me.

My breath sharpened as a low roiling pleasure began to gather and my muscles tightened. "Mindy," I groaned, voice low and full of need, as I impaled myself on his fingers, desperate.

His mouth latched onto the lower part of my spine, and he bit me. The sharp sting shoved me over the edge and my orgasm ripped through me, leaving me panting and lying in my own cum.

Serlotminden lay on top of me, licking and biting me. He lapped the beads of sweat coming off me, moaning. Carefully, he rolled me over, and I remained boneless beneath him. His hard cock pressed into me, pre-cum spreading over my skin.

"Want help with that?" I asked.

He grinned.

There was no way in hell my cock was rising to the occasion for the third time, at least not this soon, but I could suck him off.

Mindy grabbed my ankles and lifted my legs, and I frowned. What the hell was he doing? My ass was too sore for him to fuck me a second time.

At my expression, his grin widened. "Ah, my Flower, I love how little you know."

A sharp stab prodded my chest at his words. Yes, I was inexperienced, but that didn't matter. Sex did not define a person. Besides, I would learn.

He must have noticed because he bent forward, practically folding me in half, and kissed me. "I love you, and I adore discovering what you like, Bartholomew."

"Does it bother you that I can't match up to your previous lovers?"

"What match? You are my mate. They cannot compare to how I feel with you, Flower. You are everything. You hold my soul, and no one else."

I flushed. "You don't care?"

"No, and in many respects, I love the fact that I'm the only one who has ever seen you like this."

I frowned, but my face was on fire.

"Now, I wish to come all over you, marking you." Mindy straightened and rested my crossed ankles on his shoulder. My eyes widened when I realized what he intended to do. "Squeeze your legs together," he said.

Mindy thrusted, and his cock scraped along the skin of my inner thighs, eliciting the most delicious tingles. My dick twitched, but nothing. Still, I gasped in pleasure as his shaft dragged against my balls and taint.

Holding me securely, Mindy picked up speed, fucking my legs in a quick rhythm. His teeth sank into his bottom lip, and he worried at the ring there for a few moments before stilted cries broke out of him. His hair hung in a white cloud around his royal-purple scales, and his long golden earrings swayed in time with his thrusts.

Serlotminden was beautiful, and he was mine. All mine.

My fingers traced the corded muscles in his arms and the prominent veins.

"Flower," he panted.

"I'm right here. I will always be right here."

His hips stalled.

"Fuck me, Mindy. Take your pleasure."

He grew louder and louder, and I smirked. I'd learned fairly quickly that he loved to be talked to during sex. He hadn't added it to his permissions as one of the things he enjoyed, but I'd found it out anyway.

My own breath had turned jagged. "You are mine, Serlotminden."

He screamed and spurts of white cum painted me, covering my stomach, though a few globs landed on my chin.

I wiped it off and licked the substance off my fingers. The sweet and tangy flavor made me moan while Mindy growled, tackling me. Thankfully, he had the good sense to put my legs on the bed before he lay on top of me to scent mark me.

Chapter 44

YOU WON'T LEAVE ME, RIGHT?

Serlotminden

My arms were wrapped around my mate as warm water sluiced over us. I kept myself tucked against his neck as I breathed him in. I would never get tired of how good he smelled, and how much I loved my scent clinging to him. I kissed him, and Bartholomew cupped the back of my head, fingers burying into the wet strands.

He'd insisted on showering and changing the sheets, even though we weren't going to nap. I'd wanted to stay wrapped around him, covered in the scent of our sweat and seed, but he deemed it unhygienic and said we had to clean up, then take Pookie for a walk.

While I would never deny our daughter her due, I desired to spend more time with Bartholomew, alone, wrapped in each other's embrace. Soon enough there would be demands on our time and energy, but right now we were able to focus on us.

"Mindy," he said, "we're not actually getting clean. We're literally cuddling in the shower."

I did not see the problem with that. I liked the feel of my mate's soft skin against my scales as well as the warm water and humidity. Our quarters were being kept exceedingly cold, except for our bedroom, for Pookie. And I swore I felt the chill from it and the icy planet we'd left behind clinging to me. I needed all the warmth possible.

Bartholomew tried to back out of my embrace, making me groan and tighten my hold. I wanted to keep cuddling him. He cupped my cheeks, thumbs tracing my scales. I wished to fall into his brown eyes and get lost in them. I loved their depths and calmness that he exuded. So much of the time I felt as if I was racing back and forth, unable to slow down, but when I looked at him, I felt myself calm.

I didn't know what soul type my Bartholomew possessed, as he hadn't been tested and Dontilvynsan didn't have a member of the ranks or a spiritual soul on his ship to do so, and yet, I wondered. He could be fierce and protective like a warrior when he needed to be. He was knowledgeable like a seeker, though he did seem to lack their curiosity. He had assembled that tent with creativity and he had an ability to find use for random objects like a creator. And he was so calm and wise, like a spiritual.

Who was my mate at his core? I was curious to find out, though I had a sneaking suspicion. My Flower saw the heart of the matter and liked to observe. I truly wondered if he might be the first non-drakcol to possess a spiritual soul. It seemed unlikely, but when I stared into his calm eyes, I felt myself slow. Only one other person had ever been able to do that to me. Monqilcolnen, my cousin and the strongest spiritual soul ever tested in recorded history.

"What are you thinking?" Bartholomew asked.

"What soul type you have."

"Does it matter?"

"No, but I am curious."

He kissed me, and I held him tight, wanting to stay like this forever. I needed to embrace him and hold him close. No one else would ever compare to him, not ever, and yet I worried. I worried he'd be stolen from me, but more than that I worried that he would leave.

Bartholomew had promised to stay, but I perfectly recalled the longing in his expression when I mentioned returning to Earth. Bartholomew had agreed to be with me before he'd known that Earth was a possibility. I didn't want him to leave, though. I needed him, but more than that, I wanted him.

Need was important, but I chose Bartholomew. Out of every person I'd ever met, only one had made me think of forever, and I chose him. I wanted him. I liked him. I loved him.

My mate pulled back, frowning. "You are thinking very hard in there."

"What?"

"You didn't kiss me back. So either I have gotten very bad at this, or you are distracted. Which is it?"

I clutched him. We were wasting water, which Dontilvynsan would lecture me about when he saw my room's usage, and I was not paying attention to my mate, which was far worse. "I was distracted."

"About?"

"Can we not talk about it?" I refused to lie, but I wasn't ready to voice my worries yet.

"Of course." He kissed me again, his touch soft. "Sit and let me wash you."

I liked that idea very much. On the edge of the shower was a bench so we could sit as we scrubbed our wings. Bartholomew easily slid in the space between the bench and the wall and began to massage my scalp. As he washed my hair, then me, I relaxed into the familiar feel of my mate's fingers on me.

Bartholomew

As we stepped out of our room, I suppressed a shudder. It was fucking cold in the living room. But that wasn't the immediate issue. Pookie was running around, nose twitching as she snorted, dragging a ripped flag that Serlotminden had left out with the rest of his junk.

My boyfriend wasn't clean. Truly shocking. I rolled my eyes.

"Pookie," I groaned.

So she was a pig-rabbit-spider who operated on dog software. That was marvelous. She was a hunter, and like dogs, I guessed, enjoyed destroying random shit. It wasn't her fault. Mindy had left all his crap everywhere, and she had no toys left from her most recent destructive binge—not to mention, we hadn't walked her enough.

Caleb had been helping by taking her out. He adored her and wanted one of his own. Fyn had given a quick and immediate no. They were not going to ask Don to violate Maykian space a third time so Caleb could get a pet.

In truth, we probably shouldn't have taken Pookie. While she'd domesticated rather easily, we didn't know much about her or her needs. But it would've killed me to leave her on the planet; I was already so attached to her.

"We need to get her some more toys," I commented as Mindy, somewhat stiffly, bent at the waist to pick up some of the fabric.

"Agreed. I'll put all of this away, though."

I snagged Pookie and cuddled her close while she snorted into my neck. I kissed her snout, then set her down to help Mindy. Between the two of us we had the room in decent shape in no time. Then Mindy scrolled through something on his tablet, probably toys.

He'd promised to give me a tablet, and he'd already given me a touchstone—a round stone that pulsed light blue in the center. It was connected to NAID, and it allowed me to speak to anyone. I was waiting to be added to the Drakcon system, but this way, I could talk to Seth or Caleb. Or Mindy, if we ever left each other's side.

"There," he said. "I'm having some toys synthesized for her."

"Will it take long?"

"No. They're probably in our dispenser by now."

I peered at the terminal near the table, and yep, there were several stuffed toys of odd creatures and a few ropes. It was so nice not having to randomly go to the store.

I frowned at Mindy.

"What?"

"You made it sound onerous the last time you got her toys," I commented. "I distinctly remember rewarding you." I'd given him a blowjob, not that it had taken much to convince me; I liked sucking Mindy off.

He played with his lip ring, not meeting my gaze.

"You are horrible," I teased. "Come on, Pookie, let's leave the liar behind."

"No," Mindy cried, and I paused at the actual fear in his voice.

Slinging my arms over his shoulders, I kissed him. "You know I'm joking, right?"

"Of course."

From the way his tail strangled my ankle and his arms were like iron bars around my waist, I was fairly positive he hadn't known. "Let's all go together, Honey."

Taking Pookie out was always an interesting experience. People tended to shy away from her as she scurried on walls and sometimes the vines creeping over the ceiling. She'd never harmed anyone, but she was exuberant in her affection and liked everyone. And I meant everyone. Hopefully, we wouldn't bump into Seth. He was mortally terrified of her after the incident where she'd flung herself at him.

I took a single step outside and sneezed. My eyes started to itch and my nose began to run almost instantly. Pollen might not bother the drakcol, but it sure as hell bothered me.

"Hold on." I slipped back into the room; I'd forgotten my medicine. I held the preloaded injector with a frown. I had to jab it into my arm, hold it for twenty seconds, and done. However, it fucking grossed me out. Thankfully, the lone plant in our apartment was the floor. It was a moss of some type and didn't bother my allergies.

Scaled fingers took it from me, and Serlotminden tugged me close. "Let me, Mate."

He placed it against my bicep and pushed the plunger. I jolted, even though it didn't hurt that bad. In time, I'd get used to it.

Mindy growled low in his throat, chest rumbling. He nuzzled me, and I pressed into him. He hated hurting me, but there was so much damn pollen, and I was so highly allergic to the plants that Klars worried my throat would swell to the point it would stop my breathing.

After Mindy pulled the injector away, he stared at my arm with rapt attention, and I knew it was because his instinct demanded he lick the tiny puncture. I lifted my shoulder in invitation, and he grabbed my arm, fingers easily circling it, and licked me.

I swallowed at the feel of his scaled tongue dragging over my skin, and Mindy groaned lewdly. I swore he did this on purpose. Whether true or not, we wouldn't be fucking again. I doubted I could get hard, and Pookie needed a walk.

Once he was satisfied the tiny injection site was clean, he snagged my hand. Pookie bolted out, snorting and squealing with happiness. The drakcol who had gotten used to her calmly moved aside; everyone else skittered away with gasps as she raced on the wall, tongue lolling.

Pookie never left our sight, though that made her backtrack a few times, which in my opinion wasn't a bad thing, because she needed all the exercise she could get to burn her excess energy. I kept my hand within Serlotminden's grasp, and his tail was coiled around my ankle as we wandered without a destination.

Pookie wasn't the only one who needed exercise. Klars had lectured me about how important it was to rebuild my muscles, and sex wasn't what he had in mind, hence walking. When we reached Mindy's home, I imagined the doctors would prescribe different exercises, but right now, this was fine.

When I started to lag, Mindy insisted we go back to the apartment. Pookie wasn't as amicable. She stayed on the ceiling, snorting and tossing her head. Staring at her with my hands on my hips, I wondered if she was only an animal. She showed a certain level of intelligence that made me wonder. I didn't think she was sentient like Mindy and I were, but I was fairly certain she was smarter than the typical animal.

"Pookie," I called.

She gave me her furry butt, feet digging into the vines. Pookie liked to roam, but she also liked us and needed the cold, or we thought she did. We hadn't tested it yet. When we did leave her with other people, she would try to get back to us after a short while, even with Caleb, who was definitely her next favorite.

But, ultimately, she was a giant baby who wanted what she wanted.

"Come on, Pookie," I said. "We need to go back."

She didn't move more than to flick her tail at me.

Serlotminden ordered, "Come, Daughter."

Slowly, she crept down the wall, and I frowned. She always listened to him, but not me.

Mindy brushed the back of his finger over my cheek. "No need to be jealous because she loves me more than you."

"I'm not."

"You are." He grinned.

Frowning, I glanced at Pookie, then at the elevator. A revenge plan formed, and without thought, I decided to follow it. I pointed in the opposite direction and asked, "Who's that?"

Serlotminden turned, and I dashed toward the lift. Pookie tore after me, clearly excited to play. It took Mindy a second to understand what was happening, but it was too late, and the elevator door was closing.

He snarled.

"Catch me, and I'll let you fuck me again," I called.

The door slammed shut, and I smirked. I was going to make it to the room before him. Served him right for teasing me. Why did Pookie like him better? I was the one who'd rescued her... though he had fed her. A lot. I snagged Pookie, who scuttled around the walls, and kissed her fluffy face. She snorted, rooting against me. When the door opened with a low whoosh, I stepped out, putting her on the floor, and started back.

On the icy planet, Serlotminden had enjoyed chasing me, so why not here? I wasn't into exhibitionism like supposedly Caleb and Fyn were, but I had no issues with public affection. We could play, kiss, and hug around other people. As far as I could tell, drakcol were queer-normative, so we weren't in any danger if we were romantic with each other. Also, I'd seen other drakcol couples doing similar in my time on Don's ship, so we weren't breaking any rules or social norms, at least I didn't think so.

Arms wrapped around me and teeth latched onto my neck, making me leap. A low voice said in my ear, "I caught you. You did not make the chase that hard, Mate."

My heart pounded as desire flooded me. "I didn't, did I?"

"No." He licked my neck, then whispered, "Now, I am going to fuck my mate again."

I replied, keeping my voice even, "I did say you could." I wiggled and felt something hard pressing into my ass. "And you seem like you want to."

He cupped the front of my pants, and I gasped, looking around. Thankfully, we were alone.

"So do you, Flower."

Serlotminden threw me over his shoulder and slapped my ass. "Come, Pookie. I caught my prize, and I'm taking him back to our quarters." She followed along, happy as can be, and I blushed profusely.

Chapter 45

RESCUE: TAKE TWO.

Bartholomew

I gripped Serlotminden's hand and watched the monitor in front of me. It was Xome. I swallowed. I hadn't expected this to suck as much as it did. Nightmares still plagued me about what had happened and going back... I shook my head. I never wanted to see this planet again, but I had to rescue Vince and the other humans.

It had taken more time than I'd liked, but we'd finally gotten permission to retrieve Vince and any other humans, which was good because I was losing my mind. What if something had happened to him while I was gone?

But we were here, orbiting Xome. We were going to buy the humans from the different people who owned them, but that didn't help the ones who'd been sold off-world. Kalvoxrencol and the drak-col government, the Cohort, were organizing a reward for humans to be returned to them. It made Seth, Caleb, and me scoff. Humans had been reduced to lost animals, but at the same time, it would allow them to return to Earth if they wanted or stay on Tamkolvan-loknol. It would save them, and in the end, that was what mattered.

"He'll be alright, Bartholomew."

I squeezed his hand tighter, digging the ring into my skin. Serlotminden had been able to wait all of one week before he synthesized a gold ring. He'd said he would buy me another, but I liked this one and the matching one he wore.

"I need him to be safe."

"I know, Mate." He kissed my neck.

Dontilvynsan was leading the mission to retrieve the humans, as he'd refused to allow Serlotminden or I on the surface, no matter how much we both had insisted on going. The sensors had identified ten. Out of everyone, ten humans were left, at least on this planet. So many had died, and xoi had to be stealing more humans from Earth—they had to be. There was too much profit in the sale of humans to stop.

Don's voice came over the monitor. "I found Vince."

I sagged into Serlotminden's arms.

"I am bringing him and the others to the ship."

"Where?" I needed to see him, explain that I didn't abandon him.

"This way," Serlotminden said.

I saw the worry in Mindy's eyes, but I refused to talk about it. I loved Serlotminden. He understood that. I'd told him I was going to stay. He knew that. I was pretty sure me telling him over and over that he had nothing to worry about wouldn't help. He had to believe it for himself.

We wound through the ship until we waited outside the shuttle bay. Kal and Seth had joined us. Caleb and Zoltilvoxfyn were resting, but Caleb promised to entertain everyone later.

I rocked on my toes, watching the bay doors. Vince. I hoped he was alright.

Serlotminden hugged me close. "He is here. It will be alright. Everything will be perfectly fine."

I nodded, unable to speak.

Beside me, Seth looked green and was shaking as badly as I was, though for different reasons. People, as I'd come to understand, weren't his thing. I almost wanted to laugh, because he was so uncomfortable with people but he was damn good at leading.

Team Human was getting bigger, if people decided to stay, and Seth was leading the charge.

A clank sounded moments before the bay doors closed, and the airlock opened. The shuttle door painstakingly fell open, and Vince walked out. He was skinnier than ever, and his expression was drawn. I had been gone a couple of months, and it looked like that time had been pure hell for Vince.

"Vince," I called, but my voice was drowned out.

"Seth," he screamed.

Seth stiffened. The next thing I knew, he was across the cargo bay, hauling Vince into his arms. "Vince."

Vince gripped the back of Seth's hoodie, curling in tight.

Pain prodded my heart. Vince and I had been close, but clearly he knew Seth from before. Serlotminden tugged me to his side. "It's okay, Mate. He's here. That is what matters."

Kal growled, tail thrashing.

"Pest," Mindy warned; Kal ignored him, snarling.

"Vince, what are you doing here?" Seth asked, clutching him.

"I should ask you that." Vince's eyes moistened.

"It's a long story." They stared at each other, smiling.

"They know each other?" Serlotminden asked.

I shrugged. Vince hadn't mentioned it, but then again, if he had randomly mentioned an old friend named Seth, why would I remember?

Seth rocked Vince, whispering. Kal was breathing so hard I feared he'd pass out, and light gathered under his scales. Heat came off him in waves, making me sweat.

Serlotminden pushed me behind him. "Pest. Breathe. Seth loves you."

Seth and Kal could communicate telepathically with the whole Crystal-bound-mate thing, but apparently Seth wasn't talking.

"I'm so glad you're here." Vince cupped Seth's cheeks and he grinned. Vince pressed closer and placed a kiss on Seth's lips.

If I thought Kal was freaking out before, he went apocalyptic. Light exploded off him, blinding me, and the moment I was able to see again, I spotted him in front of Seth, wings sprawled and growling. Humans cowered near the ship, but Vince was squaring off. I recognized the expression. He was about to start screaming.

I rushed forward and snagged his arm. Vince blinked, eyes running over me. I said, "I'm here too."

Kal pulled Seth closer, and Vince demanded, "Let him go."

"Do not kiss my mate, human."

"Mate?" Vince asked.

Shit. He sounded hurt. Very, *very* hurt. Who the fuck was Seth to Vince?

Seth glared at his husband. "Kal, calm down." Turning to face Vince and I, Seth said, "Vince, this is my husband, Prince Kalvoxren-col, but you can call him Kal."

Even I could see the absolute devastation in Vince's whole body as he practically crumbled inward, and I wasn't alone. Kal growled, Mindy shifted, and Don crossed his arms. The one person who didn't notice was Seth, who smiled contently.

"Vince is my childhood friend. Remember, Kal? I've mentioned him before."

"I do," he said shortly, dragging Seth closer.

I draped my arm over Vince, hugging him. "I'm right here too, Vince."

He smiled, but it was fake, and his eyes never left Seth. Vince said in a forced voice, "Hey, you didn't vanish or die."

"Nope." I pointed to Mindy. "He abducted me. He's Kal's older brother. He was trying to help me, but we crash landed on an ice planet. Took me a bit to get back to you. Serlotminden, this is Vince. Vince, this is Serlotminden."

"We are also husbands," Serlotminden announced, which made me roll my eyes. They might not resemble each other at first glance, but they sure as hell proved they were brothers rather easily.

Vince's eyebrows rose. "Well, you two move quickly."

I smirked. "He's cute and has a nice ass."

He gave a chuckle, but his gaze remained firmly on Seth, who grinned. Seth disentangled from Kal and pulled Vince close for another hug. "Let me talk to everyone, then we can catch up. It's been years."

Vince nodded.

"Everyone," Seth said, facing all of the cowering humans, "if you come this way, I will explain everything."

Seth led the humans away, and only after Don practically ordered Vince and I to follow did I leave Mindy's side.

Serlotminden

I sat in the canteen, drinking. Bartholomew was curled against my side. The new humans were terrified. Most had retreated to their rooms, but a few had braved the canteen, huddling together at a single table. Seth and Vince were in the corner near the long window on the back wall, talking and laughing. Kalvoxrencol was beside them and looked like he'd swallowed a knife.

Dontilvynsan watched the pair with narrowed eyes. He was probably following more than the flow of words, planning how much he would have to protect Pest. If Seth left him, our brother wouldn't recover, but I didn't need to read Seth's mind to know that wouldn't happen. Seth loved Kalvoxrencol. He wasn't going to change his mind. Vince was pining for nothing.

Seth pulled out his screen and showed Vince his and Kalvoxrencol's kid. I grinned. Seth was not going anywhere.

Neither was Bartholomew. He was coming home with me, or so he'd said. But he might change his mind.

No. He was staying. He'd promised. After Dontilvynsan chased Vince and Bartholomew away in the dock, he'd lectured me about trusting my mate. My quick claiming of my mate hadn't gone unnoticed. My older brother was right. Bartholomew had decided to stay, and I needed to believe him, as I wanted him to trust me. We would puzzle through everything else, my work, racing—and everything it brought—later.

We would forge forward together.

"I'm ready to go to bed." Bartholomew placed a lingering kiss on my arm.

My cock perked, and I swallowed. Stars above, it took nothing for my mate to stir my body. "Don't you need to talk to Vince?"

"Later. He and Seth are busy, and to be honest, I don't have any interest in watching Kal glare at them."

Zoltilvoxfyn was currently trying to calm Kalvoxrencol while Caleb infiltrated the pair of humans with a sunny smile. It was going to be an interesting trip home with everyone and the high tensions. *Though*, I thought as I tickled Bartholomew with the tip of my tail, *that means we can spend most of it alone*. No interruptions.

"Bed sounds amazing. I'm exhausted," I whispered.

"Hmm," he said. The indecipherable noise I loved and hated. "So you're too tired for me to ride you? Too bad."

I swallowed a groan. "Mate, please."

He ducked his head. "I love when you beg."

"Then take me to bed, and I will beg prettily for you and you alone."

"Fuck, Mindy."

Laughing, I looked at his groin and noticed a bulge. "Are you having problems as well?"

"It's your fault."

I caught his chin and angled it toward me. "I love that I affect you so." I rested his hand on my own stiffening cock, grateful the table hid us from view. "You do the same to me."

"We can't move."

"No. I am not into public displays."

"You don't like holding hands, hugging, or kissing in public?"

"That I do not mind, Flower," I said. "I don't have a problem with physical affection in public, but sex, that's between you and I alone."

"I agree."

"Good." I pressed a chaste kiss to his lips. "I like playing with you in the halls, though." I had chased him multiple times through the corridors, and I enjoyed racing after Bartholomew and Pookie. The thrill of catching my mate—growling, biting, throwing him over my shoulder—stirred my blood.

"I do too."

"That is very good."

"Does it bother other people?"

"Would you care if it did?"

"Perhaps," he replied.

I kissed his cheek. "No. It does not. We are not the only couple who enjoys chasing each other, and many drakcol run in the corridors for fitness. It is fine, Teddy."

Standing, Bartholomew took my hand. "I'm tired."

"Me too."

He led me out of the tense canteen without a backward glance.

Chapter 46

BEG FOR ME.

Bartholomew

The second we left the cafeteria, I released a sigh of relief. Fuck. It was intense. Kal and Seth. Seth and Vince. Fyn and Caleb trying to fix it. Don staring at everyone. The other humans freaking out. I didn't want anything to do with any of it, so I snagged my husband to have a nice fuck.

I let go of his hand and turned around with a smirk.

"What?"

I took a step back, and his tail flicked. "Chase me."

Mindy's tail thrashed.

"If you catch me, you can have me."

Serlotminden opened his mouth to say something, but I didn't let him finish. I took off. He snarled behind me, and my pulse jumped as my dick twitched. Desire twined with a tinge of fear, not enough to bother me, but enough to make this exciting. I darted around the corner to the closest elevator. We were not far from one, and I needed to use it to get away from Mindy. He'd always caught me before. I didn't necessarily want to get away, because the sex afterward was always amazing, but I wanted the chase to be harder for him.

When I reached the end of the hall, I slammed the button, entered, then closed it. Serlotminden shouted in frustration, and I smirked, waving at him.

"NAID, floor five." The elevator moved down. There were other elevators, and he knew their placements better than me, which meant evading him was near impossible. Bouncing, I waited, ready to run as soon as the door opened. When it did, I bolted toward our room.

I rounded a corner and arms snagged me, lifting me off the ground with ease. I yelped, and Serlotminden bit the nape of my neck, growling, "Mine."

Panting, I nodded, dick hard. "Yours."

He licked me. "I am yours in return."

"Mine."

Serlotminden turned me around and lifted me, hands gripping my ass. My legs about his waist, I gripped his face between my palms as my lips found his. His tongue demanded entry, and I saw no reason to deny him. I groaned, trying to rub my dick against his stomach. Mindy nipped my bottom lip, pulling on it, then licked it.

We entered our room, and Pookie squeaked, climbing Serlotminden. "Not now, Daughter."

I laughed when she settled on his head. She didn't get why I could climb him and not her.

"Pookie," he groaned. His hard cock pressed into me and his breath was harsh from desperation.

"She wants to snuggle," I commented, kissing his neck and paying particular attention to where his scent gland was. He moaned, panting. I licked and sucked, rocking into him.

"Teddy," he cried, making Pookie snort. I laughed. Serlotminden nosed my neck. "You are very beautiful."

"So are you."

He breathed me in, huffing. "You are really staying."

"Yes, Honey. I'm staying. How many times do I need to say it?"

"My apologies."

"No." I caught his chin, so our eyes met. "I'm not mad. I am truly asking, how many times do you need me to say it? How do you need me to say it? What will ease your worry?" I kissed him gently. "What do you need?"

"This. Exactly this."

I captured his mouth in a slow kiss in an attempt to soothe him, to show him how much I loved him, to convey we had all the time in the world. Mindy started to move to our room, and Pookie squealed.

"She needs a walk," I muttered against his lips.

Mindy groaned. "I need you."

"After. I promise."

Before he had a chance to protest, Pookie leaped off and tackled one of her toys, shaking it as she started to take it back to the lair she'd made of blankets and pillows.

"She is content for the moment," he said with a smirk.

"You got lucky."

"I did. I have you, don't I?"

I locked my lips to his. Mindy stalked to our bedroom and dropped me on the bed moments before he fell on top of me. His wings sprawled and his tail whipped. I ran my fingers over the leathery membrane, tracing the delicate veins.

"You're gorgeous," I said.

Serlotminden smirked. "I know."

I laughed. God, he was so arrogant. I loved it. "I want to ride you so bad."

"Take what you desire."

"Hmm, is that so?" Arching, I kissed his chin and moved up his jawline. "I want to make you beg. I want to edge you until you are crying for me."

"Please, Flower. Please."

"You're already begging for me."

"I told you I would," he panted.

I bit my lip.

"What?" he asked.

"I don't know how."

"I will teach you."

I ripped my shirt off, and he helped me, then tossed it to the ground. I tried to pull off his shirt, but his wings were out, making it impossible. He had to draw them in so I could yank it off. The rest of our clothes followed the same descent to the floor.

Rolling on top of him, I kissed his neck and a flood of nerves rose from my gut. This was something Serlotminden loved, and I had to make sure that I was meeting his needs. I'd never done it, though, and while I knew how he looked when he started to come, I wasn't perfect at predicting it. What if I messed up?

"Flower," Mindy cried beneath me, head falling to the side to give me more room.

The nerves rushed out of me so fast I almost sagged against Mindy. He was in love with me, and he was very easily pleased. More than all that, we had time. If this time wasn't great, we would try again and again and again.

I licked his scent gland and teased his sides. He arched beneath me, whimpering. Pressing kiss after kiss to him, I muttered, "I love your noises. I love when you call for me. I love when you scream for me."

Chest heaving, Mindy groaned, "Mate."

Slowly, I tried to kiss, lick, nip, and tease every part of him. I wasn't exactly sure how to edge Mindy, but the first plan was to get him worked up. My hand slid down his taut stomach until I reached his cock. The tip was wet with his desire, and I spread the liquid to ease the glide of my palm and pumped him.

"Bartholomew, don't stop. It's so good, Mate."

"Tell me when you're close. I'm not good at this yet."

"Yes," he cried, and I wasn't sure if it's because he was agreeing or if he was enjoying what we were doing.

I cupped his balls, playing with the scales on his sack. Mindy thrust upward into my palm chasing the friction. I jerked him, watching his face, and tugged on his balls. When his cries reached epic levels, I pulled away, and Mindy groaned in protest. I kissed his knee, placing more down his thigh, tongue tracing his scales, to silence any problems he had as well as to comfort him.

"You were close, weren't you?" I asked.

"Flower, more. I won't come yet."

He'd been close. I was sure of it. I kissed his thigh, coming close to his cock, but I moved away at the last second to do the same to his other thigh. Mindy trembled, grabbing my hair. I rubbed my nose over his inner thigh. "What do you want?"

"Your mouth on me."

I sucked his tip into my mouth, and we both groaned, albeit Serlotminden's was far louder. My tongue worked the underside of his cock as I took him as deep as I could manage. I hummed around him, and he canted, sending his cock into my throat.

"Mate," he screamed, and I slid off him, coughing. Breath harsh, he asked, "Did I hurt you?"

"No." He'd been close again, I thought, so I slowed down, rubbing and kissing his scales. "Can I lick your ass?"

"Do you want to?"

"I want to try." I'd always been curious, and now, I had the chance.

"Then lick me."

"Can I put my fingers inside you?"

"Yes," he said. "But grab the lube."

I snagged the lube before returning to my spot between his thighs. "I can't see you, Honey, so I need you to tell me when you're close or if you're ready to come."

"I will."

I lapped up the sweet beads of liquid that dripped from his cock and kissed my way down the shaft to his balls. I sucked on one, then the other, making him groan, before licking from his taint to his hole. Mindy took a sharp gasp. Tentatively, I swiped his pucker, and he cried.

Mindy was so damn easy to please.

With each pass, I grew more confident until I was attacking him and making Mindy scream. His hips ground against me as I licked him. When he relaxed enough, my tongue slid inside his tight warmth.

"Yes, Mate. That's so good, but I'm too close."

"Good job." My own cock was hard to the point of painful and it was leaking all over the sheets. I wanted to plunge inside of him, but I knew he didn't want that, at least not yet. One way or another, I needed to come, but I wanted to bring him to the edge one more time.

Putting some lube onto my fingers, I circled his opening.

"Bartholomew!"

I pushed one finger in, and he groaned loudly, hips rocking instantly to ride me. "Don't you need time to adjust?" I asked, sliding my digit in and out of him.

"No. More."

A second, then third finger joined the first, thrusting in and out of his hot channel. I searched for his prostate, but I couldn't find it. "Honey, where's your prostate?"

"My what?"

"Where is the spot that makes you feel good?"

He shook his head, panting, saliva coming out of the corners of his mouth. "Too deep for your fingers."

"Do you have toys?"

Mindy paused in his rocking. "What?"

"Sex toys."

"I understand. Yes, but not here or right now. This feels amazing, Mate. So impossibly good."

I wrapped my lips around the tip of his cock and sucked, tonguing his slit for more liquid. Mindy keened loudly, rutting into me gently as he rode my fingers. He shook and trembled beneath me as my name and animalistic cries ripped out of his throat.

"Close," he snarled, his movements becoming jerky.

I pulled off him.

"No, Flower. I need it. Please. *Please*."

I kissed his glistening tip. "Let me ride you."

"Please. Please. I need you. I need to be inside you."

"You beg so nicely."

He moaned, more pre-cum escaping him.

"Help me?"

"Of course."

I climbed on top of him and gave Mindy the lube. With shaking hands, he put on the glove before coating his fingers with lube. He circled my hole, and tingles went up my spine, making me grunt. I bore down when his finger prodded my pucker; we were both too impatient to draw this out anymore. My cock was hard and leaking, and he was dripping all over his abs.

Gently, I rode his finger that quickly became two, then three. I panted at the stretch, grinding on him until I was swearing with every movement and sweat dripped down my spine. I couldn't wait any longer. I lubed his dick, then angled it toward my ass. I impaled myself in one hard motion, and a loud noise ripped out of my throat.

Serlotminden hissed. "Be careful."

I grunted. He was a worrywart. I was fine. God, I was more than fine. I was so full. It was amazing. He stared at me, eyebrows pinched. He was focusing far too hard on me. I placed his hands on my hips and began to rock, picking up the pace as I rode him.

When the first cry slipped from his lips, I grinned. Now he was focused on the right thing. I moved faster and harder, shoving down onto him. Serlotminden planted his feet wide and bucked up into me. The sound of my skin slapping against his scales mixed with his loud cries.

"Mate. Mate," he screamed on a loop. His tail curled about my leg and his wings were spread over the bed beneath me. With his messy hair and wide eyes, he looked completely undone, and I fucking loved it.

"What?" I asked. "What, Honey?"

He didn't reply, mouth open as animalistic cries escaped. With my hands splayed on his chest, I sped up even more. My own cock jerked and slapped my stomach, but I ignored it. I wanted Serlotminden to beg. I wanted to watch him come apart beneath me.

His eyes screwed shut as he called out for me even louder.

"That's it, Honey. Scream for me. Show me how much you love me."

Serlotminden complied. He thrust up into me with each of my downward movements, making our fucking even harder and more desperate as he shrieked like he was being killed.

"Husband, please."

I smirked. "Beg more."

"Please. Please. Ah, stars, please, Flower. You're so tight. You are perfect. So perfect. *Hell it all.* I need to come. Please. *Please.* Let me."

I kissed him to swallow his pleas, hips moving. His tongue slid over mine. I slammed back, and he moaned. I ate it up, not letting his mouth go.

I stilled.

"No, I'm so close," he whimpered.

"You're mine."

"Yes, Mate. Yours. All yours. Please."

I started to ride him again, pounding back. He grabbed my cock, pumping it. His thumb swiped over the tip, and my head fell back. Serlotminden thrust into me, hitting my prostate as he jerked me off.

"I'm coming, Honey."

"Cover me in your seed. Claim me. I need it, Bartholomew."

His name ripped out of my mouth and my hearing went to fuzz. Serlotminden rutted into me once, twice before his cock kicked and warmth flooded me. I groaned as his cum filled me. With a shudder, I fell on top of him, his softening cock inside of me. My breath was harsh as I lay on his chest, shaking.

He teased the slight curls that had started to grow at the base of my skull and said, breathlessly, "That was amazing. The best I've ever had."

Very doubtful, but I kissed his chest, licking one of his nipples. He wiggled, oversensitive, and yet I continued, because I liked to torture him.

"I think we should spend the rest of the trip here, alone," he said.

"If it is anything like the tension in the cafeteria, I agree."

Serlotminden rolled me over, kissing my neck. "Another round?"

"Give me a few minutes."

He grinned. "We have all the time in the world."

We did. I pressed my lips against his. Serlotminden was mine, and I was never going to let him go.

Chapter 47

NEVER WILL I ABANDON YOU.

Bartholomew

Serlotminden was asleep beside me. He had been extremely cuddly after sex and our shower. I wasn't entirely sure what was going on, but he was tense. We needed to talk about it, and we would.

I brushed his long hair, and he wiggled closer to me, whining in his sleep, which made me smile. My husband was loud no matter what we were doing. I twisted the gold ring on my finger back and forth. Mindy had been so pleased when he presented me with the simple gold band, grinning and beaming as he practically bounced. He'd been desperate for us to be official, and I wasn't sure why. We were already mates, which was the same thing as husbands, but he'd needed it more than I did. I'd told him again and again I was going to stay. He'd said he was fine. He'd said he had what he needed, but still... there was a tension in him I couldn't quite put my finger on.

Now wasn't the time to bring it up, even if sleep hadn't been easy for me tonight. I'd fallen asleep with Mindy, but not much later, I'd woken up with a nightmare filled with the ghosts of my past chasing me, screaming at me, and hating me. I'd shot awake, and I hadn't been able to sleep since.

I slid out of bed and meandered into the living room. Water. I would get a drink, then try to fall back asleep next to my husband. That was an odd yet nice thought. Pookie was curled up in her nest and surrounded by disemboweled toys. She snorted, legs thrashing, and I swallowed.

No. Please, no.

I pushed the past down, but the memories rose like the tide and swept me out to sea. I was shoved and pushed by the sights of blood and broken bodies, sounds of screams and dull thuds, scents of piss and sweat, and all the while I tried to find my way out of the mire, but it refused to release me.

Pain shot through my legs, and I jolted. Sometime in my haze, I'd fallen to the ground. My knees throbbed, but that was preferable to the hellscape that my mind had dragged me to. I didn't understand why I couldn't let it go. Even now, as I closed my eyes, the burned and broken bodies of the people who had died, the people I had failed to save, appeared.

"There are no ghosts," I whispered.

Fyn had told me so. I was the one trapping them here. While I doubted it was my fault I kept being whisked into the past at the most random of moments, I knew my guilt was keeping the faces of the dead front and center. I wanted to not see them, but... it felt like I didn't deserve to be free of them. I had failed, hadn't I? I had to be punished.

Pulling my knees to my chest, I rested my chin on my bent legs and let myself think about what happened without guilt or emotion. Logically, I accepted I had been a victim. If I had not closed that bolt, killing those who were still alive, or had chosen to stand up to Agk, I would have died. I knew it, and yet my heart continued to feel differently. It was like I could accept one thing with my brain while believing something radically different with my heart.

This was not a wound that would heal any time soon, nor would my guilt fade simply because I was done feeling it. I was going to have to forgive myself, and I didn't know how to do that yet. But I planned to figure it out. Slowly, painfully, and without hating myself too much in the process, I would forgive myself for what I did on Xome.

Letting my eyes close, I allowed the ghosts of my past to come and haunt me with their screams, but instead of fleeing, I whispered, "I'm sorry. I'm sorry you're dead. I'm sorry I locked the door. I'm sorry any of this happened to us."

Apologizing wasn't a magical cure, but it did make me feel the slightest bit better. I was more than willing to take it as the victory it was.

Painfully, I got to my feet. There was one face who wasn't among the ghosts. I hadn't truly saved Vince, but he was alive and that was what mattered.

After a quick consultation with NAID, I left the room and went down the hallway.

A chime sounded when I pressed the panel glowing with blue light next to the door. The metal door slid open, and Vince stood on the other side. His short black hair was wet, like he'd just gotten out of the shower, and he wore Drakcon clothes, though they were large on his small frame. Vince was not a big person to begin with, and he was underweight, much like me.

"Hey," I said.

"Teddy, come in." Vince hugged himself as he led me to the couch. Every light was on as bright as possible, making me wince. There was no relief from it.

We sat across from each other, and I studied him. His skin was more pallid than usual and his eyes were ringed with purple. His posture was stiff, and he was leaning away from me as far as possible while remaining on the couch. Vince looked unwell, but more than that, he appeared haunted.

"How are you?" I asked. Did he have the same issues I had? It was possible. He had been left alone with Agk for weeks.

"Fine, Teddy. Though you look thin. Has your husband not been feeding you? Punishing you for some obscure reason?"

He said it as a joke, but I heard the worry beneath it. Drakcol were new to Vince, and he had no reason to trust them, especially after everything.

I drew one leg up and faced him. "Mindy is feeding me. He's extremely paranoid about feeding me. I'm on nutritional supplements as well. I imagine Klars—that's the doctor in charge of humans—will start you on some."

Vince nodded. "Are you happy? With him?"

"I love him. I love him a lot, and I'm happy."

"So you're staying?"

"Yeah." When Vince didn't say anything else, I continued, "I didn't mean to leave you. I would've never intentionally abandoned you. Please believe me."

"I know," he said, curling in on himself and hugging his knees to his chest.

I frowned. "What happened after I was gone?"

He shrugged. "Agk sold me."

My pulse stumbled. I'd been afraid of that. "I'm sorry. Are you alright?"

"I'm alive, aren't I?"

Alive didn't necessarily mean okay; I knew that better than anyone.

After staying with Vince for a few more minutes of strained silence, I returned to mine and Mindy's apartment, pausing in the doorway. Serlotminden was in the living room, pacing with Pookie perched on his shoulder.

"Hey, Honey," I said, coming inside. "Why are you awake?"

"You were gone."

That shouldn't have instilled the tension I saw in his body. I crossed the space between us to gather him close, making Pookie squeal and leap off, and Mindy surrounded me, tail coiling about my ankle and wings hugging me. An instant heat enveloped me, making me melt against him. His forehead found its way to my cheek, nuzzling, scent marking, and he worked down to my neck.

A sure sign he was panicked. And there was no reason for him to be. I assumed Don's ship was safe to wander the halls at night, and I hadn't gone far. Vince was on the same floor as us, a few doors away. To comfort him, I tucked a hand beneath his shirt and teased the scent gland on his side. He groaned, pressing even closer to me, and continued to scent mark me aggressively.

I guessed that conversation needed to happen right now.

When I tried to shift back to see him, he grunted, refusing to let me go. "No, Flower."

Sighing, I hooked my arms around his neck and squeezed him for a moment. "Mindy, let's sit, alright?"

Finally, he released me and moved to the couch, but the second he sat, Serlotminden drew me onto his lap, and I had no choice but to straddle his thick thighs. His green eyes were wide and his breath was harsh enough to make his chest heave; it wasn't arousal riding him, but rather, fear.

"What's wrong?" I demanded.

"I awoke and you were gone."

"I went to see Vince to explain that I didn't abandon him."

"You should have told me."

"And wake you up in the middle of the night?" I asked.

"Yes."

I kissed him, trying to soothe the anxiety he was clearly having about my absence, but that wasn't going to be enough. This was something that needed to be addressed again, apparently.

Cupping his cheeks, I said, "You were asleep. I wasn't going to wake you up for something trivial." When he started to talk, I kissed him again. "No, Mindy. I can go places without telling you. I was perfectly safe. I went to see Vince. I'm allowed to have friends."

"You are. But I need to keep you close."

"Why?"

"I'm scared of losing you."

Waking up and thinking I was dead had to be traumatic. I understood that, but I was fairly certain this wasn't about that. "Are you afraid of me dying or me leaving you?"

Serlotminden looked away, but his tail thrashed.

There it was. That was the issue. He didn't believe that I was going to stay, no matter how many times I'd told him. His needing us to be husbands, his clinginess, and his quick claiming of me in front of Vince were all in line with that. He didn't actually trust that I was choosing him and this life. I could've felt insulted, but I didn't. I saw the fear in his eyes and knew the struggles he had with feeling forgotten or abandoned. Trust was a tricky thing and it took time. Mindy trusted me with his heart and his life, but he didn't trust me to stay.

I caught his chin. "You're mine."

"I am," he replied instantly, making me smile. I would have never guessed I'd be possessive, but here we were.

"I'm yours."

He did not respond.

I gripped his chin. "I am yours, Serlotminden."

"Are you?"

"Yes."

"You *want* to go home, Bartholomew. You cannot lie to me. I saw it when I told you Vince could go back. You chose me before you knew there were other options. You're staying because you feel obligated."

"I did choose you before I knew about the possibility of returning."

His head ducked.

I wrapped my arms around him, and he nuzzled my chest. I said, "I did choose you before I knew everything. But," I lifted his chin, "I'm choosing you again after I know everything. I want you, Serlotminden. Over everything. I pick you. I want you. I need you. I love you. Not your body. Not what you offer as a prince. Not your career. But you. Your bounding from place to place, your noises, your humor, your laughter, your caring, your possessiveness. I choose you."

His eyes grew wet.

"I'm not going to lie. I do miss Earth and my family. I wish I could bring them here to be with me, but I'd never leave you, Honey. Not for any reason. I can't even imagine doing that. You make me happy, and we belong together. So you are stuck with me through thick and thin and until I am a crabby old man."

"I love you so much," he warbled, squishing me to his chest. "I'm terrified you're going to change your mind. I don't want you to have to sacrifice Earth, but I cannot surrender you. I will never change my mind about you. You are my soul. My apologies for doubting you."

"Don't apologize. In the future, tell me if you're nervous. I'm more than happy to tell you that I'm choosing you or staying or whatever you need as many times as you need until you believe it. I love you, and I never want to go anywhere without you. You are well and truly stuck with me."

"Good. I don't want to be anywhere else in this universe. I shall stay right beside you, keeping you safe, and making it so you can sit and smell the flowers. I promise."

I held my husband's cheeks as I stared at his green eyes that I loved and was happy. Utterly and completely happy. Maybe Serlotminden hadn't been so bad at this rescue thing after all, and maybe I wasn't either, because we had truly saved each other and would continue doing so for the rest of our lives.

Serlotminden

Four Months Later

I held my breath, tail flicking, as I watched my mate and the priest. Bartholomew hadn't been forced to touch the Crystal, which I was thankful for. We had decided not to attempt to become Crystal-bound mates. Bartholomew didn't like the idea of being able to mind-speak and the lack of privacy; also, there was the matter of the genetic link. As of this moment, I couldn't imagine us not being with each other all the time, but in the future, he might not attend every one of my races or accompany me on every diplomatic mission.

Bartholomew glanced at me, and I gave him a smile. He didn't understand why he needed to have his soul tested. Out of all the humans that had come to Tamkolvanloknol, he was the most resistant to it. He saw it as unnecessary, for he knew who he was without knowing his soul type, but I couldn't deny I was curious. I had my suspicions, and now, we would find out for certain.

The priest did his babble about the different soul types and their colors before holding out the glowing piece of glass. Bartholomew rested his fingers against it, the light caressing him. It glowed a lovely pale gray that maybe bore a touch of pink. A spiritual soul with hints of warrior. I grinned.

"You are a spiritual soul," the priest announced. "The first non-drakcol one in our recorded history."

My mate grunted, and I laughed. He, even after our time together, wasn't much of a talker, especially in front of other people.

I surrounded him with my arms, hauling him close and nuzzling his neck. "I always knew you were special."

"You're ridiculous," he replied, but he rubbed my arm.

"Now, we can announce our mating publicly."

My parents had refused to publicly acknowledge our mating until Bartholomew had been soul tested, which had been the driving force behind this. Also, he'd needed to be tested before being added to the Drakcon network. I breathed in his earthy scent, barely paying attention to the priest who stared at us, his tail wiggling. He clearly wanted to ask Bartholomew questions. The Ranks were always so fascinated by humanity, and none had been interested in indulging them yet.

"You may leave," I said, wishing to be alone with my mate.

The priest offered me his throat and swiftly exited the terrace garden beside the palace.

I snagged my mate's hand, leading him toward the towering trees in a multitude of colors. We wound on the bark path, silent, as we observed the bright flowers, fluttering bugs, and the world around us. We had done this multiple times, and it relaxed Bartholomew each time. He was highly allergic to pollen and had to take daily injections, but he loved being outside in the quiet. The last few months had helped us both with each other and ourselves. My mate was continuing to have nightmares from his time on Xome, but he'd agreed to meet with someone to discuss them. I still worried at random times that he would leave me, but now, I asked for reassurance—reassurance that he was happy to provide.

"Tell me again," I asked quietly.

He gave me a smile, brown eyes crinkling behind his lenses. "I am staying beside you. I love you, Serlotminden."

My soul pounded as I looked at my mate, my soul, my future. "I love you too, Flower."

Vince

I'd been sold again. I didn't even react. None of it mattered. Teddy was gone. He had been for weeks, and the last few weeks had been some of the worst of my life.

What came next would probably be even worse.

The door opened, and my current owner jerked me out by my arm, throwing me. I staggered, tilting dangerously toward the floor. Strong hands caught me, steadying me, and I looked up and up and up. The largest person I'd ever seen towered over me. He was broad with black scales, deep green eyes that peered into mine, and long dark purple hair.

"Vince?"

I blinked.

"My name is Dontilvynsan, and I am here for you."

Well, that was fucking ominous.

Afterword

Writing this book was an interesting experience. I finished the first draft before I published *Cosmic Husband*, but I wasn't totally pleased with it. So I decided to leave it alone and hope that, magically, I would like the draft later. You know the whole soak-the-pan-in-the-sink-and-ignore-it thing. *Shockingly*, the draft didn't get better sitting on my computer. I ended up editing/rewriting a good portion. However, the core remained the same—sweet-puppy Serlotminden and apathetic Bartholomew falling in love on an icy planet while both dealt with their issues.

When I first started to contemplate this series as being a *series*, I wanted to have a character crash land on an ice planet where there would be plenty of cuddling for warmth (a favorite trope of mine), and Serlotminden was the drakcol for the job. Bartholomew came from the desire to have a human with a long name and Mindy needing a calming presence. And it worked out well enough!

As someone on the ace spectrum, I find it beyond nice to write a character who is as well. It has been a dream of mine to write an ace character, and I did. Teddy is so near and dear to my heart, and I love him with Mindy. The two of them have been burning a hole in the back of my mind, and I'm glad to be done with their book.

Now for the people who made this possible!

First and foremost, I would like to thank Andra for reading and giving her opinion on this book. You always give such great feedback! Next, I want to give a massive thank you to Adie Hart! You caught so many typos and grammatical errors. I also need to thank Etheric Designs for my gorgeous cover! Every single cover gets better and better! A massive thank you to Adrienne Lothy, who supported me and talked me down from anxious spirals and imposter syndrome fears. And thank you to all my RQ family; I could not do this without your support and kindness.

And finally, thank YOU for reading my book! I'm so shocked when people I don't know read my books and take the time to tell me how much they enjoyed it. This... all of this is still so surprising and humbling. I cannot thank you enough for supporting me, Martians, whether you started with *Cosmic Husband* or started with this book.

I'll see you on my socials or in my next book!

PS. I know I always say this, but I'm so excited for Dontilvynsan and Vince's romance. I love them, and I think you will too!

PPS: If you want to see pictures of the cat that Lucy was modeled after, stalk me on my socials to catch pictures of Monster.

About the author

Mars Quinn is a massive geek and an obsessed cat parent. When they are not playing with their cats, they can be found reading, gaming, and writing. They are a queer author with mental and chronic health issues who believes more representation is needed, and they strive to meet that need with their books. They welcome (and truly delight) in messages from their readers, so please feel free to reach out.

www.ingramcontent.com/pod-product-compliance
Lightning Source LLC
Chambersburg PA
CBHW030756260626
47169CB00001B/84